*Nace Jeffries and his men
met the advance with automatic fire . . .*

The creek was a deadly alley for the Federation.
Four automatic rifles could put an almost solid
wall of munitions across it. But the enemy kept
coming. Forty yards from Nace, enemy bodies
came close to damming the stream. But they
kept moving forward, and kept firing. Slowly,
they narrowed the gap.

"The next time you change magazines,"
Nace told his men, "slip your bayonets on. And
don't take too much time about it." He had no
doubt that the fighting was going to get that
close . . .

D0032103

RETURN TO CAMEREIN

Rick Shelley

ACE BOOKS, NEW YORK

This book is an Ace original edition,
and has never been previously published.

RETURN TO CAMEREIN

An Ace Book / published by arrangement with
the author

PRINTING HISTORY
Ace edition / January 1998

All rights reserved.
Copyright © 1998 by Rick Shelley.
Cover art by Dave Dorman.
This book may not be reproduced in whole or in part,
by mimeograph or any other means, without permission.
For information address: The Berkley Publishing Group,
a member of Penguin Putnam Inc.,
200 Madison Avenue, New York, New York 10016.

The Putnam Berkley World Wide Web site address is
http://www.berkley.com

Make sure to check out *PB Plug*,
the science fiction/fantasy newsletter, at
http://www.pbplug.com

ISBN: 0-441-00496-2

ACE®
Ace Books are published by The Berkley Publishing Group,
a member of Penguin Putnam Inc.,
200 Madison Avenue, New York, New York 10016.
ACE and the "A" design are trademarks
belonging to Charter Communications, Inc.

PRINTED IN THE UNITED STATES OF AMERICA

10 9 8 7 6 5 4 3 2 1

Dedicated to the memory of
Diana, Princess of Wales
and
to her sons,
Prince William &
Prince Harry —
The future of the Windsor family

THE PARADISE OF THE FRINGE
(X-DAY)

The loud, high-pitched caterwauling of a flock of cachouri birds woke everyone at the Commonwealth Excelsior Hotel, as it did virtually every morning. Except for the three weeks between the end of the birds' annual mating season and the subsequent birth of another generation of the green and orange screechers, the ritual was as inexorable as the rising of the sun. When the hotel was constructed, the colony had been quite small, its numbers kept in check by its natural predators. But the resort had thinned out those predators, and the cachouris had flourished. The last serious efforts at permanently dislodging the colony of birds from the jungle near the resort had been abandoned long before the start of the war between the Second Commonwealth and the Confederation of Human Worlds.

Shadda Lorenqui cursed the birds in a whispered monotone. He made routine efforts to shut out the squawking—wrapping his pillow around his ears, pulling the sheet over his head—but it didn't help. It never did. The noise was always there, and there was no way that he could sleep through the hellish racket.

Finally conceding defeat, as he had every morning that the birds had rioted during his seven years of isolation at the hotel, Shadda hurled his pillow away and tore the sheet off his body. He got out of bed slowly, continuing to mouth obscenities that had lost all force through years of daily repetition. He stalked over to the window and pounded against the louvered shutters. Shadda's frustrations were rarely far from the surface, but he only permitted them to show when he was alone in his room, even at the extremes of his mood swings—such as this morning. Around the others, he felt constrained to show a calm front. They expected it of him. He demanded it of himself.

After a few minutes, Shadda stopped his futile pounding and took a deep breath. He held that as long as he could, then released it and sucked in another before he turned from the window to face the rest of his room. At one time it had seemed most spacious, homey and pleasant. Shadda had never deceived himself that it was truly elegant. He knew better. But his quarters in the hotel were far better than most he had known in his years of wandering. Still, it had become nothing more than a prison cell—a venue he had passing acquaintance with.

But that had been before the war marooned him at the Commonwealth Excelsior on Camerein seven years before. It was not only the longest he had spent in one place since leaving his parents' home more than twenty-five years before, it was the longest he had spent on one world in all that time.

Shadda closed his eyes against a sudden throbbing in his temples. He massaged the aches with shaking fingers. When the pain eased enough to let him reopen his eyes, he shuffled to the bathroom. A short shower did little to help his mood, but it did give him time to start putting on his "public" face. As acting manager of the Commonwealth Excelsior, he had responsibilities.

On the third floor of the hotel, Prince George Arthur Charles woke easily to the routine cacophony. He wasted neither time nor energy with curses or vain attempts to exclude the noise of the birds. That would have been unbecoming, even in private. But George had always been an habitually early riser, so the disruption was less of an annoyance to him than it was to most of the others. He got out of bed and went to the nearest window. After opening the shutters, he picked up the shotgun that had been leaning against the wall. The weapon had been readied the night before, as usual. George pointed the shotgun toward the nearest tree and calmly squeezed off all five rounds of birdshot in the magazine, moving his point of aim with each shot. Each blast brought a momentary halt to the cachouris' screeching, but no more. The trees were too far off for the shots to do any harm, and the birds had gotten over any fear of the noise years before.

When the magazine was empty, George set the shotgun back against the wall. Although there were a dozen boxes of shells on the dresser, he never considered reloading to continue his futile assault. There would be other mornings. He had no idea how long this exile might last. After seven years, he no longer tortured himself with the stock questions: *Does the war continue? If not, who won?* And, *Will anyone ever come for us?*

"His Highness is up to it again," Marie Caffre muttered. She didn't bother to open her eyes. She had wakened before the cachouris had started their howling. That wasn't unusual. Marie had always been a light sleeper, and four or five hours was enough to carry her through the day. Once she woke, she never managed to get back to sleep.

Her husband mumbled something incomprehensible. Henri Caffre was one of the few people in the hotel who could sleep through the morning barrage of the birds, but he had never found a way to sleep through his wife's complaints. He tried to snuggle deeper into the stack of pillows he surrounded his head with. If Marie would just let it go for once. . . .

"Shadda should take his guns away." Marie opened her

eyes and sat up. She looked at her husband, started to peel pillows from his head, then poked at his shoulder until he looked at her.

"He wouldn't dream of it, even if His Highness started shooting at people instead of birds," Henri said, suppressing a sigh as he gave up on sleep. "And if anyone suggested it to him. . . ." He raised up enough to shake his head. "Leave The Windsor be, Marie. He does no harm. It's certainly not *your* sleep he disturbs." Marie had been the first to refer disparagingly to Prince George, behind his back, as "The Windsor."

"His High-and-Mightiness is no better than anyone else."

Henri sat up. "Count yourself lucky that we have him here. It is the one guarantee we have of escaping this place someday. Now, I have no intention of listening to one of your egalitarian lectures at this time of morning." There was no longer any sleepiness in his voice. Annoyance had banished the last of it.

Marie got up and walked naked to the bathroom. Now that she was in her early forties, that promenade was no longer as alluring to Henri as it had once been. The extra poundage she had put on over the years . . . among other things, it made it easier for him to remain cross with her. Marie refused to permit cosmetic maintenance. The molecular health system everyone had from birth could do that, but Marie maintained that it was artificial, and had refused to have the additional programming added at maturity. She slammed the bathroom door behind her. Henri got out of bed and started pulling on clothes. Only after he was completely dressed did he cross to the window and open the shutters.

"Camerein, the Paradise of the Fringe." That quote from the travel database had stuck in Henri's mind through the years of exile. He made it sound like an expletive now. Camerein had seemed an exciting place to visit back when it was only to be a three-month vacation—a second honeymoon. Henri and Marie had spent two years planning the trip to commemorate their tenth anniversary. Once they had settled on Camerein as their destination, it was *de rigueur* to book at the Commonwealth Excelsior, the most isolated resort on the planet, seven hundred miles from the nearest town.

The Paradise of the Fringe. There had been no warning at all that war was imminent.

By the time the residents of the Commonwealth Excelsior gathered for breakfast, the din of the cachouris was fading. No one in the hotel mentioned the birds any longer. Everyone had run out of original comments and curses.

Only seventeen people remained at the hotel. Most of the guests and employees had returned to the more civilized districts of Camerein in the first days of the crisis, before transportation became impossible. At least, they had left the hotel and no one knew that they had *not* reached their destinations. But some three dozen people had chosen to ignore the crisis and remain. "The war will never affect us here, so far from the towns and cities," they claimed. "It will blow over shortly. There's no use wasting our holiday." Those sentiments had carried most of them through the first month after the transcontinental shuttles stopped flying. After that, no one was ever quite so certain.

Communications with the outside became intermittent in the first days, then ceased completely, as quickly as the shuttles had quit flying. Twice in the first year, groups of guests and employees had attempted the long overland trip to the only town on the continent. Neither group had been heard of or from since.

Two people had died at the hotel over the years, one a suicide, the other mauled by an old bull keuvi, the largest local carnivore. The keuvi had struck and started to eat. None of the native wildlife would have dared challenge him or interrupt his feast. But that particular keuvi had no experience with humans. Prince George had killed it, but not before it had half consumed its victim. Five years later, no one could recall the dead man's name without scanning the guest register.

There was little talk first thing in the morning. Residents came into the dining room by ones and twos, guests and employees. They got tea or coffee from the beverage dispensers, then selected their food—those who bothered with food.

Although everyone gathered in the dining salon at more or less the same time, breakfast remained almost as solitary as if everyone had chosen to eat in their rooms. The dining room was capable of seating two hundred and, before the war, it had often been crowded, with people queued up for their turn. But the seventeen people who remained had taken to sitting at "regular" tables scattered around the room, leaving as much space as possible between them. At lunch and dinner there was slightly less of that, but in the morning most seemed to prefer separation to community.

The Caffres sat together this morning. That was one of the few variables. About one morning in three they were too angry at each other to share a table. The entire width of the dining room was not enough distance occasionally.

The McDonoughs, Jeige and Mai, always sat together. Even when they were fighting—which was almost always— they shared a table so that they could continue their battle without interruption.

Another morning variable was who would be the last to arrive. Prince George usually claimed that dubious honor without conscious effort, making a "regal" entrance after all of the others were in place. But occasionally Shadda did not arrive until after the prince. Shadda had duties before he could give himself over to the formalities of the dining room, and some mornings those duties took longer than others.

Shadda came down the back stairs and went to the kitchen, as he did every morning. He checked the recycling bin to make certain that it was full. He could never count on his assistant to remember. *Dacen Poriri will never be more than a flunky,* Shadda thought. He rarely considered that but for the war and this exile, his own position would likely be no better—had been no better. His years of drifting, and sometimes running, from world to world had made anything better unlikely.

He gingerly lifted the lid of the first bin, and the usual noxious odors leaped out at him. But the bin was full. Dacen had actually remembered to dump all of the organic garbage in the night before. And it appeared that he had topped it off with a couple of bundles of local vegetation.

"Thank God for the weeds," Shadda muttered with due reverence. Without the extra organics to put into the food chain, the nanotech food service system would have collapsed more than six years back. It had never been designed to be a fully closed system.

Before he left the kitchen, Shadda turned on the overhead fan and the wall vents. It would never do to let any hint of the odors from the raw materials for his guests' food reach their delicate noses.

"I do wish that someone would conceive of something novel to try," Prince George, Earl of New Britain—the primary continent of Buckingham, the capital world of the Second Commonwealth—was saying when Shadda entered the dining room. "It has been so deucedly long since anyone has come up with a truly unique diversion." George spoke loudly without putting any special effort into it.

"Why don't you come right out and say it?" Mai McDonough demanded from five tables away. "This place is a fucking bore." She used the vulgarity for only one reason. It always made The Windsor flinch.

Jeige McDonough patted his wife's hand. "Now, dear," he said softly.

Mai turned to him just long enough to snap "Fuck off."

"What a disgusting woman," Vepper Holford said under his breath. He glanced across the table at Prince George. Vepper was the prince's aide, or traveling secretary—more than servant, less than friend.

George cleared his throat discreetly, not deigning to answer either Vepper or the McDonough woman. Instead, he turned his attention to his food. The kidneys were, as always, perfect. The little cubes of cheese provided the perfect complement. There was orange marmalade for his crisp toast, tea with sugar and cream. The food service of the Commonwealth Excelsior had always been excellent, geared to please any guest, no matter which of mankind's three hundred-odd worlds they came from. George couldn't have eaten better in his brother's palace on Buckingham. Of course, the ambiance would have been infinitely more civilized there. *Still, one must make allowances for the exigencies of our isolation and the war,* he thought. Even the vulgar Madame McDonough would not disturb the royal digestion. George refused to permit that.

The McDonoughs argued for several minutes, over nothing in particular; then Mai got up and strode out of the room. George didn't bother to watch the flamboyant exit, but most of the other men did. Mai McDonough was worth watching, even though she had allowed minor slippage in her appearance over the past couple of years. She had been one of the highlights of the resort in the weeks before the start of the war. At the time, George had given serious consideration to seducing her—solo if possible, along with her husband if necessary. But now . . . In any case, the routine crudities of Mai McDonough were one of the few remaining sources of diversion. Occasionally, she managed to rise to novelty with her histrionics, but not this morning.

After his wife's departure, Jeige concentrated on his food, hiding his eternal embarrassment well. He waited until the prince finished eating before going to his table. "My apologies, sir," Jeige said formally.

The prince nodded, but said, "You owe me no apology." The way he said it conveyed more than the words. *The error was not yours. You were not responsible for the scene.*

"Thank you." Jeige was careful to nod more deeply than

the prince had. "A game of chess this morning?" he suggested.

George leaned back and considered the idea before he said, "A capital suggestion." Jeige was near the prince's age but looked a decade older. Some men preferred to show their age, at least until they were quite old, and settled for the reality of life-extending molecular maintenance. "Shall we play on the veranda?" the prince asked. "In, say, an hour?"

Jeige bowed. "In an hour, sir. I'll meet you on the porch, er, veranda." George nodded again, and Jeige left.

"One of these days, he might actually beat me," George said. "His game is improving, though at a frightfully slow pace."

"I've not noticed it, Your Highness," Vepper replied. "He has yet to beat me, and I am not your equal at chess."

Or at anything else, George thought, but that was the sort of thing one did not say—except at the greatest provocation. "He has fewer inhibitions about contesting the game fully."

"Sir?"

"Nothing. Shall we have our morning constitutional?"

"Of course, sir." Vepper kept the resignation out of his voice. He was only forty, but there were times when the prince made him feel like an old man. *Him and his damned constitutionals. What good does it do in this godforsaken place? I'm a civil servant, not a bloody commando.*

Prince George set a faster pace than usual. He wanted to get in his three miles in time for his chess game. Even after seven years of barbaric isolation, he kept appointments with obsessive precision. Vepper struggled to keep station as George strode across the trampled grasses that marked his daily route to the river and back—an isosceles triangle with the base along the river and the apex at the hotel. Vepper was sweating profusely before they had crossed the hotel's lawn. He was six inches shorter than his master and thirty pounds lighter, but had never approached the prince in conditioning or stamina.

George swung his ebony walking stick, an antique that had been in the family for generations before one of his ancestors emigrated from Earth, with studied casualness. The head of the stick was of delicately worked gold with five deep-set, pear-cut diamonds. The ferrule was ivory. George always carried the stick, unless he was carrying a rifle or a shotgun. The one thing he did not need the stick for was to assist him in walking, but the device had become so integral to his public persona that it was no longer truly an affectation. It was a habit so deeply ingrained as to be totally unconscious.

"Don't dally, Vepper," George chided as they neared the river. Even at this distance the jungle was fairly tame. The underbrush was thinner because of years of visitors trampling over the same ground. The vines that clogged some parts of the jungle near waterways were missing. And, of course, there were fewer animals about. Only the cachouri had refused to flee from the proximity of humans.

"Yes, Your Highness." Vepper struggled to find breath for the words and to catch up with his patron. *I'm glad we can't play polo here.* There wasn't a horse on the planet. It was the one advantage Vepper had found in this diabolical exile.

The river (it had a proper name, but none of the people at the Excelsior bothered with it; most would have needed time to recall it) wasn't much of a stream, except during the infrequent flooding of the winter rainy season. In the summer, it was sixty feet wide and rarely more than three feet deep. The water ran crystal clear over a rocky bed, showing the rich variety of aquatic life. Most of what passed for fish were eellike in appearance and too foultasting for humans to eat except in utter desperation. The hotel people did net a few now and then to add to the food processors. After the nanotech system finished with the fish, there was no hint of their origin or taste left.

"Look at that tree!" George commanded. He stopped and used his walking stick to point.

"Sir?" Vepper said, glad for any excuse to rest.

"There must be a hundred cachouri nests in that one tree." The tree wasn't a particularly large specimen, sixty feet high with a crown thirty feet across. The first settlers had called the species the pumpkin tree for the dull orange shade of its bark.

"Perhaps we could try smoke bombs again," Vepper said.

"You're missing the point. We've been going at this problem all wrong. Why do the cachouris frequent this area?"

Vepper hesitated. "I don't know."

"Whatever they eat must be here," George said. "Do you have any idea what those birds eat?"

"No, sir."

George harrumphed. "Neither do I. I wonder if anyone does."

"To what point, sir?"

"To what point? To get rid of the cachouris, all we need do is get rid of their fodder, don't you see? When we get back to the hotel, sound out Master Lorenqui on that, will you?"

"Yes, sir." *Always some damned nonsense,* Vepper thought.

The chessboard was set up on a table made of wickerlike reeds on the north side of the hotel, but there was no one on the veranda when George and Vepper returned. The prince checked his watch, then marched through the hotel foyer and up to his room. There were seventeen minutes left to the allotted hour, time for a quick cold-water shower and a change of clothing. In an average day, George would shower two or three times, change clothes perhaps one additional time.

"Why is he so obsessive?" Marie Caffre asked her husband after the prince swept through the foyer. There was no doubt about his destination and purpose. After seven years, there were few secrets left in the hotel. "Does anyone care about a few wrinkles in a shirt, a little perspiration?"

Henri limited his reply to a noncommittal grunt. He was daydreaming of home—his own obsession. "I want to make sure that I don't forget any detail of Loreche," he had once told Marie. Every day he chose some aspect of their homeworld and tried to encapsulate every possible fact and memory about it.

"Henri, are you listening to me?"

He hadn't been, but he rarely found any real need. Marie had to be complaining about the prince again. That was *her* obsession. Henri used his stock reply. "My dear, just be thankful that His Highness is here. If it were not for him, we could not be certain that anyone would ever come to rescue us. No matter how long the war lasts, or who wins, *someone* will come searching for the king's brother. Someday."

That was the prime canon of Henri's Camerein catechism.

The veranda, which had always been a gathering spot for guests, wrapped completely around the hotel's main building. Before the war, as many as three hundred might congregate there for afternoon tea. Shuffleboard courts were inlaid on the south side. A variety of gaming tables was available. But after seven years of enforced residence, it was a rare day when anyone could raise the enthusiasm for games.

The chess matches between Prince George and Jeige McDonough generally occurred three or four times a week. The game this day reached its thirty-fifth move. Each man had a glass of emerald green livven juice at his side. George had nearly finished his. Jeige's was almost untouched. He concentrated too deeply on the game. There were no spectators. In the constant ennui of the Excelsior, no one could bear that intensification of boredom.

Jeige moved his last knight toward the side of the board, posing a weak threat to one of George's bishops, then leaned back and took a deep breath. "Sorry I took so long with that."

George waved a hand to pass off the delay, and the apology. George had anticipated Jeige's move five minutes earlier, and had his reply ready.

The prince was reaching to move his queen to pin Jeige's knight when the late-morning quiet was shattered by a sonic boom. The building shook. George's glass toppled from the table and shattered before it hit the floor. Juice slopped out of Jeige's glass, but he didn't notice. He had leaped to his feet as the shock wave hit, tipping over his chair. Jeige reached to cover his ears but the noise was gone before his hands got to his head.

"What the hell?" Jeige shouted. He ran to the edge of the veranda and looked up. "There!" He pointed into the sky.

George got up and crossed to the edge of the veranda. He spotted the contrail flowing from west to east, well to the north. But Jeige wasn't pointing at that. George squinted and finally caught the glint of sun on metal, much lower, and some distance east of the end of the vapor trail.

"It's turning north," Jeige said. Both men strained to keep the craft in sight as most of the others poured out of the hotel.

"A sonic boom," Jeige said. "Some sort of aircraft or spacecraft." People crowded together along the railing even though they had the whole length of the veranda.

"Could you tell what it was?" someone asked.

"No, but it looks as if it's coming back," Jeige said as the craft continued its turn.

"Where is it?" one of the older women demanded. "I don't see it." Several arms were raised to point her toward it. The craft was over the hotel almost immediately, heading south now, losing both speed and altitude.

"No engines," Shadda said, almost breathless.

"It's going to crash," another voice predicted.

There was a hurried migration around the veranda to the south side. The craft was losing altitude in a hurry, and it disappeared from view as the first guests reached the southern part of the veranda.

"How far off?" "I don't see any flames." "No explosion." "Could they have survived?" "Who was it?" "Can we find it?" Questions and comments collided in destructive interference, but each was repeated often enough that they were all either voiced or heard by everyone.

"Was it ours or theirs?" Jeige asked when there was a brief hiatus in the litany. He looked to the prince. If anyone there could know. . . .

"I saw no markings," George said. "It looked a bit like our old Kappe-3 reconnaissance shuttle, but that means nothing. There are only so many practical aerodynamic shapes. And there shouldn't be any *shiny* metal on any military craft. You don't make military vehicles that are so bloody easy to see."

"Do we go looking for it?" Vepper directed the question at the prince. The others looked to George as well, apparently ready to give him the first opinion.

"I suppose we should, in case there are survivors," he said slowly, though he was eager for the adventure. "It will be a change of pace, in any event."

Several people cheered.

"I do not believe that we should all go, though," George continued, instinctively dampening the enthusiasm. "That would be most impractical. I mean, really. Perhaps there is a ship waiting to rescue us. Someone should try the radio, scan the frequencies, try to contact whoever is up there. And we do not have enough functional safari bugs to carry the lot of us and bring back any survivors we might find."

The prince scratched a line across the top of the railing with his walking stick. "We must not lose sight of the direction," he said. "That is our vector."

"Who goes? Who stays?" Mai McDonough demanded. Her words were slurred. She had already started her drinking for the day. After her behavior at breakfast, that was no surprise to the others. They all knew the pattern. Nor was anyone surprised ten minutes later when she disavowed any further interest in the matter. "I need a drink," she announced, pushing clear of the others and heading for the Savannah Room, the hotel's bar.

The arguments over who would go to try to locate the wreckage might have continued for hours if Prince George had not raised his voice and assumed leadership. "I will lead the expedition," he announced. Decades of royal training and experience at court, and perhaps also the scores of generations of royal ancestors, gave his voice an air of command that none of the others was prepared to challenge without more time.

Vepper Holford would accompany his master, whether he wanted to or not. Everyone recognized that.

"I will go," Shadda said. "Someone from the hotel must go, to look after hotel property, if nothing else."

"Your assistant could handle this," George said.

Shadda looked around the veranda, his movements slow and deliberate. Dacen Poriri, his assistant, was nowhere in evidence, as usual. And Zolsci Emmet, the services technician and only other remaining employee, was already working the radios, trying to contact the ship that had to be in orbit.

"I would not delegate this, sir," Shadda said with a formal nod to the prince. "It is my duty as your host and acting manager of the Commonwealth Excelsior."

George accepted Shadda with a nod. Jeige McDonough volunteered, and George accepted him as well. Henri and Marie Caffre were the last to be added to the party. Marie volunteered—almost demanded to be included—and her husband would not let her go without him.

"We should leave quickly," the prince said.

"If I may, sir," Shadda said. "A few moments spent stocking the safari walkers might save us considerable distress later."

"Of course," George agreed. "If you would be so good as to see to it?"

• • •

No pillar of smoke marked where the shuttle had presumably crashed. There had been no flash of fire or rumble of explosion that could be seen or heard at the Commonwealth Excelsior. By the time the expedition departed, two hours had passed since the shuttle's overflight and disappearance.

Zolsci Emmet had reported no success with his attempts to contact the shuttle's mother ship. But the narrow-focus microwave antennas had been designed to link the hotel with a satellite in geostationary orbit, not to perform search operations. It might take hours, days, to find a lower target.

The six members of the expedition left in four safari walkers—also known as walking eggs or safari bugs. Each pod could hold three people and a modest cache of supplies. Prince George and Vepper rode in the first. Shadda Lorenqui was alone in the second, carrying most of the extra supplies. The Caffres shared the third, and Jeige McDonough brought up the rear.

Before he left the veranda, George took a last check of the line he had scratched on the railing. He used the barrel of his shotgun—for a trek in the jungle he had set aside his walking stick for a more practical weapon—to hold the vector until he could walk to the bug and show it to Vepper. "Program that course," George told his aide.

The interior of a safari bug was uncluttered, utilitarian, with one wide seat in front for the driver and two seats in back. In normal times, the arrangement would have included a hotel employee to drive. But the controls were simple. Most of the work was done by computer. The driver could set a course by keypad or joystick, adjust the throttle, and override the automatics, although the coordination of the walker's eight legs would still be handled by computer. A touch pad operated the other controls, including short-range radio. The safari bug was much quieter and more versatile than floaters (ground-effect vehicles) or wheeled vehicles.

"Almost precisely south," Vepper said after he had lined up the bug's navigation program.

Prince George settled himself in the rear seat and retracted the clear canopy. "Shall we be going, then?" he said, and Vepper started the bug. The other walkers moved into line behind them.

The gait of the safari bugs looked awkward, but it was comfortable. The egg-shaped pod normally remained stable enough that tea would not slosh out of a full cup. On level ground without significant obstacles, the bugs could average fourteen miles per hour. In jungle, the bugs were unlikely to maintain half that speed, but it was still much faster, and infinitely more comfortable, than walking.

"I rather think that this must be how it felt to ride a howdah on the back of an elephant, back on Earth," George said about fifteen minutes after they left the hotel. "This is possibly even more comfortable."

"Yes, sir." Vepper had heard the comment scores of times. Sometimes he thought that the prince felt obliged to make that observation every time they rode in one of the bugs. Neither man had ever visited Earth or seen an elephant, but the prince was an ardent student of the Mother World, especially of his family and the British Empire and Commonwealth there—the *first* Commonwealth—up to the time when his ancestors had decided to reestablish the family's early glories on the galactic frontier.

"I do wish we knew how far off that ship crashed," George said, rare petulance in his voice. Vepper didn't respond. He had served the prince long enough to know when to remain silent.

George stared out, watching the jungle, letting his mind relax. There was an alluring peacefulness to the scenery, easily enough to smooth over his annoyance.

Before he had traveled three miles, Shadda was drenched in sweat even though he had kept the canopy closed and the air conditioner at maximum. *It's not the heat,* he admitted to himself. *It's never the heat.* His childhood home on Meloura had been hotter than the Camerein jungle. *Not the* outside *heat,* he qualified. If was fear that was suffocating him, and it was never "cold" fear. It was always hot—sweating, trembling hands, and stomach cramps.

Shadda had insisted on coming even though he had expected this physical rebellion. It was his duty. For once in his life he had a place, a *Position*, something that could not be taken away easily, something he would not idly throw away in a moment of rebellion or despair. Or fear.

"I hate it." *The fear.* "I never used to be like this." The unknown had been a magnet drawing him from one frontier to the next. Now, even inconsequential unknowns could provoke almost paralytic fear. The war had not really touched Camerein—as far as Shadda knew—even though the Federation had apparently taken over, destroyed communication satellites, stopped the shuttle service, and so forth. They had never come to the Excelsior, had never even overflown it. *Why has it infected me so thoroughly?* He could find no answer.

But has the war really passed us by? he wondered, not for the first time. Communications had been lost so early. There had been no news. Almost anything could have happened, and the residents of the Commonwealth Excelsior would not know. In his nightmares—garishly frightful visions that were appearing with increasing regularity—Shadda had seen the towns of Camerein totally destroyed by attack from space. In those dreams, the only humans left on the planet were the seventeen at the Excelsior, and no one in the galaxy knew—or cared—that they were there.

"We know we're not alone now," Shadda mumbled. The shuttle was proof of that. There had to be at least one starship in orbit. "There's still a chance we can get off this world." Hope for an end to the years of isolation was more powerful than any fear that the war might finally come to him.

"Shall we spread the formation out a bit?" George said over the radio. "Form a skirmish line, as it were, instead of this follow-the-leader drill? We wouldn't want to miss the shuttle, now, would we?"

Henri Caffre angled his bug to the left, between two dead feria trees. *It's a good idea,* he thought. The mark on the veranda couldn't give them a precise heading, even if The Windsor had made it. And it certainly wouldn't do to ride blithely past the wreckage without seeing it.

"Ah, perhaps a trifle more space between us?" George said after the initial maneuver was complete. "Say, fifteen to twenty yards between walkers, as the terrain allows?"

"You don't think we'll really find survivors, do you?" Marie asked her husband once the formation was spaced to the satisfaction of Prince George.

"They may have been lucky. But observe. Whether or not we find survivors is of only minor consequence, as heartless as that might sound. We find the wreckage. Perhaps we can determine to whom it belongs. We leave a message to tell the people *there*"—he pointed to the sky— "that we are *here*. If they come to investigate the crash, *voilà*, we are rescued."

"No matter who the ship belongs to?" Marie asked.

"After seven years? I think even The Windsor would accept any rescue. And who is to say what the alliances might be now?"

"How much farther do you think we have to go?"

"I have no idea. We might stumble on them momentarily. Or they might be twenty miles away."

"We could still miss them, even spread out like this."

"*C'est possible,*" Henri conceded. "But perhaps not likely, if they held a straight course after we lost sight of them. In a clearing we would have little trouble spotting them, even at a distance. In this jungle . . . well, there will be trees felled, perhaps many trees. And even if we do miss the shuttle on our way out, we merely go east or west and spread out for the trip back toward the hotel."

"I do not think that The Windsor will make *that* mistake."

They went on for several minutes before Marie asked, "Henri, will we ever get home?"

He hesitated before he replied. "More important, perhaps, will we have a home to go to?'' His voice was softer than it usually was when he spoke to her these days.

Jeige and Mai McDonough were alone in the jungle. Jeige had no idea why his wife had consented to this trip so far from the hotel's bar—sometimes she seemed to be physically chained to the Savannah Room—but she had come, and he would take full advantage of the rare opportunity.

I might never get another chance, *he told himself.*

''This looks like a good place for lunch,'' he said, stopping the safari walker under the crown of a large pumpkin tree. The branches were long and heavy, sagging, giving the area beneath the appearance almost of a tent.

''Any place's good,'' Maid said, her voice slurred. She waved a bottle of whiskey. ''Any place at all.''

''You're right, dear.'' Jeige masked any trace of his usual disgust and embarrassment at her incessant drinking. He popped open the bubble of the bug, got out, and then helped her to alight. Mai almost fell. Jeige led her to the tree trunk so that she could sit in comfort—not that she was in any condition to judge comfort.

There's no hurry, *he thought.* Show a little class. Wait for the perfect moment.

''Which do you want, dear, the beef or the chicken?'' he asked as she slid to the ground, ending up seated with her back against the trunk.

''I'll start with the scotch and finish with the gin.'' Mai laughed raucously.

Then again, the sooner the better, *Jeige decided.*

He spread a blanket by his wife. He set the picnic basket on the blanket. Only then did he drop to his knees next to her, as if he were in the process of sitting. Mai paid no attention to him, as usual. She hardly seemed to notice when he put his hands around her throat and squeezed. By then, it was too late.

I'll tell everyone that a keuvi got her, *Jeige thought as her struggles diminished, then ended.* They'll believe that. They remember what's-his-name. Perhaps a keuvi *will re-*

move the evidence. Something will. Camerein has plenty of scavengers. . . .

. . . Jeige blinked rapidly and looked around. He was still keeping station with the others, but not as precisely as he should have. His egg had drifted to the left.

"Damn, I've got to watch it." He wiped a hand across his forehead. Daydreams were fine, but he couldn't let them get out of control, not with so many of the others around. He couldn't let anyone suspect his fantasies, even though he knew they would always remain nothing more than that.

"Sometimes I wish I could do something like that," he admitted in the privacy of his safari bug. "I guess I'm still too civilized." That was easier than admitting that he still retained much of his once-fiery love for Mai.

He glanced at the bug's trip odometer. "We've come nine miles. It seems like we've been all day." According to the clock, it had been only ninety minutes since they had left the hotel.

He clicked his transmitter on. "How far off do you think they might be?" he asked.

In the next forty-five minutes, they traveled another four miles.

"Could the shuttle have veered off to the side?" Vepper asked.

"Not high enough to have gone far," George said. "I had an excellent view of their course until they were at treetop level."

"We've gone more than thirteen miles."

"Yes. The shuttle can't be overly distant now. No more than another three to six miles, perhaps considerably less."

"Yes, sir."

"The radio, Vepper," George said. Vepper pressed the transmitter button.

"You might start watching the treetops, where that is possible," George said. "Clipped tops might be our first clue to the site of the crash."

Vepper had scarcely released the transmitter button when the prince leaned forward, pointed over his shoulder, and said, ''There! What did I tell you?'' It was unmistakable. The tops of two pyon trees had been clipped. The raw wood was a clean pale tan against the dark gray of the bark.

''The radio,'' George snapped. When the transmitter was open, he said, ''There, do you see? The trees. The trees.''

There were more clipped trees, the breaks lower. Then entire trunks had been felled. The damage radiated to the sides. One wingtip had been cast aside, the first wreckage the searchers found. The natural debris became so tangled that the eggs had to detour to reach the crashed shuttle.

''Stop,'' George said. He was out before the bug's legs had folded to set the pod on the ground. The other eggs came to a stop as soon as their drivers saw that The Windsor had alighted.

George took several steps toward the wreckage, then stopped.

It could have been worse, he decided. Most of the front two-thirds of the fuselage was intact. The nanofactured skin and frame would survive all but the most extreme of traumas. But the wings and tail had broken off. One of the two engine pods had bellied out as if there had been a massive explosion within the housing. There was no sign of fire at the crash site, though, no scorched trees or burned-out underbrush.

The prince did not recognize the shuttle model. The anomaly of reflective metal was explained, though. Looking at it from so close, it was obvious that the skin had been scoured by a laser or particle beamer, destroying the dark energy-absorbing surface layer. The only visible mark on the near side of the shuttle was an anonymous serial number: 47683.

''At least we know they were human,'' Marie Caffre said.

That seemed to penetrate George's studious trance. He turned toward her, a frown solid on his face. ''Have you ever met any other type of creature that could build and fly spacecraft?''

Marie would not be put off by The Windsor. ''Not yet, obviously, but who the hell knows what's turned up in the last seven years? Do you have a crystal ball?''

''If I did have, I would hardly have been caught here, now would I? But one doesn't need crystal balls for *some* things, such as knowing that humans are the only beings who fly spacecraft.''

''Are we going to stand here talking, or do we check the inside of that thing?'' Jeige asked. He was eager to cut off the arguments. He got enough of them from his wife.

''Of course,'' George said, turning to face the wreckage again. He took one hesitant step forward. Just for an instant, he felt his resolve weaken, and he paused.

Once we go inside and confirm that there are no survivors, what then? he asked himself. One more faint hope would have been dashed. He took a deep breath and strode toward the gaping hole near the middle of the shuttle, just forward of the engine pods. Any survivors or—more likely—bodies would probably be found in that section.

The others followed The Windsor forward.

Part 1

1

(X-DAY MINUS 2)

The night had been freezing and blustery, rare for Westminster past the middle of February. The morning remained cold and breezy. There were still patches of ice. The sky had cleared, though, with only a few fair-weather cumulus clouds, scattered puffs of white in a brilliantly blue sky. The surface winds swirled and curled, seemingly unable to decide on a direction. To the southeast a bank of low clouds appeared to frost the horizon, marking the cold front that had moved through overnight.

During most of the drive in from home, Captain Ian Shrikes, Royal Navy, had kept the window open in the rear compartment of the staff floater. The bracing chill was welcome, a reminder that he was ashore. He enjoyed feeling weather of any sort. There was no weather aboard ships of the RN in space. And he would be back in space soon. Even when the cold became uncomfortable, Ian kept the window open, to the clear discomfort of his driver, a Shore Patrol petty officer.

"It could be worse, Mr. Boothe," Ian said after they cleared the security check at the gate to St. James Palace. "His Highness might have decided to go to Haven. I understand they had three inches of snow last night, and a low of twenty degrees.''

Petty Officer Boothe glanced at the captain in his mirror and tried to grin, but had trouble keeping his teeth from chattering. Boothe had the floater's heater on full blast to try to counter the cold.

"I'm from farther south myself, sir. To me, cold is anytime the thermometer drops below fifty.''

Ian smiled. "At any rate, you'll be rid of me soon and can get back to basking in the heat.''

St. James was the oldest royal residence on Buckingham. Its location had been specified on the original plat, in the center of the city, on the south bank of the river Thames. The main building covered seven acres. Another thirty-seven acres surrounded it, a landscaped oasis in the middle of the capital city of the Second Commonwealth. Parliament and the offices of His Majesty's Government were on the north bank of the river, just opposite.

The floater took Shrikes to a small entrance on the west side of the palace. Two Royal Marines stood to attention. They were a wartime addition to the king's security staff. A constable sergeant of the Metropolitan Police, the traditional security officer, opened the door from inside.

"Good morning, Captain Shrikes,'' the constable said while the Marines held their salutes. "We've been expecting you.''

Ian returned the Marines' salute, smiled and nodded to the constable, and went in. "A beautiful morning, isn't it, Sergeant?'' he asked after the constable had closed the door.

"Indeed it is, sir.'' The sergeant grinned. "Makes one think that perhaps Westminster has a little weather after all.''

Ian laughed. "I know exactly what you mean.'' The first few times that Ian had come to the palace, he had been quite nervous, but in the year that he had been aide to Prince William, the king's youngest brother, there had been many visits. Ian rarely felt truly *comfortable* at St. James, but the prospect no longer tied his stomach in knots.

He took off his overcoat and handed it to a waiting servant. "Thank you, Alec."

A butler dressed in livery that had been antique before the Windsors left Earth came out of a door a few paces along the corridor and waited for Ian to reach him. "His Highness the Duke of Haven is in the Emerald Room, sir. If you will follow me?"

The butler turned and started to walk away. Ian wasn't certain of his name. The palace had at least twenty butlers, all looking alike in scarlet and white livery with powdered wigs. The only deviation from the ancient was the small complink that hung discreetly from the man's belt.

Although there were a dozen lift tubes in the palace, Ian was led up a wide flight of stairs past portraits of King Henry's predecessors as monarchs of Buckingham and the Second Commonwealth. The succession had been unbroken, father to son, since the Founding. Although there was no constitutional or family prohibition, there had never been a reigning queen. No king had ever been without at least one son.

On the second floor, the butler led Ian along a mezzanine that overlooked the grand ballroom. The Emerald Room was on the north side of the palace, facing the river. The butler knocked at the door, which was quickly opened by a servant standing on the inside, waiting to perform just that function. As Ian reached the doorway, the doorman turned and announced him formally, as if he had come for a royal reception.

"Captain Ian Shrikes, Royal Navy."

"Come on in, Ian!" Prince William called from across the room. He turned from the windows and started toward Shrikes.

The Emerald Room was sixty feet by forty. One long wall was completely window, from floor to eighteen-foot-high ceiling. The other walls were lined by bookcases, holding actual bound books. Perhaps ten percent of the four thousand volumes in the room dated from more than a half millennium before, and about half of those had been printed on Earth. Several small tables were scattered about, with groups of comfortable chairs.

"Good morning, Your Highness." Protocol required the full honorific the first time. After that, "sir" was sufficient.

"A lovely morning." William clapped Ian on the shoulder. "Come over by the window. Tea is on the way. You look as if you've had a bracing morning. Your face is red from the weather. What did you do, walk?"

Ian smiled. "No, sir, but I kept the window open all of the way in. That made my driver quite uncomfortable, I fear."

One servant pushed the cart that held the tea service. Another walked alongside and did the serving once Prince William and Captain Shrikes were seated. The cups and saucers were the finest porcelain in the Second Commonwealth, imported from Lorenzo. The tray, flatware, teapot, and the rest of the service were of delicately etched silver. Aboard ship, Ian was accustomed to more practical tea carts, automated beverage dispensers. Along with the tea, here, was a platter with a selection of food treats appropriate for early morning.

"I hope you weren't planning to attend the lilac festival this spring," William said softly after the two servants had left. Only the doorman remained, and he was forty feet away.

"You think we'll be gone that long, sir?" Ian asked, following suit and speaking softly.

"The war has been going on for seven years. We won't end it in seven weeks."

Ian looked into his cup. As always, everything was perfect about the serving, the tea, and the food. "I've had my hopes, sir. But I've also had my worries. Do you really think that it will be possible to make an honorable peace with the Federation?"

"I think so. I pray so. Both sides have suffered, Ian. The last few years have been brutal. You know that."

"Yes, sir."

"It should be obvious to anyone that neither we nor they are likely to achieve total victory, if for no other reason than that neither side can afford the effort such a victory would require. We have received...certain signals recently that the leaders of the Confederation of Human Worlds are almost as eager for peace as we are."

"If we can agree on terms."

William nodded. "I doubt that the negotiations will be simple. The issue of sovereignty will likely remain the sticking point. The Federation does not want to withdraw its claims over all settled worlds. Other than the doctrinaire aspect, they must fear that if they make an exception for the worlds of the Second Commonwealth, it will loosen their hold on every other world that they claim, even those that recognized that sovereignty in past."

"And we can't accept any settlement that does not recognize our sovereignty?"

"Our practical sovereignty in any event, but it might take quite some time to get to that position."

"Yes, sir." In his year as Prince William's aide, Ian had learned a considerable amount of diplomacy. Negotiating with politicians on more than a score of Commonwealth worlds had been good practice for negotiating with an armed enemy. The Second Commonwealth existed only through a voluntary association of independent worlds. Only Buckingham had the dual link. It's king was also constitutional monarch of the Commonwealth. Even in the former role the king's powers were limited, though not so thoroughly as his ancestors' powers had been limited on Earth. Still, the greater part of King Henry's influence came through his ability to deal with the politicians who ran the government from Parliament. Across the river.

"Have you packed yet?" William asked after the two men had silently attended to their tea and food for a few minutes.

Ian smiled. "I believe that my wife is attending to that this morning, sir, probably has it nearly completed by now."

"My brother hasn't told me our exact departure time yet, but I suspect that that is what this morning's conference is about."

"I had the same suspicion," Ian said. "I told Antonia that she would probably only have to make up the one side of our bed after this morning."

William laughed. "How does one make up only one side of a bed?"

"Hardly even that. She scarcely disturbs the sheets on her side. I doubt that a corpse moves around less than Antonia does while she sleeps."

The prince laughed again, more expansively, but cut it off abruptly when the doorman turned to open the door.

"His Majesty," he announced.

Prince William and Ian both stood and turned to face the door as the king entered.

Henry III, King of Buckingham, Protector of the Second Commonwealth, was past his seventy-fifth birthday. There was no trace of gray in his hair, nor any age lines in his face. The hair was reddish brown, only slightly less red than it had been a half century before. The eyes were grayish blue, alert. Comfortably over six feet tall, Henry had the build of an athlete, and did remain active.

"Good morning, William, Shrikes," the king said.

The prince and captain both gave a brief bow of their heads. Their "Good morning, Your Majesty" came in almost perfect unison.

"Is the tea still hot?" Henry asked.

"I believe so," William said. There was always a place setting for the king whenever refreshments were served in the palace, just in case His Majesty should appear. William poured tea for his brother, who took one of the seats near the cart.

"Sit, both of you," Henry said. He made every show of concentrating on his first sip of tea while the others returned to their seats. "It is time, William," he said after he had set the cup back on its saucer.

"Yes, sir. That is what we both thought," William said.

"We have gone over your brief on this thoroughly," the king said. "This meeting is more to let me wish you both good luck before you leave. Your staff is prepared to depart?"

"I've had everyone on notice for a week," William said. "The ship is provisioned and needs only a few hours to get the last members of the crew aboard, about as long as it will take to get all of my staff up to it."

"Yes." Henry let that word sit alone while he took more of his tea, refilled the cup, and took another sip. Then he leaned back and made himself comfortable.

"I have every confidence in you, Will," he said, very softly. He turned toward Ian. "And in you, Captain Shrikes. I must say that I have had glowing reports of your abilities from a number of quarters. You have taken to this diplomacy dodge with admirable facility."

"Thank you, sir," Ian said.

"I have long been amazed at the extraordinary caliber of so many of the men and women who come out of our Combined Space Forces. That has never been truer than during this lamentable war. Knowing that there are people such as you serving the Second Commonwealth has been a most invaluable comfort through some of the more trying times we have experienced."

Ian was too flustered to reply coherently.

"Sorry, Ian. I did not intend to make you uncomfortable." The king smiled. "I would not have thought it possible after your time under Admiral Truscott. I've been trying to discomfit him for five years without success."

"The admiral is one of a kind, sir."

"So I have been told. But I did want to make sure that I expressed my appreciation to you for a job performed to the highest standards."

Ian's acute embarrassment had passed. "Again, sir, I thank you. I have but done my duty to the best of my abilities."

After that, the king turned his attention to his brother

again. The prince had been watching the byplay between the others with thinly disguised amusement.

"When do you want us to leave?" William asked.

"There is no call to put everyone to the test to see how rapidly you can depart," Henry said. "If you go up to your ship this evening, you should have plenty of time to make the trip to Dirigent without stressing ship or crew."

"Dirigent? The mercenary world?" Ian asked, the question out before he could keep himself from speaking out of turn.

The king turned toward him. "Yes, the mercenary world. If it were not for the Dirigenters, there might not be any talks. Their position as a neutral in the war, and their military strength, are both important. We had to have neutral ground, and we had to have a venue where our negotiators would be safe even if the Federation should happen to play us false."

"Yes, sir. I apologize for interrupting."

"No need for the apology. William's reaction was almost identical when I told him."

"We've spent so much effort trying to convince Dirigent to ally themselves with us," William said.

"And, if necessary, we shall spend more effort," Henry said. "A large part of that might have to come from you, Captain, should the talks with the Federation go poorly. With your naval background, you might well succeed where career diplomats and courtiers have failed."

"Go home and spend some time with your family," Prince William told Ian as they left the Emerald Room, after the king had made his exit. "We have a final briefing at the Admiralty at four this afternoon. That should only take thirty minutes. We'll go up to the ship from there."

"You're sure you won't need me before then, sir?"

"I believe I can survive," William said over a chuckle. "Give your wife my regards and tell her that I promise not to keep you away one day longer than absolutely necessary."

"I'll tell her, but it won't be soon enough to please her. At least, that's what she'll *say*."

"It is eminently possible that our mission will bring us back to Buckingham several times before we finish. My authority is not absolute, even with the concurrence of the representative of the Prime Minister."

The prince stopped walking, so Ian also stopped. They were in the middle of the staircase leading down to the west wing of the palace, where Ian had arrived. He had not noticed that William had glanced at his watch before he stopped.

"We really might do a lot of shuttling back and forth," William said. "It all depends on the course of the negotiations, what authority the Federation delegation has, and so forth."

"I still think it all sounds like a crashing bore, sir," Ian said. "Staying awake might prove to be a problem at times."

William laughed. "That's all part of the game. If you can't reason the other fellow around to your point of view, get him so bored that he'll agree just to escape the torture."

"And hope your threshold of boredom is higher than his?"

"Precisely." The prince had stopped where he could see the doorway. He made no move to resume his path down the stairs until a floater in navy colors pulled up in the drive outside.

"We might as well get moving," William said. "I'm subtracting from the time you'll have with your family."

At first, Ian paid no attention to the Marine lieutenant in dress blues who entered the palace. It was not until the lieutenant removed his hat and handed it to a butler that Ian really looked at him. And stopped, three steps from the bottom of the stairs.

"I'll be damned," Ian said under his breath.

Prince William was laughing softly when he turned to Ian again. "I thought you might recognize the chap."

"I nearly didn't. The uniform threw me. He was a sergeant the last time I saw him. When was he commissioned?''

''Year before last, I believe.'' William was having difficulty suppressing his laughter.

''You set this up?''

''Only when I heard that he would be coming here this morning. Come on. We might as well meet him halfway.''

David Spencer had recognized Ian Shrikes and Prince William as soon as he saw them. He wanted nothing more than to rush over and speak to them, but was too uncertain of proper behavior at the palace to do so. His hat and gloves were taken. The butler was ready to take him in tow, to lead him off . . . somewhere.

''A moment, please,'' David said as Shrikes and the prince started toward him again. The butler, who had been warned to keep Lieutenant Spencer available until the prince came down, merely nodded and stepped off to the side.

David took several steps forward. Prince William and Ian were moving more quickly. Ian was grinning broadly. The prince wore a self-satisfied smirk.

''Are you out of uniform, or are belated congratulations in order?'' Ian asked.

''I still feel like I'm out of uniform,'' David said. ''But they keep telling me that this is proper kit for me now. Good to see you again, Captain Shrikes, Your Highness.'' He paused. ''Sorry, sir. I seem to have got that twisted around.''

''Don't worry about it, Lieutenant Spencer,'' William said. ''An unexpected summons to the palace is a perfect excuse.''

''His Highness set this meeting up,'' Ian explained.

''I'm glad you did, sir,'' David said. ''It's always good to meet people you've been through tight spots with.''

''It is,'' William agreed. ''I've followed your career with interest, David. Never a disappointment. You've more than lived up to the impression I had of you back on Buchanan.''

"That's been all of five years, sir. A lifetime."

The smiles faded from all three faces for an instant. "A lifetime and more for some," Ian said softly.

"Too true, sir," David said. "We've lost a lot of mates."

"This is supposed to be a reunion, not a wake," the prince said. He made a subtle gesture, and the butler came over.

"Yes, Your Highness?"

"Harold, could you find a place close by where three old friends could spend a few minutes?"

"Of course, sir. Right this way, gentlemen."

"Er, I'm supposed to have an audience with His Majesty," David said. "Blessed if I know why, but that's what I was told."

"It's all right, David," Prince William said. "Your appointment isn't for another half hour. I asked Colonel Zacharia to send you around a bit early."

Harold led them to a room no more than fifteen paces from where they had met, on the north side of the corridor. For the palace, it was a small room, its length and width matching the eighteen-foot ceiling height. Three upholstered chairs were arranged in a narrow arc facing a fireplace. There was a fire burning. A small table held bottles, ice, and glasses.

"It seems that you arranged more than the time, sir," David said when he saw the arrangements.

"You might say that," William acknowledged. "It's a brisk day outside, and I thought a stiff brandy might be just the thing. And you do have an ordeal ahead of you, don't you?"

"Ordeal, sir?"

"A figure of speech, the meeting with His Majesty."

"Could I ask a question, sir?"

"Of course."

"Apart from this reunion, which I much appreciate, sir, could you tell me just why I was summoned to the palace?"

"You have received movement orders, have you not?"

"Yes, sir, but those have never occasioned an audience with His Majesty before."

"Quite right. But I can give you no more help on the subject. I learned long ago not to try to steal my brother's thunder."

"I'm not certain I like the sound of that word 'thunder,'" David said, and the prince laughed.

"Not to worry, lad. You haven't gotten yourself in trouble. Far from it, I would say, and that's saying more than I should. Ian, will you do the honors?"

"Already working on it." Ian had filled three glasses with appropriate amounts of brandy. He handed two of them to the prince and David. The three men sat, but only William appeared comfortable.

"I do want to congratulate you on your commission, David," Ian said. "I think the Royal Marines should have done it long before they did."

David took a cautious sip of his brandy after he had seen the prince take a drink. "I'm not so certain. I think I must be the oldest lieutenant in the RM. It feels a bit strange, if you know what I mean, sir. All these youngsters commissioned straight out of the Academy. Some weren't even born when I took the King's Shilling, and they still outrank me. Perhaps I shouldn't say it, but it's been as much a nuisance as anything else. The difference in money is nothing special, and there's bags more grief comes with it." He glanced at the prince again, to see how his statement had been received.

"It's always that way, then, isn't it?" William said. "The higher the rank, the greater the responsibilities."

"Aye, sir."

"So, what line of work have they put you in now?" Ian asked.

"They've done the odd bit of reorganizing," David said. "They took the old I&R platoons, increased the manpower, gave us more equipment, and more training. Now we're the 2nd Marine Commando Detachment, still part of the 2nd

Regiment, but more often than not, they seem to expect us to work off on our own.''

"He's being modest, our lad is," William said. "Lieutenant Spencer is the commanding officer of his detachment, and helped write the training manuals for the whole show.''

David gave an affected cough. "The colonel told me, 'This way you've got no one to blame but yourself if there's anything wrong with the drill.' ''

"Colonel Laplace?" Ian asked.

"No, sir, Colonel Zacharia. It's Brigadier Laplace now, and they've stuck him off in a staff position, last I heard," David said. "I doubt there's anyone in the regiment still doing the same job as five years ago. Some have been killed, some promoted or transferred out. You know what it's like, sir.''

"I do indeed. It's the same in the navy." Ian took another long drink of his brandy. "The next time we're both in town, we'll have to get together for more than a few minutes.''

Prince William looked at his watch. "It is near the time for your appointment, David.'' He stood, and the others hurried to get to their feet. "I want to wish you the best of luck, Lieutenant, and I want to offer my own congratulations on your commission." He extended his hand, and David took it.

"Thank you, sir. It's been good to see you again. And you, Captain Shrikes.''

Ian also extended a hand. "It's Ian at times like this, David. We're old comrades, the three of us. We went through Hell together.''

"We did indeed," the prince said. "And once this cursed war is over, I hope to have the both of you to my place in Haven, along with any others who went through that battle with us.''

"There aren't so many of us left, sir, not of the old I&R batch," David said, shaking his head.

''I know,'' the prince said, nearly whispering. ''I've done my best to keep track of the lot of you.''

''Why *was* he called to the palace?'' Ian asked after David had left the room.

''To find out what his next campaign is going to be.'' The prince finished his brandy. ''This is Most Secret, Ian. Spencer's lot is being sent to Camerein.''

Ian blinked. Hearing the name was enough to trigger the memory. ''Where Prince George was at the start of the war?''

William nodded. ''Henry wanted to talk with David personally about this. I suppose I'm to blame for him getting stuck with the job. I've bragged him up so often over the years.''

''You think it will be a rough go?'' Ian asked.

''I don't know. It might be the roughest job of work he's ever had. That's why I wanted to have this reunion before he leaves.''

''In case he doesn't come back?''

There was no need for William to answer that.

2

David Spencer tried to memorize landmarks. Harold had been waiting when he emerged from his talk with Prince William and Ian Shrikes. The butler led David along a series of corridors to a lift tube that took them to the third floor. Then there had been another series of corridors to walk. *I'm supposed to be able to find my way from point A to point B anywhere,* David thought after several turns. *It would be a disgrace to get lost here.*

He had been to the palace only once before, and on that occasion, he had needed to go no farther than the Elizabeth Ballroom on the first floor. That had been for a Commonwealth Day function the year before, his first as an officer. There had been wall-to-wall servants that day. It would have been impossible for David to get lost, even if he had not been with several other officers from the 2nd Regiment.

At least the ceiling was not so distant on the third floor, fourteen feet instead of eighteen. But there were all of the paintings, photographs, and busts that lined the corridors, the fancy chandeliers, and the rest of the trappings of luxury.

This is almost more frightening than being on patrol behind enemy lines, David thought as Harold finally stopped in front of a door. David thought that they must be near the northeast corner of the palace, about as far as possible from where he had entered the building.

The butler knocked softly. David heard no response from inside, but Harold apparently did. After a few seconds, he opened the door and gestured for David to enter before him. David was in the doorway when Harold announced, "Lieutenant David Spencer, Royal Marines," loud enough to startle him.

"Come in, Lieutenant. Over here, by the windows. Thank you, Harold. That will be all."

The door shut quietly. To David's right, near the windows, the king turned toward him. David moved cautiously forward. When he came to within two paces of his monarch, he stopped and gave a formal officer's bow, ten degrees from the waist.

"Good morning, Your Majesty."

"Please relax, Lieutenant."

"Yes, sir." David tried, but his body resisted any easing of posture. The king came a step closer.

"This is the third time we have met, Lieutenant Spencer."

David blinked. "Yes, sir. I'm surprised that you recall."

Henry smiled. "With most people, I probably would not have done so without prompting by one of my social secretaries. You would be surprised how many people I need to have around to make certain that I do not forget those who should be recalled."

The revelation had its intended effect. David relaxed visibly. The king was human, and had a sense of humor.

"In your case, I needed no reminders. The first time we met was nearly five years ago, when I pinned that King's Cross on your tunic. The second time was Commonwealth Day last April."

"Yes, sir."

"And I've had my brother, the Duke of Haven, singing your praises over all of those years. He has made certain that I remain informed of your exploits. That is why, when this current . . . affair came up, I broke one of my hardest rules and interfered in routine CSF operations."

"Sir?"

"It was I who selected your unit for a special mission, Lieutenant. I know that you have been alerted for movement, but that you have not yet been told where you are going, or why. You will receive a full briefing en route, but because of the nature of this mission, I did want a few words with you first."

"Yes, sir." David felt completely bewildered. The longer the king talked, the more desperately lost David felt.

"I wanted to be certain that the best man for the job was chosen, not just whoever's turn it was to be sent out next."

"I don't understand, sir, any of this."

Henry smiled again. "I am talking in circles, aren't I? Come. Let's sit and be comfortable. After all, we're not on parade here. These are the private apartments. Here, by the window." He gestured toward a pair of intricately carved chairs that faced a small table that had been carved to match them. David waited until the king was seated, then lowered himself carefully onto the other chair, sitting only on the edge, and trying to remain at something approaching attention.

"The first battle of this war was apparently a naval encounter over the world of Camerein," the king said. "I say 'apparently' because the Commonwealth ship that was there simply vanished, as did two others that were later dispatched to the system, in sequence."

"I know that, sir. There were Marines I knew on all of those ships."

Henry nodded. "My brother George was having a spot of holiday on Camerein at the time, at the most isolated resort on the world. That fact has not been exactly a State Secret, but it is something that has not been bruited about." He paused, and sat drumming his fingers on the arm of his chair.

"Camerein has only minimal military value to either side. It has economic value, and political value, but its population has always been rather small and there have simply been too many other worlds that required our attention more urgently. But the time has finally come for us to fully contest Camerein. That is where the 2nd Regiment will be heading.''

''Yes, sir.'' David nodded hesitantly. There was obviously more. He had to wait through another long pause, though.

''We have had absolutely no news from Camerein since the start of the war. We lost three ships there early and, since then, we have thought it safer—more prudent—to avoid sending other ships until such time as it became possible to send sufficient forces to take care of whatever may be waiting for us.'' This time, King Henry paused for only a beat.

''Your commando will be going in ahead of the rest of your regiment, but not on the type of mission you might normally be given. Instead, you are to infiltrate a part of Camerein that is one hundred eighty degrees removed from where the main invasion will take place. Your target is a hotel, the Commonwealth Excelsior.''

''That is where your brother was, sir?'' The question came out very timidly.

Henry nodded. ''Since we have had no news from Camerein, we cannot know whether George is alive or dead, captured or simply marooned in the middle of a continent-wide jungle. We suspect that if the Federation had captured him, or knew that he had been killed, we would have had some word long before now. That leads us to believe, to hope, that he has merely been stranded for these last seven years, along with the others who were at that hotel when the war started.''

''You want us to find him and bring him out?''

''Yes, if he is alive. And if he is dead, or has been captured, we would like to know the details, if possible. If there are people who have been stuck in that jungle for seven years, we want them all rescued. This is not entirely for one man, no matter who he might he.''

''We'll do our best, Your Majesty.''

"That is all anyone can ask, Lieutenant, and that is why I specifically requested that your lot draw the assignment."

The king opened a drawer in the table and took out a thin portfolio. The royal crest was on the front of the dark blue case. Henry opened the portfolio and looked at the document inside for perhaps thirty seconds. Then he nodded, closed the case, and handed it to Spencer. David took the case and stared at it, uncertain what he was supposed to do.

"Go ahead, open it," the king said. "It concerns you directly." His smile was subdued.

David opened the portfolio and looked at the top paper. He started to read but did not get through to the end. "I've been promoted to captain, sir?"

The king's smile grew. "Effective today, Captain Spencer. When I first proposed to entrust this mission to you, one of my advisors suggested that it would be improper to send a lieutenant to do the job. Before I assigned that advisor to, ah, less demanding, duties, I decided that perhaps others might feel the same way. In any event, your record certainly shows that you deserve this promotion. May God go with you."

The audience was clearly at an end. Spencer stood, bowed, took one step backward, then turned and headed for the door.

David was scarcely aware of the long trek back to the door on the west side of the palace. He followed Harold, staying close to the scarlet coat. That took only minimal attention. The rest remained focused on what the king had said, and on the implications that David could foresee. As much as the coming campaign, though, he thought about the document he was carrying under his left arm. That was the greatest shock of the morning.

When his hat and gloves were returned, David nodded absently and said something along the lines of "Thank you," but he was still barely aware of what was going on around him. The staff car was waiting. The driver got out and opened the rear door.

"You look as if you're half the galaxy away, sir," the naval rating said once both were in the floater.

David blinked several times and looked around, almost surprised to find himself out of the palace. "You may be nearer right than you imagine, lad," he said, trying to pull his thoughts closer to where he was.

The drive back to the Combined Space Forces base at the edge of the Cheapside district of Westminster took a half hour. Spencer did his best to put the king's comments completely out of mind for the duration of the ride. He stared out the side window, watching the passing scenery, buildings, and people.

It had taken a long time, but the war had finally changed daily life in the capital. At every corner, and on every advertising column, there were warnings and instructions—where civilians should go and what they should do in case of enemy attack. Constables of the Metropolitan Police had taken extensive training in emergency procedures. Units of the Buckingham Home Defense Force, a military reserve, took turns at one-month tours of active duty to provide additional manpower in the cities. There had been at least three Federation incursions into Buckingham's near space, but none of those raids had managed to strike at the world itself. The navy had intercepted the attackers and either destroyed them or chased them away first.

Two other core worlds of the Second Commonwealth had not been so lucky. Lorenzo had been attacked successfully from space twice, the target for hundreds of missiles. Those raids had left considerable damage and thousands of civilian casualties. And Coventry had suffered from a Federation invasion and occupation.

There were two separate ID checks before David got to the barracks area of the Marine 2nd Regiment. Each time, the guards took ID chips from both David and his driver and ran them through their scanners. David no longer gave that security a second thought. It had been going on for so long that he would have been shocked by its absence.

"Thanks for the ride, lad," David said before he closed the floater door outside regimental headquarters.

"Any time, sir."

Spencer climbed the short ramp to the building's entrance. The door opened automatically. David would have preferred to head straight to his quarters to get out of the formal dress uniform, but his instructions were to report to the regimental commander immediately upon his return from the palace.

Regimental Sergeant Major Alan Dockery was at his desk in the colonel's outer office. Dockery got up as soon as he saw Spencer. "I see you made it back in one piece, sir." The two had been friends since both were junior noncommissioned officers, David a corporal and Alan a new sergeant.

"I may look in one piece, Alan, but . . ." David shook his head and handed the blue velvet portfolio to the sergeant major.

Dockery did not have shock to slow his reading of the order. He grinned as he closed the case and handed it back. "Congratulations, Captain Spencer." He drew himself to stiff attention, clicking his heels noisily, and saluted crisply.

"Stuff that malarkey, Alan." There was a note of pleading in David's voice. "This morning already has me wondering if I'm one step from Bedlam and physical restraints."

Dockery laughed. "That'll teach you to go hobnobbing with the toffs."

"The colonel wanted to see me."

Alan came around the desk. "I know, and I've been remiss in my duties not getting you in there straightaway."

The sergeant major knocked at the colonel's door but did not wait for acknowledgment. "Captain Spencer back from the palace, sir," he said.

"Send him in."

Dockery held the door, then closed it behind Spencer.

"Come in, David. Have a seat." Colonel Zacharia had

taken command of the regiment when its previous commander made brigadier. Before that, Zacharia had been commander of 1st Battalion. As David sat, the colonel cleared his throat noisily. "It sets a poor example for the lads when an officer is out of uniform, Captain."

David glanced at the lieutenant's insignia on his shoulder. "I haven't had a chance, sir. I don't think it's really sunk in yet, if you know what I mean."

The stern look on the colonel's face slid into a grin. "Sorry, David. I wasn't permitted to give you any warning."

"You *knew* what was coming?"

"I knew that His Majesty planned to present you with your promotion. And I suppose that I know at least some of what he must have said to you about what's up for the regiment, and what your lot is being sent in to do."

"Yes, sir. What but not when. How much time do we have before we're off out?"

Zacharia leaned back and rotated the chair to look through the one window in his office. "If you've made plans for this evening, you'll miss them," he said after a moment. "I want your shuttles off the ground by 1600 hours."

Spencer glanced at the clock. "That doesn't give us much time to get ready. Less than four hours."

"The 2nd Commando Detachment was alerted while you were off larking at the palace. By the time you get back from the officers' mess, your people should be just about ready to go."

"I really ought to go to them straightaway, sir."

"You'll do better at the officers' mess. It's the only chance I'm going to have to give you a bit of a briefing before you start to wade through the written orders for the mission."

"Yes, sir" was the only acceptable answer.

"By the bye . . ." Zacharia opened his desk drawer and

made a show of rummaging around in it. But the small box he took out had come immediately to hand. "You'd best slip these on in place of those pips you're wearing before we go."

3

The commando detachment of the 2nd Regiment consisted of two platoons, each with a lieutenant as platoon leader and thirty-two other ranks. Ten other men were assigned to the headquarters squad. Every clerk was a fully qualified commando first. Every Marine in the unit was a combat veteran and a graduate of the commando training school. And every man in the unit had volunteered for the duty.

News of David Spencer's promotion had preceded him. The sign next to the door leading to the detachment's offices already had his new rank painted over the old. Lead Sergeant Mitchel Naughton had come from 3rd Battalion. He got to his feet as soon as Spencer entered the office.

"The lads will be ready for embarkation forty-five minutes before the lorries are due to take us to the landing field, sir," he said.

"Did Colonel Zacharia give you any details about the mission?" David crossed to his private office. Naughton followed.

"Not a clue," Naughton said after he closed the door behind them. "By the way, sir, congratulations on the promotion."

"It seems everyone in the regiment knew about it before I did. Sit down, Mitch. I'll give you a quick summary. This is Most Secret until we're aboard ship and well on our way.''

''Aye, sir. Hush-hush.'' Naughton waited until Spencer was seated before he sat.

David needed only two minutes to lay out the essentials. ''I won't know more myself until I receive our operational orders. We're going in ahead of the rest of the regiment, and we'll be on the opposite side of the world. A *real* commando operation, not any of the old I&R drill. We go in, stay hidden, reach this hotel in the middle of nowhere, find what we're there for, and get back out.''

''If there's nothing else on that side of the world, we shouldn't have much trouble, should we?''

''That is my sincere hope, Mitch, but nothing ever goes that easy for us, does it?''

''Not often enough to suit me, sir.''

''Has the orders packet come through from regiment yet?''

''No, sir, but the alert I had said that the packet would arrive shortly after you returned.''

''Get my driver to run me over to officer quarters. I need to pick up a few things to add to my kit here.''

''He's standing by. And I inspected your kit myself to make certain that you weren't missing anything.''

''Thank you. Pass the word to let the men relax once they've got their kit in order for movement. I'm not about to pull an inspection on them. Their platoon sergeants will have done a better job than I could. I might have a few words for the men when we muster for the ride to the landing field. And tell the platoon leaders that I'll want a few minutes with them as soon as I return with my gear.''

Lieutenant Anthony Hopewell led first platoon. Lieutenant Jonathan McBride had second. Neither was much more than half Spencer's age. They were reserve officers, products of the Royal Marine Reserve Officer Training Academy—six months from private to lieutenant, a wartime innovation. Each had seen combat before and after the Academy.

At a distance, it might have been hard to distinguish between the two. Each was near six feet two inches in height, muscular, athletic. Hopewell's hair was a slightly darker brown, the color of his eyes. McBride had green eyes and a slightly fuller face. The two were waiting in their commander's office when he returned. A sealed orders packet was sitting in the middle of Spencer's desk. Hopewell and McBride had been staring at it while they waited.

"Sit down," David said after a round of congratulations on his promotion. He went behind his desk and read the brief instructions on the cover of the orders packet.

"It says that the orders are not to be opened until we make our first jump to Q-space," David said, though he was certain that the lieutenants would have read that much in his absence.

"Do you have any clue where we're going?" Hopewell asked.

David sat. "More than a clue. I'll give you what I know now. Until we get to the point where I open this orders packet, though, none of this goes beyond this room. Don't even discuss it between you after you leave here. Understood?"

They nodded, and David gave them the same briefing he had given Lead Sergeant Naughton.

"That is straight from His Majesty," David said. "Then, to soften the blow, he gave me these." He gestured at the captain's insignia on his shoulder. "My guess is that he does not expect this to be a simple walk in the woods."

"How much in advance of the regiment do we go in?" McBride asked.

David shook his head. "I don't know. I presume that information will be in there." He pointed at the orders packet.

Then he opened the lower drawer on the side of his desk, pulled out a bottle and a stack of glasses. This had become something of a ritual among the three prior to leaving on a mission—and on returning. The bottle contained a single malt scotch whiskey. David poured three generous portions, and all three men stood.

"To success and a safe return." David lifted his glass to the others. They touched glasses, then each emptied his drink.

"We'll form the men for movement at 1515 hours. The lorries should be here to carry us to the landing field within minutes after that," David said.

Commando shuttles were not the standard infantry version. They were smaller, converted from other uses, supposedly as an interim measure while a totally new design was being constructed. Each commando shuttle could hold forty men with weapons, field packs, and stores to last twelve days in the field (according to quartermaster corps estimates of what "normal" usage should be in combat situations). The entire detachment could—with a little squeezing—have fit into a single standard infantry lander. But that would have put the entire commando at risk of a single enemy hit. With the men split between two shuttles, by platoons, there was a better chance that at least half of the detachment would reach the ground safely, and be operational.

Captain Spencer rode in one shuttle. Lead Sergeant Naughton rode in the other. Half of HQ squad rode with each. The additional supplies were also divided evenly, matching loads.

Since the 2nd Commando was being inserted on an enemy-held world separately from the rest of the regiment, it would not make the journey aboard *HMS Victoria*. Instead, it traveled aboard *HMS Avon*, one of several auxiliary frigates that had been modified for the purpose. Those ships carried significantly less firepower than other frigates to allow room for a commando detachment and its shuttles. Even so, it meant cramped quarters, especially for men accustomed to the more spacious accommodations aboard *Victoria* and other ships of her class.

"It's a good job these trips only take a day or two now—

adays,'' Platoon Sergeant Alfie Edwards said while he and the other platoon sergeant, Will Cordamon, were trying to fit their gear under the bunks in the tiny cabin they shared. The two were the only noncoms in the detachment left over from the days when it had been 1st Battalion's I&R platoon. They had been promoted and become part of the core of the cadre for the new unit. ''Sometimes I think this cabin is smaller than a foxhole.''

''You mean it isn't?'' Cordamon asked.

The verbal jousting went on for several minutes, but neither man had his heart in it. The words were right, but there was no feeling to them, no inflection. The men were like actors who had played the same roles for far too many years. They sounded tired.

Alfie was the first to flop on his bunk. He closed his eyes and let out a long, slow breath. His eyes didn't stay shut long, though. He stared at the ceiling, as near the light as he could. *Too bloody many ghosts in my head,* he thought. Images, memories. Mates who had died; strangers who had died, some wearing the same uniform that Alfie did, others in Federation battledress. Not all of the killing and dying had been at a comfortable distance. Enemies had died at less than arm's length . . . and friends had died in those arms. Bright light kept the ghosts away—or hid them. The hollow feeling in Alfie's stomach had nothing to do with hunger. Except when he was in combat, that feeling was present nearly all the time that he was awake, sober, and not too occupied to notice. *Maybe I ought to see somebody about it,* he thought. *Maybe they can give me something to keep them away.* But he had never been able to force himself to follow through on those frequent thoughts. It would mean opening up.

Will Cordamon sat on the edge of his bunk and unlaced his shoes. The detachment had not embarked wearing combat gear—for a change. Their departure had been low-key. The shuttles had even started off as if they were only going to one of the training ranges southeast of Westminster. It wasn't until the landers were well away from the city that they had altered heading and burned for orbit and rendezvous with *Avon*. There had been no public announcements, no fanfare. Of course, that was almost routine for the commando.

After getting his shoes off, Will sat slumped on the edge of the bunk, too tired—mentally, not physically—to flop sideways onto the mattress and get comfortable. No amount of sleep seemed sufficient to correct this exhaustion. Will stared at Alfie, waiting for him to blink. But he didn't, not for the longest time.

"How many times?" Will asked after several minutes.

That brought a blink to Alfie's eyes. He turned his head a little toward Will. "How many times what?"

"How many campaigns have we had? I can't recall. I can't pick them apart in my head any more."

Alfie blinked several more times in rapid succession. "At least six," he said after considerable thought. "It seems like more, but I'm sure of at least six. Why?"

"I don't know. Maybe because I couldn't recall them all."

"I don't remember places, just the faces," Alfie said. "Mates who bought the farm."

"Yeah."

"I think the only smart one was Tory," Alfie said. "He got out of this show in one piece. Cushy training job, home to the wife and kids every night, nothing to worry about but passing inspections and making sure the lads learn their lessons."

"He's got a third kid on the way now," Will said. "I saw him, just a few days ago. We nattered on for a bit."

"If I could find a lass who'd have me, I'd be tempted to go the same route." Alfie closed his eyes. The ghosts had suddenly become less threatening than the conversation.

Captain Louisa Barlowe was the third skipper that *HMS Avon* had had since its conversion to commando transport. An auxiliary frigate normally drew junior captains. As soon as they gained a little experience and seniority, they moved on to other ships or to staff duties ashore. A year was a long tour for a skipper aboard *Avon*. Captain Barlowe's immediate predecessor had remained less than eight months before he was transferred to one of the new Warfield-class light cruisers.

Barlowe was a petite woman who kept her cosmetic age at thirty. People who had known her for long said that she had always done that. She had been in the Royal Navy for eighteen years, and there were no flaws in her record.

She and her executive officer sat on one side of the chart table in *Avon*'s 2CC (secondary command center), which had backup controls mirroring those on the bridge, in case the ship's primary command center was put out of commission. Across the table were the three officers of the 2nd Marine Commando. *Avon* had just completed its first Q-space transit of the mission. The ship was back in normal space, eight light-years from Buckingham.

"I don't envy you your assignment, Captain Spencer," Barlowe said. They had just finished reading their sealed orders for the mission. "Camerein has been nothing but grief for us in this war—three ships lost without a trace."

"That was back in the early days, Captain Barlowe," David said, "before we knew we had a war on our hands, and before you navy people started ducking in and out of Q-space like you were simply walking from one room to the next."

Louisa smiled. "Which is why I didn't say anything about not envying my own assignment. We've always got a nice, safe place to go to in case of trouble. You and your lads don't."

"We have our tricks. With a little luck, we'll be in and out before the Feddies know that we're around. I like that part of it. Get out before the invasion if we can."

"You'll have five days. But we're not to set you on the ground anywhere close to your target."

David shrugged. "That's easy enough to understand. If we come a cropper, they don't want us to give away the location, just in case His Highness is still there. We don't let the Feddies know that we think that particular spot is important.''

"Seems a bit far-fetched to me," Louisa said. "I mean, after seven years?"

"This whole go is far-fetched. But they just give us our orders. They don't ask us what we think of them."

Barlowe keyed in a sequence on the chart table's console and a holographic projection of Camerein appeared above it, thirty-two inches in diameter, rotating slowly. As she continued to work the keyboard, a red dot appeared on one continent, and a pink circle drew itself around the dot.

"My orders are that the shuttles not approach that resort any closer than sixty miles. The dot is the resort. The circle is the sixty-mile radius. Our data are eight years old, so we can't count on clearings being in the same places. We won't be able to pick an LZ for the landers until they're on their way in.

"That entire continent is virtually empty of people," she continued. "There are, or were, perhaps a half dozen other resorts, all small, scattered along the coast, all in the tropical region, on either side of the continent. The only real town is at the far northern end of the landmass, seven hundred miles from your target. There are no roads. Two mountain chains lie across the line, and at least four substantial rivers. This Commonwealth Excelsior must be the most isolated inhabited spot on any settled world in the galaxy."

"The way we look at things, the isolation is a definite plus," David said. "There's no reason for the Feddies to show any interest. That's why it's just possible that His Highness is still there and safe. That town is no worry of ours. We'll just let the shuttles pick us up as soon as we complete our mission."

"But if something happens to us, you could have one long walk," Barlowe said.

Spencer shrugged. "We could always wait for the rest

of the regiment to arrive, let them worry about collecting us.''

"We'll try to avoid that.'' Barlowe straightened up. "We'll time our arrival to put you on the ground just after first light. I'd prefer to do the landing in the dark, but since we don't know what we're going to find in the way of an LZ, I don't want to rely totally on night scopes. It's far too easy to get false readings in a shuttle, especially during a hot landing.''

"We'd prefer the dark as well, less chance of discovery.''

Louisa studied the projection, then shook her head. "My charge is to get your lads on the ground safely, and it's much too dicey in the dark. We can't very well pop out the day before to do a recce. That would lose us any bit of surprise.''

"I wasn't trying to change your mind, Captain. I do appreciate the problem. I might make one suggestion, though. First light might not be the best alternative. Since the population centers are on the far side of the world, something closer to midday might be safer. While it's the middle of the night on the other continent. If there's nothing on this one the Feddies should be interested in, they just might not be giving it full attention.''

Avon's skipper took time to consider that, then glanced at her executive officer, who nodded. "It might work that way, Captain,'' he said. "The Feddies probably aren't going to be looking all that hard at the secondary continent. And the middle of the day? Who invades at lunchtime?''

"Very well, we'll work it that way,'' Captain Barlowe said with a decisive nod. "As soon as the navigator gives me the figures, I'll let you know the final schedule, Captain.''

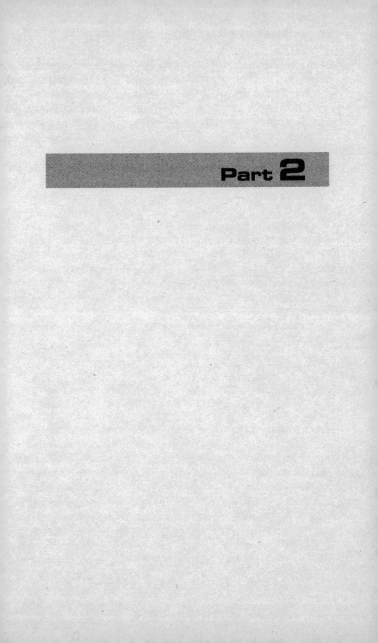

Part 2

4

(X-DAY)

A heavy odor hung around the shuttle—a mixture of ozone;
superheated metals, composites, and lubricants; and other
ingredients. The skin of the shuttle remained warm, but it
was no longer hot enough to burn the hands that touched
it. The shuttle's nose had plowed into the ground. The ex-
posed passenger deck, where the hull had broken open, was
an easy step up from the ground.

"Careful, sir," Vepper warned as Prince George started
to climb up into the lander. "Those edges look extremely
sharp."

"Yes, Vepper," George said, trying to keep annoyance
out of his voice with less success than usual. "I can see
that."

The odors were stronger inside the shuttle, and more
pungent. George needed only one glance to learn another
component of the stench.

"There are dead people in here. I see twelve bodies.
We'll have to check each of them, to make certain." He
turned to look at the others. Jeige had already climbed into
the compartment. Shadda was just stepping up. The others
waited their turns.

"Probably dead crew up front as well." George moved away from the gash in the side of the fuselage. The deck was angled steeply. Forward and starboard were down. It was difficult to move without sliding or falling.

Military men, of course, George thought as he checked the two who were closest to him. *Royal Marines, from the battledress.* Both men were dead. They had flash burns in addition to whatever other injuries they had sustained. One man's neck had obviously been broken. The head lolled over limply.

"There must have been a fire in the cabin," Shadda said. He backed away from the man he had just examined. He had touched the side of the man's neck, feeling for a pulse, and charred skin had come away on Shadda's fingers. For a moment, the acting manager of the Commonwealth Excelsior thought that he would vomit. Bile rose in his throat as he brushed the dead skin off against his trousers. The bits of flesh stuck, did not come off easily, but he worked at it until they were all gone. Then he moved farther along the aisle, looking at each man but not touching. There was no need. These men were all quite obviously dead.

Prince George had not moved from the first two men he had approached. "It looks as if they were injured before the fire, before the crash," he said, a hint almost of wonder in his voice. "We must have missed something." Looking around, he could see more traces of a flash fire on the bulkheads. The fire could have been nothing more than that, a quick flash that had singed but did little more. "This man appears to have been shot." He pointed at a bloody wound on the chest of one dead Marine. There was a bandage half peeled away from the hole.

"They were perhaps trying to escape from something?" Jeige suggested. *I know about escape.* He moved close to the prince and looked down. "That is definitely from a bullet, a very large-caliber bullet, not the sort of thing an infantryman would have."

"An aircraft cannon, perhaps?" George said. "That entrance wound is a half inch in diameter."

''They must have been on the ground,'' Jeige said, ''trying to escape when something happened to the shuttle as well.''

''Perhaps the lander was also damaged on the ground,'' Shadda said. ''It tried to reach escape velocity but lost power.''

''Why hasn't their ship sent another shuttle to check on them?'' Marie Caffre asked. She was outside, looking in, with her husband next to her. ''There's been time and more for that. You'd think they'd want to find out if there were any survivors.''

''Maybe their ship was disabled as well,'' Vepper said. He was farther outside, behind the Caffres. Only a direct order from the prince could have induced him to enter that shuttle.

''Yes, their ship might have been disabled,'' George said, not thinking about the words until they were out. *Their ship might have been disabled.*

For a time, the people from the hotel all forgot about the bodies and the wreckage. As if their reactions had been choreographed, each started to look around at the others. At first, none of the faces showed any change of emotion. The Windsor's words needed time to sink in, even for him.

''Their ship might have been disabled,'' he repeated, separating the words carefully. He blinked twice, slowly, then looked around again, meeting the gaze of each of the others in turn. ''It might even have been destroyed.''

The implications were clear. Each of them had lashed considerable hope to the evidence that there was at least one starship—hopefully, but not necessarily, a *friendly* ship—in orbit over Camerein. After seven years of isolation, any discovery would be welcome. Not a threat. But if there had been only one ship, and if it had been disabled or destroyed, then they were no better off than before.

''We'd better see what else we can learn here,'' Jeige said.

•   •   •

While the others, except for Shadda, continued to examine the dozen men in the shuttle's passenger compartment—not just checking for survivors but emptying pockets, looking for identification or anything that might indicate what ship, what *world* they were from—George moved forward and "climbed" the three steps to the flight deck. The way the shuttle had angled in at impact, the top and bottom of the stairs were almost at the same level. The door to the flight deck was jammed. The prince nearly fell from his awkward stance on the stairs as he finally managed to pry it open.

There were no signs of fire on the flight deck. The crash damage was more severe, though. The cockpit windows had been smashed, popped out of their frames, and parts of the bulkheads had crumpled inward. Both crewmen were still strapped into their seats. One pilot was clearly dead. His shoulder straps had snapped, impaling him on the control stick. But the other pilot was still alive—barely. He opened his eyes a little when George touched his shoulder, and mumbled one word: "People." Then the eyes drooped shut again.

"People," George repeated. He reached for the side of the flyer's neck, to assure himself that there was still a pulse. The beat was as faint as the one word the pilot had managed to speak before he lost consciousness. George turned his head toward the hatch leading to the troop compartment and lifted his voice just a little to say, "Vepper!"

"Sir?" It took a moment for Holford to reach the prince.

"This man is alive but badly injured," George said. He moved aside to give his aide access. Vepper had extensive training in first aid, part of the preparation for his position as George's companion. He examined the survivor, then looked up and around.

"We'd best get him laid out on the floor, sir."

George nodded. Vepper unbuckled the pilot's safety harness, and they got him stretched out on his back along the center of the flight deck. Several of the others were standing where they could look in from the passenger compartment.

No one spoke. They merely watched, and wondered if the man would survive long enough to answer their questions.

Vepper opened the front of the man's coveralls to do a more thorough examination. "There's a first aid kit in our bug," he said without looking up. "Somebody bring it. Quickly!"

"What do you think, Vepper?" George asked after Shadda left to get the medical gear.

"If we had a trauma tube here, there'd be no problem," Vepper said. "But we don't. And I didn't see one among the gear in the back, either."

"Can we get him back to the tube at the hotel?"

"We'll have to try." Vepper's voice made it clear that he didn't hold much hope that the flyer would survive the trip. "I'll see if I can stabilize him. But that's a long and uncomfortable trek in a safari bug, even if we get a dozen med-patches on him."

"Here's the first aid kit!" Shadda was breathless as he slid the case across the floor toward Vepper.

"You need my help for this?" George asked.

"Not just now, sir," Vepper said, already rummaging through the kit for the items he needed.

"Sing out if you do." George returned to the front of the flight deck. He went through the pockets of the dead pilot, then turned his attention to the shuttle's controls and gauges. There was no power at all, not even for the radios.

There's no way here to contact anyone, George thought. He knew that it had been a vain hope. Even before leaving the hotel, he had never considered the possibility that they might find the shuttle in any condition to fly, but he had hoped—in a childish, waiting-for-Christmas fashion—that they might be able to contact the shuttle's mother ship and find out just what had been going on in the years of their isolation.

If he does live, we've merely added another exile to our number. George turned and spent a few seconds watching Vepper and the wounded flyer. Vepper was working with every appearance of competence, seeking each point of injury and applying medical patches with their analgesics and molecular repair units. But the pilot showed no obvious signs of life, no promise of recovery, even temporary.

"Did anyone find anything in the back?" George asked, aiming the query at the people visible in the doorway.

"Their ship was apparently the *Avon*," Henri Caffre said. "I found that name stenciled on a couple of items. And one man had a readable ID chip. It showed Bridger as his homeworld." Henri shrugged. "I am not familiar with it."

"I've seen the name," Jeige said, "but I really don't know anything about the world."

"A Commonwealth member," George said. "A fairly new settlement, I believe. I've never been there, though. Vepper?"

"Yes, sir, new." Vepper kept working on his patient. "It's a surprise they have men to send off to the Royal Marines yet."

"A Commonwealth world," Marie said, wistfulness and deep disappointment in her voice.

"They haven't forgotten us," Shadda said. Then his stomach growled noisily, and a couple of the others looked at him. Shadda flushed in embarrassment. "I'll have a look at the rest of the wreckage," he said.

Shadda wandered around the crash site. There was no clear purpose to his route, or to the superficial inspection. He was no more than a sightseer. Looking back along the shuttle's path, he was astounded by the extent of destruction to the forest. He was even more amazed at how much debris there was from the crash itself . . . but there could be nothing useful in it, not to him or his companions in exile. *A Commonwealth ship!* Maybe there was a chance for rescue, but it looked more like a missed opportunity to Shadda, a missed chance for relief from the tensions that had so knotted him up over the past seven years.

"A chance to start *living* again," he whispered. It was too much. Shadda walked away from the shuttle and from the visible evidence of the lander's final approach and crash. He went to a pumpkin tree nearly a hundred yards from the craft, leaned his forehead against the cool orange bark, and closed his eyes.

"We've lost the only hope we've had in seven years," he whispered. "Will we ever have another?"

The prospects for rescue seemed bleaker than ever before, even though—logically—the likelihood that there was at least one friendly ship somewhere in the area should have provoked almost unbounded optimism. Shadda bumped his forehead against the tree trunk several times, each time with a little more force. The predictable pain from the masochistic act was welcome. But then his stomach cramped, severely, and that distress took his mind off everything else for a few minutes.

"If we don't get started soon, it'll be dark before we get back to the hotel," Jeige observed.

Nothing was going on inside the shuttle at the moment. Vepper was sitting back on his heels on the flight deck, just watching his motionless patient. There was nothing more that he could do for the flyer.

"I'm afraid to move him yet," Vepper said. "I don't think he could stand the strain of being carried to one of the bugs."

"Let's go outside for a moment, Vepper," George said. "Marie, will you watch over the pilot until we return?"

"Of course." For once, Marie had no argument with The Windsor. As soon as he moved away from the stairs, she moved up onto the flight deck. Vepper had not moved from his position next to the pilot's head.

George stared at him from the doorway and said, "Vepper," softly but firmly. Holford got to his feet and followed the prince out of the shuttle.

"Does the pilot have any chance at all?" George asked, whispering even though none of the others had followed them out and there was no sign of Shadda.

"I think not," Vepper replied. He glanced back toward

the shuttle. "Very little, anyway. He appears to have massive internal bleeding, and med-patches alone won't do much for that. There's just nothing else I can do for him here, and I doubt very much that we can get him back to the hotel."

"Is there any point in trying?"

"We can't leave him as long as he's alive, sir. As long as he has any chance at all, however remote, we must continue to do whatever we can."

"Of course. I was not suggesting otherwise. Do you think that he will regain consciousness before he dies, if that is to be his lot?"

"There's no way to tell."

"We really have no choice then, do we?" George asked. "We might as well move him to one of the bugs and start back. If he is to die anyway, it makes no difference, but we owe him every possible chance. Is the trauma tube at the hotel operational?"

"I presume so, sir. We haven't needed it."

"Well, let's find something to use as a stretcher."

"There's a folding stretcher on the troop deck, strapped to the bulkhead. It won't fit in a bug full-length, though."

"But we can use it to get the man to the walker without hurting him worse than he is already." George turned back toward the shuttle. *I just hope the man has a chance to tell us what he can before he dies. He must have some idea what's going on. It would be nice to have some certainty for once.*

Henri and Jeige carried the stretcher, picking their way through the debris between the shuttle and the safari bugs. Vepper hovered at the side, keeping a hand on the pulse—on the life—of his patient. George and Marie went ahead to prepare Jeige's bug to carry the pilot. Shadda had come back from his wandering just as the others were lifting the injured flyer onto the stretcher. But he did not tag along during the transfer. He spent several minutes inside the shuttle instead.

"What the blazes is he doing in there?" Marie asked while she and Prince George waited for the others to reach them.

George shook his head. He had noted Shadda's earlier reluctance to remain in the shuttle with its bodies. Now, the man seemed to court their company. "It is somewhat odd."

There was a long groan from the pilot as he was maneuvered into the rear of the walking egg. Marie and Henri collected spare cushions from the rest of the walkers to prop around the injured man. That task was nearly complete before Shadda hopped out of the shuttle and ran to rejoin the others.

"I left messages," Shadda said, as breathless as if he had just run a marathon. "I said that there are seventeen of us at the Commonwealth Excelsior and left directions. If anyone comes to investigate the crash, they'll find the messages. Anyone," he repeated, looking around as if daring the others to chastise him.

"Admirable, Shadda," George said, giving him a nod. Shadda grinned, his gastric distress momentarily forgotten.

"I had to take the chance, sir," Shadda said. "Even if they've all forgotten the Commonwealth Excelsior, they might yet come to investigate this crash."

"That is possible," George said.

"There is something else, sir."

Shadda paused, long enough for George to urge, "Go on, man."

"There were only twelve bodies in that troop compartment. It looked as if it might handle forty men. Maybe the dozen were all that it carried this time, but maybe—just maybe—the shuttle had put troops on the ground before . . . whatever happened. I admit that it's a long shot, sir. I mean, why were the dozen left aboard if the others had landed? But I thought we should not miss any chance."

"You did right, Shadda," George said. "I doubt that there were others put aground first. As you say, it seems to leave no rational explanation for those who remained aboard. But I agree. It would not do to miss any possibility, however remote.''

The sun had dropped more than halfway from its zenith, but the new clearing that had been ripped out of the jungle by the crash meant that the sun was still visible, forcing shadows from the people standing by the safari walkers. Then they all suddenly acquired second shadows as the sky brightened. The impulse was irresistible. All six looked up into the eastern sky. There appeared to be a second sun, a bright white dwarf. The new light was too brilliant for anyone to look directly at it. George was the first to speak, as the sudden light started to fade almost as quickly as it had appeared.

''It appears that their ship has exploded. *A* ship has exploded, at any rate.'' *What radiation are we soaking up from it?* he wondered, but he wasted neither thought nor time on a futile attempt to escape it. Any damage was already done. Their nanotech health maintenance systems could take care of any direct damage to cells unless the molecules of that system were themselves damaged severely.

''There goes our rescue,'' Shadda said. It was almost a moan. Tears formed at the corners of his eyes. He wiped at them quickly, almost savagely.

''Unless there is more than one ship above, no?'' Henri suggested. ''What disabled this one, neh? There must be someone else up there, friend or foe.''

''Quite,'' George said. He looked around the group, then cleared his throat. ''The sooner we get started, the sooner we can get this chap into the trauma tube at the hotel.''

If he lasts that long was everyone's common thought. The extra sun in the sky had already faded to oblivion.

George set a faster pace as the safari bugs started back toward the Commonwealth Excelsior. Potential harm to the injured flyer had to be balanced against the faint chance that a little speed might get him to the trauma tube in time to save his life. George took the driver's seat in the lead bug, letting Vepper sit in back where he could more easily keep an eye on Jeige's walking egg behind them, the bug carrying the injured copilot. There had been no room for Vepper to ride with the injured pilot; Vepper was certainly in no condition to *drive*. He was too agitated.

"His condition is so fragile," Holford muttered. "He has so little chance."

"We're going as fast as I dare," George said.

"I know, sir. Even air transport might not be fast enough to save him."

The convoy of safari bugs had covered half the distance to the hotel when everyone heard Jeige's panicked voice on the radio. "He's having convulsions, shaking all over the place!"

"Stop your bug!" Vepper shouted toward the radio. "This may be it, sir. I have to get back to him at once." He was out of the egg before George managed to get it settled on its stomach with the legs folded. Vepper ran to Jeige's bug. McDonough was just getting the canopy lifted.

"Get out. Give me room," Vepper ordered.

The flyer was thrashing around in the rear seat. His face was flushed a deep red, almost purple. Vepper knelt by the seat and tried to restrain the injured man with his body and left arm while he searched through the first aid kit with his right hand.

A sedative might stop his heart, Holford reminded himself, *but if I don't do something quickly he's dead anyway.*

"Another hour, mate," Vepper whispered as he dug out the remaining med-patches. "Another hour, please." First the sedative, on the man's neck, to stop the convulsions, then a stimulant and blood regenerator, right over the heart. "One more hour and we'll have you safe in a trauma tube," he promised.

The flyer suddenly stopped his thrashing. He relaxed and expelled one long breath. Some of the red seemed to fade from his face. He opened his eyes and looked up. The flyer stared, but the blank brown eyes did not seem to be seeing anything.

"Always hurry up and wait," he said, so softly that Vepper barely heard him. Then the pilot's eyes closed again. A strangled gurgling noise escaped from his throat.

Vepper felt for a pulse on the man's neck, but he knew that he would not find one. He took a deep breath before he looked up and said, "He's dead."

"Are you sure?" Jeige asked, his voice displaying a hard edge that might have presaged hysteria.

"I'm sure." Vepper rose and stepped out of the walker.

"What was that he said?" Henri asked. All of the others had gathered around the walker.

" 'Always hurry up and wait,' " Vepper quoted, his eyes looking back to the dead man.

"Military," Shadda said. His stomach was rebelling again, noisily and at length. He put a hand to his gut and pressed against the agony.

"We knew he was off a Royal Navy ship," George reminded the others. "Those were Marines in the troop compartment."

"The war continues," Marie said, as if she had not heard anything that had been said before.

"So it seems," her husband replied.

"How could you have thought anything else?" the prince asked. "A downed shuttle, Marines aboard. Of course the war continues. Or a second war has begun." He turned and walked away. The outburst had been unseemly. *My own disappointment,* George thought. *I wanted a chance to question the man, find out about the war.*

For several minutes, no one had anything else to say. Mostly, they stared at the dead man. Occasionally, they glanced at each other. One more corpse. They had left thirteen of them in the shuttle. Somehow, this one death seemed more personal, more important, than the others. They had witnessed this death.

"I used to fly as copilot on a shuttle, back in my military days," George said when he returned to the group. His voice was soft now, reflective, almost casual. The others understood the implicit *It could have been me* in his words. They recognized it because, one way or another, they had all felt the same thing, even though none of them were pilots. *It could have been me.*

"What do we do now?" Henri asked.

"We return to the hotel," George said. He straightened up. His voice regained some of its accustomed timbre and volume. "There's nothing else we can do here."

"What about . . ." Shadda asked, not finishing the question.

"We can't just dump him," Jeige said. "We'll have to take him along and bury him at the hotel."

"Yes," Vepper said. "It's the least we can do."

"Naturally," George said.

"I'll drive him," Jeige said, forcefully, as if there had been an argument over who would have that honor. Or duty.

It was nearly dark before the column of safari bugs emerged from the trees near the hotel. The sun was ready to disappear below the horizon. After the flyer's death, the group from the hotel had possessed neither the need nor the desire to hurry. The pilot was beyond help. He was done hurrying, done waiting, whatever might have been behind his last words.

"Can you get a blanket or tarp for him?" Jeige asked Shadda as soon as everyone had parked near the hotel's veranda and climbed out of the walkers.

"Of course," Shadda said.

"Where do we bury him?" Marie asked.

"With the others who died here?" Shadda suggested.

"Along the path, down by the river?" George asked, as if he had to struggle to recall the location. "Near the edge of the hotel lawn?"

Shadda nodded. "I'll get something to cover him with." He left the group quickly.

"Where are the shovels and so forth?" Jeige asked before Shadda entered the hotel. "I'll start digging the grave."

Shadda stopped and turned back to him. "There's no need for that. I'll fetch Dacen and Zolsci. We'll take care of it."

"No," Jeige said emphatically. "I'll do it."

The unaccustomed physical labor was a distinct relief. Jeige could not recall the last time he had done anything requiring even a tenth so much effort. He had certainly done no physical work since coming to Camerein, and it had been years before that, perhaps even before his marriage. Thinking of that, of his wife, put more force into Jeige's motions. He growled, unaware of the sound.

He had found a spot next to the path leading to the river, slightly closer to the hotel than the other graves that had been dug during the war. The first step was to remove the sod. The roots of the local grass were tightly interlocked, but the blade of the shovel was sharp and cut through without much difficulty. Once Jeige had incised the boundaries of the grave—eight feet by three—he removed the remaining sod from the center of the rectangle. The turf was set aside to be replaced later.

Dusk had faded into dark by the time Jeige got that far. The only light he had, except for the moon and stars, came from the veranda of the hotel, more than a hundred yards away. It was enough. The darkness seemed fit to the chore.

"Will that be large enough?" Jeige stepped off the length and width again, using that as a rest from the hard work. "It should be okay," he decided.

Once below the protective roots of the grass, he found the soil sandy, easy to excavate. He moved into a steady rhythm, using first one foot and then the other to plant his spade in the dirt, tugging back to free it, then tossing the load up and out of the hole. He worked from one end to the other, one level at a time, back and forth.

Jeige was surprised at how quickly the work went—and how fast the stigmata of work appeared on him. In ten minutes he had large blisters on both hands, for the first time in more than twenty years, but even those gave him little trouble. If anything, they were welcome reminders that he was actually doing honest, necessary work for the first time in decades. The dirt, the sweat, and the pain in his hands and back were badges of honor. And the pain was never severe. The medical nanosystem in his body provided pain relievers as needed.

He even felt a moment of regret when the work was done. The hole was four feet deep and he knew that he could not make it any deeper without risking a major cave-in of the sides. The sandy dirt wouldn't hold. Even climbing out brought down some of the dirt on one side.

As soon as Jeige returned to the hotel, Shadda hurried to meet him. Jeige spotted Prince George and Vepper in the foyer, seated on cane chairs. Through the archway, he saw several of the others in the dining room. And he could hear his wife's voice, loud, raucous, laughing, from the Savannah Room.

"My husband the gravedigger," Mai McDonough said, as derisively as her advanced state of intoxication permitted. She came out of the shadows to stand in the bar's doorway. "See any ghosts? Talk with Yorick's skull?"

"It's ready," Jeige said, almost in a whisper. He spoke to Shadda rather than to his wife.

"Everyone has been waiting," Shadda said. "We will all be there to say farewell to the flyer. We have not served dinner."

Jeige blinked several times in rapid succession as an idea popped into his head. He glanced toward the door of the Savannah Room. His wife had already retreated to her usual post inside.

"I need a few minutes to clean up first," Jeige said. "Will you walk upstairs with me? I need to talk to you."

"Of course," Shadda said with a quick nod.

5

The journey aboard *HMS Avon* had been quick. The Marines scarcely had time for five hours of sleep before they were roused to eat, then board their shuttles for the ride down to the surface of Camerein. It was either go immediately or wait a full day. The two captains, Spencer and Barlowe, had decided to go at once. "It will give us an extra eighteen hours, if we need it, before the regiment lands," David had said. "An extra eighteen hours to get back up here before the fireworks start, if we're lucky."

The plan was for *Avon* to stay in normal space over Camerein no longer than it would take her Nilssen generators to recycle for the jump back into Q-space. Spencer and Barlowe had worked out a timetable for communications. The ship would return periodically to maintain contact with the commandos. Those sojourns would be as brief as the first, unless something went wrong on the ground, until it was time to schedule pickup for the Marines and the people they hoped to rescue.

"Dependent on local conditions," Barlowe qualified. "We can't take on overwhelming numbers. If the Feddies have the place well defended topside, we may have to cut back on our communications forays. We might even have to wait for our battle group to arrive before we can pick you up.''

"Understood, Captain," David said.

"Good luck and God speed, Captain Spencer."

The Marines boarded their shuttles before the ship made its final transit through Q-space to Camerein. There would be no time after the ship emerged over the world, not with *Avon* planning to jump back after only ninety seconds in normal space. And in typical military fashion, the men were put aboard their landers early, just in case some unforeseen snag arose.

It was a lonely time, sitting crowded together in a shuttle waiting to be dropped on a combat run. The Marines sat with their safety harnesses tight, rifles held between their legs, at least one hand also holding the weapon. Once it was launched from its mother ship, a shuttle had no artificial gravity. That would have required a Nilssen generator, and those were too bulky for a combat lander—''unnecessary luxuries'' according to the CSF. All of the men sat with helmet visors down. The tinted faceplates hid expressions from anyone who might be looking. It gave each man almost total privacy, closed him in with his own thoughts, interrupted only by checks from squad leaders and platoon sergeants.

David spoke to all of his men before *Avon* entered Q-space for the last jump—a few words of encouragement. Then he switched to a channel that would connect him with only the platoon sergeants. "Alfie, Will, you'll have to keep your lads on their toes for this. If we've got the layout right, we shouldn't have any Feddies on our backs. It should be just us and a lot of hot walking in the jungle."

"We'll walk the whole world if we have to, Cap," Alfie said. "That's better than fighting any day."

"Amen" was Will Cordamon's only comment.

"Unless our luck goes completely south, the Feddies should never even know we're around. The ship's not sticking around all the time. And there's nothing much on the side of Camerein we're heading for, no reason the Feddies should be looking there.''

"No reason *we* know of,'' Alfie said. "Last I heard, we didn't know anything at all about the place since we lost those three ships back at the start of this soddin' war.''

"My mother always told me 'No news is good news,' '' David said. "After seven years of quiet, that's another reason why the Feddies might not be too sharp at looking for things here.''

There was the standard warning before *Avon* jumped into Q-space. Then the ship's Nilssen generators created a space-time bubble just larger than the ship's longest dimension, closing *Avon* off from the rest of the universe. Navigation determined at which point to stress the bubble and by how much to make the necessary transit—direction and distance. Then the Nilssens reversed polarity and spat the ship back into normal space. Generally, a ship took three transits of Q-space to get from one star system to any other in the explored reaches of the galaxy.

The two shuttles were launched from *Avon* six seconds after the ship emerged in normal space over Camerein.

Avon emerged one hundred seventeen miles above sea level, nearly as close to a planetary mass as the ship was designed to approach. Even as the shuttles were launched, *Avon* fired maneuvering rockets to halt her descent. Then, as quickly as her Nilssens could recycle, she jumped back to the safety of Q-space. By that time the shuttles, accelerating toward their landing zone, were clear of the zone of interference from the nascent Q-space bubble. Being caught in that could have catastrophic effects even for capital ships.

Alfie Edwards was the busiest man in his shuttle. He talked with the platoon as a whole; with squad leaders and assistants, singly and as a group; he even talked with a few of their men individually. The activity was a relief for him. It was the one time that Alfie welcomed the responsibilities of leadership. It kept him from having time to think, to brood. The five years since his first combat had aged Alfie Edwards considerably. There were times when he thought of himself as an old man, even though he was still in his twenties. On the odd occasions when he thought back to the way he had once been, the platoon clown, he could no longer recognize the bloke in his memories. That chap had been young and carefree, certain of his own survival even when his mates were being killed around him.

Just a dumb kid, Alfie thought, *too stupid to know any better.* He looked around the shuttle's troop compartment, at the blank faceplates on the helmets. There was no way to tell that the faces under those tinted visors were all new. Of the men who had been in the old I&R platoon of 1st Battalion during its first battle of the war, only three were still with the unit. The I&R platoons of all of the regiment's battalions had contributed to the new commando unit. Most of the other I&R platoons had suffered as badly as 1st's. Back at the start, Alfie had been a private, happy with his rank and lot. Will Cordamon, in the other shuttle now, had been a new corporal. David Spencer had been a junior platoon sergeant. The others . . .

It was because Alfie didn't like to think about the others at a time like this that he was glad that he was too busy to do so while the shuttle was on its way in. The heroes and cowards. The one man who had been court-martialed for killing prisoners. Those who had died. The lucky few who had transferred out.

Faces looking over his shoulder. Voices recalling the past. Screams in his brain.

"Five minutes left," Spencer said on his all-hands channel after the pilot passed him that information. "Lock and load."

In two shuttles, Marines ran rifle bolts to put a round in the chamber. For some, it was time for a last prayer before hitting the ground. Throats tightened. Stomachs churned. This was the most vulnerable time. Locked inside the landers, the Marines were helpless passengers, unable to defend themselves or escape if anything went wrong.

This is one time that nothing should go wrong, Spencer reminded himself. *Sneak in and be on the ground before anyone can do anything even if they do see us.* But he took little comfort from his attempts to reassure himself.

The pilot reported four minutes left. The words were scarcely out of his mouth before he had more news for Spencer, unwelcome news.

"We've got trouble, Captain, a blip coming in hot. It'll reach us before we get on the ground. We're working to put distance between the shuttles, make it harder for the bogey to get both of us."

"Enemy fighter?" David had no idea what else it might be over an enemy-held world, but he could not hold back the query.

"Yes, on an intercept course and accelerating."

One chance in a million and we get the short end. Spencer could hear his heart thumping. He did not share the news with his men, not even the platoon leaders and sergeants. There was nothing that any of them could do but worry, and David knew that he could do enough of that for the lot of them.

"We're running electronic countermeasures," the pilot said. "We're going in short to try to get you on the ground in one piece. It's going to be rough. We'll be landing faster than the Book says we can. Make sure your lads are strapped in tight."

"Will do." David switched to his all-hands channel. "Tighten up your harnesses until it hurts, and hold on. Brace for a hard landing. We're going in hotter than hell to try to get down before an enemy fighter intercepts us. When we ground, I want the shuttles empty in five seconds. Grab what you can, but get out fast. Get the SAMs into play if we've got a target." One man in each squad carried a surface-to-air missile launcher. Three others carried spare rockets.

There was no three-minute warning. The pilot announced

two minutes, then one. In between, he told Spencer that the enemy fighter was still closing rapidly. "It's nip and tuck, Captain. If he fires at extreme range, it could come just as we're touching down."

Yellow warning lights came on in the troop compartment. When the countdown reached thirty seconds, those were replaced with flashing red lights. When the hatches opened, green lights would come on. Regular troop shuttles had a ramp in the floor. Those landers sat on skids, well off the ground. The converted shuttles that the commandos used had wide hatchways on each side, easier for loading and unloading cargo, and the landers had skids built into the bottom of the fuselage, putting the deck no more than eighteen inches off the ground.

Red lights. "Crash-landing drill," David reminded his men. He braced himself, then took a deep breath. Seconds to go.

The landing was the roughest he had ever experienced. The shuttle skidded sideways as it plowed across a grassy field. The men were jerked from side to side. Several struck their heads against the bulkheads. Even with helmets and padding, the blows were enough to stun a couple of men.

Retro-rockets brought the shuttles to a halt in little more than three hundred yards, much less than the manuals allowed, and hard on the men who had to endure such extravagant braking. The savanna grass caught fire in several places. The bulkhead lights turned green as the hatches were opened.

"Up and out!" David shouted over the all-hands channel. "Move it! Move it!" He was already out of his harness and on his feet.

Closer to the starboard hatch, Alfie Edwards used his bayonet to slice the straps holding the extra supply packs. With one hand, he pushed men toward the exit. With the other, he picked up bundles and hurled them into the arms of the men racing out of the still-moving lander.

"Clear away from the shuttles!" Spencer shouted as he

got out. He could see the enemy fighter coming in. "Hit the dirt!"

The two shuttles had come to rest three hundred yards apart. David could not see if everyone was out of the more distant craft. It was slightly closer to the approaching Federation fighter. And the fighter had already launched a pair of missiles.

"Get the SAMs going!" David yelled. "Bring that bastard down!"

A half dozen rockets went up. The enemy fighter's missiles arrived first, destroying the shuttle that 2nd Platoon had come in on. The explosion scattered fiery debris across a one-hundred-fifty-yard radius. Screams told David that some of his men had been hit. But the fighter came down as well, hit by two rockets.

"Are your men clear?" the pilot of the surviving shuttle asked Spencer. "I've got to get out of here before that fighter's wingman shows up."

"Can you hold?" David asked. "We've got wounded. I'll need a few minutes to get them loaded. We'll give you what cover we can with our SAMs. Will you wait?"

"As long as I can. Don't bother with the crew of the other shuttle. They've had it. One of those rockets went off right against the cockpit."

It took five minutes to administer first aid and get the wounded loaded aboard the remaining shuttle. A dozen injured men were strapped in. The rest of the supplies were unloaded. Five dead Marines would have to be buried. The pilot and copilot of the other shuttle had not been located.

The grass fires continued to burn, spreading quickly, growing. Near the shuttle that was still intact, Marines beat at the flames, trying to keep them away from the lander's open hatches as the wounded men were loaded aboard.

"We're clear!" David Spencer told the pilot as he ran from the hatch. "Get out while you can." The eight seconds the pilots delayed gave David just enough time to get clear. The lander accelerated toward the edge of the savanna. The tree line was less than a mile away, but the shuttle took less than a third of that.

"Form them up!" David said over the channel that connected him to his platoon leaders and platoon sergeants. "Let's get under cover before any more Feddies come looking."

The smoke and flames would be visible for miles, a marker sure to draw the attention of any orbiting spyeyes and any planes or spacecraft that the Federation might have in position to see. The men with SAM launchers kept those weapons ready, scanning the skies as the commando moved toward the nearest cover, the tree line that the shuttle had just cleared.

Once in the air and above the ground obstructions, the shuttle turned due east. The Marines could still see the lander when it started its burn to climb for orbit, and then they saw another object moving toward it, coming in from the north.

"Keep moving!" Spencer shouted when a few men stopped. "It's too far away for our SAMs to reach it. We've got to get under cover, fast." He had had to slow down a little to talk, but as soon as he finished giving orders, David picked up his pace again. In seconds, they were all running for the cover of the trees—even the men carrying the bodies of the men who had died in the first attack.

The first two missiles that the fighter pilot launched missed the shuttle, confused by its electronic countermeasures. But the fighter fired another pair, and then started firing his RACs—rocket-assisted cannons. At top speed, a fighter could overrun projectiles from normal cannon or machine guns. One of the war's latest innovations was a cannon whose rounds continued to accelerate after being fired instead of losing speed as they fought atmospheric drag.

The men on the ground could not see or hear the impact of those shells, but a couple of men thought that they saw the shuttle seem to stutter in flight. It continued to accelerate, but it was clearly no longer gaining altitude as quickly as it had been. It passed beyond the horizon of the men on the ground before the Marines pulled up under cover of the trees.

"We'll take time to catch our breath and get organized," Spencer told his lieutenants and platoon sergeants. "See to your men and get the burial parties working, then come over to me."

"Cap, this is Will." Cordamon waited for Spencer to acknowledge his call on their private link. "Lieutenant McBride was one of the injured. We had to put him on the shuttle."

"How bad was he hurt?"

"Busted shoulder, for starters. He was one of the last men out and got hit with a bunch of shit when the shuttle blew."

"See to your men, Will. You got hit hard."

"We did," Cordamon agreed. *Cut in half before we even got started,* he thought. The five dead and twelve injured had all been from his platoon. None of the headquarters squad people had been touched. Half, just over half, of his platoon's strength was gone at one stroke. Will felt sick to his stomach. The nausea came on so strong, so quickly, that he lifted his visor, afraid that he was about to vomit. He fought it. *Got to set the example,* he told himself. And he felt that he was winning, conquering the urge. The nausea receded—until one of the men close to him lifted his faceplate and puked. That was too much. Will joined him.

The leaders moved away from their men. David Spencer, Mitch Naughton, Anthony Hopewell, Alfie Edwards, and Will Cordamon. All had their visors up. Except in extraordinary circumstances, the commandos would restrict the use of helmet electronics, including radio, until they finished their mission.

"I hope that we got all of the injured out," Spencer said, looking at Cordamon. "We're going to be doing a lot of hard moving, and some hero who thought he was doing right by sticking around with a wound could bollix it for all of us.''

"All of the wounded went out," Will said. "I just hope they made it back to *Avon*."

David nodded. "So do I, Will, but we can't help them now. And we've still got a mission."

"We should know in a minute or two," Naughton said. "It's almost time for *Avon* to come out for the pickup."

"We have problems here to worry about," David said. "The first is that we've lost nearly a fourth of our strength. The second is that we've lost about forty percent of our extra supplies. The third is that we're forty miles farther from our destination than planned. We've got to move almost a hundred miles to reach our target, damn near all of that through tropical jungle."

"I guess that puts the mockers on getting in and out in three days," Alfie said.

"Even if *Avon* can still pick us up," Spencer said. He held up a hand then, listening to a call from the ship. He pulled his visor down to bring his microphone into place and replied. The others could not hear either end of the conversation.

"The other shuttle didn't make it," David reported when he lifted his faceplate again. "The ship marked where it went down but hasn't been able to raise anyone."

Will Cordamon turned away from the others. *All of them dead,* he thought, assuming the worst.

"We're on our own for at least five days," David said, trying to keep his voice level, and working hard to concentrate on what lay ahead, not on the men who had been lost. "Even if *Avon* uses its own boats to retrieve us, we've got at least five hard days ahead of us." He paused. Up to this point, only the officers in the detachment had known the full scope of their orders, and that their mission wasn't the only operation set for Camerein. "If we can make it five days and a few odd hours, we should be okay. The rest of the regiment will be landing then, if all goes according to schedule."

"I thought there was just this one place out in the middle of the woods here," Alfie said. "What makes it important enough for the whole regiment to come barging in? I mean, I can see where there might be something, or someone, to drag our lot in, but everybody?"

"Two different operations, Alfie. Camerein is a Commonwealth world. We want it back. That's what the regiment is coming in for, and they're going to be on the other side of the world, where most of the people are. The rest . . ." David paused. It was time to let these few others know the entire story, but he still hesitated. Then he nodded to himself, took a breath, and started.

"Here's the rest of our job. Just among the five of us for now." David told them exactly why they were on Camerein early.

"After seven bloody years?" Alfie asked.

"No reason why they couldn't keep going that long," David replied. "This hotel was supposed to be self-sufficient. They'd have all the food replicators and whatnot they might need, and all the power to keep everything running. As long as the folks didn't do anything foolish, and the Feddies didn't put them in the bag, they could last a lot longer."

"Is anyone worth all the men who've already been killed?" Will asked. "Just to get the king's brother out?"

"Easy, Will," David said. "I know what you mean, but there's no help for it."

Cordamon turned and walked away, slapping his visor down over his face as he did.

"He's got a point, Cap," Alfie said. "Ain't nobody worth that, not but one of our own lads."

"We don't leave one of our own behind if there's any way to get him out," David said. "The king's brother is as much one of our own as anyone else. Remember Prince William? You thought he was a right bloke. Weren't those your very words?"

"He was different. He got right down in the dirt and fought alongside us. He *was* one of us."

"And Prince George is his brother. If it comes to it, you think he won't fight at our side as well?"

"I don't know this one. I know the other. And I knew all the lads we've lost already."

"Get your lads ready to move," David said. "We've got a lot of ground to cover. While we're here, we'll run the headquarters squad as part of 2nd Platoon. I'll go talk with Will."

6

The 2nd Marine Commando had been on the ground for fifty minutes before they started hiking toward their target. West of them, the grass fires continued to burn, but with less ferocity. The wind had switched direction, turning the flames back into areas that had already charred, starving them. There had been no further signs of enemy activity in the air.

David moved with the truncated 2nd Platoon, on the right. The two platoons were thirty yards apart, following parallel tracks. The going was not difficult. The terrain was mixed between open woodland and savanna. David had checked his mapboard—a specialized portable complink that folded in thirds—to see what sort of terrain they had to go through. The commando would not hit thick jungle, tropical rain forest, for twenty-five miles.

At least we shouldn't have to worry about mines or snoops, or anything else but nature . . . on the ground, David thought once the platoons were finally moving. It always took time for a unit to slide into proper field rhythm. With the commando, that point in time came fairly quickly. Only six of the men who had left Buckingham had not been on at least one mission as part of the unit. Two of those were already dead.

The only remaining new man in 2nd Platoon was walking just in front of Spencer. Private Evan Fox was extremely aware of the fact that his commanding officer was right behind him. He assumed, incorrectly, that it was because he was the newest man in the unit. He found it difficult to avoid glancing back over his shoulder. The urge would build, and he would fight it. At first, that distracted him. Only when he became aware that he was not being as conscientious about watching the right flank did Fox start focusing on his proper work. But even after that, the distraction returned periodically.

I wish he'd find some bloody other spot to walk, Fox thought. *Let me do my job without breathing down my neck.*

Spencer had dropped out of line and let five men pass him before Fox even noticed that the captain was no longer immediately behind him.

"Freeze!"

The command came from one of the men on point, over the all-hands channel. Every man in the unit stopped as soon as both feet were on the ground. They went as motionless as statues, waiting for more information.

David stared toward the point. It was the man heading the column on the left who raised an arm and pointed toward the sky, making two slow up-and-down motions. Then he touched the side of his helmet and made a gesture as if he were twisting a dial. Spencer cranked up the gain on his helmet amplifiers. The point men would have done that routinely, to improve their chances of hearing any threat sooner. As soon as David had the volume up, he knew why the point man had stopped the two columns. Aircraft.

The men were all under trees at the moment, but the canopy was not particularly thick. The risk was not that an enemy pilot might spot the men in their camouflage battle-dress, but that motion sensors might pick up movement. David used hand signals to order his men down, slowly. The platoon sergeants, nearer the front, echoed those signals so that everyone could see them. Like his men, Spencer sank carefully to the ground, squatting first, then stretching out into a prone position.

At first, David could not guess how many aircraft, or what type, might be approaching. He rolled half onto his side so that he could look up. *Fighters or shuttles?* he wondered. *Or both?*

David was not surprised that the Federation had sent someone to look. One or both of the pilots who had attacked the commandos' shuttles had to have radioed news of the intercept to their headquarters on Camerein. More forces *had* to be dispatched to search. The appearance of even two Commonwealth shuttles would have put every Federation soldier on the planet on full alert, waiting for an invasion, and looking for survivors.

If it was me, I'd send fighters first, and have ground troops alerted to move in next, David thought while the aircraft—now clearly more than one—continued to approach. *Look over the wreckage, then go in looking for the bodies.* A shadow against the sky moved too quickly for him to be certain what it was, just that it was larger than any bird he had ever seen.

We're not nearly far enough from the shuttle was David's next thought. *As soon as we get back to our feet, we've got to move again, and move fast. We've got to put more distance between us and the start of any search.* They had been on the move for an hour, perhaps a few minutes more. The commando was only about four and a half miles from the wreckage of the first shuttle. *That's not far enough by a long shot,* David thought.

He gave the enemy aircraft time to move away, then got to his feet. Using hand signals again, he got the unit moving. He was tempted to set the pace at a jog, but with the extra supplies the men were carrying, along with the normal weight of weapons, ammunition, and combat gear, running would be foolish. It would quickly result in the group making less progress rather than more.

David moved between the two columns, halfway between point and rear guard. He lifted his helmet and shouted new instructions. "Crank your earphones up to the maximum. As soon as those planes come back in our direction, take cover again. We've got to put as much distance as we can between us and the wreckage back there."

Less than a minute later, they were on the ground again, waiting for the aircraft to pass a second time. Up and move, then down and wait. Two Federation fighters worked a search pattern centered on the wreckage of the first shuttle, coiling out to greater distance each time around. That meant that each orbit it took longer before one of the aircraft came close to the men on the ground. But after fifteen minutes of that pattern, the commandos heard the fighter engines suddenly accelerating away.

The 2nd Commando picked up its pace, not running, but pushing the walk. Lieutenant Hopewell, Lead Sergeant Naughton, and the two platoon sergeants came back to Spencer for a hurried conference, on the move.

"We've got to put as much distance down as we can before the Feddies put troops on the ground to check the shuttle and look for survivors," Spencer said, the sentence interrupted more than once by the need to suck in air. "And we've got to avoid leaving a trail they can follow."

"We don't leave trails," Alfie said. "That's what putting a corporal at the rear of each line is all about, somebody to make sure we're not painting arrows."

"Drop back and tell them to make double sure," David said, looking at Will Cordamon as well. "We're going to veer off to the left about ten degrees and hold that course for several hours. If the Feddies do happen to spot us, I don't want us giving them a perfect vector to our target."

Three hours passed before the commandos heard aircraft engines again. The time the sound was different, lower in pitch, and the movement slower. David reached the obvious conclusion that the Feddies were sending in troop shuttles. But those three hours had taken the unit more than a dozen miles farther from the wreckage. The forest was somewhat thicker now. Even if the shuttles passed directly overhead, David would not have been overly concerned about being discovered from the air. And the shuttles did not pass immediately above the commando. They went by farther south, moving east to west. It was time for another rest, and for another conference.

"If they search for us on foot, we should be far enough ahead that we won't have to worry," Spencer said when Hopewell and the three top sergeants gathered around him. "They won't be able to travel any faster than we have, and we're not about to sit and wait for them to catch us up. And it would take almost as much time for them to do the sort of slow and sure air search that might find us."

"You're not telling us that we don't have to worry about the bastards," Alfie said. It was not a question.

"No, I'm not," David agreed. "It's bad enough that the Feddies know we're on the planet, worse that we lost our shuttles and a lot of good men. But what I am saying is that if we stay on our toes, there's no reason why we shouldn't be able to keep at least two or three steps ahead of them."

"We keep going as we have been?" Hopewell asked.

David nodded. "We must be seventeen or eighteen miles from the shuttle now. We've made damn good time. But I want to push the march hard for at least another two hours before we settle down for a decent rest. Then we'll take an hour before we push on again."

"Sir, the men can't go on indefinitely without more of a breather than that," Naughton said.

"I know, Mitch. We'll have to take four hours to give time for the blisters on everyone's feet to heal, give the lads a chance to kip out. Two hours on the march, one off, two on, then we'll stop for at least the four hours."

Naughton nodded, but said, "We won't make as good time as we've made so far."

"Mitch, you're the only man we've got who's within ten years of my age. Tell them that they can go on as long as the old man can, and be ready to run me into the ground if they have to.''

This time Naughton smiled. ''There's a few might like to give it a try.''

David returned the smile. ''I know. On second thoughts, let's save that sort of go for when things get really sticky. We might need that trick another time.''

''Yeah, don't go getting us into any foot races we don't need,'' Alfie said. ''I'm feeling twice my age already. I don't need any of the lads proving I'm as old as I feel.''

The commandos made every effort to stay under cover, except for brief exposures as they crossed clearings or the narrow creeks that seemed to lie across their path every mile or so. Still, none of them saw the brilliant glow of light in the sky that signaled the loss of a starship.

By the time that Spencer finally signaled for the promised long halt, the sun had been down for two hours. Traveling in the dark posed no extra hazards for the commandos. Marine helmet visors provided excellent night vision systems, a dual track using both available light multipliers and infrared.

Four hours. Walter Kaelich sank to the ground in relief. Four hours did not seem near long enough to recover from the day's march, but he was not about to waste any of that time in futile protests, even to himself. He sat with his back to a tree trunk. He leaned back and closed his eyes, ready to sleep. But he could not sleep yet. There were things that had to come first. He removed his boots to get air circulating around his feet, and slapped med-patches on the blisters on both heels. He pulled a meal packet from his pack, stripped the wire that opened the container and heated the contents, then ate. He was too exhausted to eat quickly, but he tried to maintain a methodical rhythm, getting the food in and down without wasting time.

Kaelich was a private in headquarters squad, the captain's clerk. That had never saved him from the twenty-five-mile hikes in training, and it earned him no special privileges on campaign. He had no red tape to generate or multiply on a mission like this. That was the only respite, and it was temporary. Once they were back on Buckingham, or in a more stable situation on Camerein, he would have that work to bring up to date.

I did volunteer for the commando. During the eight months he had been in the unit, he had been forced to remind himself of that fact quite often. *I wanted to think that I was really contributing to this fight.* Walter Kaelich was a stubborn man. He would not complain about something he had asked for, no matter how much it hurt.

The livid bruise on his left shin—although he could not see it through his battledress and the field skin underneath, he knew that there had to be a large black and blue spot on his leg—hurt more now that he was off the leg than it had on the march. The leg throbbed. He had caught a glancing blow from a small chunk of the shuttle when it was destroyed. Had he been in one of 2nd Platoon's squads, a squad leader or assistant might have checked on his slight injury, perhaps even shipped him off on the other shuttle. But in HQ squad, there were only the captain and lead sergeant, and both had had other things to think about at the time.

I should strip down and have a look, Walter thought. The field skin had not been breached. That meant that he would need to undress almost completely to see the injury. A field skin was, in effect, a living body stocking that covered everything but hands and face, a symbiotic organism built by molecular assemblers. For a Marine in the field, it was an essential piece of equipment. A field skin recycled wastes, provided insulation against heat and cold, and could help stem minor bleeding.

But if I strip to look, others will see. Too many questions to answer. Kaelich thought about it until he had finished eating, then decided to do nothing. If the leg was any worse after he slept, maybe then. He could always slap a med-patch over it to ease the ache. The nanobugs of his health maintenance system should see to the rest.

• • •

HMS Avon had made its first transits into and out of Q-space over Camerein on schedule. After launching the shuttles, the auxiliary frigate was back in Q-space before the sighting of two Federation fighters was relayed to the bridge. *Avon* would not have been able to do anything about them even if the news had reached Captain Barlowe sooner. All *Avon* could have done was launch missiles, and the range had been extreme for that. The enemy planes would almost certainly have been able to evade the weapons, and the shuttles would still have been in danger.

Louisa Barlowe sat in her command center on the bridge with gritted teeth while the ship was in the gray limbo of Q-space. There was a great temptation to return to normal space over Camerein as quickly as possible, to *see* what was happening even if she could not affect it. Not giving the order took more self-control than Louisa would have anticipated. Her imagination was not deficient. She knew what might be happening. It was possible for a shuttle to avoid an enemy fighter . . . but it was not especially likely.

I hope they get the Marines down first, she thought. *Maybe the pilots will stay down and save themselves as well, even if they lose the landers.* The shuttle crews were navy, *her* people.

"We'll stay precisely on schedule," Barlowe informed the bridge watch after *Avon* emerged from Q-space on the far end of the transit, thirty-seven light-minutes from Camerein. "We'll find out what happened then," she added more softly.

Confirmation of the losses did not make them easier to bear. "Have the boat officers ready the ship's gigs in case we have to use them for pickup," Captain Barlowe instructed as *Avon* returned to Q-space again. She had spoken briefly with Captain Spencer on the ground. "We'll maintain the communications schedule you and I set up," she had assured him.

It was a promise she would be unable to keep.

There was a scheduled link late that afternoon, local

time. *Avon* emerged from Q-space. The two captains spoke for eighty-one seconds, using all of the available window during the ship's sojourn in normal space. Precisely ninety seconds after emerging from Q-space, Louisa Barlowe gave the order to return.

Something happened.

Just as the gray of Q-space closed around *HMS Avon*, the ship shuddered violently and started to spin end over end. There was the sound of an explosion aboard ship, echoing through *Avon*'s skin and bones. Throughout the vessel, anyone who was not strapped in was thrown about by the violent contortions. In practice, that meant a few members of the duty watch, and nearly everyone else. Before *Avon* stopped spinning, more than a hundred crew members had been injured. Few got off with only bumps, bruises, and minor cuts. There were scores of fractured bones—arms, legs, ribs, clavicles . . . and skulls—concussions, internal trauma. Even those who were strapped in did not escape completely. Some were hit by flying debris. Others managed to slam heads into bulkheads, suffered sprains, or had bones dislocated.

For three minutes, the chaos was too great for anyone to do anything but hold on. When the ship finally settled down, its spinning halted by maneuvering rockets, it took more seconds before anyone could try to get back to work.

Monitors still showed the gray of Q-space around the ship. Inside, objects and people drifted around, no longer secured by the customary artificial gravity field of the ship.

"What happened?" Captain Barlowe demanded.

No one had any ready answers.

"Damage control, I need a report," Barlowe said.

"Still working at it, Captain. We have injured people all over the ship. Something happened just as we entered Q-space. I don't have any idea what." There was a pause before the damage control officer added, "All three Nilssens are off-line, Captain. Engineering hasn't been able to estimate how long repairs might take, or if repairs will even be possible."

On the bridge, that occasioned a long silence. The people in the compartment looked at each other, then at the monitors that showed the featureless gray around the ship. It was the navigator who eventually gave voice to what everyone on the bridge, including Captain Barlowe, was thinking.

"Without the Nilssens, we can't get back to normal space."

7

Vepper, Shadda, Jeige, and Henri carried the dead pilot from the veranda of the hotel to the grave that Jeige had dug. The flyer's body had been wrapped in a blanket, and a tarp had been wound around that. All of the exiles at the Commonwealth Excelsior attended the graveside funeral, not just the six who had made the trip to find the wreckage of the shuttle. Even Mai McDonough came out. Her husband raised an eyebrow when he saw her staggering along the path from the hotel toward the river, but he said nothing.

Prince George automatically took a position at the head of the grave. The stretcher was placed across two bars that spanned the open hole. The other exiles stood around the sides and foot of the hole—shadowy forms around an open grave in the dark of night that might have suggested a bizarre cult with macabre rituals. Camerein's moon was nearly full, lending strange tones to skin, casting definite shadows.

"We never had an opportunity to get to know this man, or the others who died in the shuttle crash today," George said after a moment of silent prayer. "That is our loss." He looked around at the indistinct forms of the others. *Did any man ever have a smaller kingdom to rule?* he asked himself. That was a recurring distraction. Quite often during the past seven years he had caught himself thinking of the Commonwealth Excelsior as his kingdom, and its residents his subjects . . . but those thoughts always remained private; he had never even confided them to Vepper, who knew virtually everything else about his master.

"All that we really know is that this man was an officer in the Royal Navy of the Second Commonwealth, one of the pilots of a naval shuttle, and that there were also twelve dead Marines aboard that craft. We can only speculate on what that might or might not mean for us here." He paused, glad for the dark. "But this is not the time for such speculations." It was bad form to let other concerns, no matter how vital, detract from the dignity of the moment.

"I don't know all of the proper words for a time like this," George continued. "All I recall of the traditional formula is 'Ashes to ashes, and dust to dust.' " He paused again and looked down at the stretcher. A dark lump in the deep shadows of the night was all that he could see.

" 'Ashes to ashes, and dust to dust.' That is enough, perhaps. His family will mourn him when they learn that he has been lost. His friends and comrades will remember him, for a while. The universe will move on, as it always does. In time, each of us will join him in the journey beyond, wherever it leads. We commend him to whichever god or gods he believed in, whoever is to receive his spirit now."

Dacen Poriri and Zolsci Emmet held the body while Shadda removed the stretcher and the two bars. No one had thought to bring ropes to lower the flyer into his grave, so Dacen and Shadda climbed down into the hole to lower the body gently. After they climbed back out, with help from several others, Prince George shoveled in the first load of dirt. Shadda took the spade then and pushed in considerably more, as did Jeige. Then Shadda gestured to his assistants and they took over the work, without enthusiasm but also without protest. The others started back to the hotel.

At first, the procession was silent, hushed by the sounds

of dirt being scraped and tossed into the grave. Mai McDonough tried to hurry ahead of the others, but she was so intoxicated that the faster she tried to walk, the slower her progress became, and the farther she drifted from a straight line.

"I need a goddamn drink," she said, very loudly, after managing nearly half the distance. "All thish phony crap. Jest a waisht of time."

Jeige moved to her side and took her elbow to steady her. "Enjoy yourself tonight, my dear," he said in more conversational tones as he guided her along the path.

"Wha's that s'posed to mean?" She pulled her arm free and spun to face him, almost falling in the process.

"Just what I said." He smiled and took her arm again. This time she didn't try to pull free. "Enjoy yourself this evening. I had a talk with our esteemed hotel manager earlier. Beginning tomorrow morning, none of the liquor dispensers in the hotel will fill your orders, and no one else will do it for you. You're going on the wagon, my dear— nothing stronger than the excellent tea the hotel serves."

"Goddamn you! Don' you dare!" She pulled free of his grasp again and backed two steps away, swaying wildly. "Don' you dare! I'll kill you, you sonovabitch!" she screamed.

"Sorry, dear. But if we do ever get off this world, I don't want my wife to be a hopeless lush."

Mai clenched her fists and charged at her husband, ready to do battle. But she tripped over her own feet and started to fall. He had to catch her. When she was able to stand on her own again, she turned away and went on ahead to the hotel without another word.

Shadda double-checked to make certain that he had locked the door to his room behind him. He was more exhausted than usual. He felt feverish and had a dull, throbbing headache. The medical sentinels in his body would prevent anything *serious* from developing, but they were not designed to prevent all pain. Pain was still a necessary alarm system.

There were conditions that might need additional medical treatment.

"Today, it wouldn't be normal if I didn't feel this way," he decided. "Today, I have more than earned my aches and fever."

Zolsci had been unable to raise any ship above Camerein despite the hours he had spent scanning with the radio. If there was a ship there, Zolsci had not locked an antenna on it, or it wasn't listening—or at least it wasn't *answering*.

The late dinner, following the interment, had been a terrible ordeal for everyone. Mai McDonough had screamed and fumed in a constant tirade—mostly against her husband, but not leaving out Shadda. At first, Mai had tried to get at her husband again, promising to scratch out his eyes and rip his face to shreds. But after she had been foiled at that, she had returned to her drinking, pouring as much alcohol down her throat as she could. It had taken an extraordinary amount of time for her to finally pass out.

Shadda had been tempted to applaud her collapse, as some of the guests had actually done. He had immediately gone to his office to reprogram the drink dispensers from the controlling complink. There would be no more alcohol for Mai McDonough, not even mouthwash. The machines would ignore her demands for liquor, and there was little chance that anyone else in the hotel would get drinks for her. Physical addiction was impossible, or so Shadda had always believed—a body's health implant system would prevent anything like that—but Mrs. McDonough had clearly become psychologically addicted.

There would undoubtedly be more scenes.

Shadda closed the shutters on the window in his room, then turned off the lights before he stripped out of his clothes and sat on the edge of his bed. The darkness was incomplete. The numerals on his bedside clock glowed. Some light entered the room through the louvered transom over his door. Shadda could make out objects in the room without difficulty. He looked at the pillows on his bed. Exhaustion: sleep; the ill: the cure. But Shadda did not simply keel over into bed. His exhaustion extended to a mental inertia so complete that even that simple movement was beyond him. He just sat on the side of the bed.

I saw one man die today. I saw all of those others, already dead, horribly dead. He rested his elbows on his knees and let his head sag into his hands. *At least their suffering is over.* That brought a thought that he dared not voice, even in the privacy of his room. If he ever said the words aloud, they might take control of him. Instead: *No, that's not for me. There's no escape. I couldn't do that if I tried. I don't have the courage.* He knew then what was coming next.

His body started to tremble. His stomach tied itself in painful knots, burning, boiling. Every hint of a sound, in the hotel or outside, was magnified into an unknown threat. Ghostly images floated before his eyes. Shadda could not shut them out even by squeezing his eyes tightly shut. Memories took almost physical form to taunt him. Scarcely suspected futures—dreadful, painful futures—waited to claim his body and soul. No escape was possible—or even conceivable. There was an eternity of torment waiting, his exile at the Excelsior lasting through the eons left until the universe would burn itself out.

Finally, all that Shadda could do was hold himself as tightly as possible and keep his head down, waiting for the unfightable terror to pass . . . or for it to finally crystallize and strike him down. He had no idea how long it was before he finally collapsed into nightmare-ridden sleep.

Prince George had not needed an alarm clock or wake-up call since he was ten years old. When he was a child, some of the servants in his father's palace had found him a little spooky. George always seemed to wake just before they could call him. He anticipated. The reactions of the servants provided the only feedback that George had ever needed in order to hone the talent. Causing that slight consternation became one of his secret pleasures. In time, George found that he could program himself to wake at any given time, virtually to the minute, and his mind developed an uncanny sense for time even when he was awake. Even after he left the comforts of his father's establishment for his schooling and military service, the gift had not deserted him. In fact, it had become more valuable than ever.

It didn't matter that he had managed less sleep than usual this night. George could get by with two hours a night at need, for extended periods. When he woke the morning after the expedition to the crashed shuttle, he knew that an hour remained before first light—because that was when he had willed himself to wake. The hotel was as silent as it ever got, and there were few sounds from outside. The night hunters had mostly finished their business. The day hunters had not awakened yet. And the cachouris had not yet started their morning cacophony.

George sat up and swung his legs out of bed. He stretched, then stood and stretched again, reveling in the sensations of his body—the proof of life. He moved silently about his morning routine, enjoying the anticipation of his morning plans. After his visit to the bathroom he dressed quickly, all the way up to a hunting vest with all its pockets and loops filled with shotgun shells. He had counted forty-seven shells, plus the five that Vepper had loaded into the shotgun the night before.

As he slipped into the heavy vest, George reminded himself, *I must ask Master Lorenqui to make more shells. I'll be using them rather more quickly than before.* He smiled as he buttoned the heavy vest. George picked up his shotgun and let himself out of the room. He took the back stairs down through the kitchen and went out the rear of the hotel. He cut across the lawn until he reached the path to the river. The sky was clear, and the brilliance of the late stars gave him enough light. As long as he stayed on the path after he was beyond the trimmed lawn, he would be in little danger of tripping or getting snagged by a jungle vine.

He paused at the side of the new grave. "I do wish you had survived," he whispered, "whatever your name might have been." It wasn't entirely a selfish thought. Certainly, it would have been nice to question the man about the progress of the war, and even better to have learned that there was a ship over Camerein that could take them all back to civilization. But George found himself genuinely regretting the loss of a man he could scarcely claim to have met. " 'Any man's death diminishes me,' " he said, and he couldn't recall where he had read or heard that quote.

"Rest in whatever peace you can find," George whispered. He looked around, as if to see if there were others watching. Then he went on toward the river. He followed the path to the pumpkin tree with so many cachouri nests visible that he had pointed out to Vepper just the morning before. George stood off near the edge of the tree's branches, where he still had a little light to assist him. There was no sound from the birds yet.

"We'll soon put that to rights," George mumbled.

He raised the shotgun and pulled the trigger. The explosion of the shot was followed quickly by screeches from hundreds of birds wakened from sleep. Panicked squawking obliterated the sounds of birdshot ripping through leaves and into branches and nests. George continued firing the shotgun until it was empty, pausing briefly after each blast. The shrieking of the cachouris was far different now from what it was when they went through their morning ritual. The hint of terror was welcome to the lone gunman below. And each time he heard the soft thud of a bird's body hitting the ground, his smile grew a little wider.

George slid five more cartridges into the shotgun's magazine, then pumped one into the chamber. The time that took gave the cachouris a chance to settle down a little. There was no blind flying off for them. Cachouris would not fly at night, even in terror. George moved a little, off to the side, on the edge of the path, going partway around the tree to give himself new targets. Once more he emptied the shotgun's magazine into the canopy, moving his point of aim carefully with each shot, relying more on memory than sight to tell him where the greatest concentrations of nests were.

By the time he had emptied the shotgun for the sixth time, there was a little more light. The sun hadn't appeared, but dawn had started to sketch itself against the horizon. George could see two dozen dead birds on the ground under the tree, and he had heard other bodies splash into the river. Soon he would be able to see those dead cachouris floating away—if he cared to look.

Now that he could see his targets better, George was slower to shoot, more deliberate, more selective with his aim. A single blast of the shotgun could riddle three or four nests if he were careful. More dead birds dropped. Very likely, there were also bodies in nests, or caught in the lower branches. The shrieking of the surviving cachouris was constant now, rising in pitch with each new assault. *Blast* and *shriek* were the only sounds that George could hear, all that he *wanted* to hear. His ears had become numbed to other frequencies, other sounds. Blast and shriek. It was enough.

"Quite satisfactory," George announced after he had emptied the magazine of his shotgun for the last time. He had two cartridges left in his vest. He loaded them into the gun, but he was finished with his morning's sport. The last two shells were for an emergency—in the unlikely event that a keuvi or one of the jungle's other large predators might be crazy enough to come *toward* the sounds of so much gunfire.

As his hearing started to recover from the effects of the gunfire, George heard people shouting, back at the hotel. The prince smiled while he tried to get a better estimate of the number of birds he had killed. There were at least four dozen on the ground, plus however many had fallen into the river or remained in the tree. In any case, he absolutely had to have averaged more than one dead bird for every shell he had fired.

"*Quite* satisfactory," he repeated, and then he turned and started to follow the path toward the hotel. He walked more slowly than he normally did, savoring his triumph.

"Don Quixote lives," George said softly. It was going to be a good day.

8

David Spencer begrudged every minute of darkness during which the commandos were not moving. Night was an infantryman's friend. But the men needed a rest after moving hard and fast for so long. David needed rest as well, but he had responsibilities. He was awake before the end of the four hours he had allowed for the break. Mitchel Naughton was already awake. He had been checking the sentries when Spencer noticed him.

"You know, sir," Naughton said when they came together near the middle of the bivouac, "a lot depends on how large a garrison the Feddies have on Camerein. If they've got the manpower, they'll put in whatever it takes to find us."

"I know. It's like an itch you can't scratch. And the Feddie commander will need to fill in the blanks on his report properly. 'So many enemy troops came in, so many accounted for.' Just like an accounting clerk totting up income and expenses. The sums in the two columns have to agree."

Naughton gave an almost silent chuckle. "I won't tell anyone if he wants to fudge the numbers."

David smiled. "There shouldn't be all that large a garrison here, unless they're using Camerein for something we don't know about." He shrugged. "Of course, intelligence didn't have the faintest idea what they might be using the world for."

"That rather worries me, sir," Naughton said. "They might have a dozen regiments in for jungle training, or something like that."

Spencer pulled down his faceplate just long enough to look at the timeline on the head-up display. "What worries me more is that *Avon* hasn't checked in. They're ten minutes late, and that's not like Captain Barlowe."

"There could be a reason," Naughton said.

"None that means anything good for us."

Absolutely precise adherence to the communications schedule might not be essential, but the radio link with *Avon* was the commando detachment's lifeline, its only connection to the outside, to friendly forces.

"We don't really need *Avon* until we get where we're going and do what we're here to do," Naughton said. "And if they're late for the party, we'll be able to hitch a ride when the rest of our blokes show up."

David nodded. He had considered that. It still did not ease his worry. "We've got another forty minutes until the alternate link window. Time to get the lads up, Mitch. I want to use as much of the night as we can."

The camouflage pattern of the Commonwealth battledress was even more effective at night than it was during the day, and the field skin that each man wore under his uniform minimized the infrared signature of the hot body under it. With properly fitted helmets and field skins, there was almost no leakage of heat. Only the hands were left uncovered. The 2nd Commando moved through the forest in silence, camouflaged ghosts. They even startled some of the jungle hunters.

As long as the night held, Spencer pushed his men hard, allowing only a five-minute break every hour and a half. Even with full combat packs and extra supplies, that was not a particularly onerous pace. In training, the commandos had been pushed much harder. Before graduating, every man had to complete a twenty-six-mile marathon in combat kit, sixty pounds of dead weight, in under five hours.

Avon did not call during the alternate time. Spencer only mentioned that to Lieutenant Hopewell and Lead Sergeant Naughton. They could share that much of the burden of leadership. There was no point in worrying anyone else with the possibility that they were totally on their own.

The only halt during the remainder of the night that was longer than five minutes came when the commandos reached a river that was wide enough and deep enough to pose a problem.

"We'll have to wait until we have a little light," Spencer conceded after a few minutes of moving along the bank looking for an easy crossing.

"That's nearly an hour off, Captain," Naughton said.

"We'll move along the river until then, upstream, with a man as close to the bank as possible, in case something pops up."

Naughton shook his head. "I don't think that's too practical, sir. The undergrowth is too damn thick down close to the water. Vines and thickets and trees with standing roots."

Spencer hesitated, then nodded. "You're right. We've still got to keep moving. I don't want to waste an hour sitting here waiting for light. We'll stay as close as we can stay to the river and still make good time. That shouldn't be more than twenty or thirty yards. The heavy undergrowth seems to be concentrated that close in."

The detachment continued to move in parallel columns. Where possible, they kept flankers out on either side, a single fire team, with another fire team fifty yards in front of the main body. There was no reason to suspect that they might run into enemy soldiers, but David took nothing for granted.

Dawn came slowly under the forest canopy. The treetops were higher now, and thicker. Underneath, except right along the waterway, there was little undergrowth, only a few vines that climbed tree trunks and spanned the caps between crowns looking for sunlight. The mixture of savanna and scattered stands of trees had changed into more typical rain forest.

As long as they stayed away from the river and from the occasional treefall gap where new growth struggled to win the race for sunlight, the terrain was easy, almost like marching through a massive colonnaded temple. The ground was level to gently sloping. The soil was covered with a thin layer of detritus that was being recycled to feed the growth of the trees. Mostly, it was slightly spongy, easy on the feet.

Before the Marines saw the dawn, they heard it proclaimed by the birds and small mammals of the forest canopy. Day feeders became active. Camerein had a normal variety of fauna. Like most worlds that were suitable for humans, Camerein boasted the same types of species that man had evolved alongside on Earth. There were some that might be mistaken for Earth species, while others were clearly—occasionally radically—different. But the underlying building blocks of life were always the same, the DNA, RNA, enzymes, and proteins. On any world that humans had settled, at least some native flora and fauna could be eaten without ill effects. Mankind's larder grew in variety with each new world he settled.

As soon as light started to reach down to the floor of the forest, David moved his men back toward the river. There were paths through the thick tangles that marked where animals went to drink, or to cross. With a little luck, one of those paths would mark an easy ford across the river.

The first did not. The water was clear, and too deep to wade across. "If we knew for sure that there was nothing in these waters that might enjoy a taste of Marine for breakfast, we could wade along in the shallows next to the bank until we found a place to cross," Spencer told Hopewell.

"We're going to get wet sooner or later," the lieutenant

replied. "We could send one man across with ropes to rig a bridge for the rest."

"If we have to, of course," David said. "But we've got a little slack just now. We moved far enough off the direct line yesterday. We can stay on this side of the river for a couple of hours and keep looking for an easy crossing. Going upstream, the farther we go the easier it should get."

They checked three more paths to the water's edge before they found an easy ford. The stream was wider but shallower, and rarely did anyone have to step in water more than knee deep. Moving from one bank to the other was still a slow operation. David sent one squad across to set up a defensive position. The rest forded the river one squad at a time, the men spaced several yards apart, everyone watching for the rare chance of an ambush—or the perhaps greater chance of attack by a river predator.

The river crossing had to be done slowly even though the men would be clearly visible against the water if there were any spyeyes or aircraft looking. The current was fast, the bottom slippery. It would be easy for an accident to happen, and a man swept off his feet might be in serious danger with sixty pounds of extra weight hanging off him, even if the water was no more than two feet deep. The Marines kept an eye on the sky, but even though they didn't see anything, any orbiting satellite could spot them if it were looking in the proper direction.

It wasn't until only the final squad remained to cross the river that Spencer sent his point squad on ahead. The rest of the commandos waited until the last men had crossed the river.

"We'll have at least two more major crossings before we get where we're going," David said, talking with his lead sergeant before the two men separated to take their positions in the columns. "The last one might be a proper corker. The mapboard showed that stream three times the width of this one."

Naughton couldn't hold back a wide grin. "Well, sir," he said as seriously as he could manage, "I guess we'll have to cross that river when we come to it.'' The captain's groan widened Mitchel's grin. ''Sorry, sir. I just couldn't resist.''

''You've definitely been spending too much time around Alfie,'' Spencer said. ''He's rubbing off on you.''

''More like I've spent too much time trying to get the spark back in him. He's been as dour as my maiden aunt.''

David altered the pace occasionally as a substitute for long rest breaks. It was still necessary to stop once in a while, but the continued lack of any contact with *Avon* made Spencer decide that the sooner they reached their goal, the better he would feel. Once they arrived at the Commonwealth Excelsior and learned what they had been sent to learn, the Marines' only task would be to stay alive and out of enemy hands—and protect any survivors they found at the hotel—until the rest of the regiment landed and relieved them.

With an entire continent to hide in, David thought that it should be possible even if the Federation put an entire army on the ground to hunt them down. *All we need is a little luck,* he told himself. *Not much, just a little.* Every hour they were on the move now made that luck feel a little closer. The only guide the Federation would have to locating them was the first crashed shuttle. That was their only starting point, and it was getting farther away the longer the Marines marched.

The commandos' luck expired almost exactly twenty-four hours after they landed on Camerein.

The gunfire was as much a surprise as a clap of thunder in a perfectly clear sky. Startled Marines dropped to the ground, looking for the source of the shots. Two men from the squad on point were hit in the first bursts. One was dead before he fell.

''Where did that come from?'' David asked on the channel that connected him with Lieutenant Hopewell and all of the noncoms. With enemy fire coming in, radio silence was not necessary.

"Ahead and to the left," Alfie Edwards said. "I don't think it's more than a single squad, Cap. They were waiting for us."

"Get to them quickly, Alfie. We can't let them tie us down long enough for reinforcements to join them. Tony, you take half of the platoon one way and let Alfie go the other. Will, you keep your men watching the rest of the perimeter in case it's a two-tiered ambush."

Each platoon sergeant was also leader of his platoon's first squad, one of the Royal Marines' economies of management. Alfie gestured for his squad and second squad to move with him. Hopewell and the other two squads moved in the opposite direction while the remainder of 2nd Platoon and the headquarters squad worked to keep the Federation occupied.

"They're at extreme range," Alfie reported when he finally spotted a muzzle flash. The other half of the platoon was slower to get close. "Well over two hundred yards." The point squad had been a lot closer to the enemy. The Federation had found good positions for their ambush. They had excellent cover on three sides.

"Don't waste time playing with them, Alfie," Spencer said. "Get in grenade range and drop the sky on them. Tony, you get ready to pick off any that try to escape."

It did not work out that simply. As Alfie's men closed the gap to a hundred yards, working from cover to cover, the Federation soldiers—a single squad, eight men—pulled back to new positions.

Hopewell and his half of the platoon moved toward the enemy next. They were somewhat closer after the ambushers had moved. But they did not get close enough for accurate grenade work either. The ambushers were on the move too quickly, increasing the distance between them and their pursuers.

A medical orderly worked on the commando who had been wounded in the ambush, but it was too little too late.

He died within minutes. Even if there had been time to set up the detachment's portable trauma tube and get the man in, it might not have been enough. He had taken three rounds in the chest, a tight group very near the heart.

Alfie pushed his men forward. They finally got to within eighty yards of the enemy. "Now!" he said. The grenadiers in each squad had their launchers ready, and each dropped two rocket-propelled grenades in on the Federation soldiers. As soon as the RPGs exploded, the squads surged forward, spraying bullets and needles into the enemy positions. This time there was no return fire.

The two dead commandos were buried quickly. The Federation dead were left where they had fallen, along with one wounded man. A medic patched his wounds and gave him a pain-killing patch, but there was no way that the Marines could carry him along. Nor could they leave any functioning radio equipment with him. The radios in all of the Federation helmets were disabled, as well as those in the helmets of the two dead Commonwealth Marines.

Once the burials were finished, the commandos hurried from the site of the firefight as rapidly as they could. David ordered a thirty-degree change in direction, taking them on a line slightly farther from their goal, attempting to fool the Federation as to their course and target.

For three hours, the Marines moved at the best pace they could manage, and that was very fast. Evasive tactics and speed were not enough, though. Shortly before midday, they walked into another ambush, once more a single squad strung across their line of march, eight men who opened up on them from two hundred yards or more, picking off one of the men in the point squad this time.

This ambush ended the same way as the first. The fight was shorter, though, and there were no Federation survivors.

Once more, David changed the direction of march. Again, the commandos pushed on as rapidly as they could.

Once more, it was not enough.

• • •

"At least we didn't lose anyone this time," Tony Hopewell said after the third ambush. "Two men wounded, but they'll be able to stay with us if we slow the pace a little." It was late afternoon. Everyone was exhausted from seven hours of racing through the jungle and from the adrenaline of three firefights. There hadn't even been a stop to eat all day.

"We've got to stop the attrition," David said. "Three killed today on top of all the men we lost yesterday." *And maybe our ship as well,* he thought.

"Changing directions didn't confuse the Feddies," Tony said. "You think maybe we should hold our course this time?"

"That's what I'm thinking," David replied. "Go for an hour or so, then move in under whatever heavy cover we can find and go to ground until it gets good and dark."

"We could all use the break," Hopewell said. "Some of the men are really starting to drag, and the wounded need a long break before we go much farther."

Spencer nodded. "That's the way we'll do it. Keep going the way we were headed, stop as soon as we find thick cover. Try to throw them off that way. When we start up again, we can start bending back toward our target, slowly."

"There is one good thing about the pace we've been keeping," Tony said after a pause. "We're making good distance."

"But a good part of it's been in the wrong direction. We must still be a good two days from that hotel."

Part 3

9

Officially, the ship was *HMS Prince of Wales*, but for most of the fourteen decades that it had served as the primary carrier for the royal family, it had been known unofficially (and much more regularly) as the Welsh Rowboat. It had been built to the same basic plan as the Tower-class light cruisers (the last armed ship of that class having been scrapped fifty years before the start of the war). The weight saved by eliminating weaponry and ammunition allowed for the inclusion of extremely comfortable accommodations for passengers. Three kings had used it for their quinquennial tours of Commonwealth worlds and other trips. Other members of the royal family and a few senior ambassadors had also been permitted to use the ship for trips of *special importance to the realm*—as the reports to the Chancellor of the Exchequer invariably termed them. It was inevitable that the Welsh Rowboat be used for Prince William's peace mission to Dirigent.

"I'm surprised she hasn't been turned into a museum," Ian Shrikes said as the ship's primary shuttle ferried him, Prince William, and other members of the prince's entourage and negotiating team up to the ship on the afternoon after their audience with the king.

William chuckled. "Don't let her age fool you, Ian. I'm

certain that at least ninety percent of the Rowboat has been replaced and updated since she first came out of the construction docks, some of the gear more than once. She's perfectly spaceworthy, and fitted out more luxuriously than the finest civilian passenger liner in service. Her Nilssens, for example, were replaced less than ten years ago, along with her propulsive machinery and life support systems. Nothing that really matters is more than thirty years old.''

The interior of the shuttle was more opulent than any other spacecraft that Ian had ever seen, with seats that were entirely appropriate for royal passengers. The safety harnesses were as inconspicuous as possible, but not even royal sensibilities could suffice as a substitute for gravity—real or artificial—and not even a royal shuttle was fitted with its own Nilssen generator to provide the latter. The luxury appointments meant that the shuttle could carry fewer people than its standard naval and civilian counterparts.

The trip up to *Prince of Wales* was comfortable, made without the hard acceleration of a military shuttle or the only slightly lower acceleration of a civilian passenger craft. The stresses on human bodies were kept to absolute minimums.

''I've never been to Dirigent,'' Ian said several minutes later. He had been staring out the porthole, watching the transition from atmosphere to space. ''I only know what I've read and heard about the place, and I've never been certain how much of that to believe.''

William thought for a moment before he replied. ''Dirigent may well be one instance where the reality lives up to the legend. I've been there several times. Someone from the family calls on the leaders of Dirigent periodically, have done almost since the beginning.''

''Trying to get them to join the Commonwealth?''

''Now and then,'' the prince admitted. ''But they are a real power in their own right, and it has always seemed prudent to observe the diplomatic niceties. Of late, we would have welcomed the Dirigenters as allies against the

Federation. I rather think that our efforts at maintaining friendly relations with them have already paid a handsome dividend. Without their assistance, I doubt that these talks we are heading toward would be happening."

It did not surprise Ian to find that there were layers of information that he was not privy to. He came across those reminders quite regularly. He waited to see if the prince would elaborate, but the shuttle was moving in to dock with its ship, and William concentrated on watching that.

HMS Prince of Wales was carried on the rolls of the Royal Navy. Its officers and ratings were all active duty sailors. Over the past five years there had been considerable turnover in personnel as younger officers and ratings were transferred to fighting ships, replaced with more senior personnel. It was a prestigious posting, with promotion upon completion of a tour of duty aboard the Welsh Rowboat a virtual certainty.

Prince William was received with full court honors, ruffles and flourishes, sideboys, and a receiving line of officers headed by the skipper. Captain Tobias Penworthy had a half century in uniform. He had served aboard every class of ship in the Royal Navy, including two that were no longer in service. The one mark against him was that he had never commanded a combat ship in battle. There was little chance now that he would ever do so. The only opportunity he was likely to have to make admiral was this tour as commander of the royal "yacht."

"It's good to see you again, Your Highness," Captain Penworthy said after the official rigmarole had been concluded and they were headed toward the royal suite. Penworthy's voice was high and reedy, but not because of age. His voice had always been like that, a constant drag on his career.

"And you, Toby. How have you been keeping yourself?"

"Fit as a fiddle, sir. Just waiting for a chance to get at the Feddies." He said it as if it were an old joke between them, but the way he spoke made Ian frown in concentration. If it was a joke, it was a most sour one to Penworthy.

"This little jaunt might be your chance, Toby," the prince said. The look he gave Penworthy suggested that he too had noticed something in the way the captain had spoken. "I know you haven't been given our itinerary yet. We're going to Dirigent."

Penworthy stopped and turned to face the prince directly. "Any chance yet of them coming in on our side, sir?"

"Right now, Toby, they are far more important as an independent power. We're going to Dirigent to meet with representatives of the Federation to try to end this war. Under the auspices of the mercenaries."

Penworthy appeared shattered by what the prince had said. "A negotiated peace?"

"An honorable peace," William corrected. "One that leaves the Second Commonwealth intact."

"If we don't beat the Feddies properly now, we'll just have to do it later," Penworthy said, resuming his course toward the royal suite. "They won't learn the lesson until we step on their necks, if you get my meaning, sir."

"Let's hope that it doesn't come to that, Toby. There might be some question about who would step on whose neck."

"You've known our skipper for a long time?" Ian asked when he and the prince were alone in William's quarters.

"He was the first commander I served under during my stint in the navy," William said. "And we've been thrown together now and then over the years, even before he was given command of this ship."

"Sinecure for an old and loyal retainer?"

The hint of a frown crossed the prince's face and disappeared before he replied. "I would never put it that way. Someday, when we have the leisure, I might give you a little of Tobias Penworthy's story. For now, it is sufficient that he is an excellent commander. I never have the slightest concern for my safety in his care."

• • •

"This journey will be almost like turning back the calendar to before Admiral Truscott rewrote the manuals," William told Ian and the three other staff members who took dinner with him just after *Prince of Wales* started to accelerate away from Buckingham. "Certainly closer than anything the navy does today."

"You don't mean that we're going to take two weeks to get there, do you, sir?" Ian asked. "I'd have brought along an extra change of clothes."

William gave that a gentle laugh. "No, we're not going that completely back to the old ways. But we won't make our first jump to Q-space until we're twelve hours out, and we'll enter Dirigent's system eighteen hours out from the planet."

"One transit?"

William shook his head. "No, we'll do the traditional three hops. We'll be met by a ship from Dirigent before we transit Q-space for the third time. They will make that jump at the same time we do, and we will enter Dirigent's system at coordinates that they specify, and emerge in Dirigent's space eighteen hours out. That last is at their, ah, request. Any closer and we would apparently trigger all sort of automatic defenses."

"There's one question that's been bothering me since you first mentioned this junket, sir," Ian said. "A series of questions. Do you really think that these talks can lead to peace with the Federation? If so, how long do you think it will take to negotiate an end to the war? And, one more: Why Dirigent?"

"The last question is the easiest. Dirigent offered to host peace talks." The prince smiled. "Actually, 'offered' is not quite a strong enough word, but it will do. Do I think that these talks can lead to peace? It is possible. If the Dirigenters offer the proper . . . inducements, it might even be likely. In time. That is the real sticking point. How long will it take two entities with diametrically opposed, and mutually exclusive, positions to reach some sort of accommodation, to at least end the fighting and find a new relationship—or at least return to the *status quo ante*? On that, all I could do would be to offer a wild guess, with no way to insure that my estimate might be within an order of magnitude of being correct. Days or years, or anything in between.''

''You don't sound particularly optimistic,'' Ian said softly.

''I have no basis for optimism. If I recollect my ancient history correctly, there are some extremely distressing precedents from Earth, one war that took two years of peace talks to arrive at a cease-fire, another in which the diplomats argued for a year or more over the shape of the table they would negotiate across.''

''I'm tempted to suggest that you're pulling my leg, but I don't think you are.''

''Not a bit of it, Ian. Unfortunately.''

''A lot more good people will die if it takes that long.''

''Far too many,'' William agreed.

The trip from Buckingham to Dirigent took *Prince of Wales* forty hours. That left plenty of time for Prince William and his team of negotiators to go over their plans for the talks with the Federation. Initial proposals, arguments against certain expected Federation demands, and a series of carefully honed fallback positions were scripted and rehearsed. The individuals who would be doing the actual negotiating were all experienced diplomats, including the prince himself. The Foreign Minister and St. James Palace had been working with all of them for weeks in preparation for this mission.

''I'm still not certain that I see where any real compromise is possible,'' Ian said after sitting in on one of the planning meetings. The others had gone, leaving him alone with Prince William. ''The Federation holds that it has absolute sovereignty over all worlds settled by humans, and the Commonwealth refuses to accept that claim.''

''Nonetheless, we managed to coexist peacefully for centuries,'' William said. ''We even did peaceful business on a regular basis. Despite everything that has happened in the last seven years, it should be possible to arrive at some sort of understanding.''

"But if either side concedes the other's position, it amounts to an outright defeat, doesn't it?"

"No diplomat worthy of the name would ever admit to that, Ian." The prince smiled. "You'd be surprised how many people consider the words 'diplomat' and 'liar' to be synonymous, and the former more insulting than the latter. It's all a matter of finding a formula that each side can argue the way it wants to, a way to save face and take credit for a victory."

Ian shook his head slowly.

"The headaches along the way are part of the price, Ian. And the payoff is an end to this horrible war."

Ian spent much of the final eighteen hours of the journey watching exterior monitors in what would have been the ship's flag bridge had it been carrying an admiral. Dirigent was extremely well protected against assault, better even than Buckingham. For a half million miles out, any attacking force would be in extreme jeopardy. Armed ships were only a small part of the defensive screen. The Dirigenters relied more heavily on automated systems, mines, and unmanned orbiting weapons platforms than either the Commonwealth or Federation did. That was why it had been necessary for a Dirigenter ship to escort *HMS Prince of Wales* in.

While he watched, Ian made extensive notes. He had been a naval officer too long to miss gathering any intelligence he could. Dirigent might be neutral at present, but there was no guarantee that that would always be the case, and even if the Royal Navy never had to go up against the Dirigenters, what Ian learned by observing them might prove useful in another context, against a different foe—or provide data that the Commonwealth could use to bolster its own defenses.

It would take a complete battle group a week to clear a

safe path in, even without active opposition, Ian thought after one stretch of observing the defensive patterns. *And there* would *be active opposition. They might be able to launch replacement weapons almost as quickly as we could take them out.*

He attempted to discuss the shield around Dirigent with the prince, but William put him off. "I dare say it is fascinating, Ian, but right now, I'd rather not clutter up my brain with it. I need to concentrate on the job at hand. Save your notes for after we get home with our work here done."

During the voyage, William had become increasingly withdrawn as he forced himself into the task before him. Ian recognized the signs of building concentration. Admiral Stasys Truscott, one of Ian's former commanders, had been able to do the same sort of thing, with dramatic results. By the time that *HMS Prince of Wales* approached its parking orbit one hundred sixty miles above the surface of Dirigent, Prince William, Duke of Haven, had put on the persona of the diplomat entirely. Even in limited discussions with his own people, he spoke as if he were already on diplomatic display.

Getting the entire negotiating team down to the surface required both the royal shuttle and the ship's gig. There were precise navigational instructions for the landers. Dirigent's Port Traffic Control guided the two craft down almost foot by foot. It was just past dawn in the capital. The approach of *Prince of Wales* had taken place during the hours of darkness in the most densely populated area of the world.

Dirigent City was the destination. There was really only the one concentration of people that could be called a city, even though the world had been settled before the founding of the Second Commonwealth. Dirigent's economy rested entirely on its military establishment, the mercenary regiments and a munitions industry that exported as much as was retained on the planet.

Since Prince William refused to be drawn into conversation, Ian was left to his own thoughts during the descent.

He couldn't avoid thinking about what he had learned about Dirigent.

Fourteen combined-arms regiments, each numbering over five thousand men. Support units to half that manpower. A fleet of armed transports equal to carrying all fourteen regiments at once, with the necessary escorts. A training facility to rival the Marine Commando School on Buckingham. Research and development, factories, and an infrastructure designed to support the military—to the exclusion of everything else when necessary.

Growing up, Ian had thought of Dirigent as a mythical place, the focus of scores of adventure books and vids. Most of those were historical, set in the years before the establishment of the Second Commonwealth, or in its early years, when the mercenaries were the only source of help that hundreds of worlds could look to. When Ian had learned that Dirigent actually existed, *still* existed, and flourished, he had been almost as surprised as he would have been to meet Father Christmas face to face.

The two shuttles landed and were towed to a location in front of one of the port's two large buildings. There were perhaps a hundred people waiting, including a small band. Ian turned his face away from the prince and smiled. Whether William wanted them or not, there would be distractions before they could get down to the business of negotiating an end to the war.

Getting from the shuttles to the floaters that were to carry them to their accommodations took Prince William and his staff more than an hour, even though the ground vehicles were no more than thirty yards from the shuttles. The band played. Speeches were made. The prince remained uncommunicative during the ten-minute drive, staring out through the tinted window on his side of the floater he shared with Ian. Their driver was in a separate compartment.

Ian watched the passing scenery. The portion of Dirigent City that the motorcade took them through looked functional—appropriate for such a militaristic society, everything laid out by careful military planners with little concern for anything so abstract as esthetics.

I wouldn't be surprised to see civilians marching up and down the streets to cadence-calling, Ian thought. Instead of bringing a smile to his face, the idea brought a chill to his back, a shudder he could not completely suppress. A world entirely dedicated to the practice of warfare could not be taken lightly, even when it appeared to be strongly interested in ending the war between the Second Commonwealth and the Confederation of Human Worlds.

What's their angle? Ian wondered. *What do they get out of all this?* He turned to look at the prince, but William was still staring out—or at—the other window, his body stiff and motionless. Ian did not ask his questions.

But he could not forget them either.

10

Walter Kaelich wasn't certain what had wakened him. That anything less than gunfire or a shout from one of his mates *could* wake him was something of a surprise, as exhausted as he had been. But he did come awake, immediately alert, the way he always did on campaign, when danger might be close. He did not make any sudden movements. That lesson had been drilled into every man going through commando school, if they had not learned it before. *Move before you know what woke you, and you could end up dead, very quickly,* the line from the drill instructors went. When necessary, they had not hesitated to reinforce the lesson with a swift kick to the rump—or to the helmet. *Don't move. Give yourself a chance to evaluate the threat, if there is one. Think, then respond as needed.* Walter had been on one combat mission before entering commando school, so the lesson had not been hard to learn. He had seen men who had been through several campaigns, and the way they responded to noises, even very slight noises. *Wake like a cat. Even with nine lives, he's always careful.*

If anything, Walter was more quiet when he woke than he had been asleep. His breathing was softer, less frequent. He didn't move anything but his eyes, and since he had slept with his helmet on and the visor down, not even the whites of his eyes could give him away.

How could an enemy get in the middle of us? He listened. The sound pickups in his helmet were extremely sensitive. For a minute or more, Walter listened without hearing any sounds that did not belong. He watched, but he had gone to sleep on his side, using his field pack for a pillow. His field of vision was restricted to what he could see on that one side.

That it was still dark came as no surprise. It would still be dark when they got up and started moving through the jungle again, unless the captain changed his plans.

Walter could see the form of the next sleeping man, six feet away, facing away from him. He could not see anyone walking about. That would have been difficult. The commandos had moved into the thick underbrush near a small stream before making camp. Walter had been forced to crawl into his position. That there was open space close to the ground had surprised him, but there was between eighteen inches and two feet of clearance, except close to the roots of whatever trees or bushes formed the skeleton of this thicket. There he had a little more room, almost three feet right next to the tree trunk. It was almost like being inside a dome tent, except for the open space around the bottom.

It couldn't have been anything flying over, Walter thought. They had heard shuttles or fighters a couple of times. That sound was distinct, and it would not have disappeared quickly enough to be gone in the instant that Walter had taken to wake.

After several minutes of motionless watching, Walter saw a hint of movement at the edge of his field of vision— very low to the ground. He blinked once, then strained trying to see more of whatever it was without moving, without giving himself away. Then he held his breath once he had identified the . . . thing.

Walter knew a snake when he saw one. There had been no briefings about the wildlife of Camerein, so Walter had no way to know if the specimen staring at him from two feet away was poisonous or not. Its mottled hide made it difficult to see, even through night-vision gear. It was only really visible when it moved, and it seemed to be in no hurry. The snake's body appeared to be as thick as Walter's upper arm. He could not tell how long it might be. Only the head and a section of the body were visible. The rest was cut off from his view.

A lot of thoughts, memories, and learned data flitted through Walter's brain more rapidly than he could cope with consciously, trying to assemble knowledge quickly enough for him to make an "instinctive" response to the threat. Afterward, Walter would not recall the chain of thoughts. It would just be, "I did what I had to do." If he survived the encounter.

He might have more trouble seeing me than I do seeing him. If he hunts by infrared, he might not see me at all. Under helmet and field skin, a Marine was almost invisible in infrared. *As long as I don't move, he might go on by without giving me a second thought.*

Walter's rifle was right in front of him, but even if he could get the weapon raised and aimed fast enough to do any good, he dared not use it. That would be a breach of noise discipline. In any case, it would take far too much movement to do that. The snake was too close. There would not be enough time.

I can't just lay here and do nothing. That was the bottom line for Walter. He had to do something, and faster than he could reason out the steps, his mind leaped to the only possible alternative.

He waited until the snake's head was level with his waist, looking ahead, away from Walter's head and upper body. When Walter finally moved, he wasted no time thinking through each action. Like most commandos, Walter wore a sheath knife strapped to his left arm. His right hand pulled the knife out as he lurched up and to the side. His left hand made a desperate grab for the snake, aiming for a spot close behind the head.

The snake reacted quickly, trying to twist into a coil while the head turned toward the threat. Walter did not get a secure grip with his left hand. The reptile's body was too thick, and it moved too fast. But the point of his knife, moving up and out, went through the snake's head, bottom to top, through the mouth and out the top of the snout, pinning the jaws together. Blood gushed from the wounds, but the cuts were not lethal. The snake thrashed around and started to coil around its attacker.

Walter fought to hold his grip on the knife, twisting the blade, pushing to keep the snake from freeing itself from the metal. At the same time, he worked to get a better grip on the snake with his other hand, pulling it toward him, under his arm. He had never trained at putting large reptiles in headlocks, but there seemed to be no alternative.

The snake got several coils around Walter. He could feel when it started to squeeze. *It must be twenty feet long,* he thought. Walter finally got his left hand up to the snake's head, from the side. Once he had what he hoped was a firm grip on the snake's snout, he started working the knife, twisting harder, trying to slice back from the original puncture toward a point between its eyes. But the pressure on Walter's chest and abdomen was increasing. He found it difficult to breathe. Walter feared that he was about to pass out from lack of oxygen.

Suddenly, the pressure ended. The snake went limp. Although Walter felt as if he were looking through a bloodred haze, he realized that one of his mates had come to his assistance. Someone was trying to uncoil the snake from around him. There had been another knife slicing into the reptile.

''Hang tough, Walt. The snake's dead.''

When Kaelich regained consciousness, he found that he had been moved. There were a half dozen people hovering over him, including both medical orderlies and Captain Spencer. Walter's helmet was off. It took a moment before he realized that he had been stripped and laid on a blanket.

"Not to worry, Walt," Gene Greenberg, one of the medical orderlies, said. "No bites, no poison. We're not even certain that the snake was venomous. Not many constrictors are."

Walter tried to draw in a deep breath. It hurt, enough to make him wince.

"I can't be sure, but I don't think any of the ribs are broken," Greenberg said. "Bruised, maybe cracked, but not broken. I can't be one hundred percent sure without more gear than we have here. We'll put med-patches on and tape you up so you can walk. If that doesn't do the trick we'll have to stop and pull out the trauma tube, but I don't think that will be necessary." Greenberg continued to work while he talked.

"At first, I thought you had been bit on the leg. There's one hell of a bruise, but I couldn't find any bite marks, and there were no breaks in your field skin or battledress."

Walter shook his head minimally. "That was from the explosion," he said, surprised at how hoarse his voice sounded. "Caught a bit of a bang on the shin."

"I thought it looked old," Gene said. "You should have said something right away. It might have been serious."

Walter closed his eyes. "I didn't want to get shipped back up to *Avon*."

Gene hesitated before he said, "Under the circumstances, it's hard to fault you for that. Still, you're lucky you've been able to walk on that leg. I've slapped a patch on it as well. You shouldn't even notice that the leg's been hurt while you've got your ribs to occupy your mind."

"Is he going to be able to travel?" Spencer asked the medic after Kaelich's treatment was concluded. The captain had taken Greenberg off to the side, far enough away that the injured man would not overhear. "Is he going to be able to keep up the kind of pace we've got to maintain?"

"The best I can say right now is that I think so, Captain," Gene said. "What I told him was on the level. He's going to hurt a bit, even with med-patches and tape, but he should be able to keep going. It would help if he didn't have so much weight to carry. And the longer it is before we start moving again, the easier it's going to be for him, the more time his own medbugs will have to repair the damage. If I'm wrong, we'll find out soon enough. But if I am wrong, he's going to need at least two hours in the trauma tube.''

''We can take some of the weight off for a few hours, even though everyone's already loaded down, but we have to start moving just as soon as we can. There was too much noise before.''

''I'll keep an eye on him,'' Greenberg said.

''If it becomes necessary to stop to give him further treatment, let me know.'' Spencer turned to stare at the dead snake. It had been stretched out in a small clearing. One of the men had measured it—twenty-two feet and a few inches long. It had taken four men to move it.

''There *was* one serious casualty, Captain,'' Greenberg said. ''That snake managed to kill Kaelich's field skin. The whole section around the middle was dead.''

''You got him a new skin?''

''Yes, sir, straightaway.'' Field skins were expendable. The detachment carried spares, roughly one extra per man.

Mitchel Naughton came over as the medical orderly went back to Kaelich. ''The lad did himself right, Cap,'' the lead sergeant said, nodding in the direction of the wounded clerk. ''He kept his head and performed like a proper Marine, he did.'' Naughton gestured at the snake. ''That thing outweighed him by more than fifty pounds. I've never heard of the RM giving out medals for killing a snake, but I'd like to write him up for one. They could use the tale for training recruits.''

''If we ever get someplace to turn it in, Mitch, go ahead.'' David said. ''The lad ought to get something for his pains. What were you planning, to have him write up his own recommendation?''

Naughton laughed without making a sound. ''I hadn't

thought that far ahead, Cap. I guess I'll rough it out myself, then give it to one of the other clerks to put in proper shape when we get to a complink and printer. Then you can polish it off proper.''

"I'll let someone at headquarters worry about the polish, Mitch. They didn't spend much time teaching us how to write up heroes at leadership school. In the meantime, see what you can do about lightening his load for a while. Spread as much of his gear around as you can. Give him a chance to heal those ribs.''

"Already in the works, Cap. I figured he was going to need a little help. We'll be ready to move in three minutes.''

"Make it fifteen, and make sure everybody eats first.''

The detachment moved more slowly the rest of the night, not so much because of Walter Kaelich's injuries but because Spencer decided to take more care to avoid ambushes. Two squads were sent ahead to look for roadblocks, or any signs of Federation patrols. After the third ambush the day before, the ruse of going on in the same direction had apparently worked. The commandos had moved for several hours without running into a fourth blocking force. Finding Federation troops without simply walking into range of an ambush and drawing fire was a slow process, not speeded up at all by not finding any. Proving the negative was time-consuming, cutting the detachment's speed nearly in half.

Shortly after first light, Spencer called a halt to give his men a short rest and a meal. As before, they settled into the deepest cover the jungle provided. Many of the men were clearly leery of their positions in heavy undergrowth along another stream. No one was likely to forget the snake anytime soon.

Gene Greenberg examined Walter Kaelich again before he got off his feet and pulled out a meal packet. But he didn't start eating. Instead, he went to the captain to report.

"He's in better shape than I expected, Cap,'' Gene said.

"I think I was right about there being no broken ribs. His painkillers wore off and he didn't ask for more. Sometime in the last hour he even started collecting his gear from the others."

"Thanks, Gene. Get that food down your throat and get off your feet. That's what a break is for," David told him. He waited until the medical orderly went off before he turned to his immediate companions, Hopewell and the three senior sergeants.

"That's one bit of good news," David said while he pulled out a meal packet and got ready to eat his own breakfast. The five leaders were sitting together under a tree. "I don't expect that the Feddies will give up trying to find us, especially not after we did for three of their patrols yesterday. All that did is confirm that we're here."

"Maybe they've lost the trail completely by now," Hopewell said. "It's been fourteen hours since the last contact. They might not have the manpower to do anything thorough enough."

"We can hope that we've seen the last of them, but we sure as hell can't count on it, Tony," David said. "We've also got to worry about them getting to that hotel ahead of us now. If they know about the Commonwealth Excelsior, they'll have to give it a look. Where else could we be headed on this continent?"

"That's still quite a ways off," the lieutenant said. "They might think just about anything about why we're here, and by now they should be getting awful antsy about more of us popping out of Q-space ready to jump straight down their throats."

"We would be a good diversion at that, wouldn't we, Cap?" Alfie Edwards asked. "I mean, drop a few nasty blokes like us off on the far side of the world from where everything is just to see how many of the enemy we can draw off before the big push."

"It's possible, Alfie, but again, we can't count on them thinking anything that might help us," David said.

"When do we turn straight for our target?" Will Cordamon asked. "The farther we go on the tangent, the longer it's going to take us to get in and do whatever we have to do. And the more time the Feddies will have to get there first and screw us."

"I know," David said. "And the hotel might not be as easy to find as we thought. Without *Avon* to update our mapboards, we're going on dead reckoning, and if we misidentify a stream, we might need a week to find where we're supposed to be going."

"You don't mean we're lost, do you, Cap?" Alfie asked.

"I don't think we are, but I could be wrong."

"I wish you hadn't told us that," Alfie said. "I was happier not knowing."

"Burden of leadership, Alfie-lad." David grinned despite his concern. "But, assuming that I do know where we are, at least roughly, we'll stay on this course another two hours. If we haven't had another sniff of Feddies by then, we'll change course in two steps to put us on the heading we need. Half and half. We come across any terrain features that give us a better plot on our position, we'll make whatever adjustments we need."

David had been using the brief intervals when others were talking to eat, and they had eaten while he talked. Now, he took a moment to catch up on his meal before he went back to the day's plans. "Since Kaelich seems to be fit, we'll pick up the pace again, a little now while we're still taking extreme care about ambushes, more once we change heading. My estimate is that we're still fifty miles from our target, about where we had hoped to be when we landed. There's no way we could make it there today, but I do want to be on site by dark tomorrow."

There was a pause before any of the others spoke. "We've already covered more than sixty miles in not quite two days," Lead Sergeant Naughton said. "And had our troubles as well along the way. Two more days like that . . ." He shook his head. "Even for our lads, that's asking a bit much."

"I know, but we can always tell them that it's a luxury

hotel we're going to. There might even be a chance for something better than field rations when we arrive."

"If there's anything left," Alfie said.

"The hotel is still there. *Avon* got a glimmer of it before we were half down to the ground. And the last report I had from *Avon* was that there was at least one person visible on the hotel grounds during the glimpse the ship had of it. The hotel is still there, and it's not completely deserted."

The detachment did not run into any ambushes during the two hours before it changed course. Only once was there even a hint of alarm. The Marines heard—at a distance—the sound of a fighter, just barely audible. Since the commandos were under thick cover, there was no chance that they would be spotted as long as they maintained electronic silence, and they had been doing that routinely.

David's first course change put the commandos paralleling a narrow river, just beyond the thick undergrowth along the bank. Every quarter hour he sent a fire team to look at the river, hoping that they would spot a distinctive feature that would confirm that they were where David thought—hoped—they were. It was past noon before he had his confirmation, a long, narrow island. It was time for another meeting.

"The way I read the mapboard, we're forty-two miles from the hotel now, straight-line distance," Spencer told Hopewell and the three senior sergeants. "This river flows right past the hotel, but following the stream in would add fifteen miles, and I don't think anybody wants to do that." He ignored the nods from the others. "We stay on the course we've been following for another mile. Not too far past the far end of that island, the river bends left. When it does, we turn left as well, but only about five degrees. That should put us almost dead-on for the hotel."

"You still figure for us to get there by tomorrow night?" Naughton asked. "We've already done about seventeen miles today."

"It has to be by tomorrow night, Mitch. We need to do

what we came for before dawn the next morning." Dawn that morning at the Excelsior would be sunset on the far side of the world, and that was when the regiment was scheduled to arrive.

"Can I make a suggestion?" Hopewell asked.

"Of course."

"Have you considered splitting the detachment? That could double our chances of at least some of us getting through to accomplish our mission."

"I've thought about it, long and hard. Splitting into two groups might—*might*—insure that at least some of us get through, but it also might make us easier to pick off. I think it's a toss-up, and I'll feel less nervous keeping together. We've already lost too many men on this mission. I might have decided the other way if we had all made it in safely."

Hopewell nodded. "I just had to mention the possibility."

Spencer smiled. "If you ever get to where you think you can't make suggestions, we're all in big trouble. I just hope you don't get to say 'I told you so' on this one."

"If this goes wrong, I hope we're all still around for 'I told you so,' " Hopewell said.

11

There was a second welcoming ceremony for Prince William and his party in the courtyard of Dirigent Council Headquarters. The seat of government clearly showed the military tradition that infused everything on the world. It looked like a fortress. The main portion of the structure formed one of the long sides of the large parade ground. Lower, narrower wings formed the ends, and the final side was a wall with defensive ramparts. The building was painted a stark, flat white. The only decorations were the flags of the fourteen mercenary regiments that flanked the planetary ensign, which also sported the regimental emblems in a circle. Antique cannon lined each of the narrow ends of the parade ground, the oldest dating back to Renaissance Europe.

The motorcade drove into the courtyard, following a circular drive. The floaters halted in front of the main entrance to what would have been termed Government House or Parliament on most worlds. Of the hundred or more people who were waiting to greet Prince William only a handful, all women, wore civilian clothing. The rest were in uniforms of one description or another.

"Maybe I should have worn my formal dress uniform instead of mufti," Ian said when he saw the assemblage.

"No, we're here on a mission of peace," William said. "They do present a colorful sight, do they not?"

"There are so many different uniforms the word hardly sounds appropriate."

"Each regiment regulates its own attire," William said. "Most have made a conscious effort to make certain that they can be easily distinguished from all of the others. That does not hold in battledress, of course. The Council of Regiments has the final say in that, and they are much more practical."

Ian had no chance to follow up on that. A footman was there to open the floater door.

Prince William was the first out. Ian followed. They moved out to the arc of dignitaries and officers who were waiting to greet them. The silences in the proceedings were filled by a military band that was evidently well rehearsed in providing snippets of music to cover lacunae. Eventually, the party from Buckingham was escorted inside and taken along a series of broad corridors to the south wing. A series of suites had been made available for the delegation. As aide to Prince William, Ian Shrikes was accorded a separate bedroom in the prince's suite.

Colonel Edmund Tritesse, commander of Dirigent's 3rd Regiment, had been selected as liaison with the representatives of the Second Commonwealth. He remained behind after the servants and two other members of the welcoming party had left.

"The representatives from the Confederation of Human Worlds will land in forty-seven minutes, Your Highness," Tritesse said. "They will be quartered in the north wing of Council Headquarters."

"Thank you, Colonel." Prince William crossed to the windows and looked out. "Across a parade ground with lines of cannon facing each other. Not at all inappropriate, considering."

The colonel seemed uncertain how, or whether, to respond to that. After a moment, William turned back toward him and smiled. "That was not meant as a criticism, Colonel, I assure you. I sincerely hope that, before we leave, the Second Commonwealth and the Confederation of Human Worlds can meet without the need for any weapons between them—anywhere.''

"Yes, sir. I see what you mean.'' Tritesse hid his relief better than he had hidden his uncertainty. "We share your hope. We would like to see this war end as soon as possible.''

"Our conflict must be bad for business as usual for the Council,'' William said.

Ian was surprised, almost shocked, at the tack the prince was taking with Tritesse. It seemed most undiplomatic, and most unlike William. He was always the model of proper behavior.

"Again, that was not meant as a criticism, Colonel. I have long had great respect for your regiments. You know that I have paid you several visits previously.''

"Yes, sir. We have even met before.''

William nodded. "On at least two different occasions, as I recall. The one was when I watched your regiment go through a training exercise. The other, I believe, was a reception here.'' The prince's recollections were not spontaneous. He had reviewed notes made during his earlier visits to make certain that he would recall anyone he should remember.

"Yes, sir.'' Colonel Tritesse relaxed visibly, apparently pleased that the prince remembered.

Ian hid his smile. At one time, such a device would have affected him the same way. But Ian had seen enough to make the affectation transparent. He now considered most of diplomatic usage transparent affectation.

"I fear that I let myself wander,'' William said, moving back toward the colonel. "You were telling us of the tentative schedule, I believe.''

"Yes, sir. The representatives of the Confederation of Human Worlds will arrive shortly, and be housed at the far end of Council Headquarters. This evening at 20 hours, the General will host a state dinner for the principals from both delegations, that is, yourself, your aide, and the formal members of your negotiating team. The General feels that the more relaxed atmosphere of a dinner is perhaps the most advantageous forum for introductions, before the first business meeting tomorrow."

Dirigent had only one general at a time. He was both chairman of the Council of Regiments and head of Dirigent's civilian government. The General (a formal title on Dirigent) was elected for a six-year term by the Council of Regiments, which was composed of the colonels commanding the fourteen regiments, from among their own number. At present, the General was Alvonz Partifinay, who also retained his colonelcy of the 11th Regiment.

"I have no doubt that the General is correct," Prince William said.

"You had me worried for a moment there, sir," Ian said after Colonel Tritesse left the suite.

William smiled. "How so?"

"For a time, it appeared as if you were purposely baiting the colonel, trying to get his goat, and I couldn't understand why you might be doing that."

"I was not baiting him at all, I assure you. I was just trying to pierce through any preconceptions he might have had. Lower the altitude. Make him think of us as individuals rather than merely interchangeable tokens of a foreign power."

"You think that might be important?"

"It's important to me. We do want to retain the goodwill of the Dirigenters. And I don't want to be a faceless diplomatic facade to the man who will likely be our intermediary in any number of routine ways while we are here. I want our dealings to be human to human—friend to friend, if possible."

"Yes, sir."

"Sit down and relax, Ian," the prince said, gesturing to one of three sofas in the room. "Dirigent society is far more complex than you might imagine," the prince said after both were seated. "You see a colonel and think strictly in military terms, or naval terms. A colonel is equivalent to a naval captain, and you have very definite ideas about what that means, correct?"

"Correct, sir."

"Colonel Tritesse is that, of course, but he is also one of the fourteen men who decide on everything pertaining to the Dirigent military establishment, and one of the fourteen men who decide who shall govern the entire world. Rather than being equivalent to any of the Marine colonels or Navy captains of your experience, he is more a combination of cabinet minister, privy counselor, and member of the House of Lords wrapped into one package that bears the facade of the colonel. He wields more real power than any one person on Buckingham. His Majesty and the Prime Minister acting together might almost come close to his power."

Ian waited a few seconds before he said, "Well, I knew he wasn't the doorman at the Royal Albert." That was one of the best hotels in Westminster, Buckingham.

William guffawed. It was a moment before he was able to contain his laughter. "It's been a long time since you caught me out that way, Ian." He wiped at the corner of one eye.

"If they came all of the time, they'd lose their effect," Ian said, fighting to keep from laughing himself.

The prince shook his head slowly as he stood. "I think we could both do with a drink, Ian, and then a chance to kip out for an hour or so. We'll all need to be on our best behavior at the General's dinner tonight. We'll need to keep our porcelain faces on no matter what any of the Feddies might say or do."

There were no diplomatic *faux pas* that evening. Past the introductions, there was virtually no direct contact between members of the two delegations. The dining table was wide enough that the men on opposite sides would have required the mythic ten-foot poles to span it, and long enough that they would have needed a moment to go around to get at one another.

Prince William sat at the center of one side of the table, with his counterpart, Secretary of State Yoshi Ramirez, across from him. Each was flanked by an aide and one of the Dirigent colonels. All of the regimental commanders were present. The General sat at one end of the table. His deputy, the commander of the 1st Regiment, was at the other end.

There were no women present, either as officers or with their husbands. No woman had ever risen to command one of the Dirigent regiments. Few were allowed even in the ancillary arms of the military establishment, which set Dirigent apart from the practice in both Commonwealth and Federation. Knowing the strictly patriarchal makeup of Dirigent's leadership, neither of the delegations included women among the principal negotiators.

Two string quartets took turns providing music. The only speech was a short one of welcome by General Partifinay. The introductions were formal. The width of the table prevented handshakes or other physical contact. The presence of live music limited the opportunities for casual table talk.

"I'm not certain if I understand the General's idea of an informal meeting," Ian told the prince after they had returned to their suite. "For as much real contact as there was, we could as easily have stayed on Buckingham and they on Union." Union was the capital world of the Federation.

"I got that impression myself, Ian," William said. "Still, it gave us a chance to look each other over. It always helps to have any chance to size up the other fellow before you roll up your sleeves and start the real work."

"That Ramirez is certainly an ordinary-looking fellow."

William laughed. "You're starting to sound like a right proper aristocrat, Ian. You'll have to watch that. I doubt that your wife would appreciate having to order more starch in your collars."

"No, she wouldn't. But . . . I don't know. After seven years of war, you get to thinking of the enemy one way, and then you come face to face with one of their leaders and . . . no horns, no pitchfork and red hide. He's just a bloke who looks as if he could be a bus conductor or dustman."

"As long as you don't suggest that to his face, Ian. But that's what these talks are about, getting to think of the other chaps as ordinary blokes like us, not as archvillains who are out to perform the most murderous perversities on the galaxy."

"Even if that's the way they've been acting for the past seven years?"

"Especially then."

"I don't know if I'm that much the diplomat, sir. I've been fighting them too long."

"It's either buck up and play this diplomatic dodge, or continue fighting them until everything is a shambles. Just remember that when one of them gets your dander up."

The table that the negotiators met across early the next morning was narrower than the dining table of the night before, and only half as long. People could make themselves heard from one end to the other without shouting. The room spanned the main wing of Council Headquarters from courtyard to outer wall on the second floor. Either end consisted of floor-to-ceiling windows, with only narrow mutton bars supporting the expanses of glass. The table was of a dark red, almost purple, wood, highly polished.

Five representatives of the Federation sat on the north side of the table, with Secretary of State Ramirez in the center. Five representatives of the Commonwealth sat on the south, with Prince William in the middle. On either side, there were additional members of the negotiating teams who stood or sat farther back, close enough to provide information for their principals or to run errands.

General Alvonz Partifinay sat at the east end of the table, with the morning sunlight shining over his shoulders, casting his shadow halfway down the table. He had three of his colonels as well as a number of other officers and servants on hand, some close, others scattered about the room.

Introductions were repeated. The General stood to welcome them all and to give a few opening remarks.

"It might seem strange to some," he said, "that the people of a world whose economy is tied so strictly to military affairs should take an active part in trying to end a war in which it has no part. There also might be some who would say that we wish to end the war between the Confederation of Human Worlds and the Second Commonwealth solely because that fight prevents us from conducting our own affairs as we might like. Both would be wrong."

The General did not read from a prepared text, but Ian quickly gained the impression that the General was reciting a carefully scripted speech, that he had memorized exactly what he wanted to say, and had no doubt rehearsed it, allowing his colonels to critique both the text and his delivery.

"We of Dirigent and the Dirigent Mercenary Corps do not glorify warfare or killing on any scale. We offer our services to those whose cause is just but whose means is not equal to the needs of the moment. We fight as economically as possible, both in matters of financial cost and, far more urgently, in terms of our people. We deplore flagrant waste, especially of human life.

"We regret to see a vast war fought unnecessarily, particularly when neither side appears to have the power to prevail. If this war is carried to its inevitable conclusion, both sides will suffer horribly. Both sides will be spent, obliterating any good that has come from your centuries of peaceful governance. If you insist on fighting until both sides are exhausted, financially ruined, and morally void, then in the era to follow there will be more call for our services than we could hope to fill, more than we would ever want to attempt.

"You have a clear choice. You can find the means to end hostilities while something of value can be salvaged of the civilizations and societies that have arisen over the centuries of peace, or you can lead your governments, worlds, and peoples to disaster on a scale never before seen in human history.''

The General paused for several minutes. Since he did not sit, neither Prince William nor Secretary Ramirez spoke or rose. The General looked at the faces along both sides of the table. Before he resumed his speech, he cleared his throat and took a long drink of ice water.

"Each of you have queried about the order in which you would speak this morning. Since I offered no alternative, you agreed to leave that to my discretion. I could have tossed a coin, or otherwise left the order to chance, but I chose not to do so. As I am the neutral host of these talks, perhaps chance were best given the onus of saying who speaks first. Obviously, it would do no good to have both talk at the same time in order to avoid giving one side or the other even this minimal precedence.

"The Confederation of Human Worlds asserts that this war is a civil war, a matter of it exerting legitimate sovereignty over rebellious worlds. The Second Commonwealth asserts that it and its member worlds are themselves sovereign, that the Confederation of Human Worlds has no just claim to sovereignty over them, and that they were the victims of unprovoked aggression. The Second Commonwealth asserts that it has fought only in self-defense, protecting its people and worlds from that aggression, and that it has every right and duty to do so.

"Dirigent is not a member of the Second Commonwealth. Neither do we admit the sovereignty of the Confederation of Human Worlds, or any other organization, over us. We have remained carefully neutral in this conflict. But we are not blind. We are not stupid. And we are not so dull as to have formed no opinions, based on excellent intelligence and analysis.

"Here is my decision on the order of offering introductory remarks, and how I reached that decision.

"Whatever the merits of the positions of the respective

powers, it is incontrovertible that this war was started by the actions of the Confederation of Human Worlds. Theirs were the first shots. Therefore, I have decided that the Second Commonwealth will have first opportunity to present its position here. After His Highness, Prince William, Duke of Haven, Special Ambassador for the Second Commonwealth has concluded his remarks, it will be the turn of the Honorable Yoshi Ramirez, Secretary of State for the Confederation of Human Worlds."

For a moment after the General sat, Prince William did nothing. He did not speak, did not move. He watched Secretary of State Ramirez across the table. The Federation delegates had all turned to look at Ramirez for instructions. Would they stay and accept the General's decision, object, or just get up and leave the room?

Yoshi Ramirez stared back at Prince William, as silent and motionless, as if totally unaware of the way his subordinates were waiting for some hint as to what they should do, or waiting for their leader to express outrage over the General's remarks. Finally, Ramirez gave a minuscule nod of his head, his eyes still locked on those of Prince William.

Prince William duplicated the nod, then stood, turned toward the General, and gave Partifinay a deeper nod.

"Thank you, General. I shall be brief."

William read his statement, keeping his eyes on the papers in front of him rather than looking to see how the words were received. At slightly greater length, he repeated General Partifinay's summary of the Second Commonwealth's position.

"We cannot, and will not, accept the illegal and unjust claims of sovereignty made by the Confederation of Human Worlds over the worlds and peoples who are sovereign, independent, and voluntary members of the Second Commonwealth," William concluded after he had covered the essentials of the Federation's attacks.

Yoshi Ramirez took even less time to read his statement.

"The charter of the Confederation of Human Worlds was established by the governments of Earth who authorized,

manned, constructed, and supervised mankind's coloniza-
tion of other worlds. That charter, issued seven hundred
twenty-seven years ago, in the year 2285 as reckoned on
Earth at that time, gives the Confederation of Human
Worlds full authority over all planets settled either directly
from Earth or from worlds already settled by those whose
antecedents came from Earth. A number of worlds have
failed to accept that lawful jurisdiction and have rebelled
against the authority of the Confederation of Human
Worlds. We are not only within our rights to force com-
pliance, we are duty-bound to do so by our ancient and
lawful charter.''

After Ramirez sat, the General stood. He had shown no
reaction to either statement. ''We will resume this afternoon, after lunch,'' he said. Then he left the room. After
he was gone, the two sets of delegates were escorted out,
in opposite directions. Lunch was two hours away, but
those hours would not be spent idly. Partifinay had instructed his own people to talk separately to each delegation, beginning the process of trying to accomplish some
movement.

''There doesn't seem to be much common ground,'' Ian
said when he and the prince were out of earshot of their
Dirigenter escort. ''Nothing has changed since the beginning of the war. We can't accept their position, and they
refuse to consider ours.''

''One thing has changed, Ian. We're both *here*.''

''We could be here for the next fifty years,'' Ian said.

12

David Spencer signaled a halt. A soft whistle with his visor raised brought eyes toward him. After that, hand signals conveyed the essential information. David watched as the platoon sergeants took over, showing men where to move. Even now they had to take care for defense, covering an impromptu perimeter.

Everyone was tired beyond exhaustion. By David's estimate, they had walked more than one hundred twenty miles in four days. During the last twenty-four hours, there had always been at least a few men limping, hobbled by leg cramps. Blisters were not getting time to heal properly. And the strain of carrying full combat kit plus extra supplies had sapped every man in the detachment.

David waited until most of his men were down before he allowed himself to sink to the ground. As soon as the weight was off his legs, his right calf knotted up in a cramp. The onset was so sudden and so intense that he was unable to suppress a grunt of pain. His eyes squeezed shut against the agony. He pressed down with both hands on the knee to straighten out the leg, flexed his right foot to help ease the cramp, and massaged the calf over the knot. The pain was slow to recede.

A dozen other Marines experienced the same problem.

The same thing had been happening, with increasing frequency, every time the detachment stopped to rest.

Anthony Hopewell hobbled over to Spencer and dropped to the ground, carefully stretching his legs. He pulled off his helmet and dropped it next to him. "We've just about had it," Hopewell said. "I hope we're as close to the hotel as we've estimated."

"I'm sure we are, Tony. Every landmark matches. That hotel should be about nine hundred yards, that way." He pointed. "We'll rest here for a while. I don't plan to go in until near sunset. That's about two hours. In the meantime, I want to send two fire teams out, one on either side, to get close enough to observe the hotel and give us some idea what to expect."

"Straightaway?"

David shook his head. "Let everyone get a few minutes rest first, time to get the kinks out and grab a bite. Fifteen minutes, say." He let his head droop forward and stared at the ground. "If I thought there was any difference, I'd say get Alfie and Will to pick the fire teams that are in the best shape, but . . . we're all dragging."

"I'll check with them anyway," Hopewell said.

"Yeah, do that." David stripped off his pack and harness and flopped back onto the ground. Hopewell got up and limped off to talk with the platoon sergeants. A moment later, Lead Sergeant Naughton came over and squatted next to the captain.

"If you came to tell me that everyone's beat to hell and around the corner, save your breath," David said. "I know."

"I have had two men ask if they should start digging their own graves," Naughton said.

David turned his head to look more directly at Naughton. "Please tell me you're joking."

"I'm not, and I'm not sure they were." Naughton adjusted his position, sitting and stretching his legs. "We've set some sort of record, I think, Cap. A hundred and twenty or thirty miles in four days, most of it through jungle, temperatures near a hundred every day, and survived several firefights in the process. I doubt there's a man among us who hasn't lost at least twenty pounds. A few of the lads are starting to look like walking cadavers.''

''We're almost there, Mitch. Lieutenant Hopewell is going to send two fire teams to watch the hotel until sunset. We'll move in then, unless the scouts see anything that says we shouldn't.''

''Saying we go in and find people, including the one we're looking for in particular, what then? We really haven't talked about that. You haven't said what we're going to do then.''

''If he's there, we've accomplished half our mission,'' David said. ''The rest is to keep him, and anyone else we find there, safe until we can get them off-planet or into safer hands. Since we haven't had any contact with *Avon*, we have to assume that we're going to have to wait for the regiment to arrive. Once we turn our charges over, our job is done.''

''It's not just that we've lost *Avon*, one way or another,'' Naughton said. ''The Feddies know we're in the area. If they haven't already visited this hotel, you can bet they will before much longer. Cor, they have to know it's there. Even if—by some bloody miracle—they haven't pulled all the folks out of it seven years back.''

''I know. We can't just check in and take a bit of holiday until the regiment shows. I wish we could. God, do I wish we could. Before we left the ship, I thought maybe we would be able to. This whole thing has been a bad dream. A bit crackers. Despite what I was told the last contact I had with *Avon*, I suppose the most likely scenario is that we'll find that the hotel has been abandoned since the beginning of the war, that there's nobody left and no way to guess what happened to them. If so, our entire mission is a bloody waste, and a lot of good men have died for nothing.'' Spencer was unaware of the way his voice had changed while he was talking, getting harder, louder.

''If the hotel is empty, deserted, and the Feddies know

it, then we might be safe there for a day, or at least for the night,'' Naughton suggested, lowering his voice as a hint to the captain. ''And if himself is there, then we're going to be bloody heroes. Like when your old lot saved his brother on Buchanan.''

David snorted. ''If it wasn't for that, I wouldn't be here now. Some other poor bastard would have the headaches. And good riddance. I don't think I've ever hurt so bad, not even the two times I've taken bullets.''

''Getting back to what I was saying, Cap. Supposing they are there and we make contact. What then?''

''They are there, Mitch.'' David sighed. ''*Avon* reported seeing at least one person on the lawn before we lost contact. I was just . . . letting my pessimism run away with me before, I guess. We get the civilians out of the hotel as quickly as possible and find a place in the jungle to set up camp and wait, someplace we can defend if we have to, but with any luck, a place where the Feddies won't find us before the regiment lands and gives them too many other problems to worry about besides us.''

''If the prince is there, he might not take kindly to the idea of abandoning the hotel for a night or two outside.''

David actually managed a smile. ''Then I'll have to pull rank on him, Mitch. My orders come from his brother.''

Nace Jeffries had made corporal and been given his squad's second fire team only weeks before, when his predecessor made sergeant and took over the entire third squad of 1st Platoon. Twenty years old, Nace had three years in uniform. Wartime easing of requirements had let him enlist at seventeen, and an adolescent stirring of patriotism had given him the desire. Serving in the Marines had more appeal than any of the real alternatives. His school marks had not been exceptional enough to offer much hope of achieving anything he thought he might *like* to attempt. Likewise, his athletic prowess had not been enough to offer him the slightest hope of becoming a professional soccer player, the great dream of his childhood. In his thirty-five months in uniform there had been many times when he had wished that he had been more diligent in either his studies or his soccer training. His four days on Camerein had been filled with such moments.

"There's no point arguing," he told his men after Sergeant Edwards gave him the orders. "On your feet. Let's get the job done. You can bitch all you want to later." His legs hurt enough that he didn't have to act to sound grouchy. Both calves had been cramping repeatedly.

Terry "Curls" Murphy, Zol Ketchum, and Igor Vilnuf filed past him, toward the edge of the detachment's position. As soon as the last man went by, Nace started moving as well, only slowly returning to his place at the head of the column. On the other side of the perimeter, another fire team was also moving out. Nace gave them only a brief glance.

Nine hundred yards. If we had a little more time, I'd think about crawling it, Nace thought as he led his men away. *Give some different muscles a chance to hurt.*

He did not set a blistering pace. Ten minutes of rest had not been enough to do anything but ease the first edge of pain from sore feet and cramped leg muscles. There was a good path through the jungle. Nace kept his eyes open against the chance that the Federation might have planted mines, or an ambush, on the approaches to the hotel, but he was not all that alert. He tried, but the past four days had taken too much out of him.

Before the fire team had gone a hundred yards, Nace had seen clear signs that humans had walked the trail. Footprints had dried in what had been mud. He pointed out the three impressions to his men as they went past him.

"They don't look like military boots," he whispered to each man, "but be ready for anything."

As much as it rains around here, those prints can't be too old, he thought. *Maybe only a few days.* He worried at that; it gave his mind something to think about besides the way his body was screaming for relief. *Those prints had time to dry out. Bloody miracle that anything can dry out*

in this jungle. We've hit rain since we've been here. Maybe
they didn't have any right here, though, or not enough to
turn the path back into mud.

Thoughts did not detract from watching the trail in front
and the jungle to either side. At the minimal level of alertness he could manage, the two were able to coexist. The
hotel was supposed to be just over a half mile from where
the patrol had started. There was supposed to be a wide
lawn around the hotel—if it had been kept up through
seven years of isolation and warfare. If not, the jungle
might have reclaimed that ground, moved right up to the
hotel and its outlying buildings. Vines might have covered
the structures, started to bring them down, without regular
maintenance.

Once Nace estimated that they had covered two thirds of
the distance, he slowed the pace even more, taking a few
steps and then stopping to look through every gap in the
trees ahead, wanting his first glimpse of their goal as early
as possible.

It was twenty-five minutes after leaving the rest of the
detachment before he saw anything but jungle.

Nace held up his right hand to stop the others behind
him. His first glimpse of the hotel was a patch of white
between two trees. He held his breath and listened. All he
heard were the normal sounds of this jungle, the sounds he
had been hearing for four days—when there wasn't any
shooting going on.

After a moment, he gestured to the left, away from the
path. This last stretch, there had been considerable undergrowth in the jungle, as if in protest of the wide open area
around the hotel.

Nace found a spot where his men could move away from
the path without crawling or hacking an opening through
underbrush. Getting fifteen yards from the trail took ten
minutes. But by the end of that time, the four men had a
much better view. Beyond the next trees and a last barrier
of vines and bushes they could see the manicured lawn of
the Commonwealth Excelsior, and much of the hotel itself.

"Scoot in and get yourselves comfy, close enough to see anything happening, but not out where anybody can see you," Nace whispered. "Keep a couple of yards between you, and keep your eyes open. We're not here to take a nap. I catch anyone kipping out and he'll answer to me in a big way."

Nace got down and used elbows and toes to move forward under a tangle of vines that looked nearly as formidable as a roll of concertina wire, with thorns that were as sharp as the barbs on the wire. They pricked into his shoulders and rump through battledress and field skin, but he didn't hear either ripping. Nace slid his rifle along in front of him, moving it from side to side until he had a little more visibility, and clear fields of fire—just in case.

Once he was as comfortable as he was likely to get, Nace pulled his binoculars from their case. The compact seven-power glasses had eyepieces that could be pressed against a helmet's faceplate so that it would not be necessary to lift that. The first thing he did with the binoculars was check the distance to the hotel. His eyes were one hundred twenty-four yards from the nearest wall of the building. The glasses gave the distance to within inches, but Nace wasn't interested in anything that precise.

Next he did a survey of what he could see without crawling out into the open. His location was good, giving him a view of two sides of the building and most of the lawn, down to the river on his left. The other patrol had been sent toward the right. They should be able to see the south side of the building, and some of the lawn behind. There would still be a portion of the lawn and hotel that neither group would be able to see though, a cone of invisibility if there were any Federation troops sneaking around.

But the Feddies couldn't know which side has the area we can't see, Nace assured himself.

He continued to watch, doing a series of slow scans. At first, there was no sign of anyone in or near the hotel, but the fact that there was still a hundred-yard swatch of mown grass around the building made it overwhelmingly likely that there *were* people around. Even the best automated lawn-care machinery would not operate for seven years in jungle conditions without a mechanic to perform routine maintenance.

When someone came out of the hotel and walked to the railing that bounded the porch, Nace still nearly gasped aloud in surprise. He focused on the person—a man—and looked closely, as if he thought there might be a chance that he could identify whoever it was.

They were right! There are *people here,* he thought, amazed. *Seven bloody years and some gent comes out to have a look at the bloody river.* Nace pulled the binoculars away and looked toward the hotel without them. The figure was still there.

I've got to tell the others, Nace decided, although he knew that they were supposed to maintain radio silence. *It's either call or send someone back, and I don't want to tempt a mutiny.*

He opened the channel that would connect him to Alfie Edwards and whispered, as if that might lessen the chance of discovery.

"Sarge, Nace. There's someone in the hotel. A civie from the look, out on the porch, just standing there."

"Right. Keep watching, and get off the air."

Alfie hurried over to the captain as rapidly as his sore feet and aching legs would carry him.

"I just had a call from Nace Jeffries, Cap," he said before he dropped to the ground. "He's spotted one person at the hotel, standing on the porch. Said he looked like a civilian."

David had been more than half asleep, drifted off to a level where his aches and pains had not seemed so immediate. But he sat up quickly when he heard what Alfie had to say.

"You're sure?" he asked.

"That's what he said. I didn't even holler at him much for breaking radio silence."

"I don't know if I dare believe it." David shook his head. Even the report from *Avon* had not completely convinced him. "It seemed so bloody unlikely." He squeezed his eyes shut, trying to calm himself. He was as excited as Alfie, and excitement—any emotion—could cloud judgment. His first impulse was to forget his plan to wait for sunset and take the men in now, or at least send the one fire team in to make contact immediately.

"Any change in orders?" Alfie asked.

David hesitated before he opened his eyes and shook his head. "No, we'll wait until sunset, give everyone a chance to rest. You told Jeffries to keep watching, didn't you?"

"Of course."

Spencer got to his feet slowly. He stretched, taking care to extend the calf muscles in each leg. Both still hurt, but not nearly as much as they had an hour before. "We'll wait," he repeated. "Once the shadows get thick in here, we'll move in, put a ring around the hotel." He paused. "Cover three sides at least. Then I'll go in with one squad to make contact."

"*You?*" Alfie asked.

David sat down again. "When the king gave me my promotion, he said it was because some folks thought it wouldn't be proper to have his brother rescued by a mere lieutenant. I really don't think I have any choice. I'm supposed to be the one who goes in and sees if he's really still there."

"You might be walking into a trap," Alfie said. "The Feddies have had time to go in, nab anybody there, and set up something nasty to see who walked in. Even the bloke out on the porch could be bait. Just because we haven't run into any more ambushes doesn't mean that there won't be one at the end."

"I still don't have any choice, Alfie. It goes with the territory."

"In that case, the squad you go in with will be mine, and I'll be there with you. You and I have been together since this war started. I'm not about to let you go off by yourself and get into God only knows what kind of trouble.''

David laughed softly. ''That's a dangerous habit you've picked up, Alfie, volunteering all the time. You used to know better.''

Dark green shadows were thick, edging into the blackness of night, when the detachment moved in toward the Commonwealth Excelsior. Spencer separated his platoons, sending one off on each of the trails that the first fire teams had taken. Lead Sergeant Naughton was with 2nd Platoon and the headquarters squad. Lt. Hopewell would remain with 1st Platoon when David went in with its first squad.

David had taken time to check with the leaders of the fire teams that had been watching the hotel, breaking radio silence. Both teams had seen people in the hotel. There were interior lights on, at least on the ground floor, and there were a number of people present, including at least two women.

''No way the lads would be mistaken about that,'' Alfie said when David told him.

So near the goal, the Marines moved at a casual pace. When they neared the edge of the clearing around the hotel, the remaining squads of 1st Platoon were moved to cover the west side. Farther off, 2nd Platoon would cover the south and as much of the east as they could without stretching the line too thin. The north side held the river. David and Alfie's squad waited on the path until everyone was in position. Each squad leader gave a terse report when his men were ready.

''Well, Sergeant Edwards, are you ready?'' David asked.

''Aye, Captain Spencer, as ready as I'm ever likely to be. What do we do, just walk in and ask if our rooms are ready?''

''Not to mention a drink and a hot tub,'' David said, suddenly feeling a little giddy.

''And an even hotter masseuse,'' Alfie replied, determined not to be outdone. He had not suddenly decided that there was no danger after all, but—somehow—much of the weight of the war and his responsibilities seemed to have eased, if only briefly.

David and Alfie walked across the lawn together, no more than six feet separating them. Each had his rifle at his side in one hand. Half of the squad walked on either side in a loose skirmish line, weapons at the ready, but loosely.

"We don't want it to look as if we're the first assault wave," David had said when he outlined how he wanted to approach the hotel. "If anything does happen, just go flat and let the rest of the lads take care of the immediate response."

There were stairs leading up to the porch, or veranda, on both sides of the hotel that Spencer could see. He headed toward the nearest set. No one was outside, at least not visible, but there were indeed lights on inside the hotel, and by the time that David had crossed half of the hundred-yard lawn, he could hear the faint sound of music emanating from the building.

"You don't suppose they're holding a bloody dance, do you?" Alfie asked in a forced whisper.

"I don't know. Do you remember how to waltz?"

David took a deep breath and let it out. This escapade suddenly felt incredibly bizarre, something out of a lunatic fantasy. Reality seemed to dance and spin away, faster the harder he tried to grasp it. He stopped walking for an instant, trying to gather his wits. *If they're in costume for a fancy dress ball, I'll go straight out of my head,* he thought. At the moment, it would not have surprised him.

"You all right, Cap?" Alfie asked.

David nodded. "I think so. Let's get in there and get this over with."

David went to the left side of the stairs and used the railing for support as he climbed to the porch. He found himself treading softly, as if a step might creak and bring unimaginable disaster down on their heads. Alfie was at the other side of the fifteen-foot-wide stairway, but he did not use the rail. He had both hands on his rifle now.

Here comes the crunch, Alfie thought.

Behind them, the rest of the squad moved up onto the porch and fanned out to either side, ready to flank the doorway and the nearest windows so that they would be able to cover the captain and their sergeant when they went inside.

The double doors opened inward. Each had a full-length oval windowpane in it, and there were flimsy white lace curtains on the inside. Spencer and Edwards stood in front of the doors looking in, then looking at each other.

"Together?" Alfie asked, and David nodded.

They pushed the doors open and moved inside. This was apparently the main reception area of the hotel, the lobby, but there was no one in sight. The music came from somewhere ahead and off to the left, on the river side of the hotel. David gestured toward a wide-open doorway on the left, thirty feet away.

The two men moved cautiously toward the opening. They heard a mumble of voices, and then a woman's high-pitched laughter. As the commandos got closer they could see tables and chairs, and made the obvious guess that it was the dining room. They looked at each other. David shrugged.

"We might as well introduce ourselves," he whispered.

For perhaps twenty seconds, no one in the dining salon gave any indication that they had seen the two men in military battledress standing in the archway leading to the hotel lobby. The men had helmet visors raised, and carried rifles. They simply moved into the center of the opening and stopped there.

David's quick count showed fourteen people in the room. He spotted Prince George at once. Even in profile he looked so much like his brothers that he was impossible to mistake.

Twenty seconds. Then, once one person noticed the newcomers, the others seemed to receive the message as if by telepathy. The soft music continued, coming from speakers in the corners. But the talking ceased for several seconds. Heads turned. Eyes opened wider.

Then the babel.

David ignored the confusion of voices and walked toward Prince George. David stopped across the table from the prince.

"Your Highness, I'm Captain David Spencer, 2nd Regiment of Royal Marines. His Majesty sent me to collect you and your, ah, companions here."

13

Commander Archibald Billingsley was one of a small number of officers who had spent virtually his entire naval career aboard one ship. He had reported aboard *HMS Avon* twenty-three years ago as an ensign, the most junior officer in the engineering section. Except for several short periods of detached duty, he had remained assigned to the ship ever since. Since *Avon* had been refitted to carry commandos, Billingsley had been chief engineering officer. It was only in the engineering department that an officer, or rating, was likely to spend most of his service on the same vessel. The Admiralty's rationale was "No two ships are truly identical, not even sister ships of the same class, and by leaving the same people in engineering, we are improving the readiness of those ships by making certain that the people who maintain the vital systems are intimately familiar with all of the peculiarities of their specific vessel."

"It can't be done, Captain," Billingsley reported seventy hours after *Avon*'s Nilssen generators failed. "I've tried every combination possible, and a few that aren't, and it's no go. Our Nilssens are dead. I can't even cobble together one functioning generator from the three we had. We lost the same key modules on all three, and I haven't been able to make replacements. Right now, I'm willing to concede that I never will be able to.''

Billingsley and Captain Barlowe were alone in the wardroom. The captain had chased out the few officers who had been present when the engineer entered. Zero gravity had made the wardroom a much less welcome retreat in any case. Naval crews had not had to deal with zero gravity routinely in centuries. The backup system against rare (and normally very temporary) failures in the artificial gravity produced by Nilssen generators was as primitive as it could be—boots with magnetic soles.

''Are you telling me that there is no way for Avon to escape Q-space?'' Barlowe asked, very softly.

''Not quite yet, Captain, though it may well come to that. But there might be one alternative.'' Arch shrugged, an awkward gesture for a man tired beyond all measure. ''It shouldn't be possible. Every simulation I run using Admiralty parameters fails, but that's mostly because the computers have been told that it's not just impossible but inconceivable.''

''Go on,'' Barlowe invited when the chief engineer hesitated.

''We're carrying a dozen message rockets, Captain.'' He let that hang, waiting for the captain's inevitable reaction.

''An MR's Nilssen hasn't a tenth the capacity of a ship's Nilssen.''

''That's true, Captain. And the difference is actually closer to one-twentieth. We can't simply strap an MR to the hull and use its Nilssen. All that would do is hurry the end for us. The MR would transit and break *Avon*'s back. If that weren't enough, the MR's jump would probably disrupt our little bubble so much that it would fail catastrophically.''

''You mean it could destroy the Q-space bubble around us?''

''Aye, Captain.''

''Could we rig it so that *Avon* could survive and return to normal space that way?''

Even I'm not that crazy, Arch thought. But he could not say that to the captain. "I wouldn't want to try it unless I were absolutely certain that there wasn't the slightest possibility of anything else working, and even then I'd hesitate as long as I could, because if that were to go the way I think it would, there wouldn't be any extra innings."

"Then what is it you've dreamed up?"

"Something that might be almost as drastic, I'm afraid. I did tell you right off that all of the manuals and simulations say this is impossible, but I think there may be a chance, and if you give me the go-ahead, I'll know more about the chances before we have to commit ourselves irrevocably."

"You're stalling, Arch."

"Yes, I am. It will sound daft. What I'm thinking is that I might be able to rig the lot of our MRs together to run in parallel. I think I can salvage the dimensioners from the ship's Nilssens and tie those in. With ten or twelve MR Nilssens, we might produce a strong enough field to let us escape."

"You're right, Arch, it does sound daft. All of the circuits in an MR are submolecular etchings, as I recall, including those in its Nilssen. How can you possibly patch them together and connect the lot to the ship?"

"If my thinking is right, Captain, the basics are there already. There are couplings for external test equipment. I think programming should be able to provide the necessary internal links. After that, it's just a matter of providing shielded cables to link all of the units together—after we strap them around the hull—and connecting them to the ship's control circuitry."

"Strap?"

"Well, molecular welding, actually. The connections have to be strong enough to make certain that we don't have separation at the critical moment. That would take us straight back to the other problem. Of course, it might still come to that."

Louisa Barlowe did not make a snap judgment. She sat—

hung against the lap strap on the bench—and spent several minutes thinking back over everything that Billingsley had told her, and all the other information she had gathered on the ship's condition since the Nilssen generators had blown. The engineer waited. He had explained everything as clearly as he could. The decision had to be the captain's.

"You say that you'll be able to test this rig before we commit to actually using it?" Barlowe asked eventually.

"I'll be able to run routine diagnostics on the system, tell that we've got all of the connections fit. As for the theoretical part, we won't know until we try it. But if it *does* fail, and we've got everything right up to that point, *Avon* might survive. We might just blow the MR Nilssens the way the ship's have gone."

"Will you need all twelve MRs, or can we reserve one to try to blow a hole in the bubble if this fails?"

"If we had twice as many MRs, I wouldn't be certain that we had enough, but I can try linking eleven and see what numbers the diagnostics give us. If the field looks adequate . . ."

"Do that then, Arch. Rig all but one of the MRs and get them situated. Run your tests. I'll decide then whether or not we dare try it. How long do you think the work will take?"

"At least twelve hours, and that might be an overly conservative estimate. There are two other things I think I should mention now, Captain. The first is that if we don't do *something* to get out of this bubble we don't have to worry about being stranded here until we all die of old age."

"What do you mean?"

"Ambient temperature. This little piece of infinity we call a Q-space bubble has a finite, and quite limited, volume. Initially, the temperature of the space inside the bubble was the same as outside, roughly three degrees above absolute zero. *Avon* occupies slightly more than ten percent of that volume, and the ship produces a certain amount of heat. That is unavoidable, and there's precious little we can do to minimize it. Given time, and less than you might think, our private universe could become a close approximation of a classical Hell. Very hot, that is. Hot enough that the ship's systems will be unable to cope.''

''Wait a minute. Won't we reach some sort of equilibrium?''

Billingsley shook his head. ''Not soon enough to do us any good. The warmer it gets outside, the more the life support systems will have to work to keep the inside temperature bearable, and that will simply generate that much more waste heat. Systems will fail, even if they last longer than we will.''

Barlowe frowned as she tried to think through the problem. Although her academic background was not centered on engineering, any naval officer had to survive several advanced physics courses. But those courses were many years in her past. ''How much time are you talking about?'' she asked finally.

''It's not so near that we'll have to rush our work on the MRs to beat the deadline, Captain. It's not a nail-biter out of some adventure vid. The rate of increase has already started to decline, and the warmer it gets outside, the slower the rate of increase will get. My computer models may have been too simple to be very precise, but the range I get is seventy to one hundred standard days before the temperature gets so high that the ship won't be able to compensate. Before we start to cook, literally.''

''Okay, that's something I'll have to keep in mind. You said there were two items you wanted to mention?''

He nodded. ''Saying, for the sake of argument, that this jury-rigged system does spring us free of Q-space, I wouldn't want to count on being able to make two more jumps, in and out, with it. That means that wherever we emerge from Q-space is it. We're going to be stuck in normal space until we can get to someplace or until somebody receives our radio signals and comes to collect us. And the way I understand things, nobody knows where we might come out after our, ah, unorthodox entry into Q-space. Navigation can't count on its calibrations. They won't even hazard a guess as to where we might emerge.''

The captain blinked once. ''All the more reason to reserve one MR, Arch. We come out and determine our position, then use the last MR to send our distress call. If we're anywhere in the same galaxy we started in, navigation will be able to find out where we're at as soon as we can see the stars again.''

''I'll get started on the work straightaway, Captain.'' Billingsley started to turn away.

''Just a second, Arch. How long has it been since you've had any sleep?''

Arch hesitated for a moment, then shook his head. ''I can't say, Captain. I simply don't remember.''

''Then you'd better give yourself at least four hours of sleep before you even think about starting this work. If it's as marginal as it seems, you'll want your faculties at full speed.''

''I'm okay, Captain. I wouldn't be able to sleep just now in any case. This is too much on my mind.''

''If you can't sleep on your own, have the pharmacist's mate give you a sleep-patch, Arch. I mean that. You need sleep, at least four hours. Six or eight would be even better. We're not going anywhere.''

''Captain . . .''

''That's an order. No discussion. Sleep first, work later. Get to your cabin, now. I'll send the pharmacist's mate along. She'll probably be there before you are.''

Billingsley hesitated for an instant, but he had no choice. ''Aye, aye, Captain. If you insist.''

In a naval career that spanned thirty-seven years, Master Chief Petty Officer Homer O'Neill had logged no more than ninety hours in vacuum—in a spacesuit outside a ship. At that, he had more than three times as much vacuum time than anyone else aboard *Avon*. There was simply little call for extravehicular activity in the modern navy. Virtually all outside work could be accomplished by automatons.

O'Neill wasn't even from the engineering department. Now the senior enlisted person aboard *Avon*, most of his experience was in navigation and ships' controls. But this job couldn't be done by robots, and the man with the most experience clomping around outside a ship in vacuum had to be part of it.

More than sixty people, including five officers, had cycled through the maintenance airlocks to manhandle eleven message rockets into place around the hull, and to seed the molecular welders that would secure the MRs to the ship's hull. The chief engineering officer had been out the entire time, supervising, even doing some of the physical labor. Fiber-optic cables in thick protective sheathing linked the MRs and snaked through the hull, some of them through holes that had been drilled especially for the purpose, then sealed to maintain the gastight integrity of the hull.

A bloody mess, O'Neill thought. The work had been going on for ten hours. Like Commander Billingsley, O'Neill had been out the entire time.

"This is our best hope for getting out of this mess," the commander had told him.

O'Neill suspected that the "best hope" wasn't all that good. It all sounded like something out of a poor adventure vid. *If it's time for us all to cash in our chips, why work us to death first?* O'Neill had been a noncom too long to say that, or to give his feelings away by looks or body language, especially around subordinates. If the captain and chief engineer thought that it was worth a try, *Who the hell am I to say different?*

Finally, the last MR was secure, and all of the cables linking them. Commander Billingsley had a portable testing unit plugged into one of the MRs. Half of the ratings had already been sent back inside. The others remained out with the engineer, gathered around him, watching the readouts on the tester, talking on a radio channel that O'Neill was excluded from.

"Okay, Master Chief," Billingsley told O'Neill after several minutes. "Let's get everyone inside. Make certain that no one leaves a spanner or anything else out here. We don't need bits of debris complicating this maneuver for us."

"Aye, aye, sir," O'Neill said. "I've kept a careful count and we've been sweeping. I'll be the last man through the airlock, so I'll be certain nothing or nobody is left behind."

"And I'll be at your side, Master Chief," Billingsley said.

The nearest airlock was sixty yards forward. This far back, most of the interior of *Avon* was given over to machinery and to the containment fields for the main drives and fuel storage—the antimatter that had to be held in magnetic canisters until it was routed into the propulsion chambers.

O'Neill gathered up the rest of the ratings and inventoried tools and other gear to make certain that nothing would be left behind. There would be another check as soon as everyone passed through the airlock. A yeoman had remained on station there with detailed lists of everything—and everyone—that had passed through. By the time O'Neill started moving the men toward the airlock, the officers had started cycling through, and Commander Billingsley was waiting for O'Neill and the final ratings.

"A good job, Master Chief," Billingsley said. "You and all of the men. I'll try to tell them all myself, but I'd like you to pass on my commendation as well. They'll probably take more stock in it coming from you."

"I don't know about that, sir, but I'll tell them. I just hope this gizmo you've rigged up works. I'd purely hate to end my days here in this little piece of the never-never."

"You and me both, Master Chief."

"If I've got the theory and practice right, Captain," Billingsley said when he returned to the bridge, "then our little kludge will work something like interferometry, giving us the effect of a Nilssen the diameter of the hull. It's not really that simple, of course, but it's the best analogy I can find."

"And if you've got it wrong?"

Billingsley shrugged. "Two possibilities, Captain. One is that nothing will happen—that it, nothing significant, and the only result will be that we burn out the MR Nilssens. The other . . . Well, you've studied the accounts of the space fight over Buchanan a few years back?"

Louisa Barlowe nodded.

"You'll recall that at one point two of our ships entered Q-space simultaneously, one just at either end of a Feddie dreadnought. The dreadnought was caught in the turbulence between the Q-space bubbles formed by the two Commonwealth ships and was torn completely apart. I don't think that's likely in our case, Captain, but I can't rule it out completely."

"I don't recall you mentioning that possibility when you sold me on this idea, Arch."

"I didn't think of it myself until I started calibrating the system. Fact is, I *was* too tired to think straight when I talked to you before."

"How do you assess the probabilities for your three scenarios?" Barlowe asked.

"This is mostly guesswork, Captain, but out of ten tries, I'd say three that it works and we jump back to normal space, six that we don't do anything but burn out the MRs, and one that we come a total cropper."

"We don't have ten tries, Arch. We only have one."

"I know, Captain. Believe me, that hasn't been out of my mind for a second."

"I'm going to want to see all of your notes and calculations, Arch, and I'm going to need to have you with me to explain things when I get out of my depth, which will most likely be very quickly. Let's go to my day cabin."

Louisa Barlowe lay in her berth, straps at knees and chest holding her in position. She stared at the overhead without seeing it. She has listened to the engineer's explanations, gone through every equation and note, asked questions at every point, sifting through Billingsley's complicated explanations with the patience of a barrister. Afterward, she had said that she would let him know as soon as she reached a decision about whether or not to try his jury-rigged Nilssen generator.

I really don't have much choice, she conceded. *Whether I want to or not, I'll have to go ahead with this ... "kludge," he called it. If we do nothing, the end result is obvious. We're all dead, but we might take a hundred days or more to do it. There's absolutely no chance of another ship coming into our piece of Q-space. That's a physical impossibility. If we're going to get out, we have to do so on our own. In the opinion of the most qualified officer aboard, this is our best chance, maybe our only chance. If it doesn't work, and it doesn't kill us outright, the other alternative, using the last MR to blast out of the bubble, is more likely to kill us than free us.*

She saw no alternative, from the start, but that did not stop her from taking six hours to look for other possible solutions, from waiting that long to finalize her decision. When she finally did, she unstrapped herself and returned to the bridge. As soon as she was strapped into her seat at the command console, she said, "Sound 'Call to Quarters.' "

Every man and woman aboard *HMS Avon* was at his or her duty station, waiting. Captain Barlowe spoke to the crew, explaining the ship's situation and the measures that were being taken to get them out of it. She explained what had been done with the message rockets, and why—as if the rumors had not been flying since the work had begun. While she did not lay out the odds that the chief engineering officer had suggested, she did not try to minimize their plight.

"There is no guarantee," she said. "We are taking desperate measures because those are all that remain. We do not know if any other ship has ever found itself in similar straits." *Certainly no ship has even come back from a situation like this to tell us how to deal with it.* "There is no manual on how to deal with these circumstances. If we win back through, our actions will write that manual. If not . . . it has been an honor to be your captain. I commend all of you on a job well done.''

Louisa turned off the shipwide broadcast and looked around at the other people on the bridge. Although his normal duty station was nearly two miles aft, Commander Billingsley was present. The controls for the jury-rigged Nilssens had been linked to the navigator's console. Billingsley stood next to the navigator, his hand over the pair of switches that would—probably—decide the fate of *Avon* and everyone aboard her.

For a protracted moment, captain and engineer stared at each other. There were questions, but they would not be voiced.

''Navigator, you have the course laid in?'' Barlowe asked.

''Aye, Captain, based on what little we know or can guess.''

''If anyone has any last-minute prayers they want to get in, this is the time.'' Captain Barlowe said one herself, then looked around the bridge again, her gaze finally coming to the engineer.

''Whenever you're ready, Commander Billingsley.''

Archibald Billingsley flipped the first switch. In every compartment aboard the ship, the standard announcement sounded: ''Prepare for Q-space transition in thirty seconds.'' A countdown showed at the top of several monitors on the bridge. The engineer hesitated before depressing the second switch and sliding it forward. He could do that anytime before the expiration of the countdown. The relay would not be completed until the timelines reached zero.

''Quartermaster, prepare to engage both main drives as soon as we emerge from Q-space,'' Barlowe said. ''On my command.''

Then the final seconds were gone. A muted hum seemed to vibrate through the decks and bulkheads, felt more than heard, higher-pitched than the vibrations that the ship's own

Nilssens produced when they cycled up for a Q-space transit.

Everyone on the bridge strained with the most intense—and futile—mental efforts, trying to force *Avon* to exit Q-space by dint of willpower. People leaned forward, as if the addition of some small human momentum might overcome any deficiencies in the jury-rigged generating system. Perhaps the ship itself strained in empathy with her occupants.

The uniform gray of the Q-space bubble seemed to brighten, almost to glow, for just an instant. And then . . .

The black of normal space appeared on every monitor that showed an outside view.

There was no excited bedlam on the bridge. Someone—no one was ever certain who—said, "Thank God."

Captain Barlowe took a deep breath, then closed her eyes for an instant, echoing the sentiment. When she opened her eyes again, she said, "Quartermaster, engage main drives. Navigator, I want to know where we are, right now. Engineer . . . well done, Arch. Now go check on your invention. See if the MR Nilssens have anything left to give. We won't take a chance of going back through Q-space with them, but if you can coax a little gravity from them, it would be a nice bonus."

Tears were running down Billingsley's face. "I'll see what I can do, Captain."

Part 4

14

The Dirigenters had no hesitation about showing Ian
Shrikes the military establishment that drove their world.
He had plenty of invitations to visit, tour, inspect. And Ian
found himself with plenty of free time to accept those invitations. Prince William only required Ian's presence during the formal negotiating sessions, and those took up little
enough time—perhaps two hours in the late morning and
another two to three hours in the afternoon. Ian considered
much of that time wasted. As far as he could see, absolutely
no progress was made in the first three days. Neither side
budged from its initial position. There was other work going on in addition to the plenary sessions, though. Smaller
working groups from the two delegations met—always
with the inclusion of Dirigent officials as mediators—attacking each aspect of the overall problem.

"You might as well see whatever our hosts are willing
to show you while we're here, Ian," Prince William had
told him when Ian received an invitation to dine at the
senior officers' mess after the first day. "Cultivate your
brother officers. A chance friendship struck now might have
unimagined dividends in future."

That dinner had proven to be a more relaxed affair than
Ian had anticipated. The senior officers, majors and above,

from all fourteen regiments were the only members of the mess. The food and service were as good as in any deluxe hotel. Away from enlisted men and junior officers, the leaders of the Dirigent Mercenary Corps (DMC) made themselves comfortable. They were off duty. There were cocktails before the meal, wine with it, and a broad assortment of beverages available after the majority of the diners moved to the upper story of the building. That had the appearance of a fine private club—library; bar; snooker, billiards, and pool tables; a small theater; music room.

"Nice digs you have here," Ian told his escort for the evening, Colonel Joseph Marinetto, commander of 15th Regiment. They were watching a snooker game.

"We think so," Marinetto said.

"I don't want to be impolitic," Ian said, "but there is a question I've been dying to ask since we were introduced."

"Shoot," Joseph invited.

"You command 15th Regiment, but I understood that the DMC only has fourteen regiments. Am I missing something?"

Just for an instant, the smile faded from Marinetto's voice, but it returned before he spoke. "There is no 9th Regiment. That's part of our ancient history."

"Something you don't talk about?"

Marinetto shrugged. "We all learn the story in our cadet days, if not long before. The 9th was sent to do a job on a frontier world, and managed to get itself destroyed in circumstances that did not cover the regiment with glory. It was a commission that should not, in retrospect, have been accepted in the first place, and following that mistake, the planning and execution were execrable. A lot of good soldiers paid for mistakes that should never have been made. The regiment was disbanded, with the survivors transferred to other units or released from the corps. That episode is featured strongly in our training courses."

"I suspect that if my background were military rather than naval, I might know of the engagement already," Ian said.

"The world was Wellman. I believe that it has since joined your Commonwealth."

Ian nodded. "I recognize the name, but I can't claim to know anything about it."

"I'd have to look it up myself to learn anything of the modern world. Even today it's not a planet that we're likely to have dealings with."

"Some peoples have long memories," Ian agreed.

"Still, in the long run, I suppose that our disaster on Wellman helped rather than hurt us. It certainly prevented runaway arrogance over our abilities. Our Council of Regiments was much more careful about subsequent commissions."

"That's the true test, isn't it? Being able to learn from one's mistakes?"

"That's what we're told, about our second day as cadets. Come on. Let's see if we can find some fresh drinks."

Since that evening, Ian had visited the academy where the DMC trained its officers, observed a field exercise, and met scores of officers—most of whose names escaped him fifteen minutes after the introductions. He had inspected a Dirigent combat shuttle and come away impressed. Dirigentan shuttles were armed, unlike those that the Commonwealth and Federation used, with machine guns, cannon, and rockets. And he had an invitation to visit one of their ships if the opportunity presented itself.

"Those shuttles are something else," Ian told the prince the evening after he came back from that tour. "It's really something the Commonwealth should look into."

William just smiled. Ian was puzzled, and his face showed it. Finally, the prince laughed.

"There are some things that we should not discuss here, even with our privacy insured by our own equipment." He pointed at the electronic disrupter on a table, a piece of gear supposed to reliably protect against any variety of electronic eavesdropping. "But I *have* been here before, you might recall."

•   •   •

Their fourth morning on Dirigent, Prince William's first words to Ian, other than "Good morning," were "If everything goes as scheduled, our friend Spencer should be having his reunion within the next dozen hours or so, if I've got the time conversions right in my head."

"I dare say, sir. I had completely lost track of time. Going from one world to another does that to me. I get in one way of thinking about time and forget the rest. I do hope David concluded his business successfully before the reunion. He hates to leave things undone."

William nodded. "I've been thinking a lot on that myself, Ian. Seven years. It's impossible to tell what seven years can do to people. They can be like strangers."

"Even family."

"Yes, indeed. By the way, an MR has come in for us from Buckingham. It should be noonish before we know what's in it. The Dirigenters had to physically retrieve the MR and carry the message chip in for us to view."

"Were you expecting anything, sir?"

"No, certainly not this soon. It's as much a mystery to me as to you. The only clue is that Colonel Tritesse mentioned that a Federation MR arrived in-system less than an hour after ours."

"Interesting."

"Quite. It is rather a coincidence. I think we may safely hypothesize that—one way or another—both messages will refer to the same subject."

That morning's plenary session was called off at the request of Secretary of State Ramirez. He gave no explanation, but everyone assumed that it was because he wanted to learn what message the Federation MR might be bringing him. Prince William offered no objections to the postponement.

"I'm more than a little curious myself," he told Ian while they finished a late breakfast. "I would be even if only the one MR had arrived, but with two coming in so close together, from opposite sides"—he smiled as he shook his head—"I am seething with great ferment." He did not, of course, *show* that ferment. His demeanor was as relaxed as it normally was.

"If it were just the one, I might think it could be something about David," Ian suggested.

William shrugged. "That was my first thought as well. Henry might well have decided to notify me as quickly as possible, especially if the news were good. The more so since we might be here for a considerable time. But even if it were not for the synchronicity, I think I would quickly have decided that it has to be something else. It's far too soon for the other, even for someone with such sterling qualities as David Spencer."

"Ah, I see what you mean. Then we're left to merely cast webs of possibility until the chip arrives?"

"If you like, you can take the morning to visit your new friends," William suggested.

"I couldn't take it, sir, not this morning. All I'd be doing is thinking about what might be in that MR chip."

William laughed. "I suppose a game of chess would be no good either, then."

"I think a few miles of pacing are more in order for me."

The morning seemed endless. Prince William made a pretense of reading, but did very little. Ian did his pacing, sometimes in the central room of the suite but more often retreating to his bedroom, away from the prince. The two had lunch brought into the suite, though neither had much appetite.

"Do you think it's too soon to ask how much longer it will be?" Ian asked halfway through the meal.

"It will be too soon right up until the second when it arrives, Ian," William said. "We mustn't show our impatience."

"I haven't suffered so much waiting for a message chip since I was courting my wife."

William smiled. "I guess you're just out of your element

with no subordinates to put on a show for."

That calmed Ian for a moment. "I know what you mean, sir. Putting on a stoic persona, laughing in the face of danger, all of that command mystique."

"Even when everyone knows that that is what you are doing, it has the intended effect," William said. "Generally," he amended. "But it shouldn't be all that much longer, I think."

Twenty minutes later Colonel Tritesse arrived, carrying a small package. "The message chip from your MR, Your Highness," Tritesse said when Ian led him in to the prince.

"Thank you so much," William said, rising slowly from the sofa where he had been sitting. "Ian, if you would take it off of the colonel's hands?"

Ian accepted the package—the chip was in a small cloth bag with the letters DMC embossed on it—and set it on the end table, as if it were of no particular importance.

"Will the afternoon session begin on schedule?" William asked.

"I've not been told any differently, sir," the colonel said. "If there are any changes, I'll make certain that you learn of them immediately."

"Ah, thank you, Colonel."

"Will there be anything else?"

"Not that I can think of at the moment, Colonel. We'll see you when it's time to leave for the session?"

"Of course, sir."

Ian showed Tritesse to the door. They said farewells there. Prince William did not move from where he had been standing until Ian returned from the door.

"You'll set up my complink, Ian?"

"Of course, sir."

There were large complink consoles in every room of the suite, but William and Ian each had portables that they had brought with them. Anything that might be—in any way—sensitive, they reserved for one of those two machines.

"Just form, Ian, and I apologize for the slight," the

prince said before he inserted the message chip in the reader slot, ''but until I know what this is about, I suppose you should stand on the other side, where you can't look at it.''

''Of course, sir. I should have thought of that myself.''

Ian moved away from the prince, with the complink between them. He could not see the screen, but he watched William's face closely. Almost at once, Ian could tell that the chip had come programmed with the highest level of security. After the prince entered a passcode, he was asked for simultaneous finger- and voiceprints; then he had to enter a second passcode after his identify was confirmed. Prince William leaned close to the monitor. Then, after only a few seconds of reading, he leaned back and laughed.

''Come on around, Ian. There's only the one classified message, and you might as well read it for yourself. The rest is routine blather for everyone.''

Ian moved around so that he could look over the prince's shoulder. The message was very short.

''4TH & 7TH MARINE REGIMENTS REPORT COMPLETE SUCCESS''

''All the expense and bother of an MR for *that*?'' Ian asked.

''And the other things, but this is the important information. It might well affect our work here.''

''I can tell that it refers to a victory of some sort, sir, but I wasn't aware of what those units were doing.''

''There's no time for a full accounting of their orders, Ian, and this isn't the time or place for a discussion of that nature in any case.'' While he was talking, he took out a pen and a scrap of paper and wrote one word—SHEPARD—and underlined it twice. William grinned when he saw Ian's mouth drop open.

''You see what I mean,'' William said. He carefully tore the paper into several pieces, then took a match from his pocket and set fire to the shreds, holding them by one end until the flame nearly touched his fingers. He dropped the remnants in the soil of a potted plant on the end table and stirred the ashes about to destroy the evidence more completely. Using the end of a pen, he mixed those ashes into the soil.

"I believe I do, sir," Ian said, slowly. If the histories he had read were correct, and there was some slight doubt about current "knowledge" of that era, Shepard had been the first colony world settled from Earth—*before* the discovery of a workable Q-space drive. Shepard's first colonists had made the trip over seventy years in a generation ship, with only a handful of the people who had left Earth surviving until their children and grandchildren reached the new world. Shepard had been under the control of the Federation from the beginning.

"That might indeed make a difference," Ian said while the prince thoroughly erased the message from the chip.

"You might see to distributing the other messages here to the proper recipients, Ian," William said after he had finished. The erasure was complete. There was no possible way that anyone could ever reconstruct the message—even if it might make sense to them if they succeeded.

The news Colonel Tritesse brought when he returned thirty minutes later was not particularly a surprise.

"His Excellency, the Secretary of State for the Confederation of Human Worlds, regrets that he must ask for a slightly longer pause in the negotiations. He has informed the General that he needs to send a message rocket to Union and wait for a reply before he can continue."

15

(X-DAY PLUS 4)

Time had not lessened the conversation value of the crashed shuttle and the pilot who had almost survived for the denizens of the Commonwealth Excelsior. It was the first real news they had had in seven years. They would make the most of it. Some of the people who had been excluded from the original trek to the crash site talked about going to see it for themselves. The talk, as well as the inner hopes of all of the residents of the hotel, traveled quickly from the subject of the crash to the possibility that there were other Commonwealth people close at hand.

"For all we know," one common thread went, "the Commonwealth might already be back on Camerein, fighting for the main population centers on the other continent. They might even have won that fight by now. If so, they're sure to come for us."

The veranda had become a much more popular area, and a few guests who had rarely ventured out of doors in years even took to promenading around the grounds surrounding the hotel to gaze at the sky, to look and listen for any further omen of approaching salvation. After dark, when leaving the hotel did carry some slight risk of predators, people stood at the windows of darkened rooms to look out into the night sky.

Radio receivers were on constantly, set to scan the likely frequencies for any transmissions they might overhear, even if those transmissions were coded and impossible to decipher.

Four days of hearing and seeing nothing out of the ordinary had taken only the brightest edge off the hopes of the seventeen people at the Excelsior.

"It *is* mildly frustrating," Prince George admitted to Vepper Holford as they made their way down to the dining salon for their evening meal. "Such a tantalizing tease and then nothing, absolutely *nothing*. A wisp to build a world of hopes on."

"Yes, sir," Vepper said. More mercurial in temperament than his usually phlegmatic demeanor suggested, his emotional ups and downs had been extreme since seeing the dying pilot and the dead men around him. Vepper had trained from childhood for a life at court, and he had decades of experience at suppressing his personal opinions and feelings. "I might suggest that it has been more than 'mildly frustrating' for most of the people here."

"One would have thought that someone would have come to investigate that smashup straightaway," George said, pausing in the reception area. There was no one else about. The others, those who were coming, were already in the dining room. "If not the Commonwealth to look for survivors and to ascertain the fate of the rest, then the Federation, wondering what our chaps were doing on the planet."

"Yes, sir, that's what I thought as well. I think that is what makes it so distressing. *No* one has bothered to come."

"The fact that we have been so isolated, half a world from everyone else on Camerein, has been both our salvation and our damnation these seven years. One can hardly expect it all to change overnight."

Vepper didn't bother to acknowledge that. He waited for

the prince to finish inspecting himself in the mirror, then followed George into the dining room.

Everyone else was already present, those who would show at all, even Mai McDonough. For the first two days of her enforced sobriety, she had been a wounded tigress, making life particularly miserable for her husband and Shadda and generally miserable for everyone else. Her tantrums had since waned but not disappeared. The intervening silences were welcome.

Overall, mealtimes had become more sociable than they had been in years. Especially at lunch and dinner, nearly everyone generally gathered in the dining hall, even the three employees. The latter would report on the lack of any news from the radios. The talk would move from there in predictable directions that hardly varied from meal to meal. Who had watched the skies when? They had seen and heard nothing. But soon? Perhaps. There was more hope than there had been in years. Perhaps tomorrow. Perhaps they would wake in the morning to find that their exile was over, or nearly over. Perhaps. Maybe. With a little luck.

During supper, Shadda sat where he generally did, at the table nearest the kitchen, with his back to the wall so that he could watch the entire dining room and respond instantly should someone want his services. Even more than Vepper, Shadda's calm exterior belied the maelstrom inside. His emotional highs were possibly a little higher than they had been before the appearance of the shuttle, but his lows were also far more extreme. His headache had been constant since burying the pilot. Knowing that there could be no serious physical genesis to the pain did little to help Shadda. He had long known that his problems were not physical. The blinding headaches, the times when he was scarcely in control of himself, were all attacks by his mind on itself, beyond the power of medical nanobugs to diagnose or cure.

The chance of rescue was not an unadulterated hope for Shadda. It cut to the core of his ambivalent feelings about the years of exile. He had a place, a position, some measure of importance for as long as the isolation lasted, more permanence than he had ever known. But at a cost that continued to rise.

The Caffres were sitting quietly together. Henri was content. Marie had become more sedate, almost tranquil, since the trip to the crash site. Her tirades against The Windsor and everything else had lost much of their usual force and duration. That made life much easier for her husband. Marie had even admitted that The Windsor had acquitted himself well on that expedition. It had pained her to compliment the epitome of aristocracy, even out of his hearing.

Even Jeige McDonough seemed content this evening. He kept a watchful eye on his wife, but he was satisfied that she was not finding any alcohol to drink, except perhaps the occasional drop that someone else left of a cocktail. It was not enough to allow her to resume her drunken habits. She had not reconciled herself to the situation, or forgiven her husband—or anyone else in the hotel—for forcing her to remain sober. On the rare occasions that she spoke to Jeige, it was to curse him. She had moved out of their room into one of the many vacant rooms in the hotel, as far from her husband as it was possible to get without moving to one of the outbuildings, or into a tent in the jungle.

She also continued to sit as far from her husband as the dining room permitted, and she always sat with her back to him, a pointed reminder of her displeasure. Sober now, she did not miss the fact that it was her husband who had the sympathies of the rest of her "prisonmates" (as she thought of them, when she bothered to think about them at all). The others welcomed her silence. Only Shadda made the slightest attempt to placate her, and Mai rebuffed his every approach. *He* was the one who had programmed the drink machines not to serve alcohol to her.

Prince George was especially pleased with the music Shadda had chosen to accompany this meal. It was one of his personal favorites, Beethoven's Seventh Piano Concerto (the "Galactic") by Angus Duncan. The Duncan Expansions on Beethoven, a body of work nearly as extensive as Beethoven's own, had been written in the twenty years just before Arthur Charles Windsor, younger brother of the King of England, left Earth to found the Second Commonwealth. There were seven symphonies, a dozen concertos for piano, violin, or cello, chamber music, sonatas, and scores for several movies in "The Expansions" (as they were still known). Those works were perennial favorites in the Second Commonwealth, particularly among the generations of Windsors. Angus Duncan had left Earth with Prince Arthur, forsaking a career of considerable moment to share in Arthur's dream. There was a statue of Duncan in front of the Royal Symphony Hall in Westminster.

George was a competent, though not brilliant, pianist. He had learned the solo piano music of both Beethoven and Duncan during his youth and had, by fits and starts, continued playing in private over the years. He had long held a fancy of someday performing the piano concertos with a full symphony orchestra. Concern for the dignity of the family had always kept that as nothing more than a fancy, though.

If I'd had the good fortune to be stranded here with a symphony orchestra, George thought in the brief pause between the second and third movements of the concerto, *then I could have done it for fair, with no one to complain of the impropriety.*

Just after the final movement started, George finished his dessert and leaned back to enjoy his traditional glass of port. That was when he saw the two strangers standing in the doorway.

"Your Highness, I'm Captain David Spencer, 2nd Regiment of Royal Marines. His Majesty sent me to collect you and your, ah, companions here." The helmet visor was raised, but it cast a shadow over his face, disguising the Marine's expression.

The next minutes were too chaotic for anyone to adequately describe them in detail afterward. The confusion of voices was so intense as to defy description. Everyone had questions—dozens, *hundreds* of questions. More than a few cheeks showed the tracks of tears. Mai McDonough even forgot her snit long enough to join the movement to flock around the Marine captain. Marie Caffre stood so quickly that she had to sit back down immediately, lightheaded, afraid that she was about to faint.

At first, Prince George remained motionless, one hand reaching for his wineglass, the other resting on the edge of the table. Even The Windsor felt blood draining from his face. But his moment of shock was brief, and mostly well concealed. If his hand trembled a bit as he picked up the glass of port and took a sip, no one, except perhaps the captain, noticed. The others were all too busy staring at their rescuers and talking.

The prince set his wineglass back on the table, then stood.

"I am delighted to make your acquaintance, Captain Spencer," George said, and there was nothing out of the ordinary about his voice. He was once more in full control of himself.

"I know that you must have a ton of questions, sir," David said. "And I know that everyone else has, but I must ask that you let me ask my questions first. A matter of security, sir," he said, addressing the prince directly.

"Naturally, Captain. What do you need to know?" The others quieted down, though there was still impatience— among other things—on every face.

"Have you seen any Feddies around here, especially in the last few days?"

"You mean since your shuttle crashed?"

"Yes, sir. You know about that?"

"A few of us went to see if there were any survivors. One of the pilots was still alive when we reached the wreckage. We were unable to keep him alive until we got back here, though. There were no survivors, I am afraid."

David closed his eyes briefly. "I expected that there were

none, sir. We had two shuttles and lost them both, with a quarter of my men.''

''I am sorry, Captain. Now, you have other questions?''

''You've already answered the most urgent. I fear that Feddies will be showing up, perhaps at any second. There are not enough of us to put up a credible defense of this establishment, sir, and I am charged by His Majesty—personally—to insure your safety, and that of the others here. How many are there altogether?''

''Seventeen in all,'' Prince George said. ''From what you just said, am I to infer that you plan to remove us from this hotel?''

''Yes, sir, as quickly as possible. We're just a small commando detachment sent in for this mission. There are more Marines due to land tomorrow, to take this world back from the Feddies, but they'll be on the other continent. We'll need to move off into the jungle until we're able to contact one of the incoming ships to send landers down to ferry everyone up and out of here. Until then, sir, we're on our own.''

''You wish us to leave now, at night?'' George asked.

''Yes, sir. As I said, as soon as possible. I assume that the hotel's food replicators are still functioning?''

The prince made a gesture around at the tables. ''Indeed.''

''Then if something in the way of compact field rations can be prepared quickly . . .''

''Master Lorenqui!'' George boomed, turning to gesture Shadda closer. ''Can you and your assistants take care of that?''

''Of course, sir. But is it really necessary that we abandon the Excelsior to crawl around in the bush? After all, we have been quite safe here these seven years. I don't see how one more night can change that.''

David did not wait to see if the prince would respond to that. ''The Feddies know that we are on the world, on this continent. They intercepted us as we arrived, and we've skirmished with several patrols since we've been on the ground. They are actively looking for us, and they must be wondering what a small armed detachment is doing on this continent. This is the only habitation for hundreds of miles. It's a bloody miracle you aren't already up to your necks in Feddies now. How quickly can you put together field packs for the seventeen of you, enough to last several days?''

''We were equipped to serve three hundred meals an hour. Not all of the replicator bins are loaded, but in an hour the three of us should be able to supply the amounts you suggest. We'll start straightaway.'' Shadda gestured impatiently as he started away from the group. His assistants, Dacen and Zolsci, followed reluctantly, both looking back over their shoulders, loath to miss whatever else the Marine captain might say.

''Sir, and the rest of you, I would advise that you very quickly assemble small kits of clothing and anything you absolutely cannot leave behind. And put on clothing that is practical for the jungle. The sooner we get away from this hotel, the better our chances are of evading Federation soldiers. And while you're packing, please remember that whatever you pack you'll have to carry yourselves, along with the food. My men are already loaded down with full combat kit.''

No one went rushing out of the dining room. Most remained exactly where they had been, still staring at David.

''The Feddies are as like to simply blow this hotel up from the air and not bother with landing and conducting a search, and maybe having someone fight back,'' David said, turning through a circle. When he was facing the prince again, he said, ''Sir?''

George nodded. ''Yes, you are quite right. It is that time, people,'' he said, raising his voice. ''These Marines are charged with keeping us safe, but we are all going to have to put ourselves under their orders and do what we're told until the danger is past. All of us.'' He emphasized the last three words to indicate that he did not exclude himself.

''If you would accompany me while I pack, Captain?''

George asked, as the first few of the exiles started to move—reluctantly—toward the dining room's exit.

"Of course, sir. I don't think I should let you out of my sight just now," David said. "A moment, sir, while I make a few arrangements?"

After the prince nodded, David went over to the arched doorway where Alfie was still standing. "Get the squad posted inside, around the perimeter. Send one man out to tell Hopewell and Naughton what's going on, then come back in. Stand by out in the reception area to coordinate things until we get back down."

Alfie nodded and left.

"Might I ask just how large a force you have, Captain?" Prince George asked as they climbed the stairs.

"Fifty-seven, myself included, sir. We've lost nineteen men getting here, including the wounded Marines who were on that shuttle you found. They were being flown back up to our ship for treatment. The ship seems to be gone as well. We've had no contact with her since the first day."

Vepper was right behind his master and the Marine. His room was next to the prince's, connecting. He had not said a word since the first two minutes after seeing the Marines, but he had listened intently. Halfway up the stairs, Vepper had to pause and take a couple of deep breaths. Without realizing what he was doing, he had been holding his breath—and trying to rush up a flight of stairs at the same time. He was thoroughly winded.

When they reached the passageway on their floor, Vepper started to pass the others, saying, "I'll get your things packed quickly, Your Highness."

"See to your own kit, Vepper," George said. "I think I can do for myself."

Holford stopped abruptly, as if he had run into a brick wall. "Very well, sir, but I can . . ."

"No, just pack what you'll need. You're not my footman."

Inside his room, with the connecting door to Vepper's room open, Prince George moved with quick efficiency to pack four changes of clothing and one extra pair of boots. He also changed into something more appropriate than the light-colored trousers and jacket he had worn to dinner. He continued the conversation with Spencer the entire time.

"His Majesty sent you, you said?"

"Yes, sir. Personally. I have had the honor of knowing both of your brothers. I have even seen combat at the side of the Duke of Haven."

"Willy in combat? There's a novel image."

"He acquitted himself most honorably, sir, if I may say so."

"He would. Willy puts everything into any endeavor."

"All I know, sir, is that we spent time in dire straits and came through. He would make a rare fine Marine officer."

After he had everything else ready, the prince donned his hunting vest. Its loops and pockets had already been stocked with shells for the morning. As he picked up the shotgun and his pack, he turned to Spencer.

"I am ready, Captain."

"Yes, sir. I hope we don't get in a spot where you'll need that." David pointed at the shotgun.

"But if we do, I can hardly send back for it and tell the Feddies to please wait, now can I?"

"No, sir. Of course not. I had no intention of suggesting that you leave it behind."

"As long as I'm willing to carry it myself?"

"Since you mention it, sir, yes."

"There is something that perhaps none of the others have thought of yet, Captain Spencer. We can carry much more than we could individually pack on our own backs. This hotel has a number of safari bugs, eight-legged walkers, very silent and able to move at least as fast as a man through the jungle."

"We don't dare use anything that could be scanned by Feddies, sir. That means nothing electronic. We won't even use our helmet radios except in the most immediate of emergencies until we try to make contact with the fleet coming in."

"Master Lorenqui should have a better knowledge of what sort of electronic noise the machines might leak. You might ask him if they could give us away."

"Any active electronic signals could, sir, and that includes control mechanisms of any sort."

"Very well. I accept your knowledge of such things. It was a thought."

"Yes, sir. I hope you won't hesitate any time you have a suggestion."

"Oh, I can assure you of that." George laughed. "I've never been good at keeping my opinions to myself. A family failing, I've been told."

There were plenty of backpacks for the civilians. In a jungle hotel, that was inevitable. There were also all of the ancillary devices that well-paying guests might require for their excursions, including night-vision goggles. Shadda had thought to bring those out for his guests. And, in a back pocket, he carried a small automatic pistol. It would not have much effect on the larger varieties of indigenous wildlife, but it might do against a human target—especially at close range. The remaining members of the hotel staff had taken turns going off to get ready to leave. None had taken more than seven minutes.

All of the guests were quick to make their preparations and return. Ten minutes was the longest that anyone took away from the dining hall. When they returned, they congregated in the reception area of the hotel, well away from the windows—after being chased back by the Marine sergeant, who had been fairly gruff about it. "That's it," he told one man, "go and make a perfect target of yourself. A Feddie marksman could hit a target like you from six hundred yards off." The man had moved quickly.

In less than thirty minutes, everyone was ready to leave. Only the continued flow of food from the replicators, packaged to go out into the bush, delayed the departure. The programming had been available. Shadda had known exactly what was required—food that would not spoil, that was high in calories and other dietary requirements without being overly bulky. He also found time to fill canteens for everyone, along with several spares.

"There, Captain," Lorenqui said finally. "We now have enough to last the lot of us for five days. Including your people. You didn't say whether or not your Marines needed food, but I thought that they might appreciate a change even if you have plenty."

"They will indeed. Thank you. You are most efficient," David said. "We'll be off as soon as everyone gets loaded up."

The loads were not divided equally. Some of the guests, especially among the women, were too small to carry a full share. But in remarkably few minutes everyone was ready to leave.

"Is there somewhere close where we can cross the river easily?" Spencer asked the manager.

"There is an easy ford just down the path." Shadda pointed.

"That's the way we'll go, then." David turned to Alfie. "Go out where the others can see you and get them moving. We'll rendezvous at the river, or just on the other side."

David and Prince George led the way out onto the veranda on the north side of the hotel. One fire team from the squad moved out ahead of them, jogging across the open lawn toward the river a hundred yards away. The other fire team held back to act as rear guard, and to make certain that none of their civilian charges started to straggle from the start. They also carried the bundles of food that Lorenqui had provided for the entire Marine Detachment. They had complained about the extra load until Alfie told them what they were carrying.

When Alfie returned, also jogging, he reported that the rest of the detachment was on the move.

The group was halfway to the river when the first of them heard the unmistakable sound of a military shuttle approaching. A Federation shuttle.

16

"Quickly!" Spencer called out as soon as he heard the Federation shuttle. "Across the river and into cover."

None of the civilians could run with the loads they were carrying, but they hurried as best they could. The Marines did what they could to help, but the men with the civilians were loaded down as well—far more than any of the people from the hotel. David and Alfie turned their attention to the sky, looking for the first trace of the approaching shuttle. At night, they looked for it by scanning the visible stars, hoping that the shuttle would betray its presence by occulting one or more of the stars. Surfaced in nonreflective blacks, there would be no "glint of light" off the craft, and it certainly would show no running lights.

"It's not coming in hot, anyway," Alfie commented as he moved past David. They had their faceplates down but were not using radio links. If the shuttle had been coming in "hot"—fast, the way it would for a combat landing— the first sound the people on the ground would have heard would have been a sonic boom.

Alfie sent two men ahead to cross the river and mark the goal for the rest. After they reached the far bank, the two men stood with their weapons ready, watching the sky more than the people coming toward them on the ground.

David looked back toward the hotel. The main floor, at least, was still well lighted. *Good job we didn't turn them all out,* he thought. *This way, maybe the Feddies will figure it's still just civilians inside and play it soft.*

He dropped to the rear of the line of civilians. They were strung out over thirty yards, stretching farther with almost every step. "As fast as you can," he urged the ones who were farthest back. "We don't want a firefight if we can avoid it."

Mentioning the possibility of combat lent some speed to the civilians. None of them were carrying half the load that a Marine considered routine—except perhaps Prince George with his shotgun and several dozen shells—but it was more than they were accustomed to. It had to be hard for some of them. David recognized that, but he also knew that they had to move quickly, especially now, before they were spotted by the incoming Feddies.

"Northeast, just over the trees," Alfie called out in a stage whisper. "Can't be more than two hundred feet up."

The last civilians and Marines were at the edge of the river. Alfie detailed two men to stay behind as rear guard, to cross after everyone else was on the far bank and moving under cover of the jungle. They had a path in front of them, but trees overhanging on either side, and moderately dense undergrowth on the far side of the river.

"We could take them," Alfie suggested. "A couple of rockets before they get out of the lander."

David shook his head. "No, that would just draw more of them in fast. If we do nothing, they might not be certain how long we've been gone."

He splashed out into the water. It was less than two feet deep at the deepest spot, over a firm, rocky bottom.

The last civilians were climbing out of the water when the shuttle appeared over the tops of the trees to the right and about two hundred yards away. David's rear guard hurried across the stream, moving with gliding steps that minimized the disturbance. As the shuttle settled in to a soft landing on the hotel lawn, the final Marines were disappearing into the jungle, moving to the sides of the path and hurrying forward.

The rest of the men, coming from their posts surrounding the hotel, had stayed out of view. Spencer did not worry about them. They would move around to rendezvous. Commandos would have no difficulty finding the civilians and their escort.

Once they were out of sight of the hotel, in the dark of the jungle, the civilians' pace slowed drastically. Thanks to the night-vision goggles Shadda had provided, they could see well enough, but their exertions demanded a slowdown—and begged for a halt, even after so few minutes. But David and Alfie kept them moving until they were more than two hundred yards from the river.

"Five minutes only," David whispered softly, repeating himself several times as he moved along the path. "Keep as silent as you can. The Feddies might have sound detection gear with them, and we're not far enough away to be safe."

When he reached Prince George near the head of the column, David took time to explain the situation more carefully. "As soon as the rest of my men catch us up, sir, I'll have a squad drop back as rear guard, keep them well behind us to slow the Feddies in case they do mark our trail and follow."

"Whatever you think best, Captain," George said. "I would not presume to tell you your business."

David nodded, then moved back along the column again. The other civilians watched him closely, their eyes and heads tracking his movements. Some of the people were obviously hoping for a longer reprieve before they would have to start moving again.

When he reached the tail of the column, David needed only a few seconds to tell Alfie to pick out a squad when the rest of the detachment arrived, to put them back a hundred yards behind the rest, just in case.

"You want them to rig a few traps?" Alfie asked.

Spencer didn't hesitate. "Yes, but tell them not to waste

a lot of time with it. Just enough to make the Feddies move damn carefully if they do follow. One or two the first good spot, then maybe a reminder a mile or so farther on. And get those food packets from the hotel distributed.''

''We had to leave some of them behind, Cap,'' Alfie said. ''What with the rush of Feddies coming in.''

David shrugged. ''Can't be helped.''

''How hard do you think we can push our charges?''

David shook his head. ''Not very, not without having half of them drop out by morning. We're going to have to feel this out as we go, find the best pace they can hold, with frequent breaks. We can't afford to have stragglers.''

''Twelve hours and the Feddies should have too much on their minds to worry about us,'' Alfie said. ''We could go off another three or four miles and then kip out until the invasion starts.''

''No. I want to put more distance between us and the hotel. In the morning, I'll go off to the side two or three miles before I try to make contact. If the invasion is contested strongly, it might take some time to make contact with our people, and more time for them to get shuttles down to pick us up. The fleet will be dancing in and out of Q-space if they have to.''

''It sounds like you don't think our troubles will be over that soon.''

''I just don't want to take any chances. Even with an invasion on, the Feddies might wonder what the hell we've been doing here, and who we pulled out of that hotel. Once they get a look inside, it won't take long to get some of the answers. If they do any kind of a search, they'll know about His Highness, and then we'll have as many Feddies in after us as they dare.''

Alfie gestured along the trail. ''We'd best get moving then, before our guests settle in. Here come the rest of our lads.''

Only a few of the Marines had not seen a member of the royal family in person before—at least at a distance—but apart from the three men who had been with the unit since it was the intelligence and reconnaissance platoon of 1st Battalion, the only one who had actually come face to face with royalty was Lieutenant Hopewell. He had been introduced to the Duke of Haven at a Commonwealth Day reception. David Spencer, Alfie Edwards, and Will Cordamon had all spent considerable time with the Duke of Haven. Hopewell longed for the sort of advantage that Spencer had derived from his contacts—going from squad leader, a sergeant, to captain and command of the 2nd Marine Commando Detachment in five years.

Most of the lower ranks were curious about Prince George. Those with the opportunity gave him an occasional sidelong appraisal, watching to see how royalty would perform. The rest of the civilians were merely numbers, people who had to be shepherded along and kept safe, if possible. Prince George was the purpose of the mission. Every man in the detachment knew that his own survival was secondary to protecting His Highness. So many of their mates had died just trying to get to him. If twice as many died getting him to safety, the price would be paid. That gave a deep intensity to the looks the men gave him.

With the rest of the Marines close, the civilians felt safer—in varying degree. There was a man in uniform near each of the people removed from the Commonwealth Excelsior. More Marines were out in front, and behind, human shields between the civilians and danger.

There were few words from any of the civilians, but in spite of that their sound discipline was poor. Some breathed noisily with the effort of walking and carrying their packs. There were grunts and muffled curses as people tripped over roots or their own feet. And when the jungle closed in tightly on the trail, branches occasionally snapped.

Apart from the effort of walking, and always being prodded to a little more speed by their escorts, the civilians had good cause to be tired. They had left the hotel at the end of the day. Most had been up for a dozen hours or more, some considerably more. They had been looking forward to an hour or two of leisurely pursuits, sitting around until it was time to retire, not to a forced march in the dark carrying clothing and several days worth of food.

By the time they had spent two hours walking, all of the civilians felt that they had done more than a fair day's work. Even Prince George felt tired. He said nothing about that, though. Throughout, he had attempted to be the perfect rescuee, doing whatever the Marines asked, speaking only when their captain needed a reply. He was prepared to go on for as long as necessary without complaint, until he dropped if it came to that—until they had put as much distance as possible between themselves and the immediate threat, the load of Federation troops who had apparently descended on the hotel.

The pace was not outrageous, George decided. The Marines were as solicitous as they dared be, stopping for five minutes every thirty or forty. Whenever one of the civilians stumbled, there was always a helping hand to make sure that the person did not actually fall or do serious damage to himself or herself.

Very professional, and then some, George thought. *But I do wish we could rest for more than five minutes. Some of these people simply won't be able to keep going all night.*

The same thought had been a frequent visitor to David Spencer's mind, almost from the start. The youngest of the people from the hotel had to be near forty. The oldest might be more than twice that. For civilians with the wherewithal to take long vacations at remote resorts like the Commonwealth Excelsior, being an octogenarian need pose no physical limitations, and need not offer any visual clues. Anyone could maintain the physical appearance of a twenty-five-year-old, and even those who did not bother with the cosmetic side of things would likely retain the inner vitality of youth. The only deterioration apt to show in anyone younger than one hundred would be the flabbiness and loss of muscle tone of a sedentary lifestyle. None of these people seemed to have spent any great effort at keeping fit through exercise.

After two and a half hours, David started watching the civilians more closely, trying to gauge how much longer he could keep them moving. The pace, never hard, had fallen off considerably. They had scarcely made two miles in the last hour, and the next hour the civilians would cover even less ground.

At three hours, David decided that it was time to stop. There was no hint of pursuit. The rear guard had not been caught by the Federation. There had been no sound of the enemy hitting the booby traps that the rear guard would have planted. And there had been no sounds of shuttles or fighters overhead.

"We'll rest here for a bit, sir," Spencer told the prince. "I'll send a squad off to the east to try to find us a better location close by. If possible, we'll camp and stay in one spot until we can arrange pickup. I can't guarantee that, though. If we have any enemy activity anywhere close, we might have to move on, but . . . well, sir, you know how it is."

"I can imagine," George said. "You said that your regiment is due in this morning?"

"Morning on this side of the world, but they'll be landing around sunset on the other side. I don't have any idea how much opposition they'll face, or how long it will be before whoever is in command feels that it's safe enough to send shuttles for us."

Prince George nodded slowly. "Once we go to ground, I do hope you'll find time to put me in the picture, Captain. We have all been out of touch with the rest of the galaxy for seven years. We haven't the foggiest idea what might have transpired."

"I'll try, sir. I do appreciate your patience. As soon as I think it safe, I shall give you my complete attention and try to catch you up on the war and so forth—as far as I know myself, that is."

"Thank you, Captain. I shan't ask for details of everything that has happened since I fell out of things, but whatever you can tell me now—all of us—should make our transition back to society less difficult.''

"Of course, sir.''

"You said that you were about to send a squad to find us a place?'' George said as a reminder.

"They're already off, sir. I gave my orders before.''

"Then I might as well get off of my feet and make other portions of my anatomy take their turn at supporting me.'' George took a step to the side and sat.

Alfie Edwards decided to lead the patrol himself. It was not that he doubted the ability of his squad leaders. He had trained every one of them himself and made sure that they were up to his standards. It was just that, under the circumstances, he wasn't absolutely certain that any of them would find a spot as well suited to the purpose as he might himself. And he wanted to be confident that they had His Highness in the spot with the best concealment, and the best opportunities for defense.

After they made it through seven years on their own, we can't have it be said that they came to harm because we stopped by to collect them and bollixed it up, he reasoned.

The squad moved west, parallel to the river, in more typical tropical rain forest. There was little undergrowth, except in and around tree-fall gaps and, three quarters of a mile from where the rest of the commandos and their charges were waiting, along a small stream that moved south toward the larger river.

"We might find something suitable in there,'' Alfie whispered to Corporal Ted Perth, his assistant squad leader. "You keep your fire team here. I'll take my lads in for a closer look.''

"Watch out for them bleedin' snakes,'' Ted advised. "I doubt His Highness would care for a quick cuddle with one of them.''

"The snake wouldn't dare.''

Alfie gathered the four privates of the squad's first fire team and moved closer to the thick tangle of greenery close to the stream. Between the vines and young trees trying to win their way through to the forest canopy, there appeared to be nearly a solid wall of vegetation fronting the creek. When Alfie and his fire team did penetrate, they could see that there were even stringers spanning the waterway, almost roofing it over through one stretch. They moved along the edge of the dense thickets, prodding each hint of an opening toward the water, looking for shelter and defensibility. Alfie knew that there was some urgency to the search, but he was not about to compromise on anything less than the best he could find. He took forty-five minutes before selecting a site on the west side of the creek.

"This will do." He called Ted Perth's fire team in. They had been paralleling Alfie's movements, out in easier terrain. "Get your lads in there and do what you can to make it homey. We can put all the civies in there and find our own places around about. I'll take my team back to guide them in."

After he started away from the location, Alfie stopped to look back once more. *It should do,* he thought. *We should be able to hide from anything in there for a day or so.*

Prince George and the other civilians were tired enough that no one started to ply the Marines with questions once they were settled in. Questions, and the answers to them, could wait. Sleep, or at least the chance to lie flat and renounce all exertion beyond breathing, was more important. Not all of the civilians were able to drop straight off despite exhaustion greater than they had known in many years.

The prince was one of the first to get to sleep. His last thought before losing awareness was *At least I won't have to worry about those bloody cachouris this morning.* That was a satisfying tonic. Close by, Vepper Holford watched George until the rhythm of the prince's breathing showed that he was asleep. Then he too closed his eyes, ready to escape.

Shadda Lorenqui was one of the last civilians to slide off. He would have anticipated that, had he retained energy to think beyond the instant. He was certainly as tired as any of the others, perhaps more so. Every morning at the hotel he had been one of the first to wake, and at night he was generally the last to retire to his room—and even then, sleep never came easily. What worried him most this night was the fact that he was no longer at ''his'' hotel. *I deserted my post,* he reminded himself. No matter the extenuating circumstances, the basic fact could not be changed. He had been entrusted with maintaining and running a valuable piece of property, and he had simply walked away. He had very nearly *run* from it.

Among the Marines, sleep had to be a rationed commodity. David Spencer made his defensive allocations, then put the commandos on a half-and-half watch. In each fire team, two men would sleep while the other two remained awake, watching the night for any hint of enemy activity.

The detachment was well dispersed. One squad had been left east of the stream to make certain that no one could sneak up from that side. One squad, the headquarters people, remained with the civilians. The rest were scattered around the perimeter, fifty yards or more out from the people who had been removed from the Commonwealth Excelsior, each squad charged with defending a certain section.

Once he was satisfied with his dispositions, David decided to give himself four hours of sleep. *Uninterrupted, I hope,* he thought as he settled in. There would always be someone in charge, awake. David would share watches with Lieutenant Hopewell and Lead Sergeant Naughton.

Before he slept, David went quickly through his plans for the morning, looking for any possible improvements, trying to assure himself that he had not forgotten anything essential. No amount of worry would do that completely, but a Marine learned to sleep when he could. David Spencer slept.

When Mitchel Naughton woke Spencer at four o'clock, the jungle was still firmly in the grip of night. Sunrise was two hours away, and morning would face its usual struggle to illuminate the denser areas of tropical jungle.

"Been perfectly quiet, Cap," Naughton whispered. "Just the jungle noises, I mean, nothing else."

"Let's hope it stays that way, Mitch." Another couple of hours of sleep would have been supremely welcome, but David was awake and alert, ready for another long day. On campaign, sleep was a luxury to be enjoyed rarely, and seldom for as long at one stretch as the four hours that David had managed. "Try to get a little more sleep for yourself. I'll take you and the headquarters squad when I go off to radio the fleet."

Several of the civilians were snoring, one quite loudly. David winced at the noise as he made a quick tour of the camp. A good sound detector would pick up that racket from a half mile away, and be able to home in on it with little difficulty.

Can't do a thing about it now, David thought. Besides, there was always the chance that the loud snorer was the prince.

He checked at the nearest outposts, then returned to where he had slept and sat with his back against a tree trunk. After eating a hurried breakfast, one of the hotel boxed meals, he started thinking through his plans again. Early-morning thoughts were different from late-night thoughts. Now, he kept coming back to one idea. *With any luck at all, we might be off this world in another five or six hours.*

Lieutenant Hopewell woke a little before sunrise and made his way over to where Spencer was sitting. "You still figure to go off to make your call?"

David nodded. "I'll take Naughton and the headquarters squad. You'll be in charge here and have both platoon sergeants to help. All you need to remember is that our whole reason for being here is to keep His Highness safe until we can deliver him. Him and the others, but especially him. If something happens and I don't get back, it all falls on you.

Unless there's a damn good reason for moving, I think you should stay here. You'll play hell finding a better spot than this and . . . well, you know the limits of our guests. Can't move fast or quiet with them.''

''We'll manage.''

''I'm sure you will, Tony. Once the prince wakes up, you'll have to handle all of the questions he's likely to recall. And the others are going to want to know what's been going on through all the years they've been stuck here.''

''I knew there was a reason you decided to go wandering off through the bush yourself.''

David did manage a smile.

Walter Kaelich volunteered to take the point when the headquarters squad left camp. ''That way I can be sure one of those snakes won't sneak up on me from behind, sir,'' he told Spencer. ''Have the whole lot of you behind me.''

''Okay, you've got it,'' David said, trying hard not to grin. Kaelich had sounded deadly serious. *I think that snake would have spooked me as well,* he conceded. *Anyway, whatever it takes to keep his mind on the job.* ''We cross the stream here, go east for two hundred yards from the far bank, then change to a northeasterly heading. I want to get at least three miles from our guests before I break radio silence to contact the fleet.''

Walter nodded, repeating the instructions to himself so that he would be sure to remember.

''Any time you want somebody else to take the point for a bit, just let either the lead sergeant or me know. We'll find you a cozy spot in the middle.''

They crossed the creek where there was cover from overhead vines, the stringers that reached from trees on one bank to trees on the other. The stream was no more than twenty feet wide, and less than eighteen inches deep where they crossed. The sun was just high enough to illuminate the western edge of the stream—where it could pierce the jungle canopy.

On the east side, they worked through the line of dense undergrowth and past the squad that was watching that side. The first hundred yards of the trek would be, Spencer hoped, the most difficult. Beyond the wild growth nourished by the creek, the forest floor opened out again.

There was the dark green basic color that touched everything. Even the air seemed to be tinted by the sunlight that filtered through the canopy. The mostly empty expanse on the ground was broken by the stark trunks of old trees. There was little in the way of leaves between the forest floor and the lowest branches sixty feet up. David could not tell how high the domes of the canopy might be, almost certainly more than a hundred feet above the moss and detritus of the forest floor.

Except for the Marines, the lowest level of the forest appeared to be virtually deserted, void of any animal life larger than insects. But the forest was not dead, or silent. The life was all in the canopy, and loud in the first hour of daylight. Birds and small animals made their presence known, one way or another. The predators might be silent, but their prey gave loud warnings whenever a threat was spotted. For the most part, the commandos blocked out those sounds. What they would note was any interruption to those noises that did not appear natural.

Walter Kaelich sweated, even through the first part of the journey, before the heat of the sun started to percolate through the stagnant air under the forest canopy. While the squad was in the densest area of cover, he was most nervous. He had slept little since having that snake crawl up to him—a lifetime ago, it seemed. Once away from the undergrowth near the stream, Walter breathed easier. He steered his course as far from tree trunks as possible, sticking to the most open path he could find.

What I want is open fields with the grass cut short as a cricket pitch, or paved over, he thought. *A place where I could see a snake coming a half mile away.* In his twenty years of life, Walter had never seen a snake before coming to Camerein, not even in a zoo. He had since convinced himself that one was enough to last a lifetime.

Even with occasional distractions such as that, Walter tended to business. There seemed to be virtually no chance of running into Federation troops, but he kept a sharp watch for any of the telltales that might give him even a second's warning if they *were* around, and he kept a rough count of his paces so that he would know when to make the turn and when they had covered the three miles that Captain Spencer had specified.

There was little chance of running into those other Feddies we ran into, he reminded himself. *But there they were, right in front of us, waiting. Bad as snakes.* From time to time he would take one hand or the other off his rifle to wipe the sweat from it on his trouser leg. Not for the first time in his stint in the 2nd Marine Commando, he found himself wondering how he had managed to get himself into such a fix. *I thought clerking was clerking anywhere, and having that commando patch would make me stand a little taller with the lasses.* The latter had been correct at any rate. On pass in Cheapside, the commando insignia on his off-dress khakis had brought more action with the women who frequented the area, but for the rest . . . He shook his head, reminding himself that if it hadn't been for his ego he could have opted out of commando training at any point.

My head's just too big for my shoulders, he decided.

Without out-of-shape civilians to slow them, or an enemy to bar the way, the squad made good time. The three miles took less than an hour, even at a relatively casual pace.

"This will do," Spencer told Kaelich. Then he turned to Naughton. "Get the lads spread out in a perimeter here. We'll take ten before I get on the radio." He looked up at the sky through a rare break in the canopy. "It's early days yet. If the invasion is on schedule, the fleet is liable to be busy."

Exactly ten minutes later, David switched to his primary radio frequency for contacting the fleet. He made his call and waited. There was no response. He waited a minute and tried again. When he still received no reply, he switched to the secondary channel and tried. There was no answer on that either.

It worried him, but not excessively. *They could be running a bit late, or they might just be too busy at the moment,* he told himself. *Right in the middle of the assault, after all. And they might just not have a ship in position to get a call from this side of the world yet.* There might be other reasons why there was no response to his calls, and most of those reasons would be innocuous. David shrugged, then told Naughton that there was no answer.

"We'll move on for a half mile or so, still northeast, before I try again," David told him. Movement was essential. If the enemy were using direction finders and intercepted the signal, they might think that the commandos were all moving on that heading.

Over the next three hours, David tried to reach the fleet another half dozen times. There was still no reply.

"We'll stay here another thirty minutes," he told Naughton after another series of failures. "I'll keep trying, in case they're popping in and out of Q-space all the time and we've just been unlucky with our timing. If they still don't answer, we'll head due west, all the way to that stream, before we turn south."

"What then?" Naughton asked softly.

Spencer shook his head. "I don't know yet."

17

Admiral Sir Stasys Truscott, Chief of Naval Operations, rode from the Admiralty to St. James Palace in silence. He sat so motionless in the rear compartment of the staff floater that he might have been a statue. He would have preferred to make this report by complink, but His Majesty would have none of that. It had to be in person.

A sailor for sixty-five of his eighty-five years, Truscott wore the uniform as if it had been designed especially for him. Of average height, and less than average weight, for Buckingham, he was totally unprepossessing in civilian clothes. In uniform—and few people outside of his family ever saw him any other way—he was entirely different. Today the uniform was full-dress blues, with the white and red piping, and a white hat. The left breast of the uniform jacket was covered with decorations and service medals. *Enough to make me list twelve degrees to port,* he often joked. The nautical reference was a common conceit among naval officers, few of whom had ever stood on the deck of a seagoing vessel. The navy of the Second Commonwealth had only one such ship in its inventory, a floating museum transported to Buckingham from Earth in the year of the Commonwealth's founding—and inextricably linked to that event. *USS Missouri* was permanently docked at Haven, northwest of Westminster. Truscott made the trip, pilgrimage, to Haven whenever he could find or invent an excuse—rarely in the last five years.

Truscott's current aide—he had gone through five in the not quite five years since Ian Shrikes had been promoted out of the position—sat on the far side of the compartment, equally silent and motionless. Commander Engels watched his boss, knowing that he dared not distract the admiral when he was in this sort of mood. Engels had only held the job of aide to Truscott for three months, but it had seemed an eternity.

The limousine pulled up to the west entrance to St. James Palace. Admiral Truscott was met with ceremony. The major domo was present with three butlers and the king's naval aide, a senior captain certain to make admiral soon. After a modicum of time wasted with court formalities, Truscott was escorted to an office on the second floor. His Majesty was waiting.

"You have bad news for me," King Henry said as soon as the ritual greetings had been exchanged and they were seated. Their aides, the only other people in the room, remained standing.

"I don't know for certain that it is bad news, Your Majesty," Stasys said, "but it is certainly not the good news I had hoped to be bringing you by now."

Henry nodded. "Give it to me straight, Stasys."

"The important bit is that we have no word on your brother yet, sir, neither good nor bad. What we do have is two separate items, one worrisome, the other merely a temporary annoyance. We have finally had an MR from *Avon*. They suffered some sort of mishap entering Q-space over Camerein. That destroyed their Nilssens and left them marooned in Q-space for several days. They escaped by rigging the Nilssens from their MRs, but that has left them stranded a long way from anywhere. They have had no contact with the Marines who landed on Camerein. Those who survived the initial landing." He went on to tell the king about the interception as the shuttles were going in.

The loss of both craft and an unknown number of Marines. "We assume that the bulk of the detachment did survive and are on the ground, but we have had no word from them since the first day."

"What about the fleet? Hasn't the invasion force arrived yet?" the king asked.

"Not yet, sir. That is the second item. Since nothing at all had been heard from *Avon*—she was due to report by MR no later than two days before the scheduled invasion—the First Lord of the Admiralty and I decided that it would be prudent to increase the size of the task force accompanying 2nd Regiment. The battle group returning from Shepard was sent back out at once, but that was the cause of the delay. The invasion group was originally scheduled to reach Camerein some hours ago. It will now be the day after tomorrow."

Henry mulled over what Truscott had said, then cleared his throat. "Those Marines we put on the ground five days ago must be frantic by now—no contact with their ship, lost both shuttles, and unable to get any reply from the invasion fleet because it simply isn't there."

"I have every confidence in that detachment, sir," Truscott said. "They might well be the best Marines Your Majesty has."

The king's smile was weak. "I share your confidence in them. I hope that their mission was not in vain. It pains me that a considerable number of good men might already have died in what could prove to have been a futile fancy from the beginning. I enjoyed meeting Captain Spencer, and have looked forward to renewing our acquaintance. That reunion will be difficult with him losing men, the more so if they could find nothing of my brother George." Henry looked down for a moment, sadness on his face. He blinked, then sighed before he looked up again.

"Thank you for coming personally, Stasys. Please keep me informed, as soon as you learn anything, at whatever time of day or night."

Truscott stood and bowed. "Of course, Your Majesty."

He hesitated, then added, ''It's too soon to give up hope, sir.''

The king smiled as he also stood. ''I was just telling myself the same thing. George has a positively uncanny knack of landing on his feet. If anyone could come through seven years of such total isolation, it would be he.''

Truscott bowed again and left, anxious to escape.

18

During the trek back to the rest of his command after his failed attempts to contact the fleet, David Spencer thought of a lot of possible reasons for the lack of success. The first, that there was simply a malfunction in the radio, he had quickly eliminated. He had tried with every helmet in the squad. The built-in diagnostics showed no faults.

None of the other possibilities could be tested so easily. It might be that the invasion was taking place as scheduled but that none of the ships had been in normal space during any of David's attempts to contact them. The more often he tried, the longer the odds against that explanation became, but the chance could not be ruled out completely. All he could do was keep trying. If there was a Commonwealth battle group overhead, sooner or later he would make contact.

If there *was* no fleet, that was more serious. David's imagination fed him three primary scenarios. One, the fleet had arrived and every ship had been destroyed or forced to flee before David's first call. Two, the invasion had been postponed temporarily. Three, the invasion had been called off completely.

Of those three alternatives, only the second left any hope for the people on the ground, so that was the one David spent the most time considering. The fleet commander might have decided to stage a dawn landing instead of the planned sunset assault on the opposite side of Camerein, which would mean a ten- to twelve-hour delay. That should pose little problem, only the inconvenience of spending those extra hours on their own in the bush. But if the invasion had been postponed for a day or two—or longer—life might get complicated. If there were no invasion to occupy the Federation's minds and resources, there would be nothing to keep them from putting a maximum effort into finding the commandos and the refugees from the hotel. It would also mean that the odds of a quick rescue for any of them would become prohibitively long.

By the time David returned to camp, he had come to only one conclusion. They would have to move farther away from the Commonwealth Excelsior and the locations from which he had done his transmitting. And they had to change direction.

"There's simply no help for it, sir," he told Prince George after explaining the problem. "It might just be a matter of keeping on the move today. It could get to be more, though. I don't have the information I'd need to be more definite."

"You do realize that there is no human habitation within seven hundred miles of here, save for the Excelsior," George said.

"Yes, sir, I am aware of that. And even though it might seem to be the obvious course to take, to the Feddies, I think we should head in that direction. I'm going to have to make occasional attempts to communicate, and if the Feddies continue to search for us—as I must assume they will—each attempt will increase the danger that they will find us. There is simply no escape from that."

"A pretty problem indeed."

"Understand, sir, I am not trying to shift the decision to you. Begging your pardon, but this must be strictly a military decision, and it must be mine. While I welcome your insights and advice, I have my orders direct from His Majesty, and I am duty-bound to do everything I can to keep you safe until such time as we can get you off of Camerein.''

''I know that I am not in the chain of command, Captain. I *will* observe that it might be difficult to keep everyone moving for any length of time. While I had a stint of military service, and have been bound by the demands of duty my entire life, most of these people have never been in such circumstances.''

''Difficult or not, it has to be done.'' Spencer glanced toward where the other civilians were. ''I realize that I can't ask or expect as much of untrained civilians as I demand of my own men, but we do have to move. If the others know that the choice is to continue with us or be left alone in the bush . . .''

George nodded. ''Up to a point, Captain, that will work. But if they are pressed too hard, some might well take the second option—eventually from simple necessity. How soon do you intend to start moving?''

''Immediately, sir.''

Spencer did not ask, he told. He explained why they had to move, but he squelched every attempt to discuss it. ''It's not open to debate,'' he said. ''A military unit can't exist that way, and this is a military operation. Your being civilians won't save you if the Feddies get their hands on you. You people have missed all news of the war. I haven't. I've seen firsthand what they do with inconvenient civilians, and I've seen how rarely they bother to encumber themselves with prisoners. Dead people don't have to be fed and guarded. We leave in five minutes.''

There were complaints, but David refused to respond or let himself be drawn into discussion—and he absolutely refused to reconsider his decision. ''You stay with the group, or you have perhaps one chance in a thousand of surviving. It's that simple.''

Not everyone voiced, or felt, misgivings. Prince George did what he could to ease the situation, as did Shadda Lorenqui. And no one chose to stay behind when David gave the word to move out.

"And keep it quiet," David ordered. "Noise kills. Our best chance of survival comes if the Feddies can't see or hear us."

He did not set a demanding pace, but kept the group moving longer between breaks than he had during the night. In three hours he permitted only two short rest stops. It was during the second of those that they heard Federation aircraft.

The shuttles were moving slowly, less than fifty miles per hour, which meant that they were audible for a considerable time. There was time for a commando to climb into the forest canopy and get high enough to spot the enemy aircraft. A line of eight shuttles was moving northeast to southwest, nearly a mile between neighboring landers. They were low, scarcely a thousand feet above the ground.

"They're running a search pattern," David whispered when the sentry came back down. Hopewell, Naughton, and the platoon sergeants were gathered around Spencer and Prince George. "They'll have all their detection gear running." He moved toward where the other civilians were clustered.

"Dead quiet now," he whispered. "They'll have sound gear good enough to hear anything. Stay down and stay quiet."

There was nothing to do but wait. David and the leaders who had been with him retreated under dense cover and sat motionless. Eight shuttles might carry five hundred soldiers, far more than the shorthanded commando detachment could hope to stand off.

They must have picked up one of my transmissions, David thought. His head was forward, his shoulders hunched up. He might have suggested a turtle trying to pull his head back into his shell. *It's too much a coincidence if they just happened to pull that course out of a bonnet. The center of that line is right over where I did most of my calling this morning.*

One of the shuttles passed almost directly overhead. David did not need to see it. The Doppler shift of its engine noises was enough to tell him where it was. The shuttle seemed to take forever to pass. For a few stretched seconds, David feared that it had gone into a hover. That would have meant that they had been spotted. But, slowly, the sound started to move away.

David waited until he could no longer hear the shuttles before he moved back toward the trail. He gestured, first using simple hand signs that his men would recognize, and then switching to more exaggerated motions for the civilians.

"Let's move before they come back and land," he said.

There were no complaints from any of the civilians now. Even those who had been most vociferous before had been cowed—at least temporarily—by the display of Federation power.

Jeige McDonough had not been one of the complainers. He had kept his misgivings to himself. In an almost perverse way, he was enjoying both the danger and the physical exertion, as he had nearly reveled in the labor of digging the shuttle pilot's grave less than a week before. *It gives me a sense of purpose* was as close as he could come to a reason.

The trek also seemed to be having a beneficial impact on his wife. At first, Mai had been one of the loudest complainers—about everything. During the night, and again since they had started moving again because of the Federation overflight, she had sweated profusely. Although she still refused to talk to her husband, she did not resist his occasional assistance—a hand at her elbow when she stumbled, or his offer to carry part of her load. After a short time walking, movement took so much of her energy that she had been forced to stop complaining. She didn't have the strength for both, and she did not want to be left behind.

It will do her good to sweat out the years of alcohol, Jeige told himself, watching her. He had never seen her perspire so freely, and the bedraggled look she had now was worlds different from the way she had looked in her perpetually drunken state.

This might even give me a wife back, Jeige thought. *If we ever get off of this world.*

Marie Caffre had a foolproof way to keep herself moving, to keep from saying, "The hell with it." She kept her eyes on The Windsor. She promised herself that as long as he could move, she would—and at least two steps longer. She was the smallest person from the hotel. He was the tallest. The Windsor had always kept active. She had not. But she was determined to perform just that little bit better than he did—whatever it took. *I'll sweat like a peasant and take all of the pain, and show The Windsor that I'm better than he ever could be.* Even when the Marine captain called a break, Marie made it a point of honor to stay on her feet an instant longer than The Windsor, and at the end of each halt, she was on her feet before he was. The Windsor gave no indication that he noticed that Madame Caffre was attempting to compete with him, but that did not surprise her.

Henri Caffre had noticed, early on. He watched the way his wife remained fixated on the prince, damning herself to match his performance. At first, it amused Henri. Then it started to concern him. *She'll kill herself if she doesn't relent.* As troubled as their relationship had become on Camerein, Henri could not imagine life without Marie. They would escape and go home. All of their difficulties would evaporate once they were back in familiar surroundings, with their friends, acquaintances, and neighbors. But if she destroyed herself in this vain populist mania . . .

"Calm yourself, my dear," he urged. "No one is going to get anywhere faster than the rest. There is no need to compete."

She did not bother to reply.

It was seventy-five minutes after the sounds of the shuttles vanished that they returned from the opposite direction. The line of shuttles had shifted, overlapping its previous coverage by about fifty percent. There was the same slow progress, the regular spacing, the low altitude.

"They're looking for us, that's for certain," Lead Sergeant Naughton said after the shuttles had gone past again.

Spencer nodded. "By now they must have a damned good idea who we have with us. There'd be clues enough for a brain-dead bird dog to follow back at the hotel. And the fact that they're putting so much effort into the search has got to mean that there really isn't a Commonwealth fleet in orbit."

The second passing of the shuttles seemed to have a more chilling effect on the civilians than the first had had. Once across might be coincidence. Twice removed any doubt that they were the object of an intensive search. The seventeen people from the hotel sat or lay motionless, as close to tree trunks and other cover as they could get, throughout the second passage. Most looked upward even though the canopy was too thick and constant to give them any hope of seeing the shuttles. Once more, David sent a man up a tree. This time, the scout came down without getting a look. All he could say was that they were near the edge of the search pattern this time instead of in the middle.

They're searching blind, David thought. *If they hold to the pattern, next time they'll pass off to our left.* He was certain that the shuttles would make another pass, but he could not have explained that certainty logically. *They'll keep looking until they find us.*

It was not a happy thought.

It would serve me right to die in this wasteland, Shadda Lorenqui told himself after the group started to move again. *I should never have left the hotel. Even with all of the others going, I should have remained at my post.* Fear kept his stomach knotted so tightly that it was sometimes nearly impossible to keep from doubling over in agony. *One man at the hotel could not have inconvenienced these other soldiers.* It did not bother him that the only way he might have been able to insure being left alone would have been to tell the Federation soldiers whatever they wanted to know, in as much detail as he could. Shadda had always possessed a most pliable conscience, even if it often caused suffering. His mission in life had always been to survive. Whatever that took was proper. Or so he had always told himself. *Do whatever it takes. If it gets you through the next day, it's right. You can't worry about anyone else. It's all any man can do to keep body and soul together in this galaxy.*

The comfortable years as acting manager of the Commonwealth Excelsior might have dulled his certainty about that philosophy, but it had not let him forget it. *Survive the war and maybe earn a permanent post as manager of the hotel.* That had been his goal. That was what he had thrown away by leaving.

Shadda was not overly distressed by the physical demands of the march. The pace was not that rapid, and carrying food, water, and clothing did not weigh him down beyond his limits. The seven years at the Excelsior had been the easiest of his life, but they had not erased all that he had done before. He had known hard physical labor, had even served for a short time in uniform. He knew the drill backwards and sideways, and mere physical activity would never grind him down completely. But he wondered at the purpose of this march.

Surely he can't intend to walk us all the way to Como Nairobe, he thought. Como Nairobe was the one town on the continent, seven hundred miles off, across one line of very high mountains and two dozen significant rivers, waterways that could not be forded and had no bridges. Shadda had tried to dissuade the guests who had left the hotel early in the war from attempting that passage. He had warned them that it was impossible, that they were signing their own death warrants by trying. As far as he could know, all of those people *had* died. None had come back. None had been heard from after they left.

And no one will ever know how the lot of us died, most like. It was a gloomy thought, perfectly fitting his mood.

"If we didn't have all of our guests, we could have stayed fairly close to that hotel and dodged Feddies," Spencer told Hopewell during the next break. "I'm sure the incoming fleet would try to raise us even if I didn't call. But with the civilians, our only hope is to get as far off as possible."

"We couldn't hardly go far enough that we wouldn't hear the fleet call," Hopewell said.

"Once Camerein is secure, certainly, but if there's any serious opposition, I suspect that they would use a narrow-beam transmission to cut down on the chances of an enemy intercept. That's why I've got to try calling instead of just waiting." Spencer looked down. "There's still the other possibility."

"You mean that nobody's coming at all?"

David nodded. "The civilians have been here seven years. What's to keep it from being another seven?"

"This war can't possibly go on for that long."

"Even if it ends. What happens if we're here and the Feddies still control Camerein when peace comes? There's no guarantee that we could get His Highness off safely even then."

"Our lads will come. The RM aren't going to simply forget about us, all apart from the prince and the others. One way or another, they'll come to collect us."

But when? David wondered. *It took seven years to send us to find the king's own brother.*

19

The Marine squads rotated duties at each stop. An hour after the shuttles passed overhead for the second time, Alfie's squad took over the point, moving ahead of the main body, working to keep a hundred yards between the last man in the squad and the rest of the group.

"I'd as soon it was a hundred miles," Alfie told Ted Perth when they took over the point. "Anything to get away from that lot. A herd of monkeys wouldn't make half the noise."

Perth's fire team moved out in front, walking single file along the route Captain Spencer had dictated. Alfie's fire team waited until there was a forty-yard gap between Perth's men and themselves, then formed a skirmish line spread across twenty yards. Under the forest canopy, the floor was too open for there to be much danger of ambush except when they reached water or a treefall zone where new growth was struggling toward the light and low-growing plants had a chance to survive. The point squad always took considerable care about those areas.

We should be hearing those shuttles again soon, Alfie thought after noting the time on his helmet display. *It wasn't quite this long the last time.* He didn't seriously consider the possibility that the shuttles might have given up. It was far too soon to hope for that. *They'll keep it up at least until dark, and maybe for a time after that, hoping that we'll be stupid enough to light campfires.* Sunset was still several hours off.

Visibility under the forest canopy was somewhat limited. In the distance, the accumulation of tree trunks and shadows put an edge to how far anyone could see. Everything blurred into a featureless backdrop. Paradoxically, the areas of dense undergrowth showed more clearly than the colonnaded run of uninterrupted old growth. Where treefall gaps or rivers gave run to lower plants, the greens became more intense. The scenes were often backlit even if wide shafts of clear sunlight could not be seen stretching from canopy to ground.

Ted Perth spotted the new line of undergrowth forty minutes after taking the point and waited to point it out to Alfie. "Must be another stream," Ted said, whispering. "It goes as far as I can see from one side to the other."

"Set up a line here. I'll check with the captain, see if he knows what it is. We're due for a break anyway."

"If my memory is correct, it should be a fairly sizable river," Spencer said when Alfie told him about the line of dense vegetation. "And I don't want to use a mapboard to check my memory, not with Feddies quartering the sky to spot us." Without an active link to a ship or satellite, the emissions from a mapboard would be minimal, but the Federation's detecting gear might be sensitive enough to pick it up. "I'll check with the hotel manager and His Highness. Maybe one of them will know."

Prince George nodded when David put the question to him. "If you are correct about the distance we have traveled, we should be near the Rift River."

"The data in our chart files didn't have topographical information in any great detail for this continent, sir," David said. "Apparently, there wasn't much available on Buckingham. Can you shed any light on what we can expect to find?"

"I haven't seen it myself," George said, "but from what I have gathered, the river got its name because it lies along a rift. You understand the term, Captain?" When Spencer nodded, the prince continued. "It runs straight as a laser beam for two hundred miles. I fear it might pose an insurmountable obstacle for us, though. If the reports are correct, the south bank is sheer—and as much as a hundred feet high."

"It is," Shadda confirmed. "I've seen it from the air, before the war. Before I became acting manager of the Commonwealth Excelsior, I was employed to survey remote locations to set up semipermanent camps for the convenience of hotel guests who might want more than simple day trips into the bush. There are no bridges across the Rift River, and it is too deep to ford even if you could find a way down to the bank."

"What about the north bank?" David asked.

"Like any of the rivers in this jungle," Shadda said.

"I mean, it's only on this side that there are cliffs?"

"Yes, only on the south. The forest canopy on the north is at about the same level as the ground on the south side. What difference can that make, though, if we can't cross the river?"

David smiled. "I suspect that we might be able to cross this river despite your misgivings."

"Not unless you can teach the lot of us to fly," Shadda said.

"You'd be surprised what they teach us in commando school."

Prince George arched an eyebrow but said nothing. Shadda wore a look of total disbelief on his face. He could not even bring himself to ask the obvious follow-up question: *What* do *they teach you?*

The band of dense growth was very narrow above the south bank of the Rift River, but there was almost a solid wall of greenery climbing from ground level to the canopy. A few trees grew out at an angle, over the river, claiming sunlight in that fashion; some of them seemed to be held in place by vines connecting them to upright trees above. Small trees and bushes survived at the edge of the precipice, most of their leaves on the north—the sunlit—side. Epiphytes hung from branches, some nearly reaching the ground. Rooted vines climbed along any available pathway from ground to canopy. Some spread from tree to tree. The overall effect was almost that of thatching or a basket-weave over an intricate lattice.

By the time the group reached that barrier, news of what Spencer had said had filtered through to all the civilians. None of them could answer the question that Shadda had not asked. *How?* It seemed impossible. Or suicidal.

Spencer left the civilians, guarded by most of his Marines, twenty yards south of the dense growth. He went forward with Alfie and Mitch Naughton to have a look.

Alfie whistled softly when he saw the drop to the river.

"I know what you've got in mind, Cap, and I'm not sure I care for the idea. I'm damned certain that none of our civies are going to like it at all."

"The more impossible it looks, the better," David said. "Maybe the Feddies will think it is impossible and just look for us on this side of the river."

Naughton got down on hands and knees before he ventured near the edge. He edged forward carefully, hesitating often against the possibility that he might venture out on a thin overhang that would not support his weight. "It looks like eighty or ninety feet down and maybe sixty feet across to the far side," he said. He went flat on his stomach and slid forward a little more, until his head was just over the edge. Alfie got down to hold Naughton's legs in case the ground gave way.

"Absolutely sheer," Naughton said when he slid back away from the drop. "A man would have to rappel down, then swim the river dragging a rope." He hesitated for an instant. "You weren't planning on everyone going that way, were you, Cap?"

Spencer shook his head. "Just one man to carry the line

and secure it on the far side. The rest of us will slide over one at a time. We can tie the wrists of our civilians over the transit line so there's no danger of them falling. Have several of our men waiting to put the brakes on for them when they get to the bottom. Rig a double length of rope so we can pull it in after us, not leave a sign for the Feddies to spot."

"I think Alfie had it right," Mitch said. "We might have to coldcock some of our guests to get them down a rope that way."

Without a hint of a smile, David said, "If that's what it takes, that's what we'll do. I'm not going to leave anyone behind."

"If we're going to do it, we'd best get our fingers out and start. We want good daylight for this ropey go," Alfie said.

There was no difficulty in finding enough rope. Each commando carried fifty yards of thin, strong cord. That, and a pair of clamps designed to lock two sections of rope together more securely than any knot, contributed only seventeen ounces to a Marine's combat kit. Three-sixteenths of an inch in diameter, the rope could support three tons without breaking.

After some discussion among the sergeants, Zol Ketchum was allowed to "volunteer" to be the first man across, the one who would have to do the hard work. He was the best swimmer left in the detachment and above average in mountaineering skills, both part of the curriculum in commando school.

Stripped to his boots and field skin, with his sheath knife strapped to one arm, Zol secured a doubled line to two stout trees. He rappelled down the face of the cliff carefully. There was no low bank at the bottom. It was sheer, right into the water, with the strongest current apparently close to the southern bank. Before he could get oriented, the current started to carry him west. He had to swim against that current without losing the rope.

The first twenty yards were the most difficult. After that, the current eased and Zol was able to make headway with less exertion. When he pulled himself up on the opposite shore, he still had the rope. For a moment, he rested on hands and knees, head down, dragging in deep breaths.

It shouldn't have been that hard a go, he thought. *I guess I'm not in the shape I thought I was.*

When he got to his feet, he looked for a place to tie off the rope. He knew what was needed: a strong tree not too close to the water, without too much undergrowth around it. It also needed to be as short a run as possible, as near directly across from the high end of the line as practical. He looped the end of the rope around the trunk he decided on three times, as high as he could reach without shinnying up the tree, then tied his knots before snapping on one of the clamps. Before signaling to the other side to start sending people across, Zol jumped up to grasp the line in both hands. Then he pulled himself up along it, hand over hand, until he was near the water's edge.

Can't know for sure if it's all secure till somebody comes across, but that's as strong as I can make it. He stood in clear view at the water's edge and made a pumping gesture with his right hand. On the bluff across the river, Captain Spencer echoed the signal.

"It couldn't be simpler, or safer," David told the prince and the civilians. They were all clustered together, facing him. "I'll send two squads of Marines across first to prove that the rope isn't going to give way. We'll fasten your wrists over the rope so you don't have to worry about holding on or falling off. And there will be several men to catch you on the other end, slow you down gently before you go thumping into the ground or into the tree." There were objections, but Spencer dealt with them swiftly. "There is no alternative," he said, and—after several minutes—the objections ceased.

Alfie took his squad across first. Lieutenant Hopewell crossed with 1st Platoon's second squad next. There were no mishaps. Most of the civilians had moved close enough to watch at least a few of the crossings.

"Looks a bit of a lark," Prince George said, loud enough that all the people who had shared his exile could hear. "Almost a carnival ride, don't you know."

David nodded a silent thanks. "You can go first after I've got enough lads on the other side to protect you, sir." Only three men had made the crossing at the time.

"Glad to," George replied cheerfully.

He was the first of the civilians to cross. After the Marines at the bottom slowed him to a stop and removed the length of cord that had joined his wrists and served as a runner, he moved out into plain sight and gave a thumbs-up gesture to those who were watching from the other side.

"If he can do it, I can," Marie Caffre said, moving forward to be the second to cross.

Her husband followed her, and after that there was only minimal hesitation from a few of the others. Shadda Lorenqui held back until all the people who had been at the hotel had gone. "It is my duty to be the last, to make certain that all of those I have been responsible for have made it first," he told Spencer when he finally stepped up to have his wrists tied over the rope. "Now, my place is on the other side, with them."

Once all the civilians were across, the rest of the commandos followed quickly. By the time one man touched the north bank, the next was tied in place ready to follow. Only the last man faced any greater danger. Before sliding down the rope across the river, he had to remove the clamps that held the two strands of rope together around the upper end of the circuit so the line could be pulled free and retrieved, and he made the slide holding the short cord, without having his wrists tied together over the rope. But there was no mishap.

From beginning to end, the operation—including Zol Ketchum's rappel and swim—had taken only fifty-five minutes. Sunset was still an hour away.

• • •

"Do we move on or stay here for a time?" Lieutenant Hopewell asked after the last men were across.

David glanced toward the river and the gray cliff on the far side. "I think we can afford to take time now, even spend the night here. If the Feddies know we've got civilians with us, they're not likely to think of looking on this side of the river until they've eliminated every other possibility." He had tried again to make contact with any Commonwealth ships before making his own crossing, still without success. "I'll try for the battle group again in the morning, just before we move on."

"Aren't you afraid that might give us away?" Hopewell asked.

David shrugged. "Not if I go right over by the water's edge. They'd have to be looking right down at us, so to speak, to pinpoint the transmission that closely. If they're not thinking about this side of the river, they should assume that we're still up there." He gestured vaguely. "Maybe it won't be necessary. We're still close enough to the hotel that a signal from a ship will probably reach us, even on a narrow-band transmission. Maybe the fleet will call before morning." *I hope it does. Maybe even within the next hour or two.*

"If not, well, everyone should be rested and ready to go after twelve hours here. I'll make the call in the morning, and if we don't get any response, we'll push the march as hard as we can for a few hours. By the time the Feddies figure out that we did cross the river, we should be far enough away to give them fits trying to find us. This forest goes on for another eighty miles without a significant break, if I recall the charts correctly."

"I'm sure it's at least that far," Hopewell said. "I just hope we don't have to walk it all, not with our guests."

"We'd be about out of food by then, even with the extra packets from the hotel," David said, very softly. "Living off the land, and likely not too well."

"I'll get the outposts set, tell everyone to grab a meal, and that we're here for the night . . ."

"Unless circumstances change," David interrupted.

Hopewell nodded. "If the change is our ride out of here, I doubt that anyone will object."

After he ate, David took off his boots and spent several minutes rubbing his feet. They hurt. He could imagine how the civilians must be aching. He was used to long hours of walking, carrying a heavy load. They weren't. It wouldn't take many days to really put them to the point of mutiny.

If the fleet doesn't show up soon, I'll play hell keeping everyone together, he thought. He tried to avoid the next step in his mind, but could not. *What if the fleet never comes? What do we do then?* They couldn't go back to the hotel. It wasn't just that the Federation would keep an eye on it—if they didn't like what they saw so much that they moved right in. There was simply little chance that they would be able to get the seventeen civilians back up that cliff. Marines could scale it, and simply call it part of the day's work, but the civilians made a difference. At dire need, the commandos might be able to hoist the civilians, one at a time, back to the top, but it would be extremely difficult, dangerous, and time-consuming.

Before long, we wouldn't have any choice but to look for Feddies to surrender to. That was not a pleasant thought. *If we hoped to have any chance at all to survive, we'd have to find garrison troops to surrender to, and there won't be any of those closer than Como Nairobe, and that's still close to seven hundred miles away.* Garrison troops would be more likely to take prisoners, rather than kill them to save themselves the bother. But their food wouldn't last through one fifth of that distance, no matter how frugal they were. After that it would be catch and collect whatever came within reach. No cooking fires.

Try to get close enough to Como Nairobe to send the civilians in and keep my lads out in the wild? David hated to think about surrender, knowing how rarely the Federation bothered with prisoners. *I can't even send the civilians in. I have to stay with His Highness, no matter where that leads.*

He thought his way through a short prayer. The essence of his plea was simple: *Please let our fleet show up soon!*

Once the worst of the aches were gone, David put his boots back on, though he would have preferred leaving them off through the night. If action came, he didn't want to be running around with only the field skin covering his feet.

It was near sunset, almost night-dark in the forest. Most of the civilians were asleep, or attempting to get there. David took a quick tour of the camp, then went with Mitch Naughton to check the outposts that had been set up away from the civilians. The perimeter was thin, but should be adequate. Electronic bugs had been planted farther out, and if enemy soldiers triggered them, or any of the few scattered land mines, the commandos would have time to pull back into a more adequate defensive ring.

We should do fine tonight, David told himself. *The Feddie search must be thirty miles off by now. We haven't heard any of their shuttles for more than three hours.* After returning to where he planned to spend the night, he sent Naughton off to get some sleep. "I'll take the first watch," Spencer said. The lead sergeant did not argue the point.

Little more than two hours later, David had just turned over the watch to Tony Hopewell and gotten to sleep. That was when the alarm sounded. Feddie soldiers were approaching the camp on foot.

20

The idea popped into Spencer's mind as soon as he received the warning that Feddie soldiers were approaching from two sides. *They must have spotted us crossing the river.* There was no other possible explanation. They had been caught out by a chance observation even though the odds had to have been long against it. A shuttle or an orbiting spyeye must have seen some of them sliding down the rope across the river. Then enemy troops had landed far enough away that their shuttles weren't heard, and the men had moved in on foot. *That explains why we didn't hear the searchers go by again,* David decided.

There was no mad scurrying about when the news came. This possibility had been planned for. The civilians were in the safest positions the terrain offered, in the dense growth close to the river, partly sheltered on the land side by the rotting carcass of a fallen tree that had not been completely recycled yet by nature. One squad of Marines—the headquarters squad—was with the civilians to make certain that they stayed down, and to serve as a final line of defense. The rest of the detachment was spaced around in strong defensive positions, a perimeter concentrated around a semicircle backed against the Rift River.

"I want numbers as quickly as possible. How many men

did they bring in?'' David said over a radio link that included Lieutenant Hopewell and all of the noncoms. The Federation soldiers knew where they were. There was no longer any purpose to radio silence. All that would do would cripple the Marines' ability to work together most efficiently.

No Federation soldiers had yet been seen directly. The alarms had come from the snoops that the Marines had planted farther out, small detection devices that could be buried with just motion sensors, cameras, and transmitters showing above ground. Only a one-inch knob was visible if the device was planted properly. The video could be viewed on the mapboards that officers and noncoms carried or, with slightly less clarity, on a helmet visor's head-up display.

Two groups of Federation troops were on courses that would meet at the river, almost precisely where the group had come across from the higher south bank. *They must have at least scouts in the center,* Spencer thought. *Coming in from however far out to intercept us. They couldn't have known that we would stay right here.*

It wasn't much of a stretch for David to assume that the Federation would have a decent count of his people. They might slightly overestimate the number of Marines if they hadn't taken a body count where the shuttles had been destroyed. And if the enemy soldiers had made any investigation of the hotel, they would also have a close count on the number of civilians with them.

They wouldn't send in fewer men than they estimate we have, Spencer told himself. *If it were me, I'd want no less than two-to-one odds in my favor on a go like this, and I'd like the odds even better.*

If it hadn't been for the civilians, David would not have been gravely concerned with two-to-one odds—not against any Federation troops he had fought before. His men had faced considerably longer odds and won. But the presence of noncombatants changed the equation. They couldn't fight. They didn't have the training or gear to allow them to elude the enemy. And minding them meant that David's tactical hands were tied. Using his headquarters squad as an inner defense—and to tend the civilians—diminished his effective manpower.

"Looks like a platoon on either side," Alfie Edwards said on his link to David. "Two skirmish lines in either group, the second back far enough that we can't take them all out at once."

"But not equal lines," David said, looking at the video from the snoops that was playing on his mapboard. Two platoons would mean almost even odds, not at all what he expected. "More like three squads up front and one behind. There might be another line farther back, still out of sight," he added. He switched channels to get back to Hopewell and all of the noncoms at once. "We let the first lines get within sixty yards. At that point, I want every grenadier to put a full clip of grenades down on the first skirmish line. Saturation. We account for the front lines and worry about the rear guard after."

"They can't know absolutely for certain that we're still here," Alfie said. "We might have slipped east or west, just this side of the river. Unless there are more of them moving in that way, maybe still farther off."

"We've got snoops planted on those approaches as well," Hopewell said.

"They know where we are," David said. "If they didn't before, by some wild chance, they must now, since we've been using our radios. In any case, we'll worry about any other groups of Feddies later, if we have to. For now, we concentrate on the enemies we can see. Get the grenadiers ready. It shouldn't be long now."

David made use of the time. Radio silence had been broken. The Federation apparently knew, or strongly suspected, where they were. David made several calls, trying to raise the fleet that was supposed to be on hand to land the rest of 2nd Regiment. He tried every channel that the fleet's combat intelligence center (CIC) and regimental operations should be monitoring. There was no response. The invasion was already more than twelve hours late.

Igor Vilnuf was the grenadier for his fire team. He had a new clip, five grenades, loaded, and the launcher's sights were set for sixty yards. Igor could see soldiers now, and they were getting close to the sixty-yard mark. He felt a familiar queasiness in his gut. It wasn't exactly fear, more like stage fright. The feeling came every time he knew that combat was close, and disappeared as soon as the fighting started.

He blinked twice, consciously. The launcher was in his hands, ready to fire. At his side he had his rifle where he could grab it quickly once he fired the last rocket-propelled grenade in the clip. The safeties were off on both weapons. That was a breach of SOP, standard operating procedures, but it was a breach shared by every grenadier in the unit. Routinely. No one ever faulted them for it.

Corporal Nace Jeffries, the fire team leader, slapped Igor on the shoulder. It was the signal he had been waiting for. Igor started firing, adjusting his aim slightly for each grenade. A dozen other men were doing the same thing.

The result might have appeared to be the opening of a vent from Hell—a pair of vents, one to the northeast, the other to the northwest. In each case, most of the grenades impacted within an arc fifteen yards thick centered a little more than fifty yards out from the grenadier. Some of the grenades fell well off the mark, though, deflected by tree trunks or the thick tangle of vines and branches overhead. Still, there were enough explosions in the target area to do the job. The blasts scattered thousands of fragments of shrapnel, ten percent of them white phosphorus. The explosions toppled trees and dug shallow craters. Shrapnel bit into everything. The phosphorus started fires where it hit—in a tree or a human body. Those fires were brief but intense. The forest was too damp to allow great wildfires to grow from such small seeds. The effect on human flesh could be devastating, though. No medical nanobug system could control burning phosphorus.

The forest canopy was so tightly interwoven that the fall of one tree could bring down its neighbors. Conversely, a tree might be severed low and hang in place, unable to fall because of the interwoven branches above and vines that tied it to other trees—a Damoclean blade hanging until the unrelenting stress of gravity finally brought it down.

Prince George hugged his shotgun, itching to take part in the fight. Federation soldiers were more worthy targets than cachouri birds. Those soldiers represented the cause for his seven years of isolation and exile. But the prince did remain down after the shattering series of explosions and the start of the ensuing rifle fire. He knew that he had been moved to the most sheltered bit of cover available. It was not what he would have chosen for himself. Captain Spencer had led him to the place and asked—told—him to get down and stay put. George was behind the thickest portion of a fallen tree trunk, half under it. The odors of moss and rotting wood were thick, until they were smothered by the drifting smells of burning wood and flesh, of explosive powders and their blasts.

It isn't proper for a Windsor to cower from danger, he told himself. The longer the fight continued, the more difficult it would be to contain his urge to get up and start shooting. *If the enemy gets close, my shotgun might really add something to the defense.* He realized that he was rationalizing, looking for an excuse. But there was a Marine close, with strict orders. If the prince tried to get up, the man was instructed to put him back down, quickly, with force if necessary. The way Captain Spencer had put it was "Even if you have to sit on him." Prince George had no doubt that the private would obey his orders.

There *was* incoming rifle fire. Several times, George heard bullets thunk into the tree that sheltered him. A few times, he fancied that he heard rounds flying by, not too far overhead.

How could anyone have survived that salvo of grenades? he wondered. *It should have blasted them all.* Still, there was not a *lot* of incoming rifle fire. There were clearly few of the enemy out there shooting.

"Alfie, we need to get a couple of squads out there to take care of that second line and see if there are any more behind them," Spencer said.

"We can go around from the flank on either side, but that'll leave a couple of gaping holes in the perimeter," Alfie replied.

"I sure as hell can't call in reinforcements."

"Or we could just go out on one side, sweep around and use the same lads to clear out both groups," Alfie said.

Spencer nodded. "Try that." But as Alfie took half of his platoon out of the left side of the semicircle, David thought, *You've really done it this time. Stuck on an enemy world, no escape, no retreat, and the Feddies know exactly where you are.* What did not cross his mind was *It's not my fault; I can't help it that the invasion didn't come in on time.* It simply did not occur to him to look for scapegoats. He was too busy trying to find a way, despite the setbacks, to accomplish the mission he had been given, to keep Prince George and the others safe until they could be returned to the Second Commonwealth.

Without detectors in orbit to make observations and feed information, the commandos did not have the luxury of being able to count the number of Federation soldiers with active electronics in the area. The range of the detectors built into Commonwealth battle helmets was too limited without that additional input. There might be twenty men facing the detachment—or two thousand. David hoped that there were no more than the squads that they had spotted behind the main Federation skirmish lines, because if they had additional reinforcements coming in from behind, or approaching along the river bank from either or both sides, the end might come all too quickly.

Spencer made another series of calls, praying that a Commonwealth ship would answer. But there was only silence.

He passed the word to the squads in the perimeter to try to keep the known enemy troops pinned down while Alfie's patrol worked to flank them. He worried about the amount of ammunition they were expending. There were no reserves over and above what the men carried, and there were no shuttles waiting to bring in new stocks when those were gone.

We've tried drastic course changes to throw them off the scent; then staying on the same course, he thought. *If we get rid of this lot, what do we do then? Maybe the one thing they won't expect is for us to stay right here and not move at all.*

There was no way he could guarantee that any choice would be correct, that it would make any difference. Staying put might work for a time. If the enemy put the next ambushing force far enough away, then waited before starting to move back in, they might manage a day's respite. *If I knew that the fleet was coming for sure, that it was just a day late . . .* But he did not, could not, know when or if help would come.

An explosion overhead brought Spencer's thoughts back to the immediate situation. The crown of a tree started to collapse but got caught in a tangle of vines and branches. Debris rained down, along with several birds and monkey-like creatures. The animals were all dead when they hit the ground.

"Where did that come from?" David asked on an all-hands circuit. There had been few grenades coming in from the north. The surviving Federation soldiers there were too far away for effective use of RPGs. In addition, the Federation grenade launcher was single shot.

"I think it came from behind," Mitch Naughton said. "We're taking light rifle fire too. It has to be coming from the bluff across the river."

"Get the civilians ready to move, Mitch. We're not protected on that side." *So much for staying put,* David thought.

Naughton switched to a private channel. "Cap, I think moving might be worse than stayin' here. There's a lot of wood between us and the bluffs. Not much is getting through, and they sure can't see what they're shooting at."

"No good, Mitch," David said on the same channel. "It won't take them long to open up a few holes with grenades. We'll follow Alfie's two squads around, then move past them, keep those squads between us and the Feddies we know about down here. We've got to get out of range of whatever they've got behind us, even if it's across the river."

Spencer switched channels to tell Tony Hopewell, Alfie Edwards, and Will Cordamon what they were going to do. "Will, I want you to send one squad around the other way. Tell them to be careful that they don't start exchanging fire with Alfie's lads, but get out to those Feddies. I want to put paid to the enemy in front of us in a hurry."

Vepper Holford gave little thought to Prince George. He stayed close out of habit so deeply ingrained that it did not require thought, but that was the extent of it. When the Marines told them to get up, that they had to move, Vepper resisted, silently, at first. Moving seemed infinitely more dangerous than remaining where he was, pressed into the ground and the rotting tree trunk. *Get up, with gunfire coming in from at least two directions?* But the Marines offered no choice, and Holford had no desire to find out what they might do if he refused to move. As much as he feared Federation gunfire, the Commonwealth Marines were closer, a more immediate threat.

Vepper tried to shrink within himself. He stayed crouched over, shoulders drawn in as if he might make himself a smaller target by those minimal efforts. It did occur to him that he might look ridiculous, but he was willing to suffer that indignity out here in the jungle, as long as he did not have to suffer anything more physically painful. Vepper had never known true pain, nothing beyond the minor aches that anyone might suffer temporarily. He did not want to start now.

Most of his fellow exiles were also trying to present as small a target as they could. Only Prince George seemed oblivious to the danger. He stood erect and looked around casually, his shotgun held across his body in both hands as if he were hunting game birds in some quiet preserve.

George *was* looking for targets. He welcomed the chance to get up and move. He would be even more delighted if he managed to get off a shot or two. If he saw an enemy, if any came within range of his shotgun, he would take the shots. George knew that the enemy would have to be dangerously close for his weapon to have much effect. The only shells he had were birdshot.

"Don't bunch up," one of the faceless Marines told the civilians. "That makes you too inviting a target."

People moved away from each other, if reluctantly, and only by a step. They looked around. The civilians were mostly frightened, and showed it. They had to fight the atavistic urge to herd together to escape the predators. The squad of commandos split. Half moved to either side of their charges. Lead Sergeant Naughton gestured in the direction they were to go.

"Just stay with us. Keep your ears open. If any of us yell 'Down!' just drop to the ground and ask questions later."

The squads that Alfie had led out moved quickly and quietly. This was the kind of work that they had trained for, and most of these men welcomed movement and the chance to strike at the enemy. In the dark, they had a slight advantage. Commonwealth night-vision gear was better than that used by the Federation. In the forest, moving from tree to tree, the commandos were virtually invisible. Only the muzzle flashes from their weapons were likely to give them away, and they moved after each shot.

Alfie left second squad even with the known Federation positions and took first squad on another forty yards. That would give them almost a ring of fire with what was coming from the rest of the detachment. It would be hard for the enemy to find cover from fire reaching for them from three sides.

"You put grenades in on the near squad," he told second squad's sergeant. "We'll drop on the other." Alfie allowed fifteen seconds for the grenadiers to get ready, then gave the command.

Once more an area of jungle erupted. "We're moving in!" Alfie shouted on his link to Spencer. The rest of the commandos stopped firing as the two squads ran in to finish the work of their grenades. Two minutes was all the cleanup took. Relative silence returned to the forest. Only a few scattered shots came from the top of the bluff across the river.

Five minutes later, the commandos and civilians were together, moving west, one hundred fifty yards from the river. "We've got to throw them off long enough for us to find good defensive positions," Spencer said, conferring with Hopewell and the senior sergeants. "This might give us that time."

Before moving, he had tried once more to raise the hoped-for fleet. There was still no answer. They were seventeen hours late.

Part 5

21

Dirigent's Council of Regiments had laid down strict guidelines for the delegations from the Second Commonwealth and the Confederation of Human Worlds. They might dispatch message rockets from the ships that had brought them to Dirigent at will, as long as they were launched along paths prescribed by Space Traffic Control. But any incoming MRs had to be routed to a pickup point under the control of Dirigent. "Any object arriving out of Q-space anywhere else in our system will be treated as a potentially hostile incursion and destroyed" had been the blunt explanation. The designated arrival area was a half million miles out. Even a fast courier spacecraft needed eight hours to reach the ships in orbit from that distance.

"The real problem is that we have no way to estimate how long it might take the leaders on Union to decide how to respond to Ramirez's message," Prince William told Ian Shrikes the morning after the peace talks had been suspended. "The reply might come in before the day is out, or not for a week or more."

Prior to the war, the transit time for an MR from one world to another would have been nearly as long as for a ship. The same lengthy normal space transits were imposed on MRs, sending them out five days before they were permitted to make their first jump into Q-space, leaving three-day intervals between Q-space transits, and emerging three days out from the destination. As in the case of naval vessels, the war had severely shortened the intervals for MRs, if not to the ninety seconds that a ship might now take between jumps. Still, the one-way time between worlds rarely dropped below twelve hours and often exceeded eighteen.

"And there's nothing we can do to speed the process along," Ian observed. He had spent the hour since breakfast pacing. "All we can do is wait."

"Always a large part of the duties of a diplomat, Ian. Patience is not so much a virtue as a necessity. Familiarity with one of the meditative disciplines can help."

"Is that how you manage, sir?"

"Part of my earliest training. A member of the royal family has to get used to this sort of thing even before he starts formal schooling. Anytime a royal is in public, his every word and gesture are examined with a microscope and dissected by the gossipmongers. Even in the nursery, patience was one of the first lessons I had."

"I've noticed the fishbowl effect myself, sir, ever since I signed on as your aide. Antonia has even suggested I wear a disguise when we go out together to avoid people staring and pointing fingers. I don't think she could get used to it in a thousand years."

"I suppose you have to be born to it to grow any degree of immunity at all, and even then it is rarely as complete as one would like."

"It could make a hermit out of an ant."

William laughed. "I'll have to remember that one, Ian. Henry will enjoy it immensely."

"This waiting would be easier if we had some inkling what's going on, why Ramirez wants new instructions after hearing what his government had to say about . . . the other thing. You'd think they would have told him of any changes in policy."

"My guess—and it is no more than a guess—is that part

of the message that Ramirez received was 'Tell them that you need time to send us an MR and receive a reply before you can continue the negotiations.' A stalling tactic, something to give his government time to decide how they will react to the latest events. And they might have word by now of friend Spencer's activities and so forth."

"In other words, we might wait for a considerable time."

"Perhaps. Or not. There is no way one can know until the wait ends. There is another possibility you might reflect on. Depending on what message the Honorable Yoshi Ramirez receives from *his* government, it is quite possible—perhaps even likely—that *we* shall be forced to request a further delay while we seek new instructions from His Majesty's Government."

"I have already reflected on that, at some length," Ian said, not quite with a sigh. "It could go back and forth like that for ages."

He came to a stop at one of the windows that faced the long courtyard. Somewhere over there, the Federation delegates were staying, and no doubt doing their own waiting. Ian wondered what might be going through their minds, how they were handling the wait. *It must be worse for them, knowing about the defeat their forces got on Shepard,* he thought. *One of their core worlds, part of the heart of the Federation. It would be as if we had let them take Coventry or Lorenzo and keep them.*

Ian blinked a couple of times, then turned his back to the window. "I think I'm just beginning to see what it might mean," he said. William turned his head and looked up. He had been reading from his complink, no doubt the day's news as provided by the Dirigent communications system.

"Yes?"

"I thought, 'What if it had been Coventry or Lorenzo?'"

The prince nodded slowly. "Quite. But I think we should not carry this discussion any farther."

Ian nodded and turned to look out the window again.

They're not going to simply surrender and concede everything we want, he thought. *We wouldn't have conceded any of their core demands, even without the news about Shepard. They might try to delay the talks until they've had a chance to retake it.* More fighting, more dying. Like many career naval and military officers, Ian hated the idea of war, especially since he had firsthand experience of combat. *Be prepared, but hope it never comes. If it does come, do everything you can to bring it to a suitable conclusion as rapidly as possible.* His knowledge of war had deepened his loathing for it.

"You know, sir, I can't help but think that I might do more good for the Commonwealth if I were still in command of a ship on active duty." Ian turned and took a couple of steps in the direction of Prince William. "I feel guilty being away from it, away from what I've spent my entire adult life training for."

"I know how you feel, Ian." William set his complink aside. "You probably wouldn't credit it if I told you how many times I have asked His Majesty to let me return to active duty. My little junket with you and Admiral Truscott is the closest he has permitted me to get to that, for various reasons that I understand even though I have argued against them at length. Our circumstances are not quite the same, but they are similar. If it is any consolation, you are a great help to me. You keep my mind working. You recall things I might forget. You give me an invaluable second perspective. And I expect that what you see and hear here will provide equally invaluable to the CSF. Even if this war might be in its final stages, there is still the future to think about. We'll need trained minds to help transfer the lessons we've learned."

"When this war ends, people will be so tired of the fighting and the expense that they won't even want to think about the CSF and the army for a generation," Ian said. "They'll say, 'Put the money where it will do some good for a change.' "

"Some will, but it is a matter of making certain that

wiser counsels prevail. That too will be up to those of us, such as you and I, who have been there and seen what can happen.''

''You take everything in stride, don't you, sir?''

''One tries. It's bags better than battering one's skull against a wall until it's bloody every time that the universe does not cooperate by fulfilling one's dreams and wishes. After all, the universe is rarely so accommodating.''

Prince William was not nearly as patient as he appeared, but the show was the important thing. He hid his impatience, and gave his mind free rein, letting it visit the possibilities from every angle he could imagine. Most of the scenarios were so far removed from being realistic that the game—as he viewed it—was generally relaxing. It was also helpful as a preparatory exercise. Nothing he might hear was as likely to surprise him if he had considered far more outrageous versions.

He involved himself with the minutiae of everything he did during the wait. His mind was able to grab any detail and work it. The techniques of self-distraction came easily to him. Life at court had been excellent training for this sort of task. For a time that morning, watching Ian was amusing, diversionary. When it became more annoying than distracting, the prince merely retired to his room. He showered and changed clothes, then came out ready for lunch.

During the afternoon, William occupied himself with an essay on the art of waiting, writing in quick spurts, then going back to revise. He fancied himself as a rather proficient essayist, even if few of his essays were ever read by another human being. ''Waiting'' was a frequent topic of his literary musings.

The later the afternoon became, the more intently William focused on what he was doing, shutting out all possible distractions, even from within his own mind. It worked exceptionally well. He was totally surprised when Ian came to remind him that dinner would be served in forty-five minutes. William always wanted that much time to prepare for a meal.

He leaned back and stretched, as if he were waking from restful slumber instead of just relaxing after more than four hours of concentrated mental activity.

"Ah, Ian. Why don't you see if you can't get Colonels Tritesse and Marinetto for bridge this evening?"

"I'll make the calls, sir. Are you set on those two, or should I find others if one or both can't make it?"

William shrugged. "I'd prefer those two, I think, but I would like a couple of rubbers even if they can't make it. But if you do get them, you might also ask them to share dinner with us, if they haven't already made other plans. A little company should help us both keep from fretting about other things."

"You don't seem to be having much trouble, sir."

The prince merely smiled.

The commanding officer of a regiment in the DMC could never consider himself completely off duty, even in garrison. With five thousand-plus men under his command, something could always go wrong that would require his attention—even if only for the few seconds necessary to make a decision or refer the question to the proper staff officer. And the colonels were always linked to headquarters and various staff departments, radios always set to receive any call.

Edmund Tritesse and Joseph Marinetto did not lug around bulky combat helmets. The radio gear they used in garrison hung inconspicuously from their belts under the dress tunics they wore when they came to Prince William's suite for the card game that evening. Small studs that appeared to be part of the decoration of the standing collars on the tunics could be lifted off and fitted as earphones. The microphones were attached to the knots in the officers' ties and rested against their throats.

The units were no secret. Marinetto had been quite free about showing Ian his. "The higher one goes in the DMC," he had said at the time, "the tighter the leash one must wear. I have a comm unit either on my person or within reach at all times."

"I suppose it's not much different in any organization in our line of country," Ian had replied. "Perhaps the DMC carries it a bit farther than the CSF. Even when I had command of a battlecruiser, there were times when I might be more than arm's length from a complink. But there was always a duty officer who knew how to reach me within seconds."

Colonel Tritesse joined Ian and Prince William for dinner. Colonel Marinetto arrived after the meal. The four of them played a half dozen rubbers of bridge. There was no switching of partners between rubbers. Ian and the prince took on the two Dirigenters. The colonels held their own. The scores were fairly even, going with the break of the cards rather than with any serious breaches in play.

Bridge was one pastime that could almost always keep Ian's mind from wandering to other concerns. He took pride in his game even though it had been years since he had enjoyed the leisure to be able to compete in the frequent duplicate bridge tournaments held on Buckingham, both within the CSF and in civilian venues. By the end of the first rubber, Ian had almost managed to forget the frustrations of waiting to hear what new instructions the Federation delegation might receive before the next plenary session in the peace talks.

Both sides were vulnerable in the sixth rubber. It was near midnight. There was a light haze of smoke in the room from the Dirigentan cigars that both colonels had puffed on incessantly since the start of the session. Ian and the prince had each accepted one cigar, and had made do. Neither was accustomed to the tobacco habit, though both had had an occasional smoke before. It was not common on Buckingham. The four men were also into their second bottle of brandy.

Ian dealt and opened one spade. Tritesse doubled. Prince

William passed. Marinetto bid three hearts. That was all the colonels needed. They had a part score of 30. Ian did not blink as he bid three spades. With his hand, it was a dangerous overbid without any encouragement from his partner. But Tritesse immediately bid four hearts and that was the final contract.

Ian led the ace and king of spades. When Prince William showed a singleton spade, Ian cashed the ace of diamonds, then led a low spade to let his partner trump it. When William led back the king of diamonds and Marinetto followed suit, Ian relaxed. The contract was defeated.

Tritesse, dummy for the hand, slid his chair away from the table, then stood and turned away. It was not disgust at seeing his partner go down, but a call that had come in. He was back in place before the final trick of the hand. The colonels ended up down two tricks. Tritesse waited until the last trick was collected before he spoke.

"A message was relayed to me from Space Traffic Control," he said as he offered the cards for a cut. "The MR that the Secretary of State has been waiting for has arrived. The message chip is being collected now. Secretary Ramirez will have it shortly after breakfast."

The hand Tritesse dealt was the last of the evening. The colonels had a small slam in no trump but only bid the two no trump they needed for game and rubber.

"I believe it is time we bid you good night, Your Highness," Tritesse said after the score had been tallied. "His Excellency the Secretary of State might be prepared for a meeting after he reads whatever instructions his government have sent him."

"One can only hope," William said, also rising. "I want to thank you both for an excellent evening. Perhaps one day I shall be able to offer you the hospitality of my home on Buckingham."

"God willing," Tritesse said with a nod. "It would give me great pleasure, sir."

. . . .

"I wish we could find out what the message is before morning," Ian said after the colonels had left. "The good guys in the adventure vids always seem to manage."

William laughed. "Fantasy is often more satisfying than reality. Adventure vids. You're exposing your secrets."

"Can't have a diet of just Shakespeare and Chaucer, sir."

"Well, we shall simply have to wait until Ramirez is ready to tell us what their new position is, if there is a new position. There is always the chance that his instructions are merely to continue stalling because their government need additional time to decide how to respond."

Ian shook his head. "I think I'll need a patch to get to sleep tonight."

"If you can't drop off straightaway, you should," William said, the humor leaving his voice. "If we do have a plenary session tomorrow, you'll want a clear head for it."

There was no morning session, but there was one after lunch. The General presided, as he had at the first meeting.

"I understand that His Excellency the Secretary of State for the Confederation of Human Worlds has a statement that he would like to make at this time," General Partifinay said after a round of ritual greetings. "If you have no objection, Your Highness?"

"No objection, sir," Prince William said quickly. "We are most anxious to hear His Excellency's statement."

Yoshi Ramirez stood slowly. "My government has instructed me to say the following: 'There can be no agreement concerning any end of hostilities between the Confederation of Human Worlds and the worlds of the illegal coalition calling itself the Second Commonwealth without the return of any worlds that may have been captured during hostilities.' " Ramirez looked up from the script he had read, nodded to the General, and sat back down.

Partifinay looked toward Prince William. "Do you wish to respond to that statement now, Your Highness, or would you prefer to consult with your government first?"

William stood. "I would appreciate a slight clarification, sir. Does the Confederation of Human Worlds agree that such repatriation must be reciprocal? Will they be bound by that condition as well?"

"That is how I interpret the instruction," Ramirez said without waiting for the General to put it to him.

"The Second Commonwealth certainly has no objection to such a stipulation," Prince William said before he sat. "If fact, we welcome it, so long as it is fully bilateral."

Alvonz Partifinay was silent for a time, looking first at one side and then at the other. Then he cleared his throat and took a drink of water.

"Gentlemen, might I infer that we have arrived—in theory, at least—at a basis for peace between your two governments? That basis being a return to the *status quo ante bellum*?"

William and Ramirez stared at each other. Then Ramirez switched his gaze to the General and stood again. "My government is prepared to agree to an immediate truce and the mutual cessation of all hostilities, providing that its demand for a return of any captured worlds or portions thereof is agreed to."

"Your Highness?" Partifinay turned toward William.

The prince stood. "That is certainly acceptable to the government of the Second Commonwealth. And, as soon as a final agreement can be signed, we shall communicate that to our government and to the commanders-in-chief of our various military forces. Due to the complexities of the situation, it will probably be advisable to agree on a specific date and time for the general cease-fire, allowing time for each side to communicate with all forces that might be in a combat situation."

Ramirez had remained on his feet. He nodded. "That is acceptable to the Confederation of Human Worlds."

Partifinay also stood. At that, so did the rest of the people in the meeting hall.

"I will have my staff prepare the documents immedi-

ately," the General said. "I expect that they will be ready
for your perusal within the hour. If the terms are acceptable
as drafted, it should be possible to set the time for the
formal end to the fighting no later than forty-eight hours
following the signing of the documents by the respective
plenipotentiaries. Gentlemen, you have done a good job of
work. I thank you all for your diligent efforts to achieve
an honorable peace. Once the fighting has stopped, your
governments are welcome to return here to continue talks
aiming at a permanent solution to your remaining differ-
ences. Once each side has had time to examine the truce
documents, and providing that they are acceptable to both
sides, I would suggest that we return here for the formal
signing."

"I have the nagging feeling that I missed something important," Ian said as soon as he and the prince were alone.
"Did we really just end the war that quickly?"

"So it appears," William replied. "One might be
tempted to keep one's fingers crossed until the agreement
is signed and dispatched, or even until word comes back
that fighting has indeed been halted on all fronts."

"I was prepared for this to carry on for weeks or
months."

"As was I," the prince said. "It must be the news we
both received. To the best of my knowledge, there are cur-
rently only two worlds in the hands of the other side, perhaps only one now, if Spencer's regiment has completed
its work. They had one world of ours and we now have
one world of theirs, and the Federation obviously prizes
Shepard more than Camerein. Making that demand allows
them a way out that their propaganda artists will be able to
fully exploit at home, I think."

"Speaking of home . . ." Ian let that stand alone.

William grinned. "Once we have a signed treaty, even
if it is expressed simply as an indefinite truce, our work
here is concluded—at least for the present."

•   •   •

The cease-fire documents were signed at 1720 hours, local time in Dirigent City. Message rockets carrying the news were fired toward Buckingham and Union eight minutes later.

22

HMS Avon was drifting. The ship was not within a dozen light-years of any inhabited world. It wasn't within four light-years of any star. But the ship's charts and equipment had been equal to determining *Avon*'s position. Once that was known, the last operable message rocket had been sent to Buckingham, with full particulars of what had happened to the ship and how she had managed to survive.

After that, there was little for the captain and crew to do but wait. The engineering department was managing to keep the linked Nilssen generators from the MRs that had been used to extricate the ship from Q-space functioning well enough to provide the crew areas of *Avon* with twenty-two percent of "normal" gravity. That was enough to give people some feeling of weight. The emotional benefit was greater.

"It staves off the sense that we're in a helpless hulk just waiting for space to finish the job on us," Captain Louisa Barlowe had told the chief engineering officer.

"It's the best we can do, Captain," Commander Billingsley had replied. "I might be able to coax another three or four percent from the system, but I would hate to push it that far. We could end up with nothing instead."

"You've got nothing to apologize for, Arch. You've already performed miracles. There's no need to worry because we want a little cream to pour over our strawberries.''

Barlowe had gone farther in her praise of Archibald Billingsley's actions. One of the dispatches carried by the MR launched toward Buckingham had contained her recommendation that he be awarded the Second Commonwealth's highest medal, the King's Cross. The concluding lines of that recommendation had read, ''I do not think that it is possible to overstate Commander Billingsley's courage, intelligence, and resourcefulness. He saved this ship and her crew. He provided new knowledge that is likely to prove invaluable in the future and which might save the lives of many other crews, and save their ships. A medal would be scant reward. If it were in my power, I would also recommend that he be promoted immediately and knighted.''

The MR had been dispatched before she could recant the effusive lines and recast her recommendation in the more spartan style that the CSF favored.

Thirty hours after sending off the MR, there was a reply, an MR sent to intercept *Avon*'s course. The important part of the message was news that a tug was being dispatched to bring *Avon* in. There was also a note signed by both the First Lord of the Admiralty and the Chief of Naval Operations offering a ''Well done, *exceptionally* well done'' to all hands.

Captain Barlowe read both messages to the crew.

It was another twenty-seven hours before *HMS Land's End* rendezvoused with *Avon*. The spacegoing tug—''utility repair and recovery vessel,'' on the Royal Navy's rolls—was an extremely ungainly-looking ship. Skeletal in appearance, *Land's End* was nearly a mobile construction dock. The ship's control and engineering departments, main drives, Nilssen generators, crew quarters, and workshops were spread along the outside of what was basically the hinge to a C-clamp a mile and three quarters long. The clamp was a series of girders, a framework without sheathing. It could attach the tug to any ship in the CSF's inventory.

Like a carnivorous plant, *Land's End* allowed *Avon* to move slowly into position and then closed its clamp around her. Prior to that, there had been an hour of constant communication between the two ships, often on several channels at once. As soon as the docking was complete, with airlocks mated, the skipper of *Land's End* crossed to pay his respects to the skipper of *Avon*.

"You can't imagine how happy we are to see you," Louisa Barlowe told her opposite number. *Land's End* was commanded by Captain Morris Freleng.

"The feeling is mutual," he assured her. "The skippers of the other two tugs that were in port hate me. They wanted the honor of this mission."

"Honor?"

"You're a bloody miracle, Captain Barlowe—you, your crew, and this whole bloody ship. You've done something that supposedly couldn't be done."

"That's an honor I could have gone an entire career without," Louisa said. "Can I offer you tea?"

"Let me get this operation under way first. I'll have my people take a look-see and talk with your engineers. I suspect that we'll simply haul you in as is. We have one replacement Nilssen, but installing that would be a three-day job, and the Admiralty wants you back on Buckingham as quickly as possible."

"It would be nice to return under our own steam," Barlowe said, "but I'm too thrilled to be returning under any conditions to make a fuss. But if we're going back mated to your ship, can you at least provide us with full gravity?"

"Aye, we can do that." Freleng grinned. "Once we get the links complete, it'll be as if our two ships had become one. Now, there is one favor I would like to ask."

"Anything."

"I want to meet the engineer who managed this bleeding miracle."

Four hours later, the two ships had been intimately linked. *Avon* once more had full gravity. Her own power plant was turning out only enough juice to keep life support and ancillary systems on line. Everything else was being provided by *Land's End*.

"You wound up far enough from anything that we can make the return in two easy Q-space transits," Captain Freleng told *Avon*'s skipper, who had joined him on his bridge for the first of those transits. "Even with all the fancy work being done now, we remain very cautious towing another ship. If you had ended up much closer to a star, we'd have done three standard jumps, with several hours between Q-space transits, time to perform a full suite of tests to make certain we hadn't jarred anything loose."

"You'll get no complaints from me," Barlowe told him. "I've taken all the chances I ever want to experience. I've a feeling that I've used up about all of the luck anyone can expect in a single lifetime."

Louisa Barlowe had made thousands of Q-space transits in her naval career. There had only been difficulty on one of those. But she was almost unbearably tense as *Land's End* made its first jump with *Avon* attached. She held her breath. At her sides, her fists were clenched so tightly that her fingernails drew blood from the palms of both hands. The black of normal space was replaced by the pearlescent gray of Q-space. Routine status reports came in. There were no difficulties.

Each subsequent jump, out or in, was just as harrowing for Captain Barlowe. *I'll never view it the same as before,* she thought. When Buckingham appeared on the bridge monitors after the final exit from Q-space, she felt suddenly weak in the knees, as if she might collapse.

23

There was no time to pamper the civilians. Moving west after the firefight, David Spencer pushed the pace as hard as he dared through the remainder of the night. Their only hope for safety lay in moving farther and faster than the Federation troops who would be looking for them could believe possible.

The battle did make the people from the Commonwealth Excelsior quieter, as well as more willing to do whatever the commandos demanded of them. They exerted themselves, taking what little help the Marines could provide. There always seemed to be someone close enough to keep a civilian from falling, to help them through the rough spots, to offer encouragement.

Twice during the night they heard shuttles passing above. Those were enough to give the group an extra burst of speed. But willingness and fear could only carry the civilians for so long. Stumbles came more frequently. The pace slowed. Clumsy movement made the march noisier. Half an hour before dawn, Spencer finally had to concede more than a five-minute break.

"We'll take an hour, if we can," he told the civilians. "Eat, then get what rest you can. We have to keep going, keep pushing for as long as we can stay on our feet, until we hear from the fleet or we get away from the Feddies.''

''As long as we can stay on our feet'' won't be much longer for some of these people, Prince George thought as he sank to the ground. *An hour's rest won't give them more than two or three hours on the march, if that. I'm surprised there haven't been dropouts already.* He was certain that he could keep going longer than any of the others from the hotel, perhaps almost as long as any of the Marines. He would not permit himself to give up.

The prince adjusted his position, keeping his shotgun where he could grab it and bring it into action with one fluid motion if he had to. Only when he was satisfied with that did he pull a meal pouch from his pack and start eating.

George hated rushing a meal. Dining leisurely was a mark of gentility. It calmed the soul and gave time for reflection. But he had rarely been half as hungry as he was now. He ate steadily, not *quite* bolting his food. He was also tired, and every minute spent eating was a minute less he would have for sleep—if he could manage any of that. Captain Spencer was certainly not likely to change his mind and delay the resumption of their trek simply because the prince had not yet had enough rest.

He did not waste time wishing that he had wine to go with his meal. A few mouthfuls of tepid water sufficed, most of them postponed until the food was gone. Then, without ceremony, George lay back, adjusted the position of his shotgun, and shut his eyes. He was asleep almost at once.

Shadda Lorenqui did not expect to sleep, despite his exhaustion. He went through the motions, lying back and closing his eyes after a meal that had been consumed rapidly. Slumber never came easily to Shadda. The more spent he was, the longer sleep seemed to take—and he could scarcely recall the last time he had been this exhausted. Nor was there privacy. He could not exorcise his personal demons secure in the knowledge that no one else could see his pain. He had to restrain himself, and that alone promised wakefulness.

The next time the enemy catches us up, they'll bring in more than enough soldiers to make certain that they can do the job, he thought. *I don't know why they would send in so few the first time. Don't they have any idea how many of us there are?*

Shadda had some minor experience at fighting, in his youth, but not of the sort he had witnessed the evening before. On his travels he had occasionally worked as a mercenary, never for long, never against trained opposition. He had protected miners—and raided other miners. Keeping body and soul together had often meant tackling whatever work was available. He had never been too particular about what jobs he would accept.

I suppose it will come back to that if we ever get out of this mess. He sighed, almost silently. There had been times during the last seven years when he had almost managed to forget his history, when he had thought that he might make a career out of what he was doing, even when normalcy returned to Camerein and the rest of mankind's portion of the galaxy.

If we get off of Camerein. That seemed infinitely less likely than it had when the first Marines had appeared—as if by magic—in the dining salon of the Commonwealth Excelsior. Then, Shadda had dared to hope that the ordeal was over. *But if we* do *get off, maybe I can hitch a ride to Buckingham. I've never been there. There might be opportunities for me yet.*

Marie Caffre slept a deep, dreamless sleep. She had collapsed as soon as Spencer had called the halt—as soon as she saw The Windsor sit—and would have been asleep before Spencer told them how long they were staying if not for her husband. Henri had forced her to eat first, had threatened to force-feed her if she did not eat on her own. He only relented after she had eaten half of a meal pouch.

"You can finish it after you've slept," he told her, as gently as he could. "Sleep now, while you can." He finished his meal, watching his wife sink quickly into oblivion. His sleep, when it came, was not nearly as peaceful. Those who were close heard several low moans from Henri Caffre.

Dead men waded through waist-deep snow. The fires that spewed at them from every direction did not melt the snow or burn the moving carcasses. With each step the cadavers became less opaque, more translucent. Soon, Mai McDonough could see the skeletons inside, and rotting flesh dropping from the bones even though it could not escape the sacks of insubstantial flesh that refused to lose shape. In turn, the seven corpses each downed a bottle of whiskey—including, at last, the bottle. Mai felt her mouth water, then turn desert-dry. The fire in her stomach increased, bringing real pain. She reached out toward the dead men and begged for a drink. The corpses showed no hint that they were aware of her presence. As she slept on her side, a trickle of sweat reached the corner of Mai's mouth. Her tongue licked at it greedily, trying to take ease from the salty moisture.

Mai could not explain when the nightmares had started, or why. It might have been two years earlier or six, or anywhere in between. At first, they had been rare, but they had started to invade her nights with increasing regularity. The only way to escape had been to numb her brain, to drink until sleep was a thick porridge, drowning any possibility of dreams. Enforced sobriety had not ended the nightmares. At times it had even permitted them to invade her waking mind. There had been no escape, no escape at all.

Mai tossed and turned as she slept now, thrashing about on the ground. But even that discomfort did not wake her.

An hour's break for the civilians meant a half hour for each of the Marines. They were put on half-and-half watch, fifty percent sleeping while the rest ate and stayed alert—as alert as they could. Walter Kaelich counted himself lucky that he had been in the first half to get to sleep. Thirty minutes. He thought that he had managed to sleep through twenty-eight of them. But when he was awakened, he remained sluggish. He ate, though he could not have said what he had eaten thirty seconds after he finished. He looked out into the jungle, the double images of his night-vision systems showing nothing out of the ordinary as the morning's first light struggled to penetrate the forest canopy.

Walter was far from being perfectly alert. His eyes remained open, but even as he scanned his section of the jungle, he was only a step from sleep, almost in a trance. Like the rest of headquarters squad, he was posted near the civilians, away from the perimeter. If any enemy appeared, others would see or hear them first. Walter reminded himself of that each time he felt a twinge of guilt for not being at his peak. He looked around at each of the sleeping forms he could see, then scanned farther off. He looked up into the nearer trees, moving to keep from falling back into sleep. He stifled yawns. It was more difficult to stay awake than any time he could ever recall.

Court-martial offense to sleep on duty, he reminded himself. *In a combat zone at that, and with his nibs not four feet away.* He looked at the sleeping prince. George was snoring softly. *Like he hasn't got a care in the universe.* Walter shook his head. The snoring was making him more sleepy than ever. He looked away. He tried to force himself to concentrate on other things, to shut out the soft sounds of sleep.

Can't be much time left on this break, he thought. He had not noticed the time when the captain called the halt. It wasn't vital; he didn't need to know. Someone would tell him when it was time to get up and start moving again.

Kaelich started to drift back into the trancelike state that was not quite sleep. His eyes remained open. He was, in some fashion, aware of what he was seeing. His head even moved from time to time, scanning. But his senses were dulled. He did not notice that the prince's snoring had stopped, or that George was moving—and moving quite rapidly. Walter wasn't even aware of the abrasive sounds being made by birds in the forest canopy, almost directly overhead—and he certainly could not have known that those birds were called cachouris.

Prince George stood, bringing his shotgun up as he did. He pulled the trigger five times, scattering birdshot around the canopy.

The first gunshot, scarcely a yard behind his head, almost put Walter Kaelich into cardiac arrest—figuratively if not literally. The shock stunned him so completely that he could not move until several more shots had been fired. Finally, Walter turned and lunged at the prince, coming up from his knees and knocking George to the ground, trying to wrestle the shotgun away as he did. Lead Sergeant Naughton was standing over the two of them then, and took the weapon.

"It's okay, lad," Naughton said, putting a hand on Kaelich's shoulder. "I've got the gun. You can get up now."

Spencer came running over. Although he had not traveled more than ten yards, he seemed to be out of breath.

Prince George got to his feet casually, brushing at his clothing as if trying to rid them of a few stray specks of dust. He did not seem at all discomfited. He did not particularly look at any of the others. His gaze seemed to go through them, or around them.

"What in the world was that all about?" Spencer demanded, beyond thinking of protocol, politeness, or the political faux pas of castigating a member of the royal family. "Are you trying to bring the Feddies down on us?"

"But I *always* hunt cachouri in the morning," George said, his voice innocent and surprised. Slowly, he seemed to focus on David's face. "They are such a blasted nuisance, after all. One must do *something*."

God help us, he's gone completely round the bend, David thought, squeezing his eyes shut for an instant. *That's all we need.* He let his breath out softly. *What the hell can I do?*

Vepper Holford came up to the prince's side before David had decided what to do or say next. "It's all right now, Your Highness," Vepper said softly, leaning close to the prince's ear. "These weren't *our* cachouri after all. We escaped *those* birds. These won't bother us again."

George turned. He appeared to need ten seconds or more to focus on the face of his longtime traveling companion. "You should have said earlier, Vepper. I've annoyed our host."

"I'll see to His Highness, Captain," Vepper said, turning toward Spencer. "It won't happen again."

Too bloody right, it won't happen again, David thought. *We should have taken that shotgun away right at the start. He's not about to get it back now.*

"Please stay right with His Highness, Mr. Holford," David said, controlling his voice with difficulty. "One of my men will take care of his shotgun."

Vepper nodded.

"Now we've got to get moving, quickly," Spencer said. All of the civilians were awake. Most were on their feet, staring at the scene. Too many of the Marines were also watching their captain and the prince, rather than looking out as they should have been.

"Let's just hope that there weren't any Feddies within five miles," David said before he turned and walked away.

The invasion was twenty-four hours late. All that Spencer knew was that the Federation garrison on Camerein knew that there were intruders on the ground.

We're an itch they've got to scratch, hard, David thought as the march resumed. *I might be almost ahead of the game if I picked our direction of march at random. The Feddies have apparently been able to guess my choices.* His only intention now though was to put as much straight-line distance as possible between his people and the last fight—

and the place where Prince George had started shooting at birds.

A new flash of irritation disrupted David's thoughts. He glanced over his shoulder. The prince was now closely hemmed in by Holford, Lead Sergeant Naughton, and Private Kaelich. Lieutenant Hopewell had the shotgun, and someone else had the cartridge vest. Neither item was anywhere near His Highness.

Crazy as a loon. David shook his head. *Small wonder after seven years locked away here with no news of anything and no way out. They'll all want psychiatric help, I expect.*

As he got the chance, he warned Hopewell and the senior noncoms to pay close attention to the behavior of all the civilians. Radio silence was back in order, so the briefings took some time to complete.

Spencer pushed the pace through the morning. He constantly expected some sign of the Federation—if not soldiers on the ground, then shuttles or fighters overhead searching. But there was nothing in the first three hours, and the group managed to cover nearly eight miles—an excellent distance considering the civilians, David thought.

By midmorning, when he allowed a fifteen-minute stop, the air was sweltering. It was always hot in the forest, despite the deep shadows. There was not a breath of air moving, and the stagnant heat was humid. The pace would slacken. There was no way to avoid that. Even the commandos would have moved more slowly during the hottest hours of the day under those conditions.

As long as we move faster than the Feddies think we can. That's still the ticket. David got to his feet and moved along the line of civilians. It was obvious that most of them had been moving just on willpower, or fear. Only Prince George appeared untroubled. The look on his face was one of utter serenity, as if he no longer had any idea what was going on. *Maybe he doesn't,* David thought, looking from the prince to Vepper. Holford could not meet Spencer's gaze. He looked away quickly. He seemed . . . ashamed, as if he considered Prince George's aberration to be his fault.

The easy way out, David thought, looking to the prince again. David used hand signs to get the column moving again. One squad had already been sent ahead, farther in front of the main body than Spencer had posted the point before. "If there are Feddies waiting for us, I want to know early enough that we can detour around them," he had told the squad leader and his assistant. "But don't get so far ahead that the Feddies can slip a battalion in between you and us." There were also flankers out on either side and a rear-guard squad behind.

First Platoon's third squad had the point. The fire teams were moving parallel to the line of march, about fifty yards from each other. Nace Jeffries' fire team was on the right.

Igor Vilnuf was in front, followed by Nace. Zol Ketchum was third, with Curls Murphy bringing up the rear. Terry Murphy did have quite curly hair, but it was rare that anyone got a chance to see it. In garrison, and at the start of a campaign, he wore his hair clipped almost to the scalp. In the field, it was allowed to grow until he got back aboard ship following a mission, when it was cropped again.

The point squad did not keep in a straight file. Nace and his men formed the points of an irregular quadrilateral. The jungle was open enough to permit that, except near treefall gaps and the occasional watercourse. When necessary, the fire team straightened up the column but still kept at least a dozen yards between men. That way, a single mine or grenade could not take out the entire squad at once.

During the first hour, Nace forced the pace. They didn't have to hold back to keep from losing civilians. Once they got out as far ahead as the captain wanted them, they would be able to take it easier, giving themselves longer breaks than the five minutes each hour that the main group would have. As long as nothing happened, the fire team would be effectively on its own for at least three hours. Radio silence could be broken only in case of firm enemy contact, if it was clear that Federation troops had seen them.

Nace and his men were careful even when they were moving their fastest. The men moved from tree to tree, taking some care about cover. Even without much undergrowth, visibility was limited by the accumulation of trees along any line of sight. That worked for and against the commandos. It restricted the distance at which they might be seen, but it also limited the distance at which they might see the enemy. Each man had his special responsibility, a section of the perimeter to watch.

The four men were almost absolutely silent. Sound discipline on the march was not just a matter of not talking. They were cautious about where they placed their feet and how they moved as well.

Sometime today, we're going to run into Feddies. Nace was certain of that. He had a feeling, one that took no special psychic ability. It was a logical, almost inescapable, conclusion. The Federation garrison on Camerein wasn't going to let go. They had lost too many men. That would look bad, especially if they could not even the score by eliminating the interlopers.

The only question was how soon, and Nace thought that it would be sooner rather than later, just as quickly as they could locate the Commonwealth group again and move troops into place.

"It will most likely come from deep cover," Nace whispered to his men when they took their first break on point. "Treefall gap or stream, where this turns into a real jungle." He paused. "Not that we can let up when we've got the easy going. The Feddies might be ready to try something different."

"Where the hell is the rest of the regiment?" Vilnuf asked. "They're a day and a half late. Aren't they coming at all?"

"I don't know any more than you do, but I'm not yet ready to give up. They might be delayed, but they're sure not going to leave us hanging the way Feddies might leave their blokes."

"Not as long as we've got his nibs with us," Curls said.

''With or without him,'' Nace said. They were all whispering, and even while they took their rest, each man remained alert, scanning the forest, situated so that their entire perimeter remained under observation.

''Come on, let's get moving again.'' Nace stood. He had allowed seven minutes for the rest. ''We'll have to hold the pace back a bit so we don't get too far ahead.''

It's been too long now since we saw Feddies, Nace thought as his fire team resumed its movement west. *They've had time to move an army into place, and we haven't even heard a shuttle out looking for us.* He liked to have his enemies in known positions. No matter the odds, he preferred to face them openly rather than wonder where in the blazes they might be hiding.

Two more hours brought no hint of Federation activity. They might not even be on the continent from anything the point fire teams had found. It was time for a longer break. The squad waited for the main body to reach them. Afterward, it would probably be another squad's turn for the duty.

''Half an hour,'' Alfie Edwards said when he reached the squad. ''Lunch.''

Nace didn't waste time answering. He was already sitting. Now he pulled out a ration pack.

''This is our last day on full rations,'' Alfie said, speaking just loudly enough for the entire squad to hear. ''If our lads haven't shown up by morning we go on half rations and start looking for whatever we can find to help them last longer.'' Privately, Alfie thought that they should have done that as soon as it was clear that the regiment had not arrived on schedule. He had suggested it, but David had shook his head and said, ''Not yet. Give them a bit of time. We can manage if we have to. The five days worth of extra rations we got from the hotel should make the difference.''

''Maybe one of those soddin' snakes?'' Curls suggested, only half in jest. There had been enough meat on the one that had moved in close to give the entire platoon a full meal.

"If we do, I'll see they save the ropey hind end for you, lad," Alfie promised.

By sunset, the lack of any hint of enemy troops was getting to David Spencer. There hadn't been a trace, not so much as the distant rumble of a shuttle doing a search pattern.

"It just doesn't make sense." He had Hopewell and Naughton with him, away from the civilians and the rest of the commandos. The platoon sergeants were making defensive arrangements. David had decided that it was time they took another long stop. It would be three hours or more before they moved on—unless the Federation forced a change in plans. "By now, they could have put a cordon right around us, around the entire area we might have reached since the fight last night."

"Maybe they're far shorter of men than we've allowed for," Hopewell suggested.

Spencer shook his head. "Remember all the shuttles they had looking for us? Even if they were ferrying men over from the other continent, they could have brought in as many as they might need and had us served up on skewers long since."

"I say count our blessings," Naughton said. "The whole idea *is* to evade and avoid them until our lads come to collect us, isn't it, sir?" He didn't wait for an answer. "One thing that might help, if we could get back across the river during the night, without being seen. We could even move back toward the hotel. If the Feddies haven't set up shop inside we could go in and have the staff fix up extra meal packets all round."

"We can't spare the time to scout along the river hoping to find a spot where we could get our guests up that cliff, and that supposedly runs for two hundred miles without a break."

"Just a thought, sir," Naughton said. "Are you going to try the radio again?"

David shook his head. "Not unless we've got Feddies poking up our nostrils. Not yet, anyway."

"Even if the invasion is off, for whatever reason, they'll send someone for us, as soon as *Avon* turns up way past due with no word," Hopewell said. "If this was important enough to send us in, it'll be important enough to try to collect us once they know our ship was lost."

"We lost three ships here seven years ago, and *Avon* was the first vessel sent in since," David said. "With another ship gone missing in the same place, they might decide that they can't do anything until they can put an overwhelming force in."

"You do realize that we can't keep this lark up forever," Hopewell said. "Our lads would take it for as long as necessary, but before long the civilians are going to mutiny. And who can say how much longer His Highness will prove . . . tractable."

"That's probably a damned good reason to stay on this side of the river. The problem would be worse if the civilians thought they could just hike back to that hotel and go back to life as it was before we came." David was sitting where he could watch their charges, and most particularly the prince. "Besides, our orders don't allow us to abandon our guests, especially him."

David closed his eyes for a moment of hard thinking. He knew how tired he was. He could imagine how much more tired the civilians had to be. He sighed and opened his eyes. "Unless there's a compelling reason not to, we'll spend the night here, or at least close to here. It's the only hope of keeping everyone moving tomorrow. Tony, send Alfie with a squad to find us better quarters, not more than a half mile off. The civilians won't like moving, but when they hear that it's to find a place to stay the night, I don't think they'll object too much." He rubbed at his face with both hands. "If nothing else, we'll be able to think more clearly in the morning, assess our options."

Hopewell got up and walked off to find his platoon sergeant. Mitch Naughton stayed where he was.

"If we're still here in the morning, if we're still alive," David whispered, so softly that Naughton could almost convince himself that he had only imagined the words.

24

While he ate, Prince George moved his head slightly, in time with the music he was hearing, one of Angus Duncan's Beethoven violin concertos. The music could not have sounded better if it had been real. To George, it *was* real, perhaps a replay of a concert he had heard nine or ten years earlier, in Westminster. The translucent china he ate off was heavily decorated in gold, and the flatware was also gold. Light from a half dozen large chandeliers sparkled through crystal mobiles. The wine was served in delicate crystal glasses. One held them gingerly—*so*—by the stem, because one could hardly help but think that two fingers pressed against the same spot from opposite sides might melt a hole through the crystal or crush it.

The reality was a packaged meal from the Commonwealth Excelsior and very warm water from a canteen; a background of nocturnal birds and insects making their common sounds.

Vepper Holford was the only one who suspected just how far his master had drifted from reality. He sat a few feet away and heard George's table talk—comments about the imagined banquet and the music, as well as a gently satiric critique of the clothing worn by the several dozen courtiers he mentioned seeing. Vepper did not try to tell the prince the truth. He tried to limit himself to noncommittal remarks, but when George pressed, Vepper fell into the charade. He knew the people, the music, and could respond to comments about the imagined food.

All the while, Vepper kept looking about, worrying that the others might hear. Some of them did hear parts of what George said. Since early morning there had always been at least one or two Marines close enough to intervene if the prince did anything else as bizarre as shooting off the shotgun.

Out of his flippin' mind, Walter Kaelich thought. He shook his head minutely, not wanting the prince or Holford to see. *Stuck for seven years in this hole. No wonder.* Walter shared the first watch. As before, headquarters squad's responsibilities were more the civilians than watching for the enemy. *Feddies would be a lark after watching this dotty old sod,* Walter thought.

He had already eaten, trying to savor each mouthful. Lead Sergeant Naughton had informed the squad that they would go on half rations in the morning. With that to look forward to, supper had tasted especially good. The packets brought from the hotel would run out soon, and the Marines' regular food not long after. Walter knew that it would not take long before he would miss field rations as much as he missed his mother's cooking.

The civilians and the men of Walter's squad were in a small clearing surrounded by dense underbrush. The Marines had hacked out a place, since no one had been able to find a natural clearing that was so secluded. The rest of the commandos were farther out, along a narrow creek that was completely covered over by the forest canopy, and in a semicircle extending thirty yards out from the creek. The men were dug in. Since the captain planned to spend the night, he had ordered defensive excavations.

Walter had scooped out a shallow trench for himself. Slightly better ''accommodations'' had been prepared for the civilians, trenches surrounded with the dirt excavated from them, topped by tree trunks and thick branches, with small branches stuck into the dirt to offer some slight camouflage.

Walter didn't care to have so much greenery close by. He wanted clear space, room to spot any legless intruders. Thinking about the snake gave him nightmares even when he was awake.

Before he let himself get off his feet, David toured the defensive positions his men were preparing. He inspected each section with the respective platoon sergeant. "Get every mine and snoop we have left planted farther out," he told the sergeants. "If we move in the morning and have time, we'll collect them and take them along, but I want the lot in place before anyone settles in."

"We've haven't had a glimmer of Feddies in nigh on twenty-four hours, Cap," Alfie reminded him.

"Maybe that's why I want to take such care now," David said. "We should have had something by now. There's no way they could be so incompetent as to lose all trace of us that quickly. That means they could be planning something . . . massive."

"Will you answer me one question as honestly as you can?" Alfie asked when they were momentarily away from anyone else. "What do you think happened to the regiment, to the invasion? Was it called off, postponed, or were the whole lot just zapped coming in?"

"I don't have any idea. The only thing I'm reasonably sure of is that our people will make some effort to retrieve us as soon as they know we need help, and as soon as they can. One way or another."

"But maybe not soon enough?"

"There's always that chance."

"It won't take too many more fights like the ones we've had here before the lads run out of ammunition. We're already dead short on RPGs. We've been too free with them."

"If there's another fight and we make it through it, we'll

start collecting Feddie weapons and ammo, use that and bayonets. Or make bows and arrows if we have to.''

"You want to know what I think? I think this is the one we're not going to come back from. We're in a bucket at the bottom of a deep well and the rope broke way up at the top.''

Spencer didn't answer immediately. After a moment, though, he said, ''No one promised that we'd live forever.''

The first two hours were quiet. Spencer woke Hopewell, then got ready to sleep. The lieutenant would wake Mitch Naughton after his two hours. One of those three men would always be awake.

When he lay down, David found himself thinking about what Alfie had said earlier. *He may have it right. This could be the one we don't get home from.* He felt no emotional response to that idea, to the possibility of death. *We'll give a good accounting first,* he promised himself.

He felt a temptation to try the radio, to call on all the channels that a Commonwealth ship might be monitoring. *They're almost two days late. If they haven't come by now, what chance is there that they'll ever come?* The hollow feeling in David's stomach had nothing to do with hunger.

Sleep proved elusive. David found himself recalling his home, his childhood home, and lost family—swept away in a flash flood while trying to rescue a neighbor's child. Those memories were almost unreal, a fantasy to set against the harsh, perhaps lethal, reality of this jungle on Camerein. For more than half of his life now, ''home'' had been a Marine barracks or the troop bay of a CSF ship—generally *HMS Victoria* or *HMS Avon*. Now, it seemed certain that *Avon* had been lost. *Victoria* was overdue, or lost as well.

His last conscious thought before sleep finally came was *There won't be anyone to cry for me.*

Corporal Nace Jeffries' squad had one of the corners on the perimeter, where the line of the creek met the semicircle. Nace was right in the corner, with his men on either side of him. Almost *in* the creek, they had not been able to dig in very deeply because of seepage. But they had been able to dredge a few stones out of the creek and pile them up. A little mud smeared around made it look as if the rocks belonged where they were.

Nace was not too concerned with the quality of their camouflage. Any attack, if one came, would likely come out along the arc, away from the water and the jungle tangle that bordered it, where men could move without hacking a path. The only way that an enemy could reach his fire team—without coming through the rest of the detachment or making a racket that could be heard a mile off—would be to wade down the creek. That was what Nace and his men gave most of their attention to.

It wasn't much of a stream, neither deep nor wide, but parts of the bed were diabolically slippery. Before digging in, the men of Nace's fire team had gone out to plant listening devices and two mines. All four of them had managed to fall at least once.

With half of the men on guard at all times, the squads took three-hour shifts. Two hours on and two off ended up giving no one any decent chance to rest. Four hours left the duty section with too much chance to slacken off and lose alertness. Nace had slept the first three hours. By the time his squad leader woke him, the camp was silent. No one was moving about. Even the normal forest noises seemed muted. Only the small sounds of water moving past a couple of feet away continued as usual, sounding slightly louder against the silence it flowed through.

Nace's rifle was propped between two rocks. He lay half on one side, his head just high enough to look over the low barricade. He was still tired, but he would remain awake, and alert enough to catch any movement or sound along the creek or close by on the other bank. He had already been on watch for nearly two hours. The nearest thing to an alarm had been when a family of mammals the size of house cats had come to drink from the stream. Nace had watched them, and they had watched back, taking turns drinking. Then they had withdrawn, cautious predators making almost no sound at all.

After a yawn caught him by surprise, Nace rolled over onto his back and put himself through a series of stretches, trying to pump his mind back to full alertness. Then he rolled back into proper position, adjusting himself so that different parts of his body took the pressure. He lifted the faceplate of his helmet halfway so that he could rub at his eyes and cheeks. Then he pulled the visor back into place.

Another hour and I can get back to sleep, he thought as he yawned again. *If nothing happens.*

A third of that hour passed silently. Then one of the snoops that Nace's fire team had planted sounded its alarm. There was no audible noise from the snoop, just a relay through helmet circuits to every officer and sergeant, followed by raw video feed from the snoop's camera. That could be viewed—poorly—on a helmet's head-up display or with better resolution on a mapboard. Nace's squad also had their helmets set to register anything from the snoops that they had planted.

Nace hissed to get the attention of his men, then pointed north, along the creek. The snoop that had twirped had been planted along the bank of the stream, just above water level, one hundred twenty yards out. Anything it saw almost had to be coming down the creek. Nace watched the images on his head-up display. At first, he saw nothing moving. But the camera was far more sensitive than the resolution available against Nace's faceplate. It wasn't until the figure moved that Nace spotted it—definitely human.

For several minutes there was nothing else. The one figure did not move again. No others came into view. With radio silence in the Commonwealth camp, Nace and his men could not know that four other snoops around the perimeter had also picked up movement that did not belong. The entire detachment had been placed on alert immediately, the sleeping men wakened quietly.

Nace concentrated on keeping his breathing shallow and regular. He watched the display on his visor for more movement, or for the one figure to come into focus. *How many are out there?* he wondered. *Do they know exactly where we are, or are they still looking?* The latter seemed improbable. The man spotted by the snoop wouldn't be holding so perfectly still for so long unless he had a very good idea that he was within range of an enemy. Maybe the Federation had detected the snoop's transmission and were looking for it so they could destroy the telltale before moving again.

Or maybe they're just waiting for the rest of their men to get into position before they attack. Once more Nace asked himself *How many?* He knew how many of his mates remained, and he knew that ammunition was going to be a problem before long.

He wiggled against the dirt under him, as if trying to burrow in, looking for any extra cover, even a tiny fraction of an inch. Tension built, and fear, but neither of those had ever paralyzed Nace Jeffries.

Spencer was grateful for the delay, though he too wondered at the reason. There had been no way to get a reliable count of the number of enemy soldiers who were moving toward the camp. The snoops could only show that there were several groups. There were gaps in coverage. The detachment had not possessed enough of the bugs to give thorough coverage of an entire circle, not in the forest. David scanned the video feeds. Using his mapboard, its slight glow concealed by part of a tarp, he could see clearly all the men that the snoop cameras could see.

"They obviously know where we are," David whispered on a radio channel that connected him to Hopewell and the noncoms. "It's just a matter of when they attack." Anyone standing two feet from Spencer, without a helmet radio turned to the proper channel, would have heard nothing. The whisper, muffled by his helmet's acoustic insulation, was far too soft.

"Do we sit and wait, or try to catch them out by hitting first?" Alfie asked.

''This time we wait. Save ammunition until we can do the most good.'' Keeping his people closer together to offer maximum protection to the civilians limited David's options as much as the finite reserves of ammunition. In almost any other operation, at least one squad would have been left outside the perimeter to patrol, or to be in position to hit any attacking force from behind. And David certainly would have preferred to strike at the enemy as soon as the snoops started to detect them, without giving them time to organize.

I'd also like to have the entire regiment here, and a squadron or two of Spacehawks to soften the Feddies up. But wishing wouldn't bring them. David idly fingered the safety on his rifle. It wouldn't be long now. Twenty minutes had passed since the first alert.

25

If the 2nd Marine Commando's camp had been a 180-degree protractor, Alfie Edwards would have been 45 degrees up from the left corner and Nace Jeffries' fire team. Alfie's first squad was dug in under the rotting trunk of a fallen tree. They had scooped out their slit trenches through the rot beneath. The tree had not been down long, despite the advanced state of decay. It could hardly have been down for more than a few days. The area close by had not yet become choked by new growth. A few quick-growing shoots were up, but the men still had relatively clear fire zones, limited only by the edge of the undergrowth bordering the creek to their left and the old-growth trees extending away from that barrier.

Alfie no longer needed to rely on his mapboard or head-up display to see the approaching soldiers. Federation battledress did not provide the same level of thermal insulation that a Commonwealth field skin did. The enemy was eighty yards away and had stopped advancing several minutes before. Like so many others, Alfie wondered, *What are they waiting for?*

Another two minutes passed before Alfie heard the first sounds of attack. The soft thump of rocket-propelled grenades being launched was followed by the sound of those missiles arcing through the forest canopy, ripping through leaves and snapping twigs. RPGs were not ideally suited for this sort of terrain. There were deflections and premature detonations. Still, at least a half dozen grenades exploded near or inside the Commonwealth perimeter.

Even before the first grenades exploded, a scattering of return RPGs went out from the commandos. This was not the massive volley fire they had used to such overwhelming effect before, with grenadiers expending entire clips in a concerted barrage, but more deliberate, more economical, targeting concentrations of soldiers who were within range of snoops.

Federation rifle fire started to come in from a number of areas around the semicircular portion of the perimeter. There was no enemy fire coming in from across the creek that formed the base. Alfie was too busy to notice the one quiet front. There was at least a platoon of soldiers working against his first squad's section of the perimeter. Back near the center, though, Spencer had already noticed. For the present, it was just another fact to file away in case it might prove important later.

It's not like it was a clear message, David thought. There could be a number of reasons for the gap. It might be something as simple as the enemy making sure that they did not fire into their own men. Or they might be trying to tempt the Commonwealth force into a retreat in that direction, into an ambush.

If we do have to move, I think we'll go the opposite way. David smiled. One of his grandfather's favorite clichés had come to mind, about not looking gift horses in the mouth. *If it's a Feddie horse, don't look it in the mouth, move behind and kick it where it'll hurt the most.*

He looked around, closer in. His headquarters squad was the only reserve he had. If worse came to worst, they would have to neglect the civilians and join in the fray. The civilians. . . . David looked at Prince George. The prince was down, like everyone else now, but if he was still not rational, there was no way to be sure that he would stay down on his own. Vepper Holford was almost on top of his master, and there were two Marines near enough to pile on as well if that became necessary.

As long as none of the others go crackers at a bad time, David thought, *I guess we can handle one man whose mind slipped on a banana.*

"Will, watch your flank," David said on a channel direct to 2nd Platoon's sergeant. "To the right, moving in." David had just happened to spot the enemy squad squirming along the ground, looking almost like a truly gigantic snake.

"I see them," Will Cordamon replied. "Another ten feet and they'll be where I want them. We've got a boomer planted, on command. I time it right, we should drop the whole squad. I told my lads to leave them be until then so we don't spook them."

It was dangerous to ignore the rest of the perimeter, even for two minutes, but Spencer kept watching the crawling men, waiting for the surprise that 2nd Platoon had set. *Ten feet.* It was difficult for David to pinpoint the distance the enemy point man crawled. He started to steel himself against the explosion he knew was coming, but when the mine did go off, it was still a surprise. The glare of the blast overloaded his helmet's night-vision systems with heat and light. The directional explosive had been placed high, hanging from the tree's trunk, and it unloaded its seven hundred fifty fragments in a 45-degree arc, downward, on top of the enemy soldiers.

"Looked good, Will," David said as his vision returned. "You must have got most of them." Then it was time to start watching the rest of the perimeter again.

The enemy soldiers in the creek had not done any shooting. During the first minutes of the attack they had merely crouched in the water, near either bank of the stream. Nace was certain that there were at least two squads out there trying to be coy about revealing their presence. They might be a full platoon or more.

They want us to get so caught up in the other stuff that

we'll forget all about them. Nace smiled. There was no chance of that. He had kept his fire team out of the fight and down, waiting. *We'll see who surprises who.*

He heard the mine explode on the far side of the perimeter. The noise was distinctive, deeper and louder than the sound of a grenade or the rockets the Marines carried. *Somebody got a load in the britches,* Nace thought. His men had a mine planted as well, out far enough that they would be out of the danger zone when Nace detonated it. It was hanging from a vine above the center of the creek, fifty yards from where Nace lay, thirty yards in front of the waiting soldiers. "A little hot rain in the rain forest," he had joked when his men rigged the explosive charge.

"Any movement down there?" Alfie asked a few minutes later. Even over the radio, his voice was the merest whisper.

"Not yet, Sarge," Nace replied. "They're just squatting in the water—waiting, like us. Any idea yet what the total opposition might be?"

"Looks like a full company, maybe more," Alfie replied.

Behind Nace, the tempo of the battle increased slowly, the volume of gunfire increasing and coming closer. But that was background, not his concern. Jeffries knew to focus on his own front and trust his mates to handle the other sides. If there was a breakthrough, he would be warned.

Through the gunfire and the occasional blast of explosives, Nace became aware of a distant crackling sound. One of those explosions had started a fire. It wasn't enough to cast light into Nace's position, so he didn't worry about that either.

He adjusted his rifle and moved his head so that he was looking through the gun's sights, linking them to his helmet's night-vision systems. He could see five soldiers, three on the far side of the creek, two on the near, all standing in the water, crouched low, staring toward the Commonwealth line. Their faceplates reflected nothing, and he could see nothing of the faces behind them.

How long are they going to wait? Nace wondered again.

What would they do if I let off just one shot, took out the nearest man? But he would not do that without orders or overriding necessity. The time would come. He was certain of that.

The fight had been going on for thirty minutes before the soldiers in the creek started to move. They came on slowly, almost crawling through the shallow water on hands and knees. As Nace watched, they appeared to be taking exaggerated pains to move without making noise, not the easiest of tasks in water that was almost knee-deep, over a slippery rock bed. Their progress was excruciatingly slow. *They might make better time wading through marmalade,* Nace thought. But more soldiers kept coming into his field of view as the five on point moved closer.

"They've started," he whispered over his fire team's tactical channel. "Get ready for whatever."

No one replied. There was no need. Zol, Curls, and Igor were ready. Zol was the only one who had to move. He had been turned to watch the right, out in one of the gaps where dense undergrowth made it unlikely—but not impossible—for anyone to move silently.

"Sarge, we've got at least a platoon moving down the creek toward us," Nace reported. "Their point is about sixty yards out now, moving in slowly, not firing."

"Do what you can," Edwards replied. "We're a little busy around here too."

The squad's other fire team adjusted position to add their weapons. Those men had been spread out over the next fifteen yards of the creek bank, but there was still no sign of any activity across the stream, just coming down it.

"You got that banger ready?" Teece Muldon, the squad leader, asked.

"Their point man's ten yards from it," Nace replied. "We'll let the first squads move past and catch as many as we can."

"Don't let the point get clear of the kill zone," Teece said. "We want to get the ones who are closest to us."

Almost as the point man passed under the hanging mine,

there was an increase in the volume of gunfire coming from all around the semicircular range of the Commonwealth perimeter. There were clearly new troops entering the fight for the first time, some farther off, others in the gaps that had remained quiet up to that time.

Then there was a series of grenade explosions right along the creek. The RPGs appeared to have come in from the west, over the dense jungle area on the far side of the stream. The explosions came along the entire line, but erratically because of the foliage and wood.

Nace felt a burning sting across his back. From the corner of his eye he saw Curls Murphy jerk spasmodically. Nace turned his head for an instant. Murphy had rolled over onto his side and was reaching for a bloody wound on his left shoulder. Zol moved to help, working quickly to slap med-patches over both entry and exit wound.

"He'll be okay," Zol reported. "What about you, Nace?"

But Nace had already turned his attention back to the soldiers coming along the creek. They were moving faster now, up in a moderate crouch, hurrying. The series of grenade explosions had apparently been the signal they had been waiting for.

"Mind your front, Zol," Nace said. "Here they come."

Nace was watching a mark he had made, trying to judge when the first soldiers were approaching the nearer edge of the mine's killing radius. Nace held his breath, then thumbed the remote trigger for the mine.

Nace ducked instinctively at the sound of the explosion. Hanging from a vine the way it was, the mine might have thrown shrapnel almost to the team's position. Nace had already forgotten about the pain across his back and the obvious fact that he had taken a piece of shrapnel from one of the Federation grenades—or a large sliver of wood hurled out by the blast.

There was no way he could count the enemy soldiers hit by shrapnel from his mine. A half dozen might have gone down or, if his luck was running better than usual, maybe three times that many. He glanced at Murphy again.

"You okay?" he asked.

"I'll live," Curls said through gritted teeth. "If they don't dump another one of those down my blouse."

"Hang tough. The painkiller will work in a few seconds."

The strip across Nace's back that had burned a moment before felt chilled now. He reached around to touch the one end of the cut that he could reach without difficulty. His battledress top and the field skin below it had both been sliced. Air was getting in against his own skin. His hand came away with blood across the fingers.

Must not be too bad, he thought. That was all the time he could spare on his own well-being. The enemy was moving again.

The Federation soldiers came on, moving again almost before the creek absorbed the last bits of debris from the mine blast. Those who found themselves near the front came on with rifles firing, automatic bursts that they spread along the Commonwealth line on the eastern bank of the stream. Moving three abreast, they came on as fast as they could through the water, an exaggerated but slow jog.

Nace and his men met that advance with automatic fire. Even Curls was back in action, firing his needle gun single-handed. That weapon had little recoil and less travel than the assault rifles the others carried.

The creek was a deadly alley for the Federation. Four automatic rifles could put an almost solid wall of munitions across it. But the enemy kept coming. Forty yards from Nace, enemy bodies came close to damming the stream. But other soldiers kept moving forward, and kept firing. Slowly, they narrowed the gap.

"The next time you change magazines," Nace told his men, "slip your bayonets on. And don't take too much time about it." He had no doubt that the fighting was going to get that close.

$\bullet \quad \bullet \quad \bullet \quad \bullet$

The Federation attack came in four main thrusts, from the corner where Nace Jeffries was around 135 degrees of the defensive arc. Occasional volleys of grenades came from the west, over the creek, but there was no follow-up assault from that direction. As the Federation skirmish lines moved closer to the Commonwealth perimeter, the grenade fire slowed, then stopped. It had not been overly effective, but had caused some casualties among the commandos.

Near the southern limit of the attack, Will Cordamon had concentrated most of what remained of his platoon. Without the headquarters squad to augment his force, he had less than half the number of men the platoon had left *Avon* with. To the right, three men held down the remaining 45 degrees of the arc. If another enemy thrust came, or if the one in front of Will slid around, he would be hard-pressed to shift his men in time to meet them.

"Make your shots count," Will told his men. "Keep them off, but remember we don't have any ammo in reserve." They were already stripping their casualties of ammunition as quickly as the men fell.

Will had lost track of how long the attack had been going on. It seemed hours, but couldn't have been even as long as one hour. The enemy soldiers kept coming, one skirmish line after another, taking horrendous casualties in their frontal attack, but they inflicted enough losses on the defenders to matter, and they drew enough fire to seriously deplete the commandos' ammunition stores. If the fight continued as one of attrition, the Commonwealth Marines had to lose. And it would not take all night.

Although he had two magazines left for his rifle, Cordamon set that aside and drew his pistol, a compact needler. The enemy was close enough for that to be effective, and he might need the rifle's greater range later, if there was a later. Will's touch on the trigger was light, allowing him to use minimal bursts of needles. He used a two-handed grip and rested the pistol's butt on the log that sheltered him, moving from target to target with cool deliberation, as if the targets were only silhouette cutouts on the practice range on Buckingham.

When a bullet hit the side of his pistol and plunged into his thumb, Will felt burning pain and the snap of bone as the thumb was broken—shattered. His arm came up and back. The next bullet caught him in the right shoulder. Cordamon half turned as the shot brought him up. Two more bullets struck him, one in the right arm, the other burrowing into his side. He did not feel the last hit. He had already lost consciousness.

Evan Fox was the man nearest to his platoon sergeant. He called for a medical orderly, then slid closer to Cordamon. Will was alive but bleeding badly. Fox used his last med-patches, and all that Cordamon had, to close the wounds.

No medical orderly came. Evan looked around but could see no one coming. He used his radio again. The two medics left in the detachment were both busy with other serious casualties.

"Bring him to the CP if you can," Lieutenant Hopewell said. "I'm on my way out to take over there."

Fox stripped off Cordamon's pack and web belt. The sergeant was smaller than Fox, but this was no time to be carrying extra baggage. Evan also dropped his own pack. He turned Cordamon over on his back. There was no question of picking the sergeant up and walking to the command post. Neither of them would have made it. All Evan could do was drag Cordamon along by the feet, an awkward, slow process.

"Hang on, Sarge," Evan said. "We're not out of this yet."

Tony Hopewell ran almost doubled over, occasionally dropping to all fours where the cover was particularly thin. He had made one quick stop before heading out to 2nd Platoon's end of the perimeter, to grab Prince George's shotgun and cartridge vest. He had five rounds already loaded in the shotgun.

"Might as well use what we've got," he had told Mitch Naughton before leaving.

"Close as those Feddies are, a shotgun's as good as anything, even loaded with birdshot," the lead sergeant had said. "Give them something to think about."

The closer they are, the more use it'll be, Hopewell thought after he passed Fox and Cordamon. He stopped just long enough to make sure that Cordamon was still alive.

When he got close to the line, Hopewell got down on his stomach and crawled into position where Will Cordamon had been, in the middle of what was left of 2nd Platoon. There were dead men on both sides of him. He did a quick check on the radio channel used by the platoon's noncoms to find out how many men were left. With Evan Fox gone to take Cordamon to help, there were only seven men from the platoon left.

"David, 2nd is down to less than a squad on the line," Tony reported as he lined the shotgun up with his first target. "We need help, and we need it fast."

Everyone needs help, Spencer thought, *and we've got no one to send.* He glanced around. "I'll try to get a couple of men up to you," he said. He heard the distinctive sound of the shotgun going off. *I'll have to send—*

He never got a chance to finish the thought.

"Why wasn't I invited?" Prince George demanded, very loudly. "You know how I like to hunt."

He stood, as fluid and quick in movement as an athlete. It was so sudden and unexpected that for an instant none of the people around him reacted. Then, three men tackled the prince simultaneously. Vepper hit him low, behind the knees. Kaelich and Naughton hit him higher, near the waist.

The four men landed in a heap. On top, Naughton felt a burning pain in his shoulder. The pain was familiar. He had felt it in other battles. He had been hit by a bullet. At the bottom of the pile, Prince George hardly noticed the pain of cartilage tearing around both knees. Holford's arm and shoulder had been behind the joints when the other men dumped the prince on top of him.

"I say!" George said. "What *is* the matter here?" As the others tried to free themselves, the prince neither helped nor hindered them. His body had gone limp, totally, even though his voice could not have shown more shock if the gang tackle had happened in the grand ballroom of St. James Palace.

Spencer had started moving toward the group as soon as he saw the prince get to his feet. Swearing under his breath, David helped disentangle the group. He saw the blood on Naughton's shoulder, but the lead sergeant was moving on his own.

"What is the cause of this outrage?" the prince asked when everyone had finally been separated. Then, hardly pausing, he added, "Why do my knees hurt so dreadfully?" His voice went plaintive, almost childlike. "I don't like to hurt."

Vepper bent over the prince and started fussing around the royal knees. "Nothing seems to be broken, sir," he reported. "Something must have torn, muscle or cartilage."

"Will I be fine for the dance?"

Vepper looked across the prince at Spencer. The two men shook their heads at each other.

"You'll be fine, sir," Vepper said. "We'll stick med-patches on and you'll be right in no time at all. Just stay down for at least four hours. Give the patches time to work."

"Yes, Vepper, if I must. I mustn't limp at the ball. Henry would be so disappointed."

"Nail him to the ground if you have to," David said while he applied med-patches to Naughton's shoulder. "I want someone sitting on him. If he moves, slap a sleep-patch on his neck."

"I'll see to His Highness," Vepper said. "I'll stay right with him. In any case, he won't be able to stand for a while."

"Good. Mitch, we need to pull a couple of men from

headquarters squad and send them to 2nd Platoon. Tony says they're down to seven men, and they need help right now.''

"Captain?"

Spencer turned. Shadda Lorenqui had crawled closer.

"Give me a rifle and I'll go. I might as well be of some use. Perhaps a few of the other men as well.''

"You ever fire a military rifle?"

"Perhaps not the model you lot have, but enough." He thought of the pistol he had under his shirt, stuck into the waistband of his trousers. That might also do some good, but he hoped—most fervently—that the enemy would not get close enough for him to need that weapon.

"I guess we don't have much choice. Thank you. Will you check with the others, see how many will help?"

After Shadda crawled off, David leaned closer to Naughton. "You stay here with the prince," Spencer said, whispering over their private radio link. "I meant what I said about slapping a sleep-patch on his neck if he tries to get up again.''

"Don't you think it's time we all get out to the lines, Cap?" Naughton asked. "We need every rifle we can get. Leave the prince to his flunky and the women.''

"Not yet. The headquarters squad is the only reserve we've got. As long as there's any hope, they stay here. With you. If things go completely bad, try to get out with the prince and as many of the others as you can. Remember our orders.''

Spencer stayed where he was and looked around. A thought had come to him, and he needed to work through it before he said anything. It might already be time to try to get the civilians out, sneak across the creek and try to elude however many soldiers were covering that side. The rest of the detachment could provide cover for that, while there were still men and bullets.

He squeezed his eyes shut. *No, not yet.* When he opened his eyes again, the second part of the decision came as well. *But soon. We can't wait much longer, or it will be too late.*

He tried the radio links for the fleet again. There was still no reply.

I hope Alfie wasn't right, David thought. *I hope this isn't the one we don't come back from.*

26

Mort Hardesty had spent the entire war assigned to *HMS Sheffield*, one of the Second Commonwealth's largest battlecruisers. As captain of *Sheffield*, he had served under Admirals Stasys Truscott and Paul Greene. Now, Hardesty was in the flag quarters. Admiral Greene had moved ashore, and Mort had been promoted to Rear Admiral. He was in command of *Sheffield*'s battle group, which included the troop ship *HMS Victoria*, three frigates, and the supply ship *HMS Thames*. But Hardesty was not in overall command of the Camerein operation. Rear Admiral Regina Oswald, whose flag was aboard the battlecruiser *HMS Kent*, had three years' time-in-grade over Mort. Even though the additional battle group, augmented by a third battlecruiser and four extra frigates, had been added to the operation literally at the last minute, command had to pass to the most senior officer.

Between the 2nd Regiment of Royal Marines and the crews of the ships in the flotilla, the CSF was committing more total manpower to the campaign than the prewar population of the world they were attempting to liberate. Every officer in the fleet knew why so much was being put into the operation. It was only partly the possible presence of the king's brother. More important was the fact that the loss of Camerein had marked the start of the war, and with a chance that hostilities might soon end, His Majesty's Government wanted to redress that initial defeat first. No one in the fleet knew—or could have known—that a cease-fire had already been signed. The fleet was in Q-space, ready to complete its final jump to Camerein.

For the Marines of 2nd Regiment, there was a more important, and more personal, reason for going to Camerein. Some of their mates were already on the ground there. No matter what else came of the mission, the 2nd Marine Commando Detachment needed them.

There had been one last-minute change to the operational plan, made during a conference just before the task force entered Q-space for the final transit to Camerein.

"If the commandos are still there, they might need a lot of help very fast," Osgood had observed. "They were shorthanded after the initial troubles, and we must assume that the Feddies would be looking for them. Instead of deploying strictly against the population centers on the other continent, I want to hold one battalion ready to go in to rescue the commandos and the people they were sent to save, if we can make contact with them. We would have kept one battalion as a reserve anyway. This might give them something to do while they're waiting."

Mort and Regina had already discussed the change privately. This conference, via holographic linkup, included Colonel Zacharia, the commander of 2nd Regiment, as well as the skippers of the various ships in the task force.

"Mort, as soon as we enter Camerein's near space, launch the rest of 2nd Regiment, except for the one battalion, then jump back to Q-space with *Victoria* and *Sheffield* to come out over the other hemisphere, ready to put in the last battalion and Spacehawks to cover them. We'll use the fighters from the other battlecruisers to cover the main landing." Osgood paused. "This assumes that we make contact with the commandos. We should know one way or the other by the time we make our first landings, but even if we haven't made contact yet, we'll hold the one battalion. If we don't contact them, we'll still have to land people to try to carry out their original mission.''

The resulting discussion lasted only a couple of minutes as the skippers of *Victoria* and *Sheffield* sought to clear up the few details that needed clarification.

''One other thing,'' Osgood said. ''Timetable. If we make the jump now, we can get into position two hours ahead of schedule. I do not intend to waste those two hours stooging around here when we might be doing some good there.''

27

There were more than enough rifles to equip the civilians who were willing and able to bear them. Shadda Lorenqui, Jeige McDonough, Henri Caffre, and two others collected rifles from the dead. They were each given a single magazine of cartridges. "Use them carefully," they were told. "We're all running short." The civilian volunteers moved toward the sound of the shotgun. That was a better guide than the vague arm wave they had been started off with. "Find Lieutenant Hopewell. Off that way."

Following Shadda's lead, the civilians ran in a low crouch. Shadda was bent over so far that he could almost touch the ground with his hands. He hadn't gone far before he decided that even that was too much exposure, so he went down on hands and knees and crawled the rest of the distance. The others continued to follow his lead.

Hopewell had been warned that they were coming. "Just find places and do what you can," he told them. *I hope you can hit something,* he thought, but he was not optimistic. He would be satisfied if the extra firepower just made the enemy hesitate about rushing the position.

Shadda was dismayed, but not surprised, to note that his hands trembled as he settled into a prone firing position. It had been years since he had fired a gun. A few times, back in the early years of isolation, he had accompanied the prince on a day's hunt. That normally meant that he might get one or two shots. Prince George had always done most of the firing. It had been nearly two decades since Shadda had done any extensive shooting, though, especially at men—years and light-years away, a lifetime past.

It's been a long time since I killed a man, or tried to, Shadda thought as he put a Federation soldier in the rifle's sights.

If the man had been more than thirty yards away, he would have been safe. Shadda's stomach had been tied in knots for hours, as it habitually was, and that also disturbed his aim. But after Shadda saw his target fall, the knot released, suddenly. He barely managed to get his head away from the rifle before he started vomiting. He had forgotten. His reaction had been the same the last time he had aimed a weapon at a human being.

An eerie silence came to the battlefield. The nearest Federation troops pulled back a little and went to ground, seeking whatever cover they could find or improvise. Around the perimeter, the Commonwealth Marines ceased firing as soon as they lost targets, often as soon as they saw that the enemy was withdrawing. So did the handful of civilians with rifles. Spencer started contacting people, looking for whatever they could tell him about the suddenly halted attack, their losses, and their remaining supplies of ammunition.

The news was not good on any count. There were only twenty-three Marines left in the perimeter and able to fight. If it hadn't been for scavenging ammunition from fallen comrades, they wouldn't have had any left. As it was, the average remaining was little more than a single magazine, twenty-five rounds for the slug throwers, one hundred needles for those weapons.

David had no choice but to send the headquarters squad to reinforce the most vulnerable sections of the perimeter, keeping only one man back to stay with Prince George and Vepper Holford.

The men from headquarters squad were still moving toward their new positions when the enemy started shooting, and moving, again.

Every man in the fire team had been wounded, two of them more than once, but all four were still on the line. Nace Jeffries had come up with his own plan for conserving ammunition. The men in his fire team took turns shooting, two at a time, and they were firing single shots. "Unless they're crawling in on top of us, I don't want any more than that" was the way Nace had put it. The attack down the creek had slowed. Nace's estimate was that there had to be at least forty dead Federation soldiers in the water. Loaded down with combat kit, the bodies could not float. Finally, they did virtually dam the stream some twenty-five or thirty yards out from Nace's position.

Thank God it's dark, Nace thought. *I don't want to see all of that blood flowing past.*

"Maybe we ought to let a few of the bastards crawl right in with us," Igor Vilnuf said during the brief hiatus in fighting. "Let them get close enough for us to grab their rifles and ammo. I'm getting awfully near the end here."

For an insane instant, Nace was tempted by the idea. "No, that would mean trading our lives for a few bullets. Even two Feddies could take us all out before they got close. We just have to make every bullet count. One bullet, one Feddie. After that, it's bayonets and knees."

And then they were coming again.

Alfie Edwards had been working hard to meet the "one bullet, one Feddie" goal for some time. His first squad had already been cut in half meeting one of the heavier concentrations of Federation troops. Four men were trying to cover a section of front that had been too large for eight, and they were all low on ammunition. There wasn't a single grenade left in the platoon—in the entire detachment, as far as Alfie had been able to determine—and the last shoulder-operated missiles had been expended within the last few minutes. The SAMs were not intended as antipersonnel weapons, but that did not stop the Marines from using them that way.

The mess of dead enemy soldiers out front seemed scant measure for the losses inside the lines. There seemed to be no end to the enemy, and no lack of will. They kept coming. If there were fewer of them now, and if they came on more slowly, the balance was still in their favor, more than before, because there were also fewer Commonwealth commandos, with much less ammunition.

Alfie was caught by surprise by another pause in the assault. The few who could withdraw did. From a distance, there was light rifle fire, but just a scattering, enough to make men remember to keep their heads down.

"David, lad, we've about had it," Alfie said on his private link. In these straits there wasn't even the quasi-formality of calling him "Cap." They went back too far together. "The only thing I can think of now is to pull back into one tight wall in the center, maybe try to get across that creek."

Spencer had been thinking much the same thoughts. "They've got to have a trap laid on for us there, Alfie. But . . ." David paused, briefly, then almost shouted, "They're here! Hang on!"

The wait seemed eternal to Alfie. His body started to shake. *Who's here?* He feared that it was some cruel hoax, or a mirage, some last kick in the face before the end. *God, David, what's taking you so long? Tell me something, anything.*

"Twenty-eight minutes," David said when he returned to the channel. He cut in Lieutenant Hopewell and the rest of the noncoms on the circuit. "Our relief force is here. In twenty-eight minutes we'll have two flights of Spacehawks and the entire 1st Battalion in to help us. The men are already in their shuttles, ready to head down as soon as

Victoria gets into position. We just have to hold for another twenty-eight minutes.''

Alfie felt an instant of giddy elation, but it could not last. *Twenty-eight minutes or twenty-eight hours. Not much difference,* he thought. He had no more than a half magazine of ammunition left in his rifle, and two clips of needles for his pistol. If the enemy started coming again, the ammunition wouldn't last for half of the necessary time.

Tony Hopewell passed the news to the civilians on the line with him. They had no radio links. The men who had come from the Commonwealth Excelsior reacted much more positively to the news than most of the Marines did. The civilians had little conception of how difficult it might be to hold on long enough for the close air support and the battalion of Marines to get in. The short break in the enemy assault gave the civilians a chance to quietly exult. But they did remain down, and silent. Only Jeige McDonough said anything that the others could hear.

"Maybe the Feddies will figure out that we've got help coming down and leave us alone." By that time, the pause in the enemy attack had lasted for nearly four minutes.

Hopewell said, "Don't count on it. Feddies don't give up that easily."

It was almost as if his words were the signal for the next wave of Federation soldiers to start moving in.

Shadda had met the news of impending rescue with no more than a blink. He heard the words, but they did not seem to register. The concept was too abstract to assimilate. A long, soft sigh, another blink. His mind seemed to throttle down, his senses dulled. Sound seemed muted, the way it can be with water in the ears. His sight lost focus, as if thin sheets of gauze had been drawn across his eyes. When the enemy troops started in again, they appeared to move in a most exaggerated slow motion, a series of stop-action photographs, a surreal ballet.

Shadda lined up the first of them in his sights and pulled

the trigger. *Everything* seemed to be in slow motion. For an instant he even fancied that he saw the bullet in flight, inching toward its target. He watched in captive fascination, certain that the bullet was going to strike the soldier, that the wound would be lethal.

Impossible though it was, Shadda could swear that he did see the bullet strike the soldier high in the chest on the left side, saw the shudder of impact, the spurt of blood, and the start of the soldier's fall. In his peculiar state of awareness, Shadda thought—briefly—that the soldier would fall on top of him. The idea was absurd. Despite Lorenqui's perceptual anomaly, the soldier dropped thirty yards away.

Shadda's eyes followed the man to the ground. The appearance of unnatural slowness continued until the helmet hit turf and rebounded slightly. Then time seemed to resort to its normal speed. Shadda glanced around. There was another target. He fired quickly, but poorly, missing the man completely. Shadda took a deep breath and tried again.

Twenty-eight minutes? he thought as that shot also missed. *We should live so long.*

Jeige McDonough felt a fluttering in his chest after hearing the news that relief was coming. He had feared to cheer, afraid that showing any reaction might negate the possibility of survival—an atavistic superstition. He wondered if his wife remained safe, but could not glance in that direction. He was afraid to look away from the front, certain that the instant he did there would be a soldier standing right over him, ready to finish him off. The break in the attack had given him no relaxation. Those minutes had passed with incredible speed, and once the soldiers started coming again, time was both fast and slow, simultaneously. The enemy advance seemed speeded up, but there seemed to be virtually no passage of the time required for the new Commonwealth force to arrive.

I hope Mai has finally realized that I cut her off from liquor for her own good, he thought.

Jeige was a terrible shot. He had never fired at a human

being before, had rarely hunted lesser animals. Even on Camerein, on the few occasions when he had gone out on a hunting expedition, he had never shot to hit any of the animals that they hunted. Now, the soldiers were sometimes no more than twenty yards away before they fell. Jeige pointed his rifle toward the middle of the torso. He tended to close his eyes and jerk the trigger, both traits deadly to marksmanship. As far as he could tell, he only scored one hit, an embarrassing bullet to the groin of a hapless Federation soldier.

None of the Marines had really noticed Marie Caffre crawling around, going from body to body to find a rifle and ammunition. If anyone *had* noted her crawling toward the perimeter, generally along the route her husband had taken some minutes earlier, they had not said anything or tried to stop her.

I'm no helpless child, Marie thought as she moved toward the perimeter. *And I'm no crazy parasite like The Windsor, either.* She had watched his display of insanity with habitual scorn. His outbursts came as no surprise to her—not that she would have admitted it if they had. Her grudge against royalty in general, and the royalty of the Second Commonwealth in particular, had its roots a thousand years before the first men had left Earth to settle new worlds. The medieval disputes between France and England, the series of wars that had extended through centuries, all were grist for her political fervor. That her own world, originally French-speaking, was a member of the Second Commonwealth—and had largely switched to English as a first language—had rankled since she was a schoolgirl. Before her marriage to Henri, she had dabbled at political activism, organizing protests, publishing diatribes against aristocrats, the Commonwealth, and anything else that happened to rouse her ire. She had even managed to get arrested during a demonstration once. She had been only partially relieved when the charges against her were dropped. That had deprived her of a small martyrdom.

I'm better than any royalty, and The Windsor most of all, Marie assured herself as she found a spot on the perimeter. *I'll prove it right here, once and for all. The cringing fool.*

Marie Caffre had never fired a rifle in her life. But she had been watching the Marines. She remembered the steps, taking the safety off, making certain that there was a round in the chamber. She sighted, and pulled the trigger.

The recoil was more than she had counted on, and there was obviously something wrong with her technique. Her thumb had smashed into the right lens of her night goggles. But she settled back into position. Now that she knew what to expect, she did a little better. After a half dozen shots, she thought she might actually be doing some good. After all, the Federation soldiers were so close that she could almost have spit in their faces.

She was not at all prepared for the terrible pain that came as two bullets slammed into her back at a very sharp angle. Marie screamed in terror and pain before she lost consciousness.

Zol Ketchum was dead. That bothered Nace Jeffries, as much because he didn't know when or how it had happened as from the fact of the death itself. Terry Murphy was unconscious. He might or might not survive, depending on how long it took to get him into a trauma tube. Igor Vilnuf was still fighting, but like Nace had been wounded more than once. Teece Muldon was the only one left from the squad's first fire team. He had moved to the corner with Nace and Igor. So far, they were still keeping the enemy from reaching them. That wouldn't last much longer, though. They had only four rounds of ammunition left apiece.

"We're going to have to let them come on in," Teece told the others. "Save those last rounds for the last few yards, then get up and use our bayonets."

"How 'bout we pull back instead," Nace suggested. "Do what we can to last until 1st Battalion gets in."

"I'll check with the captain." That conversation lasted no more than ten seconds. "We pull back to the next cover," Teece said. "Igor, you cover us while we haul Curls."

There was no way to avoid it. All along the northern half of the perimeter, David pulled his men—the last few survivors—back. Shortening the line was their only hope, and not much of a hope at that. The attacks were still coming mostly from the north and east. There had been nothing but scattered shots and grenades from the west and south. The commandos pulled back toward the dense treefall undergrowth that sheltered Prince George and most of the civilians, dragging their wounded along.

After the four-minute pause, the enemy started forward again, but only in two spots, roughly opposite Tony Hopewell and his few civilians on the right, and against Alfie Edwards' squad on the left. It was clear that the Federation force had also taken considerable punishment. This assault was lighter than any that had gone before, fewer men, fewer shots.

There was another difference. The soldiers did not try to storm all the way in to the Commonwealth line. They took cover fifty or sixty yards out, often behind piles of bodies, trying to cut down the opposition from that distance.

David glanced at the timeline on his visor display. There were four minutes left in the promised twenty-eight. *We've got a chance,* he thought. *As long as they don't rush us.* His throat was dry. He had been unable to raise any spit. He wasn't certain how much longer he would be able to talk. There were three minutes left when he received a call from the Spacehawk flight leader.

"We're coming in just ahead of the shuttles," the pilot said. "I've got some bad news for you, though. Three more Feddie shuttles just grounded three hundred yards east of your position. They were in before we could launch any munitions at them. We'll do what we can, but you're going to have a few minutes that could get hairy, until 1st Battalion gets to you.''

"Do what you can.'' David's voice cracked and threatened to seize up completely. He coughed. "We're about out of ammo. They take very long, and all they'll be able to do is count bodies.''

"I've got twelve birds here, and we see your positions. We'll put as tight a ring around you as we can. Get your heads down when the shooting starts. Under two minutes now.''

David had to waste several seconds sipping water before he could pass the news to his men. *Pull back and hunker down.* Then the lead shuttle pilot was on line to tell him where the landers would put down, where his reinforcements would be coming from.

"As close as you can get them,'' Spencer said. "I wouldn't even object to a platoon rappelling down in the middle of us.''

"I wish I could help you, but we're going to have to land in the same place the Feddies just did, after a few Spacehawks make sure none of them are left there. There's just no other open space within reach.''

The Spacehawks came two at a time, in quick succession. Each launched a pair of high explosive air-to-surface missiles on each pass, working their way around the Commonwealth perimeter. The fighters killed speed until they were traveling slow enough to use cannons. Each had two six-barreled guns that could spew out eighteen hundred .50 caliber rounds a minute.

For the commandos and the civilians they were guarding, it was like being at the eye of a hell-storm. Scores of rockets tore at the forest around them, felling trees, ripping vines, digging up craters. Hot shrapnel flew. Dozens of small fires started, though nearly all failed to survive longer than a few minutes. Smoke rose from charred wood and leaves. Trees fell in every direction, some splintered and falling in two directions. The smell of explosives was thick.

The noise was beyond belief. Marines turned off the external microphones on their helmets. Some clapped hands over the sides of those helmets, as if that could help. All the civilians could do was press hands against ears, trying to keep out the worst of the din.

Spencer did not even hear the first word that the shuttles carrying 1st Battalion had landed safely and that their reinforcements were moving toward the commando detachment. He didn't hear the news until the aerial assault had ended and there was relative silence around him.

The radio call seemed to come out of a cave, the voice strangely damped, distant. First Battalion was on the ground and moving toward them. The Spacehawks would remain on tap for any additional help that might be needed. The pilots could see no trace of Federation soldiers moving; no enemy helmet electronics were active.

David could not get rid of the hollow ringing in his ears. He was not aware that the pilot had been shouting, that he had been shouting back. When he started to hear rifle fire again, it seemed to come from miles away.

Finally, he could hear that gunfire more clearly. Most of it *was* some distance off, and had to be coming from the Marines of 1st Battalion. Some of the rifle fire was closer, though. The enemy soldiers were retreating from the reinforcements, and that was carrying them directly toward the remnants of Spencer's command.

"Oh, no!" Alfie Edwards said when he saw the soldiers coming in again, across the zone of incredible destruction that the Spacehawks had plowed around the Commonwealth perimeter. The enemy was facing away, mostly, and when they did turn toward Alfie, they were more interested in climbing over or through obstruction, trying to get away from the new force on the ground, than in continuing to fight the commandos. Even when they started taking fire from the commandos who still had a few rounds of ammunition left, the enemy soldiers were slow to react.

They came on in a daze, slowly, haltingly.

Alfie whistled over his squad channel as he got to his feet. He was moving forward, toward the enemy, as he fired the last two rounds from his rifle. All he had now was the nine-inch blade of the bayonet on the end of that rifle.

Only ten commandos on that side of the perimeter were able to follow Alfie forward. With one exception, the civilians stayed where they were. None of them had bayonets, and even if they had, they had never been trained on how to use them.

The nearest enemy soldiers seemed shocked—though nothing could be seen of their faces—at the way the commandos advanced on them with bayonets. A few of them had no choice but to try to block those attacks. None of them had bayonets fixed. Behind the leaders of the enemy movement, the rest stopped. Although there were only a few Marines in front of them and many behind, they hesitated. Most broke to one side or the other then, trying to escape both groups of the enemy. Those who could not disengage fought as long as they could, until they fell.

Alfie was the first to close with an enemy soldier, feinting with his blade and then swinging the rifle butt around and up, knocking his opponent's rifle out of position. Alfie pressed forward, stock blocking stock, and kneed the man between the legs. When he bent over in automatic reflex, Alfie brought his bayonet down, slicing into the shoulder and neck. As the man fell, Alfie kicked at the helmet to help free his bayonet, then stepped over that man and started for the next.

The second enemy had time to bring his rifle up. He had started to squeeze off a burst before Alfie's rifle knocked his off line. Edwards grunted in pain as a bullet tore into his thigh, but he still moved forward. In three quick motions, he planted the point of his bayonet in the man's chest as he lunged forward, then tumbled over the top as the man fell backwards. The blade ripped free in a fountain of bright arterial blood.

When Alfie tried to get back to his feet, his injured leg refused to support him. He fell back to the ground.

• • •

Shadda Lorenqui started back toward the fighting. He had just thrown down his rifle. It was out of ammunition. Now, he had the automatic pistol in his hand. It was cocked, with a round in the chamber. Shadda moved back toward Prince George and the other civilians who had not moved into the line with weapons. Enemy soldiers were coming in.

There was no clear thought to Shadda's movements. His mind had long since fallen to instinct—of some sort. All he felt was an impulse, a need to continue protecting his guests from the hotel. He intended to put himself between those guests, especially Prince George, and the enemy.

He was no longer conscious of the bullets flying around him. Nor was he aware that he had been slightly injured. A round had grazed his arm, cutting his sleeve and scoring the skin beneath. He felt no pain. More important, he no longer felt fear. He was no longer capable of that.

Shadda moved past the guests. He saw a couple of the Marines using their bayonets. He saw Alfie Edwards go down and not get back up. Although Shadda could not identify Edwards by sight in battledress, he went over toward him as two more enemy soldiers moved toward the fallen Marine.

He fired twice, once at each of the men. From no more than fifteen feet away, his aim was sufficient. Both men went down with wounds to the upper torso. Shadda moved toward them. He wanted to check, wanted to know whether or not he had killed them. The first man was either dead or close to it.

The second . . . was not.

Shadda leaned over the man, then reached to lift his faceplate. At that point, the man swung his rifle up. Shadda saw the movement but could not block the swing or get out of his way. He did pull the trigger on his pistol again, just before the rifle butt connected with the side of his head.

The world seemed to explode as Shadda collapsed on top of the man he had just killed, falling into a limitless darkness.

• • •

The fight was over for the men of the 2nd Marine Commando Detachment and their civilian companions before any of the men from their relief force came into sight. The last enemy soldiers who could had faded away to one side or the other.

Two squads of Alpha Company, 1st Battalion, 2nd Marine Regiment moved across the area that had been hit by the Spacehawks. They came cautiously, weapons at the ready, in two skirmish lines, still looking for the enemy.

People stood, commandos and civilians, slowly. Most simply stared at the oncoming Marines, too numbed by what had happened to give any other reaction. Some could not even stand.

At the center, David Spencer was in radio contact with the battalion commander and two company commanders. Medical orderlies were being routed in to care for the wounded. David sank to the ground near the feet of Prince George. The prince was oblivious to what was happening. Someone had slapped a sleep-patch on the royal neck. George lay on his back, smiling at the universe, or at some mad dream. David closed his eyes, unaware that he was crying, sobbing out loud.

"Captain Spencer?"

David looked up slowly. Although the man standing over him had his visor up, David needed a moment to recognize him as Lieutenant Colonel Marc Olivier, 1st Battalion commanding officer.

Spencer nodded once, dully. "Yes, sir." He did not try to stand, not immediately.

"We've got your wounded in hand. Some are already on the way over to the shuttles. We have a half dozen trauma tubes. If that's not enough, I've had one shuttle alerted to take off as soon as we get the most seriously hurt men—and one woman—loaded."

"Woman?"

"Madame Caffre," Jeige McDonough said. He had just

come up behind the colonel. "She had a rifle and was fighting along with the rest of us. A most spirited woman."

Finally, David struggled to his feet, needing to use his rifle as a crutch to make it. "Do you have a count yet, sir?" he asked, focusing in on Olivier. "How many survived?"

"No, I can't give you numbers yet, Captain. As soon as possible, I promise." He pointed to the sleeping figure on the ground. "His Highness?"

"Yes." David glanced at the prince, then looked back at Olivier. "It was necessary to sedate him. I'll explain later, to Colonel Zacharia."

"Yes, of course. He's anxious to hear about your lot." The colonel lowered his visor to get the benefit of its night vision. "First impression, Captain. You did remarkably well, no matter how serious your losses. Under the circumstances. . . . And succeeded in your primary mission as well. An astounding performance, one might say."

David nodded slowly, the compliment missing him entirely. "If you'll excuse me, sir. I need to see to my men." *Those I've got left.*

HAVEN

According to the official account published by the Combined Space Forces, the battle for Camerein lasted seven hours, marked from the time *HMS Victoria* and her escorts launched their attack. The week that David Spencer's band of commandos spent on the world was mentioned only in a footnote.

> *The 2nd Marine Commando Detachment was infiltrated in advance of the primary landings. Their mission rescued a number of Commonwealth citizens who had been trapped on Camerein since the start of the war and paved the way for the quick liberation of that world.*

The fact that Prince George was one of those citizens was never officially acknowledged. Everyone involved was cautioned that any mention of his presence on Camerein throughout the seven years of war would be a violation of the Official Secrets Act—even after the end of hostilities. The official silence about the prince had lasted throughout his years on Camerein. It would continue until he was released from a specialized treatment facility on the grounds of the Royal College of Medicine, Westminster University.

Only twenty-seven members of the commando detachment survived their footnoted engagement. Of those, twenty-three had been wounded, sixteen seriously enough to require hours in trauma tubes. Of the seventeen civilians, only one man died, and no one was quite certain how or when that had happened; even alive, Homer Keating had been something of a nonentity among the exiles. Of the surviving civilians, Marie Caffre was the only one to suffer serious wounds, though several had minor injuries. The psychological effects of the long isolation and of the stresses of their final week on the world took longer to treat.

Little more than an hour after 1st Battalion reached them, Spencer and his group were all aboard *HMS Victoria* being treated. They were still in the shipboard hospital when news arrived of the cease-fire signed on Dirigent. That news came just minutes before word came that the last Federation troops on Camerein had surrendered—before hearing of the cease-fire.

No one in the hospital cheered.

Eight hours after reaching *Victoria*, the commandos and the civilians they had rescued were transferred to *HMS Sheffield*. Quarters had been prepared for them. An hour later, *Sheffield* jumped to Q-space, on her way back to Buckingham.

The war was over, its last battle a victory for the Commonwealth.

ii

David Spencer fell asleep before the commuter shuttle took off from the civilian airport east of Westminster. He had been lethargic through the three months since his return to Buckingham from Camerein. He tired easily and had little energy even after a full night of sleep. Batteries of medical tests had determined that there was no physical reason for the lethargy.

The doctor who had approved the formal diagnosis seemed inordinately proud of his deductions. "After seven years of war, and a number of battle campaigns, you are a warrior without a war now. There is bound to be a reaction. It will most likely pass in due course, with or without counseling. Counseling will likely shorten the period of adjustment, though."

Spencer had not bothered to offer his opinion of the doctor's cleverness. It would have taken far too much effort, even for a string of monosyllabic words.

A warrior without a war. Debriefing, medical screening, writing letters to the families of the dead—or paying them personal visits—and the bureaucratic necessities of returning to garrison had taken most of three weeks after David's return from Camerein. There had been two visits to the palace, two private audiences with His Majesty. Then David had taken a month of his accumulated furlough time and done as close to nothing as he could manage. For once, it wasn't at all difficult to be completely idle. At the end of his leave, he had spent a week back on duty, then had taken another thirty days of holiday.

That had ended two days before this flight. David was on administrative leave now—which would not be deducted from his remaining leave time. There had been few opportunities to use that time during the past seven years. He still had seventy days left that he could take at any time, subject to military necessities and convenience. After considerable internal debate, David had decided that he would not bother to take those days. It wouldn't be necessary.

"Captain?" The voice and the gentle shake of his shoulder woke David. He looked up and smiled at the flight attendant. This was a much nicer way to wake than he had ever known in the Marines. The first time she had called him by rank, David had been surprised. He was traveling in civilian clothes. He had needed a moment to remember that his ticket had been procured by regimental headquarters and had listed his full name and rank.

"We're due to land in Haven in just a couple of minutes, Captain. Time to fasten your lap strap."

"Yes, of course." David straightened up and pulled the belt around into position. "Thank you."

Haven was on the seacoast north of Westminster. The city of Haven was situated on a broad bay. The duchy of Haven extended over twelve thousand square miles. Except for the duchy's capital, most of the population was scattered about in a score of small towns and large villages.

David glanced out the window at his left in time to see Havenheights, the home of Prince William, on top of the bluff on the west side of the bay. The city was below, centered on the seaport. The east side of the bay had extensive beaches—beautiful, but with water seldom warm enough for swimming.

The shuttle circled over the city and settled in gently at the airport just to the south. Like most such facilities, the

Haven airport had a fairly informal layout. The terminals were low and spacious buildings with automated transit systems so that passengers had little walking to do. The hangars and maintenance sheds were considerably distant, and looked decorative rather than purely functional.

As the shuttle taxied toward the terminal, David spotted a bright blue limousine with the crest of the Duke of Haven on the skirt. The figure standing next to the floater looked familiar, but the shuttle passed too quickly for Spencer to be certain.

The flight attendant returned just before the aircraft came to a halt. "If you'll follow me, Captain. There's a limousine here to collect you. You can exit through the cockpit door."

David unstrapped and stood, a little unsteadily as the shuttle braked to a stop. "My luggage?"

"Will be sent along straightaway, Captain."

She led him to the front of the passenger cabin, then past the service area where the in-flight drinks and snacks were prepared. The door to the cockpit beyond was open. On the right side of the fuselage, the exit door was already open as well, with a ramp in place.

"Thanks for everything," David told the flight attendant before he started down the ramp. "I could get used to this sort of service."

One step out on the ramp, David recognized the figure waiting beside the blue floater. He hurried away from the shuttle. The other man hurried to meet him.

"Alfie, I thought you had gotten yourself lost," David said. "You're looking fit."

Alfie grinned and flipped a salute that many officers would have considered insubordinate. "I've been here for a week, Cap. The prince's people have been fattening us all up."

"All?"

"You'll see. God, it's good to see you, David. There have been some nasty rumors going around."

"You know better than to believe everything you hear, Alfie-lad." David gestured at the floater. "Do we have a driver, or have you signed on as a chauffeur for His Highness?''

''He asked me to collect you and apologize for not being here himself. I'm not the regular chauffeur, but I did sign on to work here, assistant to the head of security.''

''I knew you left the RM. They told me when I came back from leave. I was upset that you didn't wait until I returned.''

''I was afraid you'd try to talk me out of it.'' Alfie shrugged, then turned away just for an instant. ''It was time for me. If nothing else, the fact that it took a civilian to save my arse would have convinced me.''

''No shame in that.''

''Maybe. I'm glad he survived, anyhow. I don't think I could have lived with myself if that hotel manager had died saving my life. Now, we'd best be going. His Highness is keen to see you. If you're going to be hoity-toity, you can sit in back. Else you can ride up front with me.''

David rode up front.

There was no direct road from the airport to Havenheights. Alfie drove north on the main turnpike, into the city, then along the waterfront. Just opposite city hall, an immense gray ship lay moored to Commonwealth Pier. That ship, more than a thousand years old, was Haven's primary claim to fame. It was not just that *USS Missouri* had been built on Earth and lifted to orbit for the transit to Buckingham. That feat, spectacular though it had been, had only been part of the story, lost in the intrigue that had led to the establishment of the Second Commonwealth.

Alfie turned left and followed the waterfront past the fishing boats to the long road that climbed to the top of the hills and cliffs that sheltered the harbor.

''They tell me this road is really fun during the winter,'' Alfie said after twisting the floater around one of three switchbacks. ''It's impossible for wheeled vehicles if there's any snow or ice at all.''

"This is close enough to impossible for me. We survived a war, Alfie. Don't kill us here."

Alfie laughed. "I could do this with my eyes closed."

"That's what I'm afraid of."

Havenheights was an amalgam of styles—medieval castle, colonial hacienda, and baroque palace in approximately equal shares. The twelve-foot-high curtain wall enclosed one hundred twenty acres. Disproportionately large towers stood at the corners and at intervals along the sides. A variety of outbuildings were backed against that wall as well. The parapets were not manned, though there were automatic sentry systems. In the front, east, half of the enclosure stood the main building, the palace, on a knoll that had been prescribed by the architect. The palace was similar—except in scale—to the style of building common on most frontier colonies, built around its own interior courtyard. One side of the structure was all baroque palace, four stories high, exaggerated in decoration, with rooms and corridors two to three times the size that they needed to be. The flanking wings were more modest in scale, and the fourth side was primarily a covered walkway, with a wall only on the outer side.

The only security visible as David arrived amounted to two guards decked out in the antique finery of the Coldstream Guards, red uniform blouses, black shakos, white gloves and trim. The weapons they carried were as modern as anything the Royal Marines carried into combat, though.

The limousine was passed straight through the outer gate.

"I see they know you already," David commented.

"Yes, and they let me in anyway."

They drove straight through into the inner courtyard and parked at the bottom of a wide formal stairway leading up to the main entrance of the "palatial" side of the building. There were footmen to open the doors of the floater. Alfie hurried around and gestured up the stairs.

"His Highness has really been keen on getting you here," Alfie said. "You were off on holiday and nobody knew where you had gone. He was afraid that this would all have to be postponed.''

"What do you mean?" David asked, hesitating on the stairs. " 'This all' what?''

"Oops. Nearly put my foot in it there.''

Alfie was saved from further explanation by the arrival of Prince William, Duke of Haven, at the top of the stairs.

"David!" the prince called, starting down the stairs. "I was afraid we weren't going to be able to find you in time.''

"Good afternoon, Your Highness," David said with a proper bow of his head. "I'm beginning to think I've been shanghaied and I'm not sure why.''

The prince laughed. "I was afraid that your friend wouldn't be able to keep the secret.''

"I didn't say a word, sir," Alfie protested.

"He didn't let on anything but that there is some sort of secret, and some sort of schedule," David confirmed, "and that just in the last few seconds. I was about to grill him when you came out, sir.''

The prince and the captain shook hands. William took David by the elbow, as if to guide him up the remaining stairs and into his home.

"It's not all that much of a secret, actually," William said, humor clear in his voice. "This is just a little something I've been promising myself ever since we survived that minor set-to back on Buchanan.''

"Sir?"

"I only wish there were more," William said—quite cryptically, David thought.

The double doors were both opened as they approached, William in the center, David at one side—his elbow still firmly in the royal grasp—and Alfie a half step behind on the other side. The foyer they stepped into was huge. And crowded.

David stopped just inside the doorway. All of the people, guests, in the foyer were in civilian clothes, but David recognized most of them at once. There were clearly more people present than would fit comfortably in the entryway, even though it was twenty-four by thirty-six feet. The crowd seemed to extend into the rooms beyond and to either side, framed by doorways large enough to let a private floater drive through.

"What is this, sir, old home week?" David asked.

The prince grinned. "Something like that. Come now, no call to stand here in the draft."

The round of applause as William led David through the foyer embarrassed him considerably. Brigadier Laplace, who had been 2nd Regiment's colonel through half of the war, stood with Colonel Zacharia, who had succeeded him. Admiral Truscott was with Captain Shrikes. But the guests weren't all brass.

"We collected everyone we could find who was with us on Buchanan," the prince said. "Everyone who is still around. And all of your lads who made it back from Camerein."

The civilians rescued on Camerein were there as well, all but Prince George. David did not mention his absence. He was almost beyond speaking at all. People came over to shake his hand or to offer compliments. There were claps on the shoulder, and more attention than Spencer would have cared for in a lifetime.

The next two hours were a blur to David, and an emotional roller coaster—part joyful reunion, part painful nightmare. He was relieved when he was finally allowed to escape to the room that had been prepared for him, to rest and change for dinner. Alfie showed him the way, then left him alone.

David's room turned out to be a large suite, better than the best available in the finest hotels in Westminster. *In the RM, we'd fit two platoons in this much space,* David thought as he wandered through the three rooms. *And they'd cut the height in half and fit two more platoons on the floor above.*

The bed looked tempting, and large enough for six people to share without crowding. David stared at the bed. He was tired—again, or still. He closed his eyes and let out a long sigh. He almost missed the soft knock on the entrance to the suite. The door was in the next room. But the sound did bring him out of his reverie. He crossed into the other room.

"Come in."

That it was Prince William was as much a surprise as anything else that had happened since he had landed in Haven.

"Your Highness."

"Not in private, David. No formalities, please."

"Yes, sir."

"Let's sit over by the windows." After both men were seated, the prince stared at Spencer. "You appeared, ah, somewhat distressed downstairs," he observed finally.

David hesitated. "It's with too many ghosts, I think. All the lads who didn't make it back. Friends, comrades, men I had shared everything with. It was like they were all hanging on my shoulders, weighing me down."

" 'The dead are always with us.' "

"Sir?"

William shook his head. "I don't have the foggiest notion who said that first. Someone or other, before we left Earth. I've been more than a little worried about you, David."

"Me, sir?"

"I understood that you had been having a spot of bother adjusting since coming home this last time."

David shrugged. "I can't deny that, sir. Everything has been just too much to handle. I've been tired all the time, no enthusiasm about anything. Twice, sir, I lost more than half of the lads I was responsible for. I can't escape the feeling that I should have done a sight better. I was responsible and I failed, but people treat me like a bleeding St. George, like I'd been out slaying dragons, rescuing maidens in distress, and all that rot."

"You *have* slain your ration of dragons, David, I assure you, and rescued people as well. You and your lads, those who came back and those who didn't. And, though some in this Commonwealth of ours might fault you for it, you have saved the lives of two members of the royal family."

David looked up quickly, caught by surprise by the way William had said that last. The prince was smiling.

"No, we are not universally loved. That Caffre woman, for one, has voiced definite opinions to the contrary. After she had spent seven years isolated with brother George, one can hardly fault her."

"Sir?" David was beginning to feel extremely confused.

"I have the deepest respect and affection for my brother George, but I do understand him as well."

"Yes, sir. Seven years of that life would have been near impossible for anyone. May I ask how His Highness is doing?"

William hesitated. "Improving. But what about you? Are you improving as well?"

"I don't know. I can't tell. Perhaps I'll require treatment myself before . . ."

"Before you go completely round the bend?" William suggested when David stopped talking in the middle of his sentence. "Like my brother?"

"Begging your pardon, sir, but yes. I do worry about it."

"It is possible. Combat veterans sometimes do require counseling, often for many years. But the fact that you worry about it might be the best sign that you don't need to worry about it. Have you made any plans for your future? You've taken a lot of time to yourself since Camerein."

"As a matter of fact, sir, I have. It's something I've been thinking about for weeks, I guess. Just this morning I realized that I had already made up my mind without realizing it, and that I'm comfortable with the decision. As soon as I get back to barracks I intend to file my request for retirement. I've got my twenty years in, and with peace all over the place, I'd likely end up passed over for promotion eventually anyway. There are too many officers looking for advancement for the likes of me to have much chance."

"I can't say that I'm surprised by your choice. I accept that you've thought it over at great length."

"Yes, sir, I have."

"Have you given any thought to what you'll do on civie street, as Master Edwards calls it?"

David tried to grin but failed. "To be honest, not much, sir. With my pension, back pay for leave not taken, and standard maintenance allowance, I shan't need to do much. I suppose I'll give some thought to finding a wife and settling down. And try to put my ghosts to rest." *As if that will ever be possible,* he thought.

"I do hope you'll keep an open mind about that future, for a bit longer, at least," William said as he stood. "As a favor to me, if nothing else."

There was another half hour of mingling with the other guests before dinner. The meal was formal, with the seating in the dining hall arranged in as egalitarian a fashion as possible. Good food and more than a modicum of alcohol lifted David's spirits a little. It was hard to remain glum among so many old comrades, even with the ghosts they shared.

As servants came in to clear away the last course of dinner and make sure that everyone had drinks, Prince William stood. He used a spoon to tap on the rim of a crystal goblet for attention.

"I intend to break with tradition," he said. "I know that it is customary in military and naval messes for the first toast to be to His Majesty. Tonight, however, there is one other toast that should come first." He raised his glass. "A moment of remembrance for those who are not here. To fallen comrades."

His guests stood silently and raised their glasses toward the prince. William drained his drink, then set the glass, upside down, on the table in front of him. Everyone else imitated those actions. Waiting servants quickly collected the downturned glasses and replaced them. Nothing was said at table, but Prince William had already instructed his staff that the glasses used for that toast were never to be used for any other purpose.

The party lasted until well past midnight and remained generally subdued. In the morning, it was ten o'clock when a servant came to wake Spencer.

"His Highness requests that you join him for breakfast at eleven o'clock, sir," the servant said once David was awake.

"Of course. Where?"

"The Bay View Gallery, sir. I shall return to conduct you there at five minutes before the hour."

That room proved to be at a considerable distance from David's suite. It was on the top floor of the main wing, the northeast corner. Prince William was already there. He stood when David was shown in.

"Good of you to come, David. I trust you don't have a hangover this morning?"

David smiled. "I stuck a killjoy-patch on before I slept last night, sir, to make certain I wouldn't."

"I had better warn you straightaway that we won't be breakfasting alone. There are a couple of people who couldn't make it up here for the festivities yestereve."

David cocked an eyebrow but did not speak.

"Just remember, this is a purely informal, private breakfast, no need for fancy manners or such."

David nodded, knowing that his suspicions were almost certainly correct. It was no surprise when the door opened a minute later and both of Prince William's brothers entered. Despite William's warning, the greetings were still awkward and uncomfortable for David.

"I didn't have a chance to properly thank you for rescuing me from that place," Prince George said once they were all seated. His voice was little more than a whisper. "I know that I was a less than perfect guest. I apologize for that."

"This is only the second time in more than seven years that the three of us have been together in the same place,"

King Henry said before David could find a response to George's statement. "We have you to thank for both of those times. Without you and your people, I might easily have lost both of my brothers to this war. I know that I have given you my thanks before, Captain, but it is not enough. It could never be enough."

"I was only doing my duty, sir. As best I could."

"Far more, and far better than anyone could rightfully ask," the king said. "Enough for now. Shall we eat? I find myself possessed of an immense appetite this morning."

It was nearly an hour later before the breakfast dishes were cleared away.

"William tells me that you intend to retire from the Royal Marines," the king said as he leaned back in his chair.

"Yes, sir. At least, I intend to request retirement."

"My first thought was to attempt to dissuade you, but further reflection changed my mind—as long as you are absolutely positive that you *want* to leave the service."

"My mind is as clear as could be on that, sir."

Henry nodded slowly. "William said that you were certain. He also said that you had no clear plans for what you will do after you leave the Marines."

David shrugged. "I figured there would be plenty of time to decide, sir, and no particular rush about it. I have time now, if nothing else."

"I fear that I am going to impose on you again, if you will permit me to," Henry said. "The Commonwealth needs people like you. Buckingham needs people like you."

"Sir?"

"You do realize that as a result of your medals for heroism, you will retire as a major instead of as a captain?"

"I hadn't thought about that at all, sir."

"It is true, standard policy dreamed up by the Admiralty and War Ministry. My brothers and I have spent rather a considerable amount of time debating what else we might do for you to ease the debt of honor and family we owe you—as well as what more we might ask you to do for us, and for the Commonwealth. Please hear me out before you say anything.''

''Of course, sir,'' David said when the king paused.

''We decided quite early that a knighthood alone would not be sufficient reward for your deeds, nor would that address the possibility of retaining your services in some fashion.''

David had to struggle to keep from interrupting.

''Although they are not, and in our Commonwealth can never be, identical, you have performed great services both to the Commonwealth and to our family. The family wants to reward you in suitable fashion. The Commonwealth needs your continued service, perhaps more than ever now that the war has ended. We believe that we have discovered a way to reach both of those goals simultaneously.'' He paused to look at each of his brothers in turn. Each nodded, as much to David as to Henry.

''There will be a formal investiture ceremony in Westminster next week—rather a bother and a bore, I freely admit, but the public show is necessary. You will be named first a knight commander of the Commonwealth, and then created Baron Malden. That is to be an hereditary peerage which will give you a seat in the House of Lords for Buckingham, and you will be a royal nominee to the Commonwealth House of Lords. I hope and trust that you will continue to serve your world and the Second Commonwealth in that fashion.''

''I don't know what to say, Your Majesty,'' David said, nearly stuttered.

''In case you weren't aware,'' William said, ''Malden is in the southern part of Haven, bordering Westminstershire. My steward will go over the accounts of your holdings there. It comes to a bit more than a military pension and basic maintenance.''

For David, there was nothing but stunned silence.

•   •   •

Hours later, after forty minutes with Prince William's steward and a first session with his protocol secretary, David was still in shock, glassy-eyed, scarcely able to believe what was happening. But, alone in his suite of rooms, there was one thing he could not resist. He took pen and paper and wrote his signature the way the protocol secretary had instructed.

David, Lord Spencer, Baron Malden

He stared at the paper. It was all too unreal. After a time, he crumpled the paper and tossed it in the trash can.

Either my troubles are over, he thought, *or else they are only beginning.*